Francesca

DONALD FINNAEUS MAYO

First published in the English language worldwide in 2013
by Betimes Books

www.betimesbooks.com

ISBN-13: 978-0-9926552-3-5

Cover design by JT Lindroos

To Renée, with love

PROLOGUE

Jakarta, Indonesia, 5ᵗʰ December 1975

"I would now like to speak to you, Mr President, about another problem." Suharto paused for effect before enunciating the single word with visible distaste. "Timor."

Kissinger glanced quickly over to Ford before returning his attention back to Suharto. So the Station Chief had been on the money after all. He'd been wondering if the sly old bastard would bring it up. He just hoped the President could recall his own briefings on the subject.

Suharto paused to allow them all to shift gears from the implications of Vietnam and potential communist infiltration through Cambodia, Thailand and Malaysia, took a sip from his tea, then continued. "When it looked as if the Portuguese rule would end in Timor we sought to encourage the Portuguese to an orderly decolonisation process. We had agreement with them on such a process and we recognised the authority of Portugal in the carrying out of decolonisation and in giving people the right to express their wishes."

In Kissinger's opinion Suharto was like most other dictators he'd met, in that he'd long since forgotten what it was to be contradicted. As a consequence, he tended to ramble on in long winded sentences that meandered all over the place. Did the man not realise he was taking up the valuable time of the President of the United States? Who gave a damn about the orderliness or lack of it displayed by the Potuguese?

Kissinger stifled a yawn as Suharto continued waffling on. "Indonesia has no territorial ambitions. We are concerned only about the security, tranquility and peace of Asia and the Southern Hemisphere. In the latest Rome agreement the Portuguese Government wanted to invite all parties to negotiate. Similar efforts were made before but Fretilin did not attend. After the Fretilin forces occupied certain points and other forces were unable to consolidate, Fretilin has declared its independence unilaterally. In consequence, other parties declared their intention of integrating with Indonesia. Portugal reported the situation to the United Nations but did not extend recognition to Fretilin. Portugal, however, is unable to control the situation. If this continues, it will prolong the suffering of the refugees and increase the instability in the area."

For all his verbosity, Kissinger had to concede Suharto's strategy was sound: the Americans, of all people, would have little sympathy for any lingering ambitions of colonialism held by once powerful European nations.

President Ford leant forward from the deep recesses of his cushion backed cane chair, almost spilling his coffee all over his lap. "The four other parties have asked for integration?"

"Yes," Suharto replied, in a slightly injured manner that seemed to imply he was somehow the wounded party in all this. "After the unilateral declaration of independence, Indonesia found itself facing a fait accompli. It is now important to determine what we can do to establish peace and order for the present and the future in the interest of the security of the area and Indonesia. These are some of the considerations we are now contemplating. We want your understanding if we deem it necessary to take rapid or drastic action."

Ford paused a moment, glanced across at Kissinger, trying to read his thoughts, then replied. "We will understand and will not press you on the issue. We understand the problem you have and the intentions you have."

"The use of US-made arms could create problems," interjected the Secretary of State.

"We could have technical and legal problems," agreed Ford. "You are familiar, Mr President, with the difficulties we had on Cyprus, although this situation is different."

Ford looked again to Kissinger for help. Ever the manipulator, the Secretary of State could see his President appealing to him to find a way of twisting them around Congress's dictates. "It depends on how we construe it," Kissinger said eventually, "whether it is in self-defence or is a foreign operation." He turned to look straight ahead at Suharto. "It is important that whatever you do succeeds quickly. We would be able to influence the reaction in America if whatever happens happens after we return. This way there would be less chance of people talking in an unauthorised way. The President will be back on Monday at 2pm Jakarta time. We understand your problem and the need to move quickly, but I am only saying it would be better if it were done after we returned."

Once again he looked Suharto directly in the eye. "Do you anticipate a long guerilla war there?"

Suharto seemed to breathe a small sigh of relief at the Americans' apparent lack of concern at his plans. "There will probably be a small guerilla war. The local kings are important, however, and they are on our side. The Timorese Democratic Front represents former government officials and

Fretilin represents former soldiers. They are infected with communism, the same as is the Portuguese army."

Of course he knew that always shut them up. The subject appearing to be closed, Suharto moved on. "I would like to say a word about trade relations. There are severe economic pressures on our countries. We must do all we can to maximise our income. In this connection there is an imbalance of profits between the oil companies operating in Indonesia and those operating in the Middle East. Indonesian companies make as much as $2.50 a barrel whereas the profits in the Middle East are under $1.00 a barrel."

Ford looked up. "Are they reinvesting and expanding operations?"

"Yes," Suharto replied. "We don't want to interfere with that. But we believe they can stretch out their profits. What we do should not be interpreted as nationalisation. We are seeking an understanding and negotiations are underway. Prospects are encouraging. We also want the understanding of the US Government, however."

"They should be grateful that they are treated well here in Indonesia, much better than in some other countries. I hope that your negotiations with them will be beneficial and that they will support your effort."

Why was the President always such a pushover, wondered Kissinger? But he dared not contradict him directly in front of the Indonesians. "Our main concern is that whatever you do does not create a climate that discourages investment. Basically, the matter is between you and the companies. We are not involved in such problems."

"We have taken these views into account and everything that we do will be based on existing laws," replied Suharto smoothly. "We want to find a way of obtaining revenue which will not jeopardise fair profits for the companies."

"We appreciate your clarification of this matter," Kissinger said frostily.

Smiling, Suharto moved to wind up the meeting. "Once more, I thank you for this visit. We are a country that has many needs and we continue to look to the United States to help us."

Here it comes, thought Kissinger, the begging bowl and the pitch for cash. In that respect, the wily Suharto was as predictable as any tent preacher. He looked across at the President, he could handle that one.

"We will do what we can," stumbled Ford, uncertain if he could commit to anything. "Our problem is to convince Congress. We have great difficulties here, although our prospects may be a little better than we had thought earlier. We will also try to get Congress to modify the trade act which excludes OPEC countries from generalised preferences. We realise that Indonesia did not participate in the oil embargo. Congress has, unfortunately, treated all OPEC countries in the same fashion."

At the cue of the US ambassador, whom Kissinger could see had spent the past ten minutes nervously looking at his watch, they all stood up and there was the usual round of bowing and hand-shaking before the American delegation made its way to the door. Just as he was about to leave, Ford turned to Suharto.

"I would like to mention also, Mr President, that I want to maintain a direct relationship. If you have anything special, I hope you will communicate with me directly by whatever means seems appropriate."

Suharto smiled and nodded, escorting them through the lobby to the waiting motorcade of limos and secret service agents. He'd got what he wanted, or most of it anyway. As Kissinger settled into the back of his air conditioned car, he reflected that compared to the fiasco of Vietnam and the looming threat of communism across the rest of Asia, not to mention what the hell was going to happen to China once Mao finally fell off his perch, East Timor was the least of his problems. He really couldn't see why Suharto was so nervous about what they might think. Most people back home had never heard of the former Portuguese colony now nervously sitting in a power vacuum following the collapse of the Salazar regime in Lisbon. It was hardly going to be a big election issue next year. He'd be surprised if one American in a hundred could stick a pin in the place on a map and be accurate to within a thousand miles.

DILI, EAST TIMOR
7TH DECEMBER 1975

1

The shooting finally stopped. It was a miracle she had not been struck by any of the bullets ricocheting around the house. Not that she believed in miracles any more. Chances were she had survived only to be saved for something worse around the corner. But she did know she wasn't waiting for them to come back.

How long she remained as she was, tucked in a foetal ball, she wasn't aware, but eventually she summoned up the strength to move. Her mother's body had taken several bullets in and around her abdomen, and Francesca could feel the sticky warm blood trickling up against her back. It took her several minutes to raise herself to her hands and knees. Each movement sent stabs of agony through her wounded internal organs; combined with the pain was an overwhelming nausea. Part of her wanted to curl up and die, but a stronger, more elemental side to her was already planning what to do next. She managed to stagger to her feet and find a towel from the kitchen. There was some water in the kettle, and slowly she began cleaning herself off as best she could. It was painful, but she forced herself to concentrate on the single task ahead of her, willing herself oblivious to the corpses around her and the sound of sporadic gunfire from outside. When she had finished, she went over to the chest and picked out some clothes to wear. She chose the most shapeless garments she could find, an old pair of tracksuit trousers, a pair of tatty gym shoes and one of Marco's football jerseys. She had to travel light, she knew.

Every movement hurt, but walking was particularly excruciating. If she thought about what had happened to her she became paralysed, reduced to a piece of meat that had been used, abused and spat out. So she didn't think about it, relying instead on the irrational will to live driving her forward. She wanted to tend to the bodies of her family spread out in their gruesome death poses, only she lacked the strength to do so. A line from the Bible popped out at her, Jesus' admonishment to the living to "let the dead bury the dead", and she realised she didn't want to touch the bodies at all. She simply felt she ought to. The imperative right now was to get out of the house before the soldiers realised they'd forgotten the TV and the radio and returned for their loot, or a fresh platoon appeared on the scene for another round of hell.

She stripped the beds of their sheets and covered each body, hoping that some neighbour would eventually come along and see to a decent burial before any dogs managed to break their way in. She was about to cross herself and pray for absolution of their souls when she checked herself. Instead, she piled her long hair on top of her head and stuffed it under one of Antonio's baseball caps. If she stooped and shuffled along, not too difficult given her current physical condition, passing soldiers might mistake her for a harmless old peasant.

Finally, she packed half a loaf of bread, some bananas and a bottle of water into a canvas shoulder bag and prepared to set off. The last thing she felt like doing was eating, but she knew she would be hungry later. She was astonished at herself, at how the calculating, survival orientated part of her brain had muscled in to cauterise her emotions, forcing her to apply clear logic and animal cunning to her situation. She hobbled back into the main room, past the shrouds, already blood-stained, to the door. Amazingly, it was still on its hinges. She cracked it open and peeped outside, adjusting her eyes to the early morning light. She could hear machine gun fire from the harbour, and also from the direction of the town square, but her own street seemed deserted. Where was everybody? Were they huddled inside their houses, terrified to go out while this firestorm passed over them? Were they dead, butchered in their homes like her own kin, or had they been rounded up and taken somewhere? How many of them had escaped while they still could and made for the Falintil lines before the Indonesian paratroopers had dropped in? She doubted very many. Like her father, they probably hadn't been able to conceive how awful things could get, or how barbaric the Indonesian soldiers would be. In their optimism they had set themselves up for their end, so all the Indonesians had to do was pull their triggers. Too late, she wished now that she had run off and joined a Falintil group. At least there was some dignity in going down fighting, taking some of the bastards with her instead of huddling down at home unable to resist as they pulled her from limb to limb, each mocking taunt degrading her yet another notch, until all vestige of humanity was torn from her. So, she was an animal now, and if she was an animal, she had to think like one to plan her own escape.

Her thoughts turned to Baby Angelica, now the sole surviving member of her family, if indeed she was still alive at all, and she felt a sharp wrench of grief. She wanted to chase after her, to track down this first aid tent the officer had ordered her to be taken to. She wondered how disciplined the Indonesian army was, and whether the soldiers would actually obey an order given by a junior officer. But she could hardly wander up to the Indonesian rear lines and ask if anyone had seen a baby she was looking to claim. She could only rely on the faint prospect that some spark of humanity still resided somewhere in an Indonesian heart. She certainly didn't trust God to protect her baby sister. His existence was likely limited to the pathetic imaginations of the nuns who had indoctrinated her with their teachings.

Think like an animal. Where should she head? The obvious, natural answer was to run for the mountains like everyone else, and hope to hook up with a Fretilin or Falintil patrol. But would they be able to provide any shelter, or would their very presence attract the Indonesians in greater number, with correspondingly greater savagery? She knew, like she had never known before, the bitter fiction of safety in numbers. She had to be smarter, stay one step ahead. Quickly she padded down the same steps she had walked up without a care in the world less than twenty four hours earlier, crouched under the porch with her canvass bag, and examined her options.

The gunfire from the square and the harbour was intensifying, and it had an almost musical rhythm to it: silence, followed by a sharp burst, followed by silence, before another burst. It didn't sound like an exchange between two positions, more the start stop start stop of a percussion solo. She very much doubted whether there were any Timorese forces remaining in the town centre. If she walked straight into it, there was every chance she too would be sucked into the grisly massacre again. On the other hand, it was the last move anyone would expect someone in her position to make, and hence it possibly became the right thing to do. It was also the last place anyone would think of looking for her. Everyone, from the Indonesian army to Fretilin, would assume any stragglers would run south. Now she had been left alone her best chance was to remain alone. So long as she could steer clear of marauding patrols, the safest place for her might well be behind Indonesian lines, where the soldiers weren't expecting any resistance because they had crushed it all.

There was another, deeper reason why she was reluctant to follow the tide of refugees into the mountains. These were her people, and how could she look them in the eye after what had happened? Even if she said nothing they would know, they would know because similar things had most likely happened to many of them. They would become a stigmatised group of victims, untouchable objects of pity, but untouchable none the less. No Timorese man could possibly want her now, and whilst the thought of any man, Timorese or otherwise, being inside her ever again made her shudder, she had no wish to be an outcast amongst her own people. If she was to live, it would have to be somewhere else, some place where no one had seen or knew of what had just happened . Maybe then she, too, could wipe the slate clean, eradicate the nightmare of the past day. It was a long shot, she knew, but she also knew it was her only shot. Suddenly, she was filled with a sense of gratitude for the first time since the Indonesian artillery bombardment had begun; grateful for her passion for languages and the curiosity that had led her to learn not just the usual smattering of Portuguese, but conversational English on top of the Bahasa she'd picked up from the Chinese coffee traders over by the waterfront. She knew she'd never be able to pass herself off as an Indonesian, whatever that meant these days, but she knew enough of the dialect to understand what people were saying around her, and that alone might be sufficient to keep her alive.

She was decided. She would make for the waterfront, keeping in the shadows between and underneath the houses. She didn't have a plan beyond that, although she was vaguely aware of the pull of the sea, as if somehow its purifying powers could cleanse the abomination her poor battered body had endured.

Checking for soldiers, she set off along the street. With her awkward gait and instinctive caution, progress was slow. She took the back streets, avoiding the main thoroughfares where troops were most likely to be combing through houses. Halfway down the street adjacent to hers a kampong dog, its curled tail high up in the air, stood in the middle of the road gorging on a corpse whose entrails had been ripped open by machine gun fire. Pieces of flesh flicked out from the dog's greedy mouth and when it glanced up at her she saw its entire snout was covered in bright red gore. The dog stared her down, reluctant to abandon such a feast. Enraged, Francesca reached down, picked up a stone from the gutter and hurled it at the animal as hard as she could. The stone struck the beast square on the shoulders and it jumped with a sharp yelp, scurrying away from the corpse as Francesca reached for another stone. It was a futile symbolic gesture, she knew, the dog would return to finish off its grisly meal the moment she was gone, but she had needed to do something to take a stand against the horror unfolding all around her.

She continued her shuffle in a broad northerly direction through the routes she knew so well. There was an eerie quiet to these normally bustling back alley ways and side streets. Shops were either boarded up or spilt open, their contents looted by the invaders who could only carry so much and had discarded the rest. Where were all the inhabitants? The machine guns had kept up their sporadic firing ever since she had left her house, presumably shooting at someone. She wanted to bang on the shutters to see if anyone was inside, to find out what was going on, but she knew she couldn't.

Eventually, she reached an alleyway that led out onto the harbour and she stopped, her heart racing in terror. An Indonesian platoon was directly in front of her, less than fifty yards away, marching at double time to the command of an NCO jogging along at the side. Rifles were shouldered, as the troops struggled to keep up the pace whilst hauling their bulky packs. Darting under a set of wooden steps, Francesca waited for the soldiers to pass, convinced she would be spotted. She tucked her head under her arms and crouched herself into a ball, desperately making herself as inconspicuous as possible, even though the stance was agony for her injured body. She heard the steady rhythm of the platoon as it pounded by almost on top of her, two dozen pairs of rubber soled boots slamming down on the dusty road overlaid by the metallic rattle of loose magazines and mess tins. So this was what invasion sounded like, this was what it meant to be embraced into the fold of mother Indonesia. Her thoughts turned to her own mother, and tears welled up from her heart. Perhaps she was looking over Francesca right now, guiding her hand, willing her to make good decisions, seeing her through to safety. Out of habit, she fingered the tiny silver crucifix around her neck, astonished now she thought of it that none of the soldiers had seen to rip it from her throat. She would keep it as a talisman, the only touchstone she had in a world gone crazy.

Think, girl, think, she admonished herself. They've all abandoned you now. She tucked the crucifix back inside her shirt and looked up through the slats of the stairs. The soldiers had moved on, for now there didn't seem to be any more. She remained still for three or four minutes more, then darted out from under the steps to a house three doors down. She took up a similar hiding place under the steps, from where she could see the harbour.

Suddenly, the sporadic machine gun fire made sense, consistent with all she had witnessed so far during this excursion into hell. A heavy machine gun had been set up on the wharf pointing out to sea, a long ammunition belt snaking out of the side into a large tin below. Two soldiers were operating the weapon, one firing while the other fed the belt into the mechanism. For now they stood casually around the gun smoking and kicking the occasional spent cartridge into the sea. While they chatted, two other soldiers led a group of a dozen Timorese Chinese up along the jetty, occasionally prodding one with their rifles, until the men (she could see they were all men, from kids barely out of their teens to grandfathers) were standing in line at the end of the wharf, facing out towards the sea. The soldiers then withdrew to behind the machine gun, and the gun burst into life.

From her hiding place under the steps the condemned men looked like toy soldiers being knocked down at the end of a childish game. The bullets ripped through the bodies, each hit whipping its victim off his feet before continuing its trajectory to splash into the sparkling sea with a pop of white foam. The massacre was over in seconds. She watched the machine gunner don a pair of gloves and remove the barrel from the gun, replacing it with another he had resting at his feet. He turned to exchange a few words with his comrade, his face animated by the power temporarily handed to him.

Already, Francesca could see, more soldiers had a fresh group of victims waiting to be escorted to the execution point. Suddenly, she put her hand up to her mouth to suppress an involuntary cry of horror. Fourth from the left, stooped in silence, staring at his feet stood Miguel. He had lost his glasses, presumably not wanting to be identified as an intellectual, but it was definitely him.

She knew then that it really was all over. She couldn't watch any more. Crouching into the darkest recesses of her hiding place, she tried to close her ears to the next burst of machine gun fire, then shut her eyes. This time there were no dreams of walking hand in hand with Miguel along the beach, just a blessed nothingness. Oblivion.

It seemed like she had closed her eyes no more than a minute or two, but it must have been hours for when she woke the sun was high in the sky. The steps, which had been in dark shadow when she crawled under them, were now exposed in bright daylight. She squinted against the glare and rubbed the dust from her eyes, looking up as she remembered with a dull sense of dread where she was. Oblivion had been a blessing, and for the first time she envied her fellow citizens who wouldn't have to wake up again and face a fresh round of horror.

Because she had been discovered. Standing above her was a middle-aged man, smoking a cigarette and observing her as an object of curiosity. He wasn't a local: he had that Javanese look to his eyes and his stance bore the casual confidence of the victorious invader. He wasn't crouched in fear or bothering to hide himself from the soldiers, yet neither was he dressed in uniform. From her position on the ground she could see a pair of oil-stained training shoes, giving out to a pair of dark blue and equally besmirched trousers. On top he wore an open-necked white shirt and a pair of sunglasses.

"Good day, my little sleeping beauty," he began with a smile.

She turned her head towards him and looked up suspiciously.

"Who are you?" she replied in Bahasa.

"Hasan Budiarko is my name. And you are?"

She looked at him guardedly. He seemed friendly enough, but she had learned never again to take a smile at face value. "I used to live here," she said simply.

"Well, you don't want to be walking around the streets now. It's not safe."

She gave him a look which he must have interpreted as contempt, for he softened his jovial façade and reached down, ignoring her flinch, which she realised was a type of movement you'd expect from a cornered dog used to beatings..

"Do you have a name?" he asked kindly.

"Why should I tell you?"

"Because I can help you."

"I don't need your help. Or anyone's."

To her surprise, he didn't rise to her hostility. Instead, he reached a hand out to her to help her onto her feet. She felt wobbly, her bruises aching all the more for the rest she had given them.

Around them the firing had stopped, the wharf was clear of bodies and the machine gun crew were gone. Instead the harbour was now full of boats, boats of every size from large naval ships to small fishing boats and cargo tramps. There was still sporadic gunfire in the distance, while nearby soldiers oversaw motorcycles, TVs and bicycles being loaded on to other vessels.

"Come with me," he said simply, and for some reason she didn't understand, she took his hand. She stood up, holding her bag with her free hand, and gave him a closer look. His face, though weather-beaten, seemed kindly enough, certainly not the face of a murderer or a rapist.

"Who are you?" she asked again.

"I told you, my name is Hasan."

"Yes, I know that, but what are you doing here?"

"I'm just a passing through on a job."

"Are you with the Indonesian army?"

He let out a little laugh. "Do I look like a soldier?"

She looked at him guardedly. "Not especially," she replied after a moment's thought.

"I don't think the Indonesian army would have much use for someone like me in their ranks."

"Then is it safe for you to be out on these streets?" she asked. "They are killing everyone, you know."

"I know," he said quietly, and she could see the sorrow in his eyes. "But they won't hurt me, and if you are with me, they won't hurt you either."

"Where are we going?"

"Away from here."

"How far away?"

"Oh, a long way. Is that alright with you?"

"I have nothing left here," she said, and hobbled alongside Hasan, trying to keep up with his jaunty pace as he sauntered towards the harbour.

BANDAKAN, INDONESIAN BORNEO

15TH DECEMBER 1975

2

Benny Surikano was not a happy man. If there was one thing he hated above all else, it was being interrupted while he was eating. Damn them all, he thought, his substantial pot belly grumbling, bloody Yanks and their piss-ant problems. He reached into his breast pocket and ripped away the cellophane from a fresh pack of Dunhill International; if nothing else it would momentarily suppress the hunger pangs. He mourned the lost steak sandwich the way he imagined some people might grieve a departed friend. He hadn't even seen it, let alone had time to take a quick bite, wrap the remainder in a paper serviette and stuff it in his pocket. He'd barely placed the order when the waiter had obsequiously sidled up to his table to tell him there was an urgent message for him at the front desk. Something about Mr Bird. In other words, something that couldn't wait.

Through the double-fronted plate glass doors he could see the driver waiting for him in the familiar blue air-conditioned Datsun, engine idling, not even bothering to park. The thought of wrenching himself away from that strip of sirloin, cooked medium rare, just ever so slightly bloody in the middle; the whole shooting match liberally spread with caramelised onions and ketchup, and wedged between two thick toasted slices of white bread, it was enough to make him want to weep. Not to mention the accompanying platter of freshly cooked french fries, still dripping with succulent grease and too hot to pick up with his fingers. This had better be good, he thought, as he took the telephone handed to him by the receptionist.

It wasn't good. It was far from good, a stinking piece of shit so far beneath his dignity it beggared belief, let alone a Chef's Special Steak Sandwich. But it had to be sorted out, and sorted out fast. And, as with so many other catastrophes, large and small, there was no one who could do it quite like Benny. Screw them all, he cursed to himself as he sent instructions for his order to be cancelled. Fucking bus boy would probably end up eating it on his break, he thought bitterly as he strode out of the club into the sweltering mid-day heat.

Twenty minutes later they were stuck in the middle of downtown Bandakan, surrounded by honking horns and overladen motorbikes nipping between the cars and vans.

"Why didn't you take the road round the back of the hotel?" he demanded impatiently of the driver. "We're going to be sitting in here all day."

"I'm sorry, Mister Surikano, sir, I thought this way would be quicker." As if to emphasise he was doing everything in his power to get them to their destination as quickly as possible, he pressed his hand down on the horn.

"Don't do that!" snapped Benny. "My headache's throbbing hard enough as it is."

"Sorry."

Benny helped himself to another cigarette, stuffing it between his lips. With his right hand he felt into his pocket for the sleek black lacquered electronic lighter embossed in 18 carat gold with an italicised *BJS*, clicked the button and savoured the crackle as the tobacco took hold of the flame. He didn't offer one to Stephen, who was no more called Stephen than Benny had a middle name beginning with J, but when you'd reached his position in life you could hardly go down to a jewellers with a brand new lighter and have them engrave BS on the back. Even the Benny was a fiction, a westernised affix designed to supersede the humble Abdurin he'd been saddled with from birth. He'd thought long and hard about how to stylise himself in his new incarnation, and eventually settled on Benny after the English comedian Benny Hill. It lent him a cuddly, jovial and harmless aura guaranteed to bring out a bitter chuckle in anyone who really knew him. He'd never tired of watching old reruns of the comic genius on the large grainy television in the officers mess, and he was delighted to give his reverance an added twist, confident the master of slapstick would, if he ever found out, surely approve.

He glanced at his watch, a Breitling liberated from a Texan roughneck who'd been arrogant enough to think he could teach the dumb Indo a thing or two about poker. Quarter past one. He'd heard the plane fly over the club just before midday, which meant by the time he arrived at the airport the little bugger would have had almost two hours to sweat it out in an airless locked room with the delightful Captain Durijarian for company. Benny knew the slimy shit would be looking to extract every last rupiah from the situation, which was why he'd had Stephen stop at the company offices before they left the ridge. Marching into accounts, he'd demanded a million and a half in cash.

The finance clerk was new and unused to Benny's ways. "I am very sorry, sir, we do not have that much in here."

"Yes you do," retorted Benny. "Go get your boss to open the safe, and put it on my expense account."

Benny watched as the clerk retired to consult with his superior in a back office. Five minutes later he returned, the trained book-keeper in him clearly affronted, holding a thick bundle of 20,000 rupiah notes, which he started to count out on the desk in front of them.

"I haven't time for that crap," Benny snapped at him, "just give me the money and a chitty to sign."

The clerk proffered a note typed on company stationery, and Benny scrawled along the dotted line at the bottom.

"What shall I put it down as?" asked the clerk.

"You ask a lot of questions," replied Benny, a menacing tone entering his voice. The clerk shrank back, sliding over the cash along with a manila envelope.

"OK, maybe I just put sundry expenses?"

Benny allowed himself a smile. "You're learning. Now, if you've got any more questions, you go speak with Mr Bird."

"No more questions, Mr Surikano, sir," replied the clerk giving Benny an obsequious look.

Benny returned to the car. Already he was calculating percentages. Durijarian may think he was sitting in a strong position, but there was no way Benny was going to hand over anything like a million and a half. They both knew the outcome was pre-ordained by forces greater than either of them; in that sense neither party was more than a puppet playing his allocated part in the broader drama. The only freedom lay in the squalid details, where the directors permitted a level of improvisation providing it didn't upset the direction or structure of the overall narrative. Benny's fortune was founded on hundreds of similar improvisations - some big, some small; each overlooked crumb squirrelled away for a rainy day. From previous dealings Benny guessed Durijarian would start high, a million, perhaps a million point two, and they'd settle somewhere around the six hundred thousand mark, which would include a hundred thousand for the officers who'd made the discovery in the first place. Which left nine hundred thousand for him. On reflection, well worth forsaking a steak sandwich over, he could always send out for a late lunch once he'd handed the peckerwood over to his father.

He reminded himself of the thought again as the car in front of them stalled on an orange light, condemning them to sit out yet another sequence at the crossroads on Pasar Saru. What was the point in sweating, the little brat would be doing more than enough of that for the two of them? What did it matter if he, Benny Surikano, took an extra half hour, an hour even, to make his entrance as the white man's saviour? Momentarily he contemplated ordering Stephen to stop at the Atomic for some Dim Sum, but thought the better of it. He could all too easily be seen and, contemptuous though he was of the boy's predicament, a balance had to be found. Whilst he didn't want to demean his dignity by running around in a flap, he had to be seen to be taking the situation sufficiently seriously to justify the million and a half he'd deemed it demanded.

The light changed, but still they were moving barely faster than a brisk walk. Scooters and little two-stroke Japanese bikes continued to weave around them like pesky hornets, while pedestrians thought nothing of jumping out in front of the car, carrying striped plastic bags full of fruit from the market, or the cigarette trays and sweet tea urns favoured by the street vendors. Cocooned in his air-conditioned cell, Benny watched the scene dispassionately. Unlike some of his fellow countrymen, he felt no shame at the shambles and chaos, no urge to apologise for the backwardness and all too visible poverty. Neither was he moved to anger or the need to blame. All he saw was the raw struggle of human beings to rise above their circumstances, the same struggle he found everywhere he went. Despite this, he still felt the patrician phobia of proximity to the masses, perhaps more so than a genuine aristocrat for he had been born amongst their number. He had no desire to taste any of it ever again, neither did he allow himself the sentimental indulgence of empathising with the unfortunates who'd not managed to rise above their origins. He kept the window firmly shut, unlike the westerners who leant their elbows on the door rest while they sipped from a can of Tiger held in their hand, only to express astonishment and horror when some street punk sidled up to them at a stop light with a pair of bolt-cutters and snipped their watch from their wrist. Though it would be a brave thief to pull such a stunt on a fellow Muslim, especially one influential enough to command his own driver. He thought of the old 9mm Browning he still carried in the locked glove box whenever he ventured off the ridge, more a hangover from his army days than a measured response to any perceived threat. He couldn't even remember where he'd put the spare clip, so long it was since he'd had occasion to use it, and whilst he thought there were at least eight or possibly nine rounds loaded in the magazine, he certainly wouldn't have wanted to stake his life on it.

Once through the centre of town the traffic cleared and they were able to proceed at a decent pace. They passed a convoy of Datsuns coming the other way, each driver chauffeuring a family laden down with the trophies of a Singapore spending spree. The drivers raised their hands from their steering wheels to acknowledge Stephen as they passed, delivering their occupants to cool showers and cold drinks by the swimming pool. It was another good reason to have held back. Durijarian would be more amenable to cutting a reasonable deal if they were alone.

They approached Kendalakkan around the perimeter road, eventually reaching a dirt car park behind the single storey hut that constituted the heart of Durijarian's empire. The airport itself was quiet after the rush of the scheduled Garuda flight from Jakarta and the Constar charter service. A four engined Hawker Siddeley 148 sat on the apron, the pale blue Bouraq livery almost bleached away by age and the sun. A flight crew huddled outside the building, gossiping and smoking cigarettes, while an engineer was patching together the front undercarriage motor to see the 148 through a few more take-offs and landings. Old parts cannibalised from a written off sister aircraft lay spread out in front of him in the shade afforded by the wing; Benny paused a moment to watch him scratch his head before forcing himself to attend to the matter in hand.

The hut didn't benefit from air conditioning, and the sole fan gently turning from a rafter in the ceiling was woefully inadequate for the task of dispersing the cigarette smoke and stale anxiety filled air. Unlike up at the club the smell of locally produced cloves predominated, reminding anyone, should they need reminding, that here they were in Indonesia. Durijarian's Indonesia. Two customs officers looked up as Benny opened the door and let it shut on its spring behind him. They didn't stand, and neither did they stop eating their lunch, a steaming curry ladled into enamel dishes from one of the canteens. It was at moments like this that Benny most missed his colonel's epaulettes. He wanted to kick the chairs from under their fat arses, teach the lazy slobs a bit of respect, remind them who he was. Focus, he told himself. Restrain yourself, keep the objective in mind.

"Where's Captain Durijarian?" he barked at them.

Both customs officers continued eating, though one jerked his thumb towards the single door set in the middle of the far wall.

"And what about the kid?"

"He's in there with him," replied the other officer, who was the older of the two, through a mouthful of rice.

Benny turned away from them and crossed the empty hall to the door to Durijarian's office, which he gave three soft but firm knocks.

"Come in," called the familiar voice from the other side.

The kid was slumped in a wooden chair placed in the opposite corner to Durijarian's desk. Benny found it hard to tell whether the posture was one of defiance or defeat. There was no mistaking the expression on Durijarian's face. Like a caged python that's just had a huge rat introduced into his quarters he was savouring his prey, whilst pretending other matters of consequence demanded his attention. Benny wondered whether the kid saw through the act, whether he had any inkling as to how invulnerable he actually was to Durijarian's posturing. He looked about fifteen, although Benny knew he was in fact only a few months shy of his seventeenth birthday. His mousy hair was well below the collar of his adidas sports shirt, leaving Benny to wonder how he'd managed to avoid being strip searched and sheared by Immigration in Singapore. He was at least fifty pounds overweight and his face, which had the well bred structure of his father, was puffy from too much junk food and too little exercise. If ever there was a poor little rich boy, Benny thought, here he sat.

The boy's suitcase rested on a small trestle table in the centre of the room, the top unzipped and flung back. Piles of clothes had been carelessly shoved back in, along with some pirated cassettes and a couple of tatty western paperbacks. The prize itself, the cause of all this fuss, had been separated from the rest of the possessions and placed to one side, far enough to single it out for attention, close enough to be incriminating.

Benny didn't bother to acknowledge the boy's glance, but simply walked over to the magazine and picked it up. Briefly he flicked through the pages, taking care not to reveal the slightest hint of lasciviousness, tossed it to one side and stared straight ahead at Durijarian.

"Is that it?"

His dismissive tone caught Durijarian off guard, and had the desired effect of placing him on the defensive.

"What do you mean, is that it? Don't you see what it is?"

"It's a copy of *Men Only*, for Christ's sake." Benny switched to Bahasa to exclude the kid from the conversation. "It's hardly the Communist Manifesto. If he'd brought in pictures of a bunch of homos bumming each other I might be a bit more worried, but I bet you've got a whole stash of this kind of stuff tucked away in these cupboards of yours."

"Benny, if you think this is such a trivial matter, maybe I should just play it by the book and send him straight down to Bandakan jail."

"You know who the kid is, don't you?"

Durijarian picked up a US passport, which he had on his desk and smiled, as if he'd just been dealt the missing card to a royal flush.

"I not only know who he is, I also know what he's done. Why else would I be honoured in my humble customs house by a visit from the great Benny Surikano?"

"Well, now I'm here, what are we going to do about it?"

"This young man has, by his acts, deeply offended the religious sensitivity of our great nation and directly threatened its moral integrity."

"If this crap's for his benefit, he can't understand a word of what you're saying. Why don't you just get to the point and tell me what it's going to cost to get him out of here?"

Durijarian shaped his hands on his desk like a tent, pausing as if to calculate a figure sufficient to atone for such an insult. "A lot of people saw it," he began. "The hall was full, the whole shift was present. That's a lot of officials to hush up. I can't see it costing less than a million and a quarter."

Benny snorted, not just for effect, as he sat down in the chair across from Durijarian's desk. "A million point two five! I could cut a deal with Sidi for half that and freeze you out of the picture altogether."

"I don't think so, Benny. Times have changed, inflation's caught up with us all. You've been up on the ridge too long, hiding in that fancy club of yours."

"I could have been to the fucking moon and back, a million and a quarter is completely out of the question."

"What are you offering then?"

"A damn sight less than that."

"Name a figure."

"Try chopping a million off the one you came up with."

"Two hundred and fifty thousand!" Durijarian seemed genuinely affronted. "What do you take me for?"

"Do you really want me to say?"

"Sure. Go ahead."

"An over-promoted pen pusher who's about to wander out of his depth."

Durijarian banged his fist on the desk, causing the cup of sweet tea to rattle on its saucer. Out of the corner of his eye Benny noticed the kid start from his trance like state and sit up. "I don't have to take this shit from you, Surikano!" he yelled. "You may think you're some kind of hot shot with your Constar paymasters and your friends in high places, but you're not in the army any more. This is my customs office, and what I say round here goes!"

Benny waited for the force of Durijarian's anger to diffuse of its own accord, knowing full well how little of substance lay behind it.

"Then I guess you'd better send him off to Bandakan jail," he said simply. "And we'll see what happens then."

Durijarian allowed himself a smile. "Surely you don't mean that, Benny. Think how it would look if you went back to the ridge empty-handed and had to tell Harry Bird his precious boy is stewing in a rat-infested cell surrounded by communists and thieves. What would Mrs Bird say? I hear her nerves are shaky at the best of times."

"Captain Durijarian, I think we both know this boy is no more going to Bandakan jail than I'm about to enrol in the next intake at Harvard Business School. It's just not going to happen. Sure, if I go back to the ridge and tell Harry Bird I couldn't cut a deal with you he's going to be pissed at me, but he'll just get on the phone himself to Sidi, or General Roullah. Or even Suharto himself, if that's what it takes to sort it out. God knows he's got the contacts in Jakarta through the American embassy. It may cost him more in the end, but the outcome won't change. The boy will go free, and someone will get paid. If we can agree on a figure," and here Benny tapped his left breast pocket into which he had split a third of the banknotes from the envelope, "that someone can be us. If not, it strikes me as a bit of a wasted opportunity all round, don't you agree?"

He knew Durijarian wouldn't be able to fault his logic, just as he knew the Captain's greatest fear lay in being taken for a chump. Benny had to think of a convincing way of showing him his true ceiling. He pulled the money from his breast pocket and laid it out on the table, taking care to watch for Durijarian's face to betray his greed. Sure enough, the man's gaze locked onto each sweat stained note as Benny counted it out, unaware of the way the tip of his tongue licked the edge of his upper lip.

"There's half a million there, and that had included my share."

"How about what's in your other pockets?" demanded Durijarian sharply.

"What other pockets?"

"You think I came down with the last shower of rain?" Durijarian looked at Benny incredulously. "I'm not expecting you to walk out of this empty handed, but neither am I about to let you take me for a ride. Go on, empty all your pockets, I'm curious to see just how much Harry Bird thinks his precious boy is worth." He gestured towards the desk. "Let's have it all out on the table."

Something told Benny to acquiesce. Perhaps it was the stories he knew circulated around the barracks downtown, tales embellished in every recounting of the fabulous opulence up on the ridge, perhaps it was his long experience of plodders like Durijarian; cunning enough to realise they were being taken advantage of, stubborn enough to cut their noses off to spite their lost faces. Besides, Durijarian was right – Harry Bird would be mad as hell if Benny returned empty-handed. Sighing at the second and third half million he'd now have to split, he pulled the envelope out from his trouser pocket and flopped it down on the desk along with his cigarette lighter and a few coins, just to make a point.

Durijarian picked up the fat envelope with a look of glee, tipped open the money and counted it out. "You sure know how to hold back, Benny," he said when he'd finished.

"If you think you're getting all of that, you can think again."

Durijarian smiled. "Don't worry, I'm not greedy. Fifty fifty split. That's the wonderful thing about the oil, there's enough to go round for everyone to be happy." He paused, looked up at Benny's crestfallen face and smiled. "Be happy, Benny! So, it's not as much as you wanted, but this is your lucky day too."

Benny tried to smile, but the best he could manage was a watery grin. He watched helplessly as Durijarian divided the notes into two equal piles, one of which he slid across towards himself where it disappeared into the cracked open desk drawer like a stake stuffed into the safe box by the croupier on a roulette table, the other of which he passed back to Benny along with David Bird's US passport.

"He's free to go," announced Durijarian in English, standing up and gesturing to the boy with a dismissive nod. David, who had seen his fortunes rise in line with the stakes on the table, now looked hopefully across at Benny, who motioned him to follow. He turned back to Durijarian. "Do you mind asking one of your men to fetch us a porter?"

"Of course." Durijarian opened the door to let the pair of them out, then barked an order at one of the officers slouched down in a wooden armchair. There was a momentary flurry as three underemployed minions jumped to his bidding, vying to wrestle the suitcase from the now bemused David. Benny stood aside in an attempt to recover some of his dignity. Thinking about the deal Durijarian had driven made him want to be sick. He knew he should have left the last half million in the car. Perhaps Durijarian was right, he was spending too much time up on the ridge. Too many Johnnie Walker Blacks on the rocks, too many sixteen ounce rib eye steaks, too many lazy Sunday afternoons by the pool soaking up the good life. He was going soft, he was losing his touch. It wouldn't do at all.

3

The porter was loading the suitcase into the boot of Benny's car as Eddie Vandeberg glided the Bell Huey directly over their heads past the control tower, throwing up a cloud of dust that spread out across the entire car park. Sitting alone in the cockpit, Eddie remained oblivious to the finger Benny gave him as he kicked the machine into a sharp 180 degree turn fifty feet above the apron then flared the nose to set the chopper gently down in front of the company hangers alongside a sister Huey, three Puma workhorses and a Gazelle. Through the soles of his boots pressed against the metal pedals he felt the skids first make contact with the asphalt and then take the entire weight of the craft. Satisfied the machine was stable he shut down the engine and yanked the sweat lined headset from around his ears. Still, after all these years flying he never tired of the sweet quiet that followed an hour of having his ears bombarded by a 6,000 rpm engine screaming at full tilt six feet behind his back, or the stillness around his body once the vibration of the thousands of bolts and screws holding together this mechanical defiance of gravity ceased. Leaning forward, he rubbed the knuckles of his right hand against the small of his back, feeling the familiar sweat stain spreading out across his white uniform shirt. As always, he experienced that momentary recoil of disgust at the thought of all the other backs that had been there before him, seeping their beer tinted aquateous molecules into the sun bleached teal canvas seat to lend the cockpit its singular ubiquitous aroma.

Above his head the blades began to slow, gradually brought to a halt by the resistance of their weight against the gearing. He waited until he could make out individual lines from the whirring disk before pulling on the catch and flinging open the door to catch the last of the downdraught. At the same time, he unclipped his harness, shut down the electrical systems and removed the key from the ignition box. Climbing out, he slammed the cockpit door behind him and crossed the tarmac to a series of portakabins bolted together underneath a large wooden frame topped out with a brushwood roof. The accommodation area took up less than half the floor space, the rest was given over to a veranda dotted with a dozen or so tables. A bar ran the full length of one end, behind which sat two enormous glass fronted fridges racked up with bottles of Anchor and Bintang, as well as a long shelf stacked with every imaginable brand of dark and clear spirit. At the other end of the veranda was a worn-out pool table with a large strip of duct tape covering a rent from a missed cue. Four fans hung from the rafters, slowly circulating the breeze wafting in from the sea less than a quarter of a mile away. It was too early for the hardened regulars, and Ming, the Chinese bar manager, had taken over a table in front of the large incongruous looking, fully decorated Christmas tree while he worked on a pile of stock and order sheets spread out around him, periodically stabbing his pudgy fingers at a calculator as if sheer willpower could make the figures more to his liking. Not that he had anything to complain about, mused Eddie, thinking of all those tax free dollars nobly intended for savings accounts in Houston or Melbourne that had short-circuited their way into Ming's coffers, the consequence of boredom, addiction, lack of moral fibre or whatever the hell else you wanted to attribute it to.

Ming glanced up as Eddie climbed the three steps onto the veranda, past a cut-out tin Santa tacked to the railings, and they nodded politely at each other. So far as anyone could discern, Ming didn't have any friends, he just had customers, and you either were one, in which case you were entitled a modicum of respect so long as your slate was cleared at the end of each month, or you weren't, in which case you might as well not exist. Eddie then walked over to the nearest portakabin and poked his head around the door of the Ops Room, where Shaky Mick sat slouched in an easy chair smoking a cigarette. A Harold Robbins thriller rested to his side, its spine balanced over the arm of the chair. Though Eddie saw no physical evidence, the smell of stale alcohol filled the air conditioned room.

"You're back early," Mick muttered in his west Australian drawl, barely bothering to look up as Eddie walked in.

"There ain't exactly a whole lot to hang around for in Katapulu."

"How was the Reverend?"

"He asked me how well I knew the Lord."

"Jesus Christ!"

"Yeah, him too."

"Man's on a mission."

"You can say that again. Did you see the stuff we sent up with him?"

"He's got good old uncle Benny to thank for that."

"I never knew he had it in him," replied Eddie.

"Dennis Cole was the one who signed it all off, and I think he had instructions from Houston. Normally you'd expect

Benny to flog at least half of it to the pharmacies downtown, but this time he seems to have behaved himself."

"Maybe he's been overcome by the spirit of Christmas."

Mick snorted, sending a waft of stale alcohol in Eddie's direction. "Isn't he a Muslim?"

"I dunno. Probably, somewhere back in the dawn of time. But you know Benny, he'll be whatever it takes to get along in the world."

"You got your paperwork?" asked Mick, suddenly seeming to tire of the conversation. Eddie pulled a sheaf of papers out from his side pocket, and tossed them on the desk along with his log book and the Huey's ignition key.

"Thanks," muttered Mick. "You might as well knock off early, have a shower and get the drinks in."

"Sounds good to me." Eddie retired to his cabin, shuddering at the prospect of a drinking marathon with Shaky. Shaky may have been one of Constar's most experienced pilots, but it was one of the great unmentionable facts of life in Base Camp that he no longer flew. The pilots had thrashed out an agreement with the rig crews after a terrifying incident over the Mahakam River in which Mick, who had been up drinking until five that morning, rolled back the collective with his left hand at five thousand feet, opened the side door and threw up while the helicopter, suddenly devoid of mechanical power, auto-gyrated downwards into the jungle, a trail of vomit streaming from his mouth up to the blades where it disappeared in a vortex. For a pilot of Mick's skill there had been plenty of time to bring back enough revs to recover the craft, but it was a close call too many for the rig crew, who had insisted the price of not reporting the incident to management was that Shaky be removed from the flying roster. Fictitious entries were made in his log book, signed and counter-signed to keep his licence current, and Mick ran the Ops Room. There was no logic to the way the other pilots instinctively covered up for Mick – after all it meant more work for them. Eddie suspected it was something to do with the way Mick embodied a broken-down future that could await any one of their number.

He wondered if there was a way to slip out undetected, perhaps go up to the club for an early supper and a scratchy censored-for-television movie on the video. These days he found it hard to know what to do with himself after a day's flying. There was none of the euphoria of surviving another mission, the relief of being another day closer to the end of a tour, the sense of purpose from having achieved an objective that might nudge history onto a barely discernible but still different arc. The reality was, he was no more than a glorified bus driver, ferrying geologists and seismologists in and out of exploration sites slashed out from the jungle, spots deemed to have potential on the back of a hunch or an educated guess in some air conditioned map room in Houston. This was a jungle which contained no native more threatening than the occasional machete wielding Dayek, yet still he flew with the mindset of a combat operational army pilot, anticipating anti-aircraft fire, machine gun tracer from some nest positioned on top of a hill, or worst of all, a rocket propelled grenade whooshing out from the shadows while he exposed the vulnerable belly of the craft in the final approach to the ridiculously tight landings he was compelled to execute, often little more than a hastily constructed wooden platform twenty five feet in diameter. Most of his passengers knew none of that, passing the flight preoccupied in their private daydreams, quietly smoking away or staring out of the window, following the helicopter's course along the river Eddie used as the simplest means of navigation. He still found it strange to look back upon such a benign payload, commuters really, these bored itinerant workers from places like Texas and northern Queensland, squirreling away what wages weren't blown with Ming into some retirement condo in one of the sunshine states.

For Eddie each trip still carried the ghosts of infantrymen waiting to pounce onto action, loaded down with M16s, spare ammunition clips, bulky field radios and canteens. Leaping out at the LZ with silent prayers on their lips, not knowing if they would be climbing back in when the firefight was over or travelling prone in a tagged body bag like a sack of potatoes on the floor of a medivac ship bringing up the rear.

Yet what had any of it achieved, beyond more doubt to add to the vast amounts he had already accumulated? For doubt had been his constant companion for as long as he could remember. He'd cherished it, celebrating it as a virtue in the pursuit of truth. Doubting Eddie, they'd called him at school, and he'd borne the moniker with pride. Even growing up in a household of academics, where scepticism was the norm, Eddie's doubt had stood out. "Why can't you ever accept anything I tell you?" his exasperated mother had bewailed on more than one occasion, as yet another answer was challenged with the inevitable why.

Why. It wasn't a question they necessarily encouraged in Champaign-Urbana, Illinois, not really, and especially not if you went beyond a certain acceptable point and objected to the fundamentals underpinning the way people lived which, as everyone was hell bent on telling you, offered an abundance and level of freedom hitherto unwitnessed by human civilization. Nursery school, grade school, middle school, high school, college, law school, a place in the family firm, the country club, the golf club, the split level home in the premium new development on the edge of town, maybe if it hadn't been so neatly laid out for him, maybe if it hadn't been forced down his throat he might have wanted it. Like if he had turned up on American shores as a refugee from Vietnam or Cambodia.

Any of them would have grabbed the life Eddie turned his nose up at in a heartbeat. Because if he thought about it, what really stuck in his throat wasn't so much the dream in itself or the burden of living it, but the lack of choice, the assumption that he, Eddie Vandeberg, would embrace it solely because they told him it was good, because they told him it was right.

And where had all that questioning and challenging got him? Vietnam, that's where. Because if you were cursed with the perverse logic of Eddie you didn't dodge the draft like any other self-respecting rebel or have your family connections secure you a nice cushy post in the National Guard thousands of miles from any likely action, oh no, that was far too neat and justifiable and self-contained, you went ahead and volunteered. Looking back, he could see the existential act for the half-assed piece of adolescent nonsense it was, but at the time the decision had seemed loaded with significance. What a fuck-up, what a pathetic, moronic way to protest against the torpor of affluence! But by the time he'd found that out, it had been too late, too late by far.

If he thought he was alienated from middle America when he joined up, it was nothing to the utter isolation he experienced when he returned. Applauded for his patriotism by worthy burghers he despised, shunned by the counter culture whose acceptance he craved, misunderstood by his family, their relief at his safe return expressed in a suffocating deaf love, he'd sought out the company of Cindy, the one he thought would understand. Yet Cindy had changed. Or maybe it was him. He sensed it the first time they went out again, in her irritation at his confusion, in her inability to accept why he couldn't just put the whole thing behind him and get on with his life. He tried telling her about some of it, but then he saw the glazed look come across her eyes and changed the subject. They were sat in a booth at Deluxe, down by the university on the corner of 6th and Green Street, the same bar he'd sought refuge in during countless cut classes as a student, shooting pool with other GDIs or educating himself in a corner with dog-eared paperbacks by Camus and Sartre. She'd just told him she was doing some voluntary work for the Junior League and he could tell she was stung by his laughter. Who the hell was he, baseball cap pulled tight over his head to conceal the fading military haircut, to judge her?

Only later did he discover she had only gone out with him to spur one of her favoured suitors into making a firmer commitment. It had worked, too. Biff was his name, Biff or Boff or something equally inane, the kind of nickname frat-rats desperately cling onto when they metamorphose into clubby, chubby accountants and bankers. Even Cindy, clever beautiful artistic articulate Cindy, had turned to a Biff, opening her arms to embrace the predictable security that lay mapped out in front of her. He knew then it was time to leave town for good. Biff and his ilk hadn't gone to Vietnam, oh no. Unlike Eddie, they weren't fucking stupid. For all their narrowness and hypocrisy, they seemed to have some kind of grasp on the essential truths about what it took to succeed in life, what you had to do just to get through. Truths that seemed to elude Eddie, even as he rested in a wicker chair later that evening up at the club on the ridge, a bottle of Bintang at his side and a Camel between his fingers, still struggling after all these years to contemplate the essence of being.

4

I've been here a week now, and yesterday I conducted my first service in the main hut that doubles as a school room and church hall. We had a congregation of about forty, and I preached from the Parable of the Sower. As I spoke I felt the power the Lord has channelled through me and through all of you who have made this dream, which was but a vision less than a year ago, a reality. Without your generous support and your prayers, I would not be able to continue doing the work I have been sent here to do. Believe me when I say there is plenty to be done. The Christian community out here is strong, but it is also still small, and we struggle against the dark forces of paganism and other forms of idolatry, as well as the ever present Islam. Yet we are nothing if we are not front line soldiers in Christ's army, and our spirits are more than up to the task. I have been blessed in having an extremely talented and committed team around me, aided by a trusty ency-clopaedia of tropical medicine and a supply of drugs generously donated by Constar Oil of Texas, who have a large presence in our nearest large town Bandakan, some 100 miles away. It is just one of the countless miracles that have been bestowed upon us, each one a further confirmation, if it were needed, that we are indeed doing the Lord's work. I have been ably assisted by Hallie, whom *many of you know, and by Yusuf whom I baptised at yesterday's service and is now known to all at the mission as Joseph. He has been working here full time since the beginning of this month and doing a magnificent job. I don't know where I would be without his practical skills and tireless enthusiasm, which never fail to lift me on those occasions when the challenge of what we have set out to do seems overwhelming and I succumb momentarily to the temptation to get downhearted.*

For it would be wrong of me to conceal from you the scale of the task ahead of us. Many of the children in our Sunday School were born out of wedlock, a situation I can assure you we are doing our best to remedy. Three ceremonies are planned for the next month, and negotiations are underway to arrange a further two. It pains me to tell you that promiscuity is rife amongst these people. We are working hard to convince them to repent from these sinful ways, and with the power of the Lord behind us I have no doubt that we will eventually triumph, but there is no room for complacency and our small band values every one of your prayers...

Ron put down his pen and re-read what he had just written. It struck the right note, emphasising solid accomplishments whilst leaving the casual reader in no doubt of the need to keep the cash pipeline open. So far as his own role was concerned, he felt he'd drawn a rounded picture of a seasoned missionary who was possessed with sufficient worldliness for the job but wasn't about to allow it to dampen his enthusiasm for the ideals that had brought him to this place. It was good on the specifics, too. The Sunday School, health outreach work, pagan couples joined together in Christ, these were all measurable results you could point to when, inevitably, the time came to pass the hat round once again. In acknowledging his team he could draw attention to these early achievements without sounding boastful. As much as anything, though, if he was honest about it, the upbeat missive was designed to cheer himself up, to convince himself there was any point to it all.

Because frankly, it had been a week from hell. Diarrhoea, lassitude and indifference had been his constant companions. He'd arrived at the mission station on the edge of the village of Katapulu after a five mile walk through jungle paths from the drilling platform where the helicopter had dropped him off, his feet in blisters, his shoulders chafed from the brand new rucksack, his arms, legs and face covered in scratches and mosquito bites. Yusuf, or Joseph as he had to learn to call him, had been there to meet him, accompanied by a large straggle of volunteers, who had to be restrained from fighting each other over each box as it was unloaded from the helicopter. Dripping sweat in the equatorial humidity, he'd arrived to find the mission in the middle of its siesta. Joseph showed him to his quarters, a single room hut built on stilts, devoid of any furniture bar a rusty fold-up camp bed tucked away in one corner, then left him to freshen up. With what? There was no running water, the only place to wash was a stream at the end of a well worn path, where a guide warned him by making wild snapping motions with his arms and gnashing his teeth, to watch out for crocodiles. As he stripped to the waist and splashed the cool river water over his face and chest, he thought of the early apostles by the Jordan, tougher and better men than him.

Ron had often contemplated the trials of Job during these difficult past two years, how that Biblical giant had never wavered when God stripped him of all he held dear, how he had held firm and finally been rewarded by God for his resolve, not just in the next life but in this one too. Like Job, his faith too would hold fast in the face of all he had lost. Each night he forced himself to pray for the souls of Germaine Greer and Gloria Steinem, along with all those other feminist disciples of the Evil One whose blasphemies had so poisoned Patti's mind and aroused an anger from which she seemed incapable of ever returning. Like an Old Testament prophet, he had repayed anger with anger, which hadn't solved anything, just as it hadn't solved anything with Sue-Ann, who had run off with a bunch of hippies four days after her seventeenth birthday, which also happened to be three days after he discovered the diaphragm in her bedside drawer, or two days after the first hearings by Congress into the Watergate burglaries, and the day after the hideous row they'd had over dinner about the right to abortion.

Piece by piece his family had fragmented, each blow yet another test of his faith. Before Sue-Ann it had been Ron Jr., who had chosen to slink off to Vancouver with his tail between his legs rather than face the draft and fight for his country like a man. Then finally it was Patti's turn. It was still a source of deep and abiding shame when anyone asked. Was this the pain the Lord had asked him to endure so he could know the suffering and humiliation Christ had borne for him on the cross? How he had tried to reason with her, to make her happy, to give her what she wanted. But none of it was ever enough, and he couldn't have done any more without betraying who he was and the commitment he had made to God. His mind wandered back, as it did whenever he was feeling down and sorry for himself, to that dreadful night in the fall of '74 when she'd announced she was going. He could still remember every insult she'd hurled at him, every unjust accusation, every weak reply as he oscillated between fighting back and pleading with her to give their marriage another chance. How many times since then had he questioned his motives, as the seditious thoughts popped up from his nagging conscience that his real motive for holding her hostage in her misery was to save his own face? What minister wanted to stand in front of his congregation and preach the virtues of family unity whilst back at home the lawyers were busy serving the divorce papers on each other?

The truth was, and it was a truth he had had to come halfway round the world to see, Patti and he hadn't really loved one another for years. While his faith had deepened from the rigid certainties of callow youth to form mature roots that anchored his entire being, hers had dulled until it became little more than dutiful ritual, and then not even that. He knew she despised him for it, for she was incapable of concealing the barbs behind her teasing ripostes to yet another rant of his against some fresh assault on the pillars of decency perpetrated by the hippies waging their war of attrition on any standard he had been brought up to cherish and defend. She mocked the same fifties haircut he'd worn since he first courted her, she mocked his cornball patriotism, she mocked his reluctance to turn on President Nixon, delighting in his eventual fall with childlike glee, until it seemed she not only mocked everything Ron stood for, but everything he was.

The most vicious battles were reserved for the children, and here her betrayal was at its most painful. How he had agonised over the best way to bring them up, to inoculate them against evil by instilling a love of Christ and a respect for his church. What's more, he had done it all out of love, a genuine love that went to the core of his soul. He recalled the day he'd given Ron Jr the first and only real whipping of his life, for an act of childish sadism carried out on a neighbour's cat, vomiting in the bathroom as he heard his eleven year old son's whimpers from the bedroom across the hall, remembering how he had held the boy as a vulnerable baby, and asking God how it could have come to this. And then he had to face Patti's look of pure loathing as she accused him of being a hypocrite, of failing to teach the boy anything more than the simple barbaric lesson of violence begetting more violence. She had refused to speak to him for a week after that particular episode other than to exchange the bare bones of information essential to the management of their household. A truce had followed, during which she pleaded with him to yield a little, to bend with the winds of change, to see that he didn't always have to be right for his family to love and respect him.

But Ron just couldn't do it. Compromise was Satan's olive branch. He sought solace in the knowledge that the apostles were not easy men to deal with, just as he focused on Jesus' outbursts against human frailty and refusal to negotiate with the temptations of an easy life. For if he gave in, he reasoned, what was the point of any of it? What would it all have been about, all the years of preaching, of winning souls, of trying to reach out to the blind, the indifferent and the uncaring? No, he could not budge, and even now, deep in the Borneo jungle, he still believed he was right not to have budged.

As the children failed him in each test of their emerging characters, inevitably they gravitated towards Patti, who was more inclined to offer solace to their weaknesses. After the notorious beating Ron Jr had withdrawn from active confrontation but Sue-Ann remained vocal in her defiance, correctly sensing that he wouldn't dare lay his hands on her. Their fights, over the usual territory – boys, make-up, what TV shows and movies were deemed suitable for a budding adolescent – became set piece spectaculars which only ended when one or the other (usually but not always Sue-Ann) stormed out of the house. Over the years their front door had accumulated a number of cracks which soon ran the entire length of the timber behind the bamboo fish, each scar punctuating a new low in a family disentanglement rapidly deteriorating beyond repair. Ron knew things weren't going well but the end, when it finally came, took him by surprise.

He'd returned home earlier than expected, having postponed a staff meeting after the treasurer rang in sick, to find Patti in their bedroom packing a suitcase. On the dressing table was an envelope with his name written on the front in her familiar handwriting.

"What on earth's going on?" he asked, picking up the envelope and looking across at his wife, who was guiltily holding several pairs of panties.

"You weren't meant to find that until I was gone."

"Gone?"

"Yes Ron, gone."

"Where were you planning on going?" His guts had tautened, his pulse sped up, the full implication of what he had interrupted dawning upon him.

"What does it matter where I'm going?" she replied.

He tried to force himself to sound reasonable, as if this were something she did every week. "So, when are you coming back?"

"I'm not."

Silence, as the irrefutable reality of the situation aired itself for the first time.

"Not at all, not ever?" Desperately, he tried to stuff the anger down, beneath the incredulity and the fear.

"Ron, please don't make this any harder for me than it already is. I can't take this discussion, my mind's made up, you can't talk me out of it, that's why I left you the note." Helplessly, he watched her spit each thought from her mouth as she tried to maintain the coherent logical chain that had taken her to this point.

"So, what does it say?" he began slowly, sliding his fingers under the flap and ripping the envelope open.

"For God's sake don't read it now!" She almost screamed at him. He sensed himself taking the advantage, suitcase not yet packed, him positioned between her and the doorway. He was damned if he was going to step aside and help her with the case into her car, and he could tell she knew it. He pulled open the single piece of paper and unfolded it. Across the room Patti's brittle frame crumpled as she collapsed onto the bed, still gripping her supply of panties.

"Dear Ron," he read aloud, ignoring her move to cup her hands over her ears. "By the time you read this I'll be gone. Ha! Please don't try and come after me, I will write to you within the next few days with my lawyer's details. It is my sincere hope we can conduct the unpleasant business we need to carry out between us amicably and with dignity. We both know our marriage has become a sham, just as we both know your beliefs would not allow you to do what has to be done. So it falls on me to take charge, for both our sakes. If ever there was a reason for us to stay together, that reason no longer exists now Sue-Ann and Ron Jr have left home. I believe I have a right to a happy life, and I intend to exercise that right. You may not think I care, but the collapse of our marriage truly saddens me, even more so when I remember the man I married, before the intolerance and the bigotry set in, before you decided you had to act out this patriarchal role in which you took charge of all our thoughts, beliefs and deeds. Your refusal to entertain any viewpoint other than your own has already alienated you from your children and caused them considerable pain. Now it has become too much for me to bear as well. I accept you are sincere in your beliefs, however those beliefs are no longer mine. For this reason, and many others too numerous and complicated to list here, I can no longer be your wife. Signed, Patti. Whoa," he continued, holding up the letter with a flourish, "Fighting talk!"

She didn't look up. "It's not just talk, Ron. I mean it, every word. I've made my mind up, I'm not going to play games with you, and neither am I going to falsely raise your hopes. I feel for you, honestly I do, but it's not enough. I don't love you in that way anymore, and I haven't for a long time. I know it sounds brutal, and the last thing I want to do is hurt you, but I have to speak the truth. Otherwise I'll disappear down the drain like all those other valium popping zombies I see down at the hair salon. This is my last chance and I'm going to take it. I have to."

Speechless, he had little choice but to follow her out to the car where he wedged her case in the back, behind the driver's seat. He stood awkwardly to one side while she clipped on her belt, conscious he could be mistaken for someone cheerfully waving his wife off to a weekend reunion with some college girlfriends. She started the engine and dropped it into reverse, meshing the cogs with a clumsy shift on the clutch, staring straight into the rear view mirror. He heard the handbrake spring release and watched helplessly as she slid down the drive, a ship cut adrift on its slipway to find a new life under its own steam.

Since then, he'd not been able to contemplate the abyss that had become his life. He'd shielded himself from it by filling his waking hours with dutiful activities, praying in between to a God whose lead he no longer understood. For the first time he had to take his saviour's will on trust, incapable as he was of seeing any good in the larger picture. Once or twice he came close to doubting that too, but he brought himself back, knowing that if he lost Jesus on top of Patti he really was finished.

It was about this time he heard about the Indonesian job. In the wake of his turmoil and grief it seemed like the first indication that there could be a future beyond his despair. Perhaps God had a use for him after all. There really was no going back, he knew that. Whatever the shortcomings of the situation in Katapulu, and right now Ron could identify plenty, this was where his future lay. He had no choice but to make a go of it.

5

Amanda Cole had been standing just behind David Bird when one of Captain Durijarian's men had seized upon the now notorious copy of *Men Only*, and had witnessed both the delighted expression on the customs officer's face as well as David's reaction, which rapidly shifted from embarrassment to fear as the consequences of his transgression set in. Her first thought was for her own suitcase, resting on the trestle table beside David's. Thank God she hadn't tried to sneak in any dope, not that anyone other than a complete numbskull would bring anything through Singapore these days, not since they'd started hanging smugglers, even nice white middle class hippies from Australia. She didn't think a carton of duty free cigarettes, some Estée Lauder perfume and a few pirated cassettes picked up in the Orchard Road malls would raise any eyebrows, though you couldn't tell with these thieves. You never knew what to expect coming into Bandakan, and today was one of those days when they were opening everything. Someone up at the ridge must have been late with the monthly pay-off, unless this was just their way of celebrating Christmas. Guiltily she acknowledged a momentary tingle of pleasure at David's predicament. Of course he would be alright, anyone could have told you that, they were probably just picking on him because he was travelling on his own. She didn't wish the poor boy any harm, it was just nice for someone else to be on the receiving end of whatever trouble was going round for a change.

The holiday had not started well. Unbeknown to Amanda, a letter had preceded her arrival by a week and a half, personally addressed to her parents from the headmistress of Cheltenham Ladies College. In it, the headmistress, a mean spirited spinster with what Amanda suspected were suppressed lesbian tendencies, outlined her reasons for taking the almost unprecedented step of requesting that Miss Cole not return in the new year for her final two terms of A level study. It was a step taken, the headmistress conceded, with great reluctance and amidst much sorrow, for she appreciated full well how this disruption to Amanda's education, coming at such a critical moment, would impact upon her prospects for university and beyond. However, the letter went on, the common welfare of the other young ladies had to be considered, and this was one of those regrettable occasions when the interests of the one had to be sacrificed for the good of the many. Amanda had become a destabilising influence at a time when the virtues of self-discipline, industry and order were of the utmost imperative. Several incidents were alluded to, including one involving some boys from the neighbouring Cheltenham College that had caused both institutions no small embarrassment, and whilst the *prima facia* evidence necessary to justify an outright expulsion wasn't in the headmistress's hands, she and the governors were of a single mind in deeming it best that Amanda discontinue her education under their tutelage.

The letter was pompous in tone, and was waiting in Barbara's handbag when she greeted her daughter at Payer Lebar airport. Jetlagged and jaded from an eighteen hour flight in a clapped out British Airways VC-10 smelling of sick, Amanda failed to register her mother's coolness as anything out of the ordinary. It was only back in their room at the Hyatt, fortified by a double slug of Gordon's from the minibar while Melanie was downstairs at the reception desk trying to put in a call to her parents to let them know she had arrived safely, that Barbara delved into her bag for her little incendiary bomb and detonated it in Amanda's face in the form of a sharp slap across her right cheek.

Barbara's reaction, as she conceded in a tearful reconciliation the following morning, had been wildly excessive, especially as she hadn't even given Amanda a chance to defend herself or offer her side of the story. And Amanda had forgiven her mother partly because she understood, more than Barbara realised, that her anger was directed at Amanda not for the alleged offences she was supposed to have committed, but for foolishly handing the headmistress and the governors the ammunition to humiliate her family so publicly. Amanda had never forgotten the one occasion her mother had turned up at a Parents Day, when they were still living in Bahrein. With her deep chestnut suntan, flash clothes, hoops of gold jewellery from the souks dangling from her wrists, and rich Barnsley accent, Barbara had become an instant object of ridicule for the girls, who delightedly mimicked her West Yorkshire brogue within earshot. Even the staff had barely bothered to conceal their condescension. Prole Cole the girls called her after that, and the hateful moniker had stuck.

But Prole Cole had seen enough from weekend visits to the homes of the small cluster of friends who continued to stick by her, to know what demons lay behind their snobbery. Amanda's mother might not have a smart home counties accent, but she did have two servants at her beck and call, as opposed to a surly cleaning lady who came in once a week to stroke the furniture with a duster and make a half-hearted effort at a bit of vacuuming. Carefully, and subtly, she let reports of her lavish lifestyle seep out, knowing they would go a long way towards ameliorating some of the faux pas she'd made in her early days. She recalled the humiliation of being instructed in front of her entire table on the correct way to use a knife and fork. "Not like a pencil, Cole, where on earth did you learn to hold it like that."

The young ladies dismissed her as a nouveau riche parvenu, but she noticed the eyes in the most well-bred of them still lit up when they saw her collection of duty free perfumes (which they were happy to borrow for a school dance) or her Panasonic stereo cassette recorder, which was used to tape the top 40 each Sunday night. To hell with them all, she thought, happily exchanging these expat trophies for their friendship. If it came down to it she'd rather be nouveau riche than nouveau poor. How different it was for her father, who simply glanced at the termly bill, made some dry comment about the unauthorised extras Amanda had managed to rack up on taxis, clothes and stationery, then passed the whole thing on to the accounts department to be settled and promptly forgot about it. Amanda knew some of the expat women out here complained of the hardship of their posting, citing the sweltering heat, the inaccessibility of good shopping and the way everything, from a bar of chocolate to a magazine, was months out of date. Not her, nor her mother, when it came down to it. Both of them went home often enough to appreciate what a sorry state their country was in. Britain was so, so shabby these days, especially when your eyes were used to the shiny shopping plazas and hotels of Singapore, its people so downtrodden, overweight and pasty faced from a diet of cheap carbohydrates, struggling with their plastic shopping bags through mildewing concrete town centres rebuilt after the war in the architecture of the new brutalism. Who in their right mind would exchange a privileged life on Constar's famous ridge for that? What other seventeen year old girl in her class had breakfast made for her by her servant? Or could snap her fingers and demand whatever took her fancy – be it a glass of iced water, a trip to the fish market to fetch some live lobsters, a skirt hand washed and ironed in time to go out for the evening? It was partly why she'd invited Melanie to join her for the Christmas holidays; the descriptions of expatriate opulence would have greater credibility and wouldn't be seen as vulgar bragging if they came from the lips of her titled friend. Now there didn't seem much point to the visit, and besides, what would Amanda say to her?

It hurt to be asked to leave. And it was so unfair, too, as she tried to point out to her mother when they had both recovered sufficiently to be able to discuss the matter coolly. They were sitting alone in the Hyatt coffee shop, casually people-watching as hungover flight crews drifted in and out in twos and threes to pick away at the buffet, Amanda sipping at an orange juice while Barbara stirred a cup of black coffee and lit her first cigarette of the day. Having accepted Barbara's offer of a Mogadon to see her through the night, Melanie was still fast asleep in their adjoining rooms on the 11th floor, along with Amanda's younger brother James.

"That night we went to the party at the boys' college," Amanda began, "there was a whole group of us, but none of the other girls have been asked to leave."

"I know, darling, but that's the way it is. They singled you out because you're different."

"But I'm not different," protested Amanda. "I look just like them, I sound just like them."

"I should jolly well hope so too," Barbara interjected. "We didn't go to all that trouble and expense to have you speaking like your Nan. The fact is, they needed a scapegoat to make their point and get the girls to knuckle down and put their noses back to the grindstone, and so they picked on you. It makes my blood boil."

"What am I going to do?"

"There's always the International School here in Singapore. It may not turn out refined young ladies but it'll get you through your exams, if that's what you want. But before any of that happens, we have to decide what to say to your father."

"Tell him the truth."

"It's not that simple. He's a good man, your father, but he never had to pull himself up by the bootstraps the way I did. He doesn't see the world in quite the same way."

"How does he see it?"

"He misses things. He's always giving people the benefit of the doubt, when really it's plain to see they're out to take advantage of him. I've had to protect him a lot over the years. I can tell you, if I hadn't we'd have never got where we are today."

Amanda reached over for her mother's cigarettes, half expecting to have her wrist slapped aside. When it wasn't, she helped herself to one, lighting it with a book of matches from the centre of the table. "I still don't see why you can't just tell him what happened. Otherwise he'll think it's all my fault."

"He so wanted the best for you when he chose Cheltenham. If he knew what a snake pit it really was, it would hurt him terribly."

"What about how it's hurt me?" asked Amanda.

"You'll get over it."

"No one said a word to me, not my housemistress, not the head, not any of the staff. They must have known, and they quite happily watched me say goodbye to all my friends and tell them we'd meet up again in the new year."

"It's the way they are. They didn't want a scene, just have you quietly disappear off into the sunset."

"To hell with them."

"The truth is, Amanda, they're not your friends, not really, and they never will be. The main thing is, you got what you needed out of the place. You can go anywhere in the world and pass yourself off for the real thing."

"What's wrong with who I am?"

"Nothing, it's just the world is so quick to judge, and there are certain opportunities in life that were closed to me and always will be, but will open up to you because of what you've learnt there and how it's shaped you. And believe me, it has nothing to do with A levels. That's what your father can never accept. Oh, he knows it, but deep down he doesn't really believe it. He thinks I'm exaggerating, or I've still got a chip on my shoulder, whereas in fact I know. I know what they're really like, and I know the lengths they'll go to keep hold of what they have. I know here," and she pointed to her heart.

"So, what are we going to tell him?"

"Leave it to me, darling, I'll think of something. But don't worry about it, he'll be fine. Come on, let's get something to eat. I wonder if they've freshened up that dish of pancakes. I know I shouldn't, but I don't get to come here that often."

Dennis had been waiting for them on the tarmac, but as soon as David Bird was apprehended and carted off to a side room, he'd had to excuse himself and make a couple of telephone calls.

"That's definitely one for Benny," he remarked cheerfully as a couple of porters loaded their bags into the boot and they climbed into the two cars. "Darling, why don't you take Melanie and James?" he called over to his wife, "that way I can have a few moments alone with Amanda."

Until that moment they had been surrounded by people they knew, so all her father had been able to do was fling his arms around her and make small talk about the flight and the humidity. Amanda was dreading the moment they would be alone and she would no longer be able to evade the one matter she knew he was waiting to discuss. He'd caught her by surprise, and she hadn't had time to prepare herself. On the other hand, there was something to be said for getting it over and done with. Desperately, she tried to think of something, anything, to distract his attention. Yes, there it was, a snippet she'd read in the paper shortly before leaving England.

"Daddy, what's all this about the Indonesians invading East Timor?"

"Oh, that," her father replied in an offhand tone as the driver led their procession out of the airport, "it was just a little local difficulty they had to sort out with some communists nipping in and out across the border. I shouldn't worry about it, it was inevitable and it won't affect anything important, certainly not round here. What I'm more interested in hearing about is what you've done to get yourself kicked out of Cheltenham."

"Psst! Amanda."

"What?"

"Don't turn round, but behind you, out there on the balcony."

"Where?"

"End table. Blond hair, smoking a cigarette. Who is he?"

As subtly as possible, Amanda turned her head to peer out of the restaurant window. "I think he's one of the pilots. I don't know his name."

From across the table Melanie reached to her frosted glass of Seven Up and lifted it up to her lips. "Bit of a dish," she whispered.

"Definitely," her friend agreed in a voice low enough for no one else to hear.

"Don't whisper," Barbara barked sharply from the end of the table.

"Sorry, Mum. I was just saying something to Melanie."

"Perhaps you'd like to share it with all of us?"

"No, it's okay, thanks."

"Go on."

"It's nothing."

Realising she wasn't about to be privy to whatever her daughter found so entertaining, Barbara decided to let the matter drop. Instead she turned to her husband, who was chewing thoughtfully over a piece of grilled red snapper.

"Isn't it wonderful about the new girl Benny's found."

"What new girl?" asked Dennis absent-mindedly.

"The new amah," Barbara replied, not bothering to conceal the exasperation in her voice. "Finally, I'm going to have someone working in the house who actually understands English. It'll be such a relief not to have to shout in words of one syllable to make myself understood."

"You say Benny found her for you?"

"I told you I asked him to find someone when Ida left. I don't care where you have to look, I said, just get me someone who can speak English."

"I didn't know Ida had gone," interjected James.

"I'm sure I told you, darling."

"No, you definitely didn't," protested her son. "What happened to her?"

"She kept breaking things, and she was so slow."

"You sacked her?" James was incredulous.

"She left," his mother retorted firmly. "It was for the best, for everyone."

"Where did she go?"

"I haven't the faintest idea," said Barbara in a tone that made it clear to all this was not a matter with which she had felt it necessary to tax her conscience. "Back to where she came from, I imagine." To further emphasise the fact that this was her last word on the subject she resumed picking the lobster flesh away from the shell draped across her plate, deliberately dipping the white morsel of flesh into the ramekin of molten butter before popping it into her heavily rouged mouth.

There was a pause while they all concentrated on their food, then Dennis piped up.

"What I'd like to know is how on earth Benny found someone who can speak English and is prepared to work on an amah's wages."

"You know Benny," his wife replied still chewing. She paused to take a large slurp from the glass of chilled Californian Chardonnay at her side. "Whenever I want something and everyone tells me I can't get it, I always go to him. He never lets me down. Just a pity there aren't more like him."

"He had to sort out David Bird at the airport today," said Amanda with a mischievous grin.

"Who's David Bird?" asked Melanie.

"I pointed him out to you on the plane. You remember, the fat kid with the black T-shirt and the bad skin. He's the general manager's son."

"Amanda, don't be so unkind!"

"It's true, Mum, there's no point denying it. Customs went through his bags and found a porn mag."

"I didn't see anything," said James.

"Well, you wouldn't," retorted his older sister. "You were too busy writing down aircraft registration numbers. Anyway, he was well behind us towards the end of the queue. Stephen told me this afternoon. Apparently Benny had to bribe the customs men a million rupes or they'd have carted him off to Bandakan jail."

"How much is a million rupes?" Melanie asked.

"About two and a half thousand pounds,"Amanda replied.

"Bloody hell! I mean, goodness, that seems an awful lot of money just to fix something like that."

"That's how it is round here. Welcome to Indonesia."

"I think we should have a toast," interrupted Dennis, rapping the table sharply with the handle of his knife. "I propose we drink to our family, reunited again, to a wonderful Christmas holiday, and to our guest Melanie. Welcome to Bandakan, Melanie." Amanda seized the opportunity to refill the one glass of wine that was supposed to constitute her ration and which she had already drunk dry, and together they raised their glasses.

"Did Benny really have to cough up a million rupes to get that Bird brat off the hook?" Barbara asked her husband later that night when they were alone in their bedroom.

"Add a half and that's about the size of it. Or so he told me. I don't doubt he kept a clip for himself, but I've no way of finding out exactly how much." He shrugged his shoulders as he unbuttoned the loose cotton shirt he'd worn to the club. "Anyway, who cares, Harry Bird's not about to start asking for receipts."

"At least it wasn't drugs."

"I imagine that sentiment's being expressed in the Bird household as we speak," replied Dennis. "Even Benny would have had his work cut out hushing that up."

"He really is a spoilt little jerk. Stupid with it, too. I blame his mother, I'm sure he wouldn't have turned out half as bad if she hadn't clung on to him like a baby for so long. Thankfully, Amanda doesn't seem to have much time for him."

"Speaking of Amanda, what was all that business lighting up at the end of the meal? I didn't realise we'd agreed to let her smoke."

"Oh darling, she's been sneaking cigarettes for almost three years now. We came to an agreement in Singapore. She could smoke at home if she kept it to ten a day."

Dennis snorted. "So she smokes half a pack in front of us, and the other pack and a half is business as usual at the end of the garden!"

The air conditioning unit hummed quietly in the background, blocking out the sound of the crickets and the toads from the other side of the sealed glass doors, as Dennis digested this compromise negotiated without his consent.

"I know it's not ideal," his wife went on, "but it does seem rather hypocritical, darling, seeing as we both puff away."

"She's seventeen, for Christ's sake!"

"It's how they are these days. According to Amanda, they're all at it at school."

"Which reminds me, have you had any further thoughts about how we're going to handle that particular situation?"

"I guess she'll have to finish off her A levels at the International School in Singapore. There's nowhere in England I could think of that would take her at such short notice except for some hideous crammer. Did you talk to her about it in the car?"

"She insists she was made into a scapegoat. With no other evidence from her or the school, I don't have much choice but to believe her."

"It's my fault," replied Barbara.

"In what way?"

"It's me they couldn't stand, not Amanda. Asking her to leave was their way of getting back at me."

"What on earth are you talking about?"

"You don't go there, you don't see the way they look down their noses at me. Oh, they're happy enough to take our money, but I can tell they feel the world has gone to the dogs having to let people like us in."

"You're exaggerating," Dennis replied, stifling a yawn. "This is the nineteen seventies, the world's changed, people don't think like that any more."

"All I can say is, you didn't have to face that frigid bitch of a headmistress at the beginning of each year."

"She didn't seem too bad to me."

"On the one occasion you met her."

"It's history now, unless you think there's any point in making an appeal."

"I'd rather die than grovel in front of them," Barbara replied with vehemence. "So far as I'm concerned they can stick their bloody Ladies College. Amanda will be fine, she got what she needed out of the place."

"She's still to get her qualifications."

"That's a minor detail."

"In the meantime, I don't want her having an adverse influence on James, especially with this smoking."

"She won't. I made her promise. I told her if I found out she'd been giving him cigarettes I'd cut off her allowance."

"Why not just cut it off anyway?"

"Darling, the last thing I want to do is alienate her. I miss them so much when they're away, I hate to have a huge row the moment they arrive. I'll keep an eye on her, if it starts getting out of hand, I'll come down on her."

"What do you make of her friend, Melanie? She didn't have much to say for herself at dinner."

"I think she was overwhelmed by it all. They're still jet-lagged."

"Have you had a chance to talk to her?"

"A bit. She seems a sensible enough girl. I think she'll be a good influence on Amanda."

"If I were Lord Brancock, I think I'd be more worried about what kind of influence Amanda's going to be on her."

Down at the end of the garden, Amanda and Melanie could make out the silhouetted figures of Dennis and Barbara preparing for bed while they enjoyed a last cigarette before retiring themselves.

"I wonder what they're talking about?" mused Amanda, pulling heavily on her Marlboro.

Melanie contemplated this while she blew a series of smoke rings that were clearly the result of extensive practice. "I don't know, what do parents talk about?"

"Boring old stuff, mostly. Money, things they want to buy, what people are saying up at the club. Or at least they do whenever I'm around. Maybe they have scintillating conversations about philosophy when they're on their own, but I doubt it."

"She seems so worldly."

"My mother?"

"Compared to my mother, she is. All she ever talks about is points to point and what the garden club are up to. Whereas your mother, well, she's lived."

"I guess that's one way of looking at it. Whenever I asked her what it was like growing up all she ever talked about was wanting to get away. If she did what her father wanted he told her she was dull and stupid, if she went her own way he accused her of getting above herself. She couldn't win."

"That's what comes of trying to please other people all the time. Speaking of which, I think you should go for that helicopter pilot."

"He's so old."

"No he's not," scoffed Melanie. "Besides, you need someone with a bit of experience for something like this. The last thing you want is some kid who doesn't know what he's doing shooting his load the second he touches you."

"Like David Bird?"

They both giggled. "He's probably tucked up in bed wanking over you right now. Especially now they've confiscated his porno mags."

"He can dream on," replied Amanda. "Ugh, the thought of doing it with him."

"That's exactly my point," Melanie persisted, pulling on her cigarette.

"What about you? Aren't you interested in him?"

"Who?"

"The helicopter pilot."

"Sure, he's good looking, but he's more your type."

"How do you know what my type is?"

"Just a feeling. Besides, right now your need is greater than mine."

"I thought you'd split up with Frederick."

"I have."

"Then what's going on, Mel? I've never known you to be unselfish about a guy, unless there was something seriously wrong with him."

"There's nothing wrong with him. It's just you need to have this experience."

"Why?"

"You just do. So we can talk about it properly and we both know what we're talking about. It's like, right now there's this divide between us: there are things I want to talk to you about, but there's no point because you can't fully understand. It's not your fault, it's just the way it is. So you see, I'm not really being unselfish, I'm just being me, thinking of a way to fill those dull rainy January afternoons."

"I'm not going back."

"What?"

"They've asked me to leave."

"You've been expelled?"

"Not technically, just asked to leave. They said they'll give me a good reference for wherever I want to go, but they don't want me back."

"But that's outrageous! Why?"

Amanda shrugged. "They didn't give a real reason. Just said they thought I was a bad influence on the other girls."

"But they can't do that to you, with your A levels coming up in a few months!"

"Apparently that was the whole point. They think I'll disrupt the others."

"That is so wrong! Do you want me to get Daddy to talk to someone? He's friends with a couple of the governors."

"There's no point."

"There's every point. You can't lie down and let them do this to you."

"I don't want to go back. Not if they don't want me. I'll stay here, I'll be fine. Really, I will."

"But what about university?"

"What about it? I never really much fancied it anyway, I was only applying because I couldn't think of anything else to do."

"But what will you do here?"

"I don't know. I'll think of something."

"That makes it even more important we set you up with that pilot."

"He wouldn't be interested in me."

"Amanda, only you could say something like that. It's one of the things I love about you."

"We don't even know his name."

"That shouldn't be too hard to find out. Do they live up here?"

"Who?"

"The pilots."

Amanda shook her head. "No, they're down at Base Camp next to the airport. They just come up here to use the pool and the club."

"Then the pool and the club it shall be." Melanie flicked her cigarette butt onto the grass then ground it out with her heel. "Come on, let's get inside. I'm getting bitten half to death."

THE FLORES SEA, INDONESIAN WATERS

8TH DECEMBER 1975

6

They were onto her again, coming at her with their disgusting leers, attacking her from every angle, soiling her hair and her face with their foul emissions, laughing as they oversaw her utter degradation. On and on it went, for nothing seemed to exhaust these barbarians, until she woke with a scream.

She realised she had been thrashing from side to side, for the single sheet was twisted all round her body. Opening her eyes, she looked around the tiny cabin, just big enough to house the single bunk bed on which she lay with a tiny space to squeeze past. Daylight seeped in through a porthole set into the wall at the end of the bunk, but it was the gentle rocking motion and the vibration from the noisy diesel engine the other side of the warm metal wall behind her that told her they were no longer in Dili harbour but far out to sea.

Hasan had been vague when she had asked where the boat was destined, simply saying "back to Indonesia" before turning to give more orders to the crew. An argument was raging between two soldiers on the bow, one of whom wanted several motorcycles looted by the other unloaded and replaced with a dozen chests full of coffee beans liberated from a nearby warehouse. The boat was perilously overloaded as it was, and eventually Hasan was called upon to intervene. After a short exchange the coffee won the day, some compensatory notes changed hands and the first soldier sulkily called out to two colleagues to find another berth for the bikes. At this point Francesca shrunk back from her vantage point on the bridge; the last thing she wanted having come so far was to be deemed excess cargo herself and dumped back on the dock, which was quickly filling up with more and more soldiers, many of them disembarking from a couple of warships now tied up against the harbour. As things stood, she didn't particularly care where they were heading, just so long as they got away from here. Hasan had been right, with him at her side not a single soldier had even looked at her in that chilling, predatory manner, let alone touched or threatened her. They assumed she had been earmarked for bigger fish than them, and for all she knew, she had. But Hasan was the first Indonesian to have extended to her anything other than unadulterated brutality, and if his kindness was no more than a momentary respite before some greater, hitherto unimaginable terror, she was happy to accept it at face value for now. So she had stood there in Hasan's shadow, watching as he issued orders to the crew scurrying up and down the single deck of the rusty cargo tramp.

All along she had kept an eye out for anything that might resemble a first aid tent or field hospital, or even someone carrying a baby, but there had been nothing to give any clue to her tiny sister's whereabouts. She knew she had to assume the worst and move on, and try not to think of some of the grislier fates Angelica might have suffered. All she hoped, whether she was in this world or the next, was that her torment was over. Perhaps some day she would be able to return and seek her out properly, but for now she had to follow Hasan wherever he was going to take her.

Eventually the boat would take no more, and Hasan ordered the gangway to be drawn up and the ropes cast off from the shore. By now the harbour was teeming with traffic, much of it military, along with cargo vessels like theirs loading up with plundered goodies. There was a considerable amount of tooting from ships' horns and cheerful waves between crews of different vessels. She noticed the blackened muzzles on the warships and wondered whether these were the guns that had pounded her home town before the parachutists arrived. By day there was a carnival atmosphere to the flotilla, with men cheerfully going about their business on board, scrubbing down decks or wringing out buckets full of washing. It was hard to see these young faces as ruthless killers, just as it was probably hard for the mothers of the men who'd been in her house to imagine their precious little angels as the hideous monsters the army had turned them into.

Those men. She knew she had to find a way to come to terms with what had happened, but she also knew it would be the most difficult obstacle she would have to overcome. On the one hand she knew she was lucky, she had seen enough slaughter around her to know that relatively speaking she had been spared. She was still alive and her physical injuries would in all probability heal. She still shuddered when she recalled the agonising screams emanating from a burning building she and Hasan had walked past on their way back to the boat, Indonesian soldiers laughing while they stood guard outside, her fellow Timorese citizens shrieking while they burned to death inside. Who was she to complain about a little rough handling? Yet the violation struck to the core of what it was to be a woman, for she supposed that was what she was now. And what if one of them had made her pregnant? How could she go through with having a baby, let alone loving it and nurturing it, if she saw one of those soldiers every time she looked into its face? She would know soon enough, she thought, and if it had happened she would deal with it then.

For now she had had enough of men to last a lifetime. Those who hadn't abused her; Miguel, her father, Antonio, precious little Marco, were all dead. And whilst Hasan may have saved her life, the fact remained she was a prisoner on his boat. She didn't regret the decision to follow him away from almost certain death, but he was still to reveal his full hand. Vaguely she recalled an expression she'd learnt in her English classes about stepping out of the frying pan into the fire.

So far, though, Hasan had been nothing but kindness, showing her to the tiny cabin next to the engine room in which she now lay, and ordering his cook to bring her some food and water. At his suggestion she had moved away from the bridge to confine herself below decks, "at least until we are out at sea". She had tried to eat but only managed to swallow a few morsels of the rice and fish stew brought to her cabin. She had accepted the tray from the boy without a word, and he had been too shy or uninterested in her to attempt to initiate a conversation. The remains of the meal now lay on the floor beside her, where she had put it before falling into that deep sleep. Momentarily it been a refuge, but with the nightmare it seemed even that avenue of escape was denied to her. If she killed herself, she wondered, would her spirit go to some place where the horror she had suffered was revisited upon her again and again, in some circular loop of terror, her own private hell that lived up to everything the nuns had promised lay ahead if she sinned? She wondered what had happened to them, and her resentment at her perception of their harsh judgements of her was momentarily overcome by concern for their welfare, especially the younger ones. Sister Isabella, for instance, who had taught her Portuguese and English, didn't have a malicious bone in her body, and she was far too pretty for her own good. Stripped of her habit, in a manner Francesca could now all too easily picture, she would be just another terrified young woman like herself, reduced to an object that momentarily satisfied the lust and power cravings of these vermin high on their victory. Francesca wondered how Isabella's faith would have stood up against her own. Perhaps she had fought for her honour with every ounce of strength left in her body, embracing death in the sure knowledge she was about to be reunited with her precious Jesus. If so, she was a more devout woman than Francesca, who felt nothing more than a sense of utter abandonment. Fingering the crucifix around her neck, she wondered why she hadn't ripped it from her throat and tossed it into the sea. It was only because it had been a gift from her dear, dead parents, its symbolism was no more than that, on its own it was nothing. Still, it was a mystery how her supposed saviour could have let her down so badly. By rights she should be furious at him, but how could you be angry at someone you had just decided did not exist? She would save that one for later, she thought. She had hardly been top of Jesus's concerns these past twenty four hours, why should he be amongst hers?

She sat up and looked out of the porthole, which was screwed firmly into place. Every so often a wave would splash over the glass, causing her to flinch. From her side of the vessel at least no land was in sight, and from the angle of the sun she supposed it to be late afternoon. Soon the sun would set and it would be another night, the first night to live through since the horror her life had become.

As she had feared, he came to her cabin later that evening, tapping softly on the door then opening it before she had a chance to answer. So this was the score. He'd saved her life only to have her for himself later, at his time and place of choosing. He was no better than the soldiers, only more discerning in the way he went about satisfying his appetites.

"Francesca," he whispered, for by now he had learnt her name. She pretended to be asleep, keeping one eye open ever so slightly so she could see him close the door behind him and move towards her.

"Francesca," he whispered again, now at her side. She had chosen the lower bunk and he was leaning over her. She smelt beer and tobacco on his breath. Should she try and stab him with the fork at her foot, gouge his eyes out as he came onto her, or bite that thing of his off if he tried to put it into her mouth?

Shifting half a pace so he could crouch down by her face, he placed his right foot firmly down in the middle of her half eaten bowl of rice, causing it to flip up and spray the remains of the stew over the bottom of his trouser leg. The enamel bowl made a clanging sound as the edge hit the metal floor.

"Shit!" he exclaimed into the dark. Francesca, who could no longer feign sleep, tried to suppress a giggle.

"So you are awake," he said, the irritation clear in his voice.

"How could I not be, with you stomping around my cabin like that?"

"I came to see if everything is alright for you?"

"Yes, it's fine thank you," she replied guardedly.

"How about your supper? Was it okay?"

"It was until you stepped in it." Splattered in oily stew, he was impossible to take seriously. "Would you like some?"

"Thank you, I've eaten already." His attempt to recover some dignity through his formal tone just made her laugh even more.

Sitting on the edge of the bunk, staring disconsolately at his greasy foot and trouser leg, Hasan looked the picture of misery.

"What's so funny?" he demanded.

"You," she replied without thinking.

"I save your life and that makes me an object of ridicule, someone you can make fun of?" He was angry now, and she realised she had gone too far.

"No, Hasan, I don't mean it like that. I'll never be able to say how grateful I am to you for saving me. Just as I will never be able to repay you for your kindness."

"I am not asking to be repaid," he said quietly. "I have a daughter at home about your age."

"I just thought maybe you expected something from me. And I can't do that. I just can't. I can work, I can cook, I can mend things, I can clean, I'll make myself useful to you, but not that. I'm sorry, I just can't do it."

"The soldiers?" he asked. "Did they?" He let the sentence hang in the air and she turned away from him, staring firmly out of the porthole.

He touched her gently on the shoulder, letting his hand rest on her for a few moments before lifting it away. "You don't have to do anything, Francesca. Just rest and recover your strength. You are going to need it."

"Where are we heading?"

"Eventually Jakarta. But before that we're making a detour up the Macassar Strait to a place called Bandakan where I have to dump most of the stuff we loaded up. I plan to drop you off there too."

"Why?"

"Two reasons. It's an out-of-the-way town, you're less likely to fall into trouble than in a big city like Jakarta, and I know people there who can help you. Find you a job, a proper job, if you know what I mean, something you can use to start a new life."

"I don't think I can ever go back to Dili."

"I know. Bandakan may not be the most exciting place on earth, but you'll be safe there. My boss lives there, he'll look after you."

"Your boss?"

"Yes, he's the one who owns this vessel, I'm just hired to sail it wherever he wants it to go."

"Oh."

"Don't worry, he'll take good care of you. Especially when he sees all the other goodies I've brought him."

"Is that what I am? Some trophy to be handed over along with the motorcycles and TVs and all the other things you people robbed from my country!"

"What you call your country is part of Indonesia now, and the sooner you get used to the idea the better. Would you rather I left you at the waterfront?"

"And deny you the chance to sell me into slavery?"

"Who said anything about slavery?" He was exasperated at her now, she could see. "Bandakan's a rich town, it's full of oil and logging companies, there are plenty of opportunities for someone as smart and as pretty as you. I promise you, I'll make sure you're looked after."

He made to stand up, removing the soft plimsoll he'd stepped into her supper as he did, holding it in one hand.

"I'll leave you in peace now," he said when he was at the doorway. "You won't be disturbed any more for the rest of the voyage. We should be in Bandakan in around six or seven days. If you want, you can join us for meals in the crew mess, otherwise I'll have a tray delivered to your cabin."

"Thank you, Hasan." She paused, then seeing he was waiting for something, added, "I am grateful for what you've done for me, honestly I am. I saw enough to know what happened to the people who stayed behind."

"I had nothing to do with any of that."

"I know."

She realised in that moment that he knew the extent of the wrong perpetrated by his army against her people and somehow needed absolution from one of their number for what had happened. She wasn't in a position to absolve anyone for anything, but she might be able to find something out.

"There's another thing you could tell me."

"What's that?" he asked wearily, now leaning against the open doorway.

"When you were walking around the harbour front, before you discovered me, did you by any chance see a baby?"

"Just a baby? On its own?"

"She would probably have been with a soldier."

He shook his head sadly. "Your baby?"

"My baby sister."

"I'm sorry, I didn't see any baby."

"They were talking about taking her to a first aid tent."

"The only first aid tent I saw was full of Indonesian soldiers. Some of those Falintil boys were pretty well dug in, they gave the paratroopers a good run for their money."

She looked away, as the full implication of her loneliness slammed into her properly for the first time. Hasan must have seen her face fall in the dim moonlit cabin, for he reached over again and gently placed his arm on her shoulder.

"It was chaos out there, casualties were being ferried all over the place, and I know there was a hospital ship due in to take some of them back to Jakarta. Just because I didn't see her doesn't mean she wasn't there." He paused a moment before continuing. "Look, I know some of the soldiers went too far, but underneath they're human beings like you and me."

"You wouldn't say that if you'd seen what I saw."

"Maybe, but they're not baby murderers."

"So you think my sister may be on that hospital ship?"

"Don't raise your hopes too high, but it's possible."

"I want to go to Jakarta. If she's there I want to find her."

"No!" he barked.

"She is all I have left in the world."

"It's too dangerous for you there," he continued, his voice suddenly hard. "I can protect you in Bandakan, in Jakarta you'll be eaten alive. I won't take you there, that's my final word. You get off this ship when we dock in Bandakan, no further argument."

"What will happen to my sister if she's on that hospital ship?"

"My guess is she would be given to some childless military couple with connections."

"The army that murdered my family will bring up my sister as one of its own!"

"Hush! Don't raise your voice so. She will have a good life, she will have opportunities she would never have enjoyed had she stayed, she will have much more than you could ever give her."

"But what of her family? Her roots?" Francesca was pleading now, her voice cracking against Hasan's authoritarian shell.

"She will remember none of it. It's better that way. Now, listen to me, Francesca. Your sister has her own destiny, you have yours. Maybe one day your paths will cross again, perhaps in this life, perhaps in the next."

"I don't believe in any next."

He shrugged his shoulders. "Whatever. Either way, you must think about staying alive and looking after your own future. For now that future is in Bandakan. I promise you, it is the best place for you."

"Can I ask one more question?"

"Go on." His voice seemed weary, as if she were about to confront him with yet another atrocity for which he would be obliged to find a justification.

"There were some Portuguese nuns working at the school in Dili. Have you any idea what might have happened to them?"

"I believe they were evacuated. One of the Australian oil companies sent some helicopters to rescue them."

"Oh." It wasn't what she had imagined at all, and suddenly her resentment at the nuns welled up so strongly from within her she thought at first she might choke. Not only had they deceived her with their fairy tales, when it came to it they hadn't even been there to share her suffering.

"Let me tell you one thing about the world you're going in to," Hasan said softly. "You may think it's a man's world out there after what you've seen, but the fact is, it's really a white man's world, and the sooner you accept that, the easier you'll find it to live in that world and make it work for you. Goodnight," he added, smiling briefly before stepping back out of the cabin and shutting the door softly behind him.

After Hasan's visit no one bothered her, and she gradually settled into an onboard routine of sleeping, eating and staring out of her porthole at the Flores Sea. For the first two days she remained in her cabin, recovering her strength while the worst of her injuries healed. Hasan provided her with a bucket of warm water and a bar of soap, and she cleaned herself again and again, trying to scrub away all physical evidence of her attackers. Soaping her ripped flesh was agony, but she forced herself to continue until she saw herself bleed again. When she was done, she lay down in her bunk and fell asleep, utterly exhausted.

By the third morning much of her strength had returned, and she could walk without each step reminding her of her ordeal. She found herself marvelling at the recuperative powers of the human body. She was finding the confines of the cabin claustrophobic too, and that afternoon she resolved to muster up her courage and venture out on deck.

Not knowing what to expect, she clambered up the steep metal stairway and opened the heavy metal door to step out on the main deck. The equatorial sun was still strong, causing her to squint as she took in the first restorative gulps of sea air. There was a gentle breeze which acted like a healing balm over her entire body, enveloping her in its breath. She looked out at the bright blue sea and experienced a momentary urge to run to the side of the boat and dive in. Instead, she gingerly made her way up the port side past the laden crates of loot to the bow, where she wedged herself between the converging railings. Turning round, she caught a glimpse of Hasan in the wheelhouse, cigarette firmly clenched between his teeth. He offered her a jaunty wave, which she shyly returned. A crewman was lazily painting part of the stern railing, but apart from him the deck was deserted.

Being up there in the bows felt good. With each wave that crashed against the metal skin of the boat she felt another fathom being placed between her and the horrors of Dili. She felt curious about this place Bandakan that Hasan was so adamant should be her destination. Jakarta, Bandakan – neither meant anything to her. Now she'd had time to think about it, she was happy to defer to his judgement, especially if he had friends there who would help her. Alone in a hostile world for the first time in her life, she was discovering a newfound appreciation for any friends she could get. She wondered if she should ask Hasan not to tell anyone what had happened to her. Was it a good idea to raise the subject, or should she just let it rest and trust to his discretion? She would think about the best way to approach it, for it was important, she knew. If no one in this Bandakan place knew her past, it would be a great deal easier to create a future there.

Over the next few days she spent hours at a time wedged into her little triangle at the bows, so much so the crew began to refer to her as their little figurehead. Hasan insisted she wear a large floppy hat to protect herself against the sun, as each morning she picked her way across the deck to secure her spot after breakfast, which she now took with the others, squeezed around the small table bolted to the floor in the crew mess. At first, she offered to help clear up or perform other chores, but this seemed to upset the invisible order running throughout the ship, so eventually she took the hint and kept to her own private routine.

Facing forward into the sea where no one could observe her face, she allowed herself to give in to her grief. Racked by howls heard by no one apart from the porpoises that played their games around the bows, she gripped onto her memories of each one of her family; her gentle, well-intentioned father, her mother, Antonio, Marco, and finally Baby Angelica, whose fate she would probably never know. Each one heralded more pain, as she oscillated between picturing them as a happy family who didn't know how happy they were, and as massacred corpses sprawled out in the front room of their home. Somehow the survivor within her knew that these long peaceful days at sea represented her chance to let slip these anchors in her old life, and that when they reached their destination she would have to leave them behind. She would need all her strength and her wits to make it through those early days and weeks while she found her new bearings. Knowing this, she let herself wail from the pit of her soul in priovate expressions of grief that left her feeling utterly exhausted but strangely exhilarated. Then she would retire to her cabin to sleep some more, before joining the crew for another meal.

She would sit up in the bows at night time too, gazing at the moon and the stars. Sometimes Hasan would sidle up to her and they would stare at the heavens side by side, Hasan occasionally pointing out a star or a constellation. Mostly she just leant against the rails and looked out. It gave her a new sense of her own insignificance, quite different from being the victim of an Indonesian soldier's casual whim.

"It's what I love most about being at sea, the way everything resumes its proper perspective," he said softly.

She turned to him. "How did you know what I was thinking?"

"It has that effect. If only more people stepped back to examine their lives the way being out here forces you to do, the world might be a happier place."

"It couldn't get much unhappier."

"For now, yes. But you're strong, little Francesca, I can see that. It won't always be like this for you. You're young, you will heal, even if it seems to you now that you can never recover from what's happened to you. But you will."

She said nothing, turning to face the sea and the heavens once again. "What's that star there?"

"That's the north star."

"Tell me about your family, Hasan."

"What's there to say?"

"You said you had a daughter my age."

"Yes, I do."

"What's her name?"

"Burpina."

"That's a nice name. What's she look like?"

In response, he reached into his shirt pocket and pulled out a well thumbed photograph wrapped in clear tape. In the moonlight she saw a formal family grouping, and she forced herself to stuff down the fresh wave of grief welling up from inside.

"That's her," said Hasan simply, "second from the left. Naughty little thing, always causing me or her mother trouble."

Francesca squinted at the picture. "Do you miss them?"

"Of course. But you've got to do what you've got to do. My work is here. It won't be long, I'll be back with them in a few days from now."

"Until you leave them again."

"That's right. Always leaving, always coming back, always leaving again. You get used to it after a while."

"Until one day you don't."

"Exactly. Until one day you don't."

She was resting at her usual spot the following afternoon when she noticed the vessel change from their northerly course up the Macassar Strait to a westerly bearing into the sun. Feeling thirsty, she decided to fetch herself a glass of water and stop in at the wheelhouse on the way. Perhaps they had made better progress than expected, she hadn't thought they were due to dock in Bandakan for another day and a half. Hasan was at the wheelhouse, but he wasn't at the wheel; instead he was giving orders to a crewman while he stood at the doorway with a pair of binoculars at his eyes, staring out to the stern, where Francesca could just make out a little dot on the horizon.

"What is it?" she asked.

"I don't know, but they're coming towards us," he replied without moving.

"Is that why we've turned away?"

"Yes. I don't doubt they can catch us, but I want to make sure they're chasing us, and I want them facing into the sun if they are."

"Are they pirates?"

"It's possible. There are plenty of boats operating out of Sulawesi, and we make a tempting target."

"What are we going to do?"

"Flush them out." Hasan turned to the crewman at the wheel. "They're flying the Indonesian flag."

"Doesn't mean anything," muttered the crewman.

"Hold your course. And when they do get up close, keep turning away to keep them on our stern. Whatever you do, don't expose our midriffs to them. I'm going below deck for a minute. Francesca, you might not want to watch this."

"I'd rather stay up here, if you don't mind," she replied. "I promise I won't be in anyone's way."

"Okay, but you jump to when anyone gives you an order." She noticed how his voice had adopted a hard edge to it, the efficient captain at work.

Hasan disappeared below decks, returning a couple of minutes later with two crewmen carrying a large wooden case one at each end, which they set down on the raised deck above the stern. Francesca moved over to the metal stairway and climbed two steps so she could peer her head over the deck floor and watch. They opened the case. It contained a machine gun and a number of accessories. Under Hasan's guidance, they placed the gun on a bipod, loaded it from the top with a magazine and cocked the mechanism. In the meantime, the boat had closed in noticeably upon them. To Francesca's naked eye, it was no longer a speck but now discernible as a motor vessel of some description.

Hasan looked out towards it with his binoculars and then spoke to the crewmen. "Remember, keep the bursts short and neat – it's a machine gun not a hosepipe. We won't have time to mess around changing barrels, so don't overheat it. There are six magazines in the case with that gun. I want you to fill the lot, twenty-eight rounds each – don't try to jam in the full thirty – then lay each one on the deck in line beside the gun. As soon as a magazine is emptied, one of you take it off, bang on the next one and refill it while the other one keeps firing. I doubt we'll need all six, but I don't want to be caught short. Got all that?"

The gunners nodded.

"Good." Hasan continued. "Now, the most important thing is, absolutely no shooting until they're up real close. I want you to keep that tarpaulin on until the very last minute, and don't fire until I give the command. If they start shooting at us, shoot straight back at where they're coming from, but otherwise I want you to fire along the hull right at the waterline. Don't shoot short or the water will disperse the force of the bullets, but don't aim too high either. Start around the engine room, then work your way left and right. Don't try and pick out individual targets, just concentrate on disabling the vessel. Understood?"

Again, the gunners nodded.

"Good. Once those magazines are loaded get a couple of mops and pails from below and look as if you're cleaning the deck. Don't get into position until I say so, and remember, keep that tarp on until you see me remove my cap, then let them have it. I'm going to let them come up close, real close."

"Do you think they'll shoot us first, Captain?" asked one of the gunners.

"Not if they don't see the Bren," replied Hasan. "My guess is they'll try and bluff their way on board. That's their usual tactic, spin us some bullshit about a sick crewman."

The boat was gaining on them quite rapidly, and already Francesca could discern its shape. It obviously had powerful engines, for it was creating quite a wake in its path. Hasan was right, there was no chance of outrunning it anywhere. She looked up at her protector, who was staring intently at the vessel through his binoculars.

"They've got her decked out as a customs boat," he remarked to no one in particular.

"Could it be a real one?" asked Francesca.

"In these waters?" Hasan let out a little laugh. "I very much doubt it! What I mean is, it's highly possible the boat is real, but those won't be customs officials on board. They could have captured the boat or even stolen her from a berth somewhere, but they're pirates for sure. And we're one fat juicy mango sitting bang slap in the middle of the sea, ripe for plucking."

Within a few minutes it was possible to pick out several men on the boat with the naked eye, and Francesca could see one of them standing upright in the cockpit staring at them through a pair of binoculars. Hasan had taken over the wheel and continued to manoeuvre their boat at about three-quarters speed ahead, constantly adjusting their course to keep their pursuers behind them and looking into the sun as much as possible. The boat was closing in on them rapidly, and was only a few hundred yards off their stern when it cut its engines to avoid overtaking them.

Hasan poked his head out of the wheelhouse. "Okay boys, keep mopping and don't take that tarp off until my cap comes off."

Francesca looked across at the sun-bleached red cap with an equally faded Shell logo printed across the front. "As for you," he continued, seeming to notice her presence for the first time, "you can either go down to your cabin or stay in the wheelhouse."

"I'll stay here, please."

"Fair enough, but don't step out on deck until this is all over."

Francesca nodded, and Hasan handed the wheel over to the crewman with an order to throttle back to quarter speed. The figure in the cockpit had replaced his binoculars with a megaphone, which he raised to his lips. They heard the amplified click of the speak button followed by a burst of static.

"You are ordered to stop your engines and make ready to be boarded! You are in Indonesian waters, this is a Customs vessel and we have reason to believe you may be carrying contraband cargo."

"He's lying," muttered Hasan quietly.

"How can you be so sure?" asked Francesca.

"His accent for a start. Most of these customs skippers are from Java, and his accent is Sulawesi." He turned again to the crewman at the wheel. "Okay, let's pull them in. Dead slow ahead, then slip her into idle when I say."

"Dead slow ahead, Captain."

Francesca glanced through the small window looking out to the stern. The two crewmen had put their mops to one side, they now squatted over the bulky tarpaulin, glancing between Hasan and the other vessel, which had cuts its engines to a crawl. It was so close now Francesca could make out the expressions on the faces of the uniformed crew. They bore the same grins she had last seen on the faces of the soldiers in her front room, that lascivious anticipation of pleasure handed to them at the barrel of a gun. Come on, Hasan, she silently urged. They'll be jumping over the rail in a minute! She watched the man in the cockpit lift his megaphone back up to his mouth.

"Prepare to be boarded! Please drop your engines into neutral now!"

Francesca looked across from the customs boat to Hasan, who was standing in the wheelhouse doorway. She watched him reach up to his head and take hold of the peak of his cap with his forefinger and thumb. Hardly daring to look, she gripped the edge of the wheelhouse table and waited. Out of the corner of her eye she saw the two gunners watch their captain with the intensity of ravenous dogs about to be served their dinner.

The customs boat floated closer still towards them, its skipper struggling to reach their amidships without over-shooting. Francesca estimated it to be less than sixty feet away. A uniformed figure standing at the bows was reaching for a boathook when Hasan flicked the cap from his head to expose his receding hairline and balding pate. Francesca heard a rustle as the tarpaulin was whipped away, followed by a clatter of metal as the gun was hastily repositioned to face the customs boat which was now almost directly amidships. A second later came the ear shattering burst of machine gun fire.

The Bren proceeded to rake the boat from end to end, systematically perforating the wooden hull as if it were a sew-ing machine running across a piece of muslin. Although the gunner kept his aim low as instructed, the figures on the deck instinctively dived for cover. She watched, mesmerised at the machine gun's efficiency. There was a muffled explosion as some bullets found the fuel tanks, followed by a scream and a large pall of black smoke rising from the boat's stern. A quick metallic pause followed while magazines were swapped over, during which she heard the men on board the stricken ves-sel shout desperately for the shooting to stop. She could see four or five of them scarpering about in blind panic, unable to decide whether to reach for cover or hold up their hands in surrender.

More ruthless shooting followed from the Bren as a second, then a third magazine fed itself through the weapon. Francesca found it a bizarre and disturbingly empowering experience suddenly to be on the other side of the trigger. After being caught unprepared at the hands of the Indonesian soldiers in Dili, it was sweet exhilaration to lure these pirates into an ambush and let them have it. So far not a single shot had been fired back at them; it seemed the crew, if they were armed, had no wish to provoke another onslaught from the Bren.

With their victim now listing at a thirty degree angle in the water and orange flames visible from the engine room, Hasan gave the order to cease fire. Once it became apparent that the shooting was over and the stricken vessel had another minute or two at most before it sunk, the crew reappeared on deck, their hands held high above their heads, shouting for help. Hasan briefly looked the scene of his devastation up and down, then turned to the crewman in the wheelhouse.

"Full speed ahead."

The crewman put his hand down on the throttle and their engines roared to life.

Francesca looked across at Hasan. "Aren't we going to pick them up?" she asked in a shocked voice.

Hasan shot her a scornful look. "You're joking, right?"

"We can't just leave them here to drown."

"The sharks will find them before that happens."

"But that's murder! It's one thing to defend yourself against an attack, another to leave those men to face certain death."

"And what, Madam, do you suggest I do with them? Do you want them on board here causing trouble, ready to slit our throats at the slightest opportunity? Have you any idea what pirates operating in these waters do to people on the vessels they seize?"

Francesca shook her head. In the distance the wreckage of the customs boat receded, and although she could no longer hear their cries above the engine noise, their flailing arms left no one in any doubt as to the extent of their despair.

"All I can say," continued Hasan, "is their behaviour makes those Indonesian paratroopers in Dili look like guests laden down with house gifts. Do you want to live through that again, only a hundred times worse?"

Again, Francesca shook her head.

"Then forget about those scum, put them out of your mind and thank whatever God you do or don't believe in there is some justice left in this world."

Chastened, Francesca retired to her cabin, taking one last glance at the remains of the customs boat. The rising water had extinguished the fire, but the bows had already disappeared, and she could see the five pirates huddled around the stern, each reaching for the highest piece of railing. So far as she could see, no effort had been made to launch the sole life raft, which had been shredded by the Bren, leaving them nothing but orange inflatable jackets and pieces of foam mattress to hold on to. Shutting the door to her cabin, she forced herself to do as Hasan had bid and put their suffering out of her mind, hardening her heart to the realities of the world. If this was what one had to do to survive, then so be it. Hasan was right, she realised: stripped of all niceties, she knew that if it came down to it, she would rather have the murder of five pirates on her conscience than go through the nightmare of Dili once more. It was simple. It was elemental. It was survival.

Two days later they docked in Bandakan. Still dressed in the same loose clothing she had left her home in, she leant against her usual railing in the bows as they entered the harbour. The huge oil refinery with its silver tanks neatly laid out dominated the skyline of what otherwise appeared to be little more than a large, sprawling shanty town. Behind the town the ground rose through a series of ridges, each one dotted with clusters of neat modern bungalows. Francesca looked out nervously at the place destined to become her new home. Was it big enough to disappear in? What kind of life would she be able to make for herself here? Hasan had promised to help her, but who were these friends of his and how would they treat her once he had set sail again for Jakarta?

There was quite a crowd to greet them when they finally found a berth to dock alongside, including a small convoy of army trucks. Francesca was about to make a dash for her cabin when she realised not one of the soldiers lined up along the wharf was armed. Of course, she remembered, they were too busy salivating over all the plunder they were about to unload. She just hoped she wasn't on their manifest as well. As if sensing her unease, Hasan tapped her on the shoulder. She jumped and turned to stare straight into his smiling face. He was holding out her small bag of possessions.

"Come, it's time to go now. You don't want to forget these."

"Thank you."

"Follow me. I'll introduce you to my boss."

"Is he here?"

Hasan laughed. "Oh yes, Benny wouldn't miss a party like this."

He led her over to a rickety gangway bordered by a single rope railing on either side. After being so long at sea her legs felt wobbly against the concrete dockside, and Hasan held out his hand to steady her.

"Welcome to Bandakan, town of oil and timber."

She looked up at him suspiciously.

"Don't worry," he continued in his breezy tone, "you'll be fine here." Already people were coming up to Hasan, most of them in uniform, smiling, shaking his hand, asking after his health and his journey. Politely he brushed them off, keeping a firm course towards an official looking single storey building the other side of a busy thoroughfare, as if he were still at sea following a compass bearing. Somehow they picked a path through the motorcycles and hooting cars coming at them from both directions. All that time at sea had left her senses both open and attuned to the faintest shifts; both the noise and the smells were too overpowering. If Hasan hadn't been there to guide her, she was sure she would have been hit by a passing vehicle.

Safely across the road, they made a direct line for the building where Hasan assured her Benny would be waiting for them. Just outside a vendor had set up a stall, where he had laid out packets of cigarettes and bottles of brightly coloured soft drinks, as well as a pile of newspapers. Following Hasan around the corner, her eye caught the single sentence boldly printed above the fold of the top paper: **NAVY FINDS WRECKAGE FROM MISSING CUSTOMS BOAT**. Below it a grainy photograph of a shredded life jacket leapt out to accuse her, alongside a smaller heading: **MINISTER PROM-ISES TOUGH ACTION AGAINST SULAWESI PIRATES**. She wanted to grab Hasan, to drag him back and show him how their world and all they believed to be true had been turned upside down yet again, but he had already moved on inside the building and she had no choice but to follow him, lest she lose him forever.

BANDAKAN
14ᵀᴴ DECEMBER 1975

Benny was never a man to pass an opportunity, especially when it was handed to him on a plate. Delighted as he was with the contents of the manifest Hasan handed over to him, which exceeded his wildest expectations, Francesca was the icing on the cake whose fortuitous arrival promised to place Dennis Cole in his debt for months to come. What a ball he would have! No more pesky auditors sticking their noses into affairs that didn't concern them, and as for his grand plan for young Rollo, the timing couldn't have been better. He could hardly wait to drive up to the ridge with his trophy and announce the wonderful news. When Francesca was finally ushered into the room Benny commandeered whenever he had shipping business to conduct downtown, he politely shook her hand and showed her to a chair in the corner.

"Great work, Hasan, great work," he said, slapping his skipper on the back.

"You look after her, Benny, like I said. She's had a rough time thanks to your old buddies, and I don't want her ending up in some massage parlour. I'll be checking up on her next time I'm in town, and if she's not happy I'm going to give you a serious hard time."

"Hasan, I give you my word, she will be treated like a princess."

"Just make sure she's not mistreated."

"If anyone lays a finger on her, they will have me to answer to." A wolfish grin spread across Benny's face, and he glanced over to Francesca. "See, your troubles are over now, Uncle Benny will take good care of you. Now, if you will excuse me, I need to speak to Hasan in private for a moment."

"Would you like me to wait outside?" Francesca looked confused.

"Manzoor!" Benny yelled through the open doorway. There was a shuffling of feet in the corridor, followed by the appearance of an elderly asthmatic man dressed in a sarong and a pair of flip flops. "Take this young lady over the road and get her something to eat and drink." Benny reached into his pocket and peeled a five hundred rupiah note from a silver money clip.

As soon as the pair of them had left, Benny closed the door and sat down, leaning back in his chair and resting his hand made leather boots on the desk. He reached into his breast pocket for his cigarettes, extracted one and tossed the pack over to Hasan, who had sunk into an armchair by the window.

"So, what was it like over there?"

"You want the official version or the truth?"

"Just tell me what you saw."

"It was a fucking mess."

"What do you mean? I heard Dili fell without any problems."

"Who told you that?"

"I had lunch with General Roullah yesterday."

"All I can say is that General Roullah must be as out of touch with reality on the ground as the over-promoted idiots who put this shambles together in the first place."

"Careful what you're saying, Hasan."

"You weren't there, Benny, it was a complete cock up. They dropped half the paratroopers in the sea to drown under the weight of their equipment, and most of the rest on top of the Fretilin forces, instead of behind their lines. And if that wasn't bad enough, the paratroopers then came under fire from our own marines. It didn't exactly put them in the best of temper when they finally hit Dili. They went berserk, they were like animals. I've never seen anything like it, it made me ashamed to be Indonesian."

"What did you expect them to do? It's a military operation, not a Sunday school picnic."

"I know that, Benny, I know. I just didn't expect them to cut up so rough with the civilian population."

"That's the way it is with these commies. It's not like fighting a regular army. They blend in with the people, then the people wonder why they end up getting a bloody nose."

"This was more than that."

"What kind of fight did the Timorese put up?"

"In Dili itself, nothing we couldn't overcome when we finally got our act together. We pretty much had the town to ourselves. But I think it'll be a different story in the countryside, which is where they're going to take the war."

"There won't be a war. There might be the odd isolated outburst, but we'll soon mop up any resistance."

"Maybe."

"Either way, it's not our problem. You've done a great job, Hasan, I'll make sure you're properly rewarded."

"What's wrong, Benny? You look worried."

"No, it's nothing."

"Come on, I know you better than that. What is it?"

"The paratroopers who were dropped into the sea. Do you know which brigade they were from?"

"Kopassandha, I think."

"Oh."

"Why?"

"Nothing, just curious, that's all. I used to know their CO."

"There's one other thing I need to talk to you about, Benny."

"The girl?"

"Apart from that. You know that customs boat that was attacked?"

"The one on the front of all the papers?"

Hasan nodded. "I was listening to the VHF radio this morning on the way in. That was us."

"Shit." Benny took a deep breath and momentarily closed his eyes, rubbing his forehead. He looked up to face Hasan. "What happened?"

"They were chasing us, and I thought they were pirates. We drew them in, then when they were about to board us we shot them up."

"Did a pretty good job of it from the pictures I saw. Were there any survivors?"

"Nope."

"You sure about that?"

Hasan nodded. "Definitely."

"No one could have got into the water to be picked up by the Navy?"

"No chance. The boat went straight down and they didn't manage to launch the lifeboat. There's no way they would have made the night."

"So you didn't finish them off?"

"There was no need. I just wanted to put as much distance between us and the scene as possible."

"What about the crew?"

"They won't say anything, especially now it turns out it was a genuine customs vessel. But you might want to remember them come payday."

Benny ignored the hint. "Genuine or not, they're still a bunch of thieving cocksuckers who got what was coming to them. You did the right thing, Hasan, if they had boarded you they'd have just impounded my ship and stolen everything for themselves. They're no different from the pirates that way."

"I just thought you should know."

"Thank you for telling me. I'd forget about it if I were you. But what about the girl? She must have seen it."

"She understands we did what had to be done. You can trust her to keep her mouth shut. Just make sure she's well looked after."

"She might have to have an accident."

"Benny," Hasan growled with a menace Benny hadn't heard before.

"Are you and she, like... you know?"

"No, it's nothing like that."

"So, what is it?"

"I can't explain. It's just important to me that she isn't harmed."

"Have it your way, it'll be your balls in a vice if any of this gets out."

"It won't get out."

"Good. Then we won't talk about it any more. You must be hungry, I know I am. How about I treat you to lunch?"

The following afternoon Benny had Stephen drive him and Francesca up to the ridge. Francesca sat beside him, behind the driver, her miserable pile of possessions wedged between them. As the car snaked its way up the hill, the shambles of downtown Bandakan gave way to an opulence she had barely imagined existed. They passed a small guardhouse, which led them past a high cyclone chain fence topped out with barbed wire stretching to the left and right as far as she could see. Once inside the compound, it was like stepping into another country. Most of the houses downtown looked similar to her old home; knocked up from old planks of wood, with tin roofs, intermittent electricity and certainly nothing as sophisticated as running water. Up here they even had sprinklers to keep the grass a lush shade of green. As for the houses, they were more akin to palaces than anything she had ever been inside. They passed a group of white children mooching about on bicycles, and she fought back the tears as she recalled all the hours Marco and Antonio used to spend kicking a football in their dusty back yard, driving her mother mad by persistently bouncing it against the kitchen wall. *Slam, slam, slam*, she'd never forget that sound: how many times had she sat at the table trying to concentrate on her homework while the boys messed around outside. All of it gone, her life reduced to a grubby little bag and the four five thousand rupiah notes Hasan had pressed into her palm when he said goodbye and wished her well.

Sleek bungalow after sleek bungalow slipped before her eyes, nestling between expensively cultivated shrubs and trees of bougainvillaea and jasmine, until they turned into a cul-de-sac dominated by a three-storey office building. The car slowed down and pulled up alongside a bungalow similar to the ones they had just passed, whereupon Benny climbed out and beckoned her to follow. Shyly she let him lead the way into an empty car port, which divided the main house from a small ancillary building. Clearly servants' quarters – she could discern noises of domestic industry and rich cooking smells emanating from within. Benny strode up to the door, removed his sunglasses and rapped the slatted woodwork four times.

"Who's there?" called a male voice in Bahasa.

"I've come to see Suki," Benny replied, clearly not feeling the need to announce himself.

"She will be with you in one moment!" the voice replied. There was some scuttling and shuffling, and finally the door cracked open. Francesca saw a diminutive woman, perhaps ten years older than herself, peer out suspiciously before opening the door fully to stand in the entrance. She had once been good looking, but hard work and disappointment had chiselled away at the edges of her face, so she now just looked ageless and tired, her hair scraped back into a bun held in place with a tortoiseshell skewer.

"Colonel Surikano," she said in a deadpan monotone.

If Benny was put out by her indifference, he didn't let on. "Suki, good afternoon, I have good news for you."

"Abdul?" she asked, a note of hope entering her voice.

"Alas, not," Benny replied, shaking his head. "But good news, none the less. I have found someone to replace Ida."

Suki looked confused. "But I have already found someone. She starts Monday, it is all arranged."

"Then unarrange it."

"I don't understand. You signed her papers yourself."

"Meet Francesca." Benny turned on his heel to make the introduction. "Francesca, this is Suki, who will show you everything you need to know. Suki, Francesca is the answer to all our prayers."

"How come?" To Francesca's eyes, Suki looked distinctly sceptical.

"Because she can do something that neither you nor Hamid nor any of the other girls you've had here working for you have ever been able to manage."

"What's that?"

"She speaks English." Benny was triumphant in his smugness, as if he had just laid out a poker hand he knew it was impossible to trump.

"Oh, yeah?"

"Not perfectly, but well enough to be able to talk with Mrs Cole. You know how it drives her crazy that none of you understand what she is saying. She thinks you do it on purpose to avoid carrying out her wishes. Now Mrs Cole will be very happy. And if Mrs Cole is happy, Mr Cole will be happy. And if Mr Cole is happy, then Uncle Benny is happy and you, Suki, will be happy too."

Suki certainly didn't look very happy to Francesca. "What will I say to this girl?" she persisted.

Benny seemed annoyed at Suki's lack of enthusiasm. "I don't care, tell her whatever you like. Things have changed, a better candidate got the job. And one other thing, Francesca is to work here in the house, but none of the other stuff."

"What?" Suki was clearly appalled.

"You heard what I said. She can do a bit of cooking for you, but no tricks."

"Why?"

"Because I say so."

"How am I going to manage on my own? That was the whole point of getting the other girl in. I don't need another amah in the house, I need someone out here. There's at least twenty construction workers on that new extension to the office block, and they're going to be around for most of next year."

"I don't care," Benny replied firmly. "And if I find out you've gone behind my back and put her to work, you and Hamid will be out on your arses in the street. What's more, you can kiss goodbye to seeing Abdul again for a very long time, a very long time indeed."

"What's so special about her?"

"Never you mind, you just do what I say and everything will be fine. You two have a nice little thing going on here, just don't do anything dumb to screw it up for yourselves. You get what I mean?"

Suki nodded with a surliness that led Francesca to wonder how she was going to survive once her benefactor had left.

"Now show her where to put her things," Benny continued, "I've got work to do. Is Mrs Cole in?"

"She's sleeping," replied Suki with a smug look.

"Mr Cole?"

"He flew up to Gunpura. He won't be back until tonight."

"Is anyone else at home?"

"Miss Cole."

"Then I guess I'd better speak to her. Could you tell her I'm here?"

Amanda was reading a heavily annotated and cross-referenced copy of *Great Expectations* when Suki glided into the sitting room and indicated through a series of hand and facial gestures that someone wished to see her. She rested the book face down on the armrest and stood up, extending an arm to keep her balance against the dizziness from this sudden exertion. The dog-eared Penguin paperback, until recently a text to be filleted, decoded and analysed, had lost its imperative and was now simply a story to be enjoyed.

Benny was waiting for her in the front hall. He seemed ill at ease in their home, the aura of authority she had seen when he ordered underlings around suddenly diminished. Up close she could see he was really quite tacky with his slicked back hair and the weird gait he adopted, a consequence of the concealed raised heels so beloved by Indonesian men who felt their physical height didn't quite match up to their social status. And those silly Playboy glasses he was twirling made him look simply ridiculous. She'd heard the stories, of course, the expats all called him Backhand Benny behind his back, but how could anyone take such a caricature seriously?

"Good afternoon, Miss Cole. I hope I have not disturbed you."

"Not at all. My mother is taking a nap, but can I help you?"

"The new girl I told her about is here. The one who can speak English." He paused, then seeing Amanda's nonplussed expression, felt compelled to continue. "It was not easy, most girls are not taught to speak a foreign language, and the ones who are generally get good jobs with the government. But I have found someone." He flashed her a triumphant smile, revealing several gold crowns towards the back of his mouth.

"My mother will be delighted. Where is she?"

"Suki is with her now, showing her her quarters. But come, let me introduce you."

Amanda followed Benny through to the kitchen, where he opened the door to the carport.

"Suki!" he called, clapping his hands twice. Amanda stood behind him as the door opened and Suki emerged, followed by a girl Amanda estimated to be roughly her own age. She was pretty, very pretty in a petite way, and her dark hair ran all the way down her back, but she seemed withdrawn, and refused to look Amanda back in the eye.

"Miss Cole, this is Francesca." He switched back to Bahasa. "Have you shown her everything, Suki?"

Suki nodded, then thrust the girl forward with a hostile shove, as if she never wanted anything more to do with her.

Benny turned to Amanda. "Francesca has come a long way, and she travelled light. Do you have any old clothes you don't need that she could wear?"

"Of course." Amanda reached her hand out to the girl. "Here, come with me."

"I will leave you two alone, then," said Benny. "Please tell Mrs Cole I will call on her later."

Amanda led Francesca into the house, through the kitchen and reception rooms, to her own bedroom, where she slid open the door to her built-in closet.

"Where have you travelled from?" she asked, flicking through the rail laden with skirts, dresses and blouses. Francesca was several sizes smaller than her, but luckily Amanda hadn't got round to purging her wardrobe of some of last year's garments she'd outgrown.

"Far away, the other side of Sulawesi," Francesca replied.

"On your own?"

Francesca nodded.

"What about your family?"

"I have no family," she said in a controlled voice. "There is just me."

"Gosh, Benny wasn't making it up, your English is good. Mother will be thrilled. Now, if we took this in a bit, I think it would just about fit you." Amanda held up a thin cotton print to Francesca's delicate frame. "What do you think?"

"I think it is a nice dress. But it is too good, it is nearly new. You cannot give it to me."

"Nonsense," protested Amanda. "Go on, try it on." She pointed towards the ensuite bathroom.

Reluctantly, Francesca took the dress and went in to the bathroom, locking the door behind her. While Amanda waited for her, she returned to the closet and pulled out some more items. None of her trousers or shorts were going to work, but there were several tops that would fit with a little taking in, some skirts and a couple more dresses. There was something about the girl that drew Amanda to her, the awe with which she handled a five dollar garment was such a refreshing contrast to Melanie's jaded sense of entitlement. She was glad Melanie had decided to take a stroll to the commissary for some cigarettes and chewing gum. If she had been around she could all too easily have taken it into her head to turn the whole thing into a joke at Francesca's expense.

The bathroom door opened, and Francesca reappeared wearing the dress.

"It's fabulous!"

"It is too big, I think."

"It just needs a belt, that's all," replied Amanda, pulling open a drawer to rifle through a large pile of accessories. "Here, try this one."

Francesca wrapped the thin burgundy leather around her waist and slipped the buckle pin through the last notch.

"See! It's perfect. I wish it had looked that good on me. That's one down, let's see what else we can find."

8

As ever, Ron woke from his siesta drenched in sweat. Gingerly he rolled over onto his side, taking care not to collapse the canvas camp bed with any sudden movement. Pulling aside the mosquito net, he glanced at his watch. Three twenty. He'd been asleep nearly two and a half hours. He hadn't realised how tired he'd been. As a rule Ron disapproved of siestas, a decadent Catholic habit, but out here in the jungle you really had no choice. A world away from the nearest air-conditioned office, it was insanity to do anything other than rise before the dawn to capture the most pleasant hours of daylight before the sultry heat kicked in. Early on he had realised the futility of trying to run the station around a North American schedule. By midday, following literacy classes, bible instruction, a drop-in health clinic and prayer sessions, he was well and truly beat.

There was a gentle tap at his door.

"Come in," he called. The door opened to reveal Joseph's thin frame and amiable face. He was holding what looked like a cup of tea. "Is that for me? Oh, thank you. Gee, I slept a long time."

"You were tired. Here, drink this."

Ron took the cup and raised it to his lips. The tea was sweet, with a sickly aftertaste from the tinned condensed milk that strangely enough had turned out to be one of the hardest adjustments to make. Oh, a cup of decent coffee with a spoonful of fresh dairy cream swirling around the surface... At least the beverage was hot and refreshing, a reviving balm to his dehydrated carcass.

"Joseph, that is the finest cup of tea I think I've ever tasted."

"You are welcome, Mister Ron."

"All I need now is a quick dip in the river and I'll be ready to resume the Lord's work."

"You're not afraid of the crocodiles?"

"I try not to think about them."

"God is watching over you, yes?" Joseph smiled.

"I guess he is, keeping those pesky crocs distracted while I take my swim. Care to join me?"

"No, thank you. Maybe when I have achieved your level of faith I, too, can swim in crocodile-infested waters."

Ron stood up and wrapped a towel around his waist, before slipping off his boxer shorts and replacing them with a pair of cotton trunks. His feet reached out for the pair of flip flops by the end of the bed, which he wiggled into with his toes. "I've yet to see one, and I've been taking a dip pretty much every day since I arrived."

"Ah, but they are watching you. Watching and waiting."

"Pah! Anyway, suit yourself." Ron slurped down the rest of his tea and placed the cup down on the small tea chest that contained his entire wardrobe. "We need to get together to talk over a few things before I fly to Bandakan. Have you completed that list of medicines yet?"

"I think it is ready."

"Excellent. I can't believe how much we've got through. I thought those supplies would last at least a couple of months."

"There is much sickness all around."

"Of every degree," Ron agreed. "Shall we say four o'clock?"

"I will pray for your safe deliverance from the crocodiles."

"Then I shall be there as living testament to your faith."

Ron walked past Joseph onto the veranda, squinting against the sunshine, which still radiated a dangerous degree of bite to someone as fair skinned as himself. He descended the four wooden steps to the ground, where half a dozen scrawny chickens were going about their business, pecking at anything that looked vaguely edible. He picked up the long stick resting against the guard rail, the shepherd's crook he carried to ward off snakes, then turned towards the well-worn track leading out of the settlement towards the river, enjoying the gentle breeze against his chest. Faith aside, he knew the danger from crocodiles in these waters, though present, was wildly exaggerated. A more immediate albeit considerably less dangerous hazard were the leeches that suckered onto his legs, which at the last count sported more than sixty sores from assorted parasites, all in various stages of recovery. Looking down at the angry pink bites, he marvelled at the fortitude of the early missionaries who had blazed a trail through similar terrain without recourse to the chloroquin, antibiotics and antiseptic creams in his rapidly depleting medicine chest. Fortunately for Ron, he was blessed with a strong constitution, essential for this kind of work, and he shook off the jungle maladies to which his western body was so susceptible as nothing more than another trial to overcome.

Crocs or no crocs, he wasn't about to abandon his daily immersion in the cool river that snaked past Katapulu. From the trail, he'd found a pleasant sandy spot several hundred yards upstream from the bend where the villagers washed their clothes and their bodies. He placed his towel and crook on a log and waded into the rich brown water, keeping his flip flops gripped tight between his toes. The other side of the world from the Jordan, the healing powers of the river worked on his body, soaking up his worries and the baggage he'd left behind. It never failed to recall the time more than twenty five years ago he'd stepped into the Illinois River along with thirty other freshmen to receive the blessing of the Holy Spirit. Sinking into the middle of the river, where the water was at its coolest, he knew he would never have come here had his marriage not collapsed. It was as if God was saying to him, let Patti walk her path, I'll be looking over her, I have work for you to do. He'd forgotten, though he'd repeated it often enough from the pulpit, how exciting a life following Christ could be. Weighed down by endless finance committees and leadership team meetings, he'd allowed the blade of his evangelism to dull. Of course, the work he had been doing was important; for services to happen and outreach work to take place, people had to be organised and accountants satisfied, but it was all too easy to lose sight of what it was for. And he had been more conscientious than most, retaining almost all of his preaching commitments and not just the Sunday morning star turn, as the worldly obligations filled out his desk diary. From being the senior minister in charge of a fifteen hundred strong congregation, the head of a family with a mortgage, two cars, two children, various dogs and cats and numerous other possessions, including several thousand books (now in storage), it was quite refreshing to be able to pack his entire worldly belongings into a medium-sized tea chest. Arriving at Katapulu had been a terrible assault on his comfortable rhythms and routines, but the longer he was here the more he viewed it as a much needed jolt to what had become a complacent and unchallenged life. Of course the mission station was rudderless and a bit of a mess. If it had been running smoothly as a perfectly tuned evangelical machine, what would have been the point in sending him there in the first place? A week or so ago it had suddenly dawned upon him shortly after his morning prayers that he needed Katapulu every bit as much as Katapulu, with its deficiencies staring him in the face, needed him. At that moment he had been overcome, with an intensity he had experienced on only a handful of occasions in his life, by the awesome might and majesty of God's plan for his world and his people.

From that point on, his attitude towards everything had undergone a fundamental change. No longer a shameful penance for a broken down minister to retreat into and lick his wounds, conveniently out of sight from anyone whose opinion he valued, it became the latest offering in a constant stream of gifts handed to him by God. Maybe it was the jungle working on him, wearing away at his zeal as it had corrupted so many fine souls who had gone before him, including his own predecessor. Being out here was shaping and redefining him in ways that not many men were privileged to experience at the age of fifty three. There had been moments, too, when the validity of some of Patti's complaints had exposed themselves to him with painful clarity, followed by periods of mourning and regret at the way he had handled Sue-Ann and Ron Jr's journeys through adolescence. Maybe when his work here was done he'd have an opportunity to make things right with them, just as he prayed for peace and harmony between himself and his ex-wife.

Fifteen minutes later, he towelled himself dry on the river bank, picked up his crook and returned to the station. Once back at his hut, he quickly changed into his cream cotton slacks, a light short-sleeved shirt and a pair of leather sandals, and made his way over to the schoolroom where Joseph and Hallie were waiting for him. Joseph stood up when Ron entered, but Hallie remained in her seat, poring over a sheaf of notes. For now he decided to ignore the disrespect in her gesture. While she was a link with his predecessor and the bad old days, more dope-smoking Peace Corps hippy than committed evangelical, she knew too much about the way the station was run, and was too popular amongst the villagers for him to alienate her just yet.

The three of them drew up chairs around the large desk in front of the blackboard still chalked up with the names of the four Gospels. There was no fan, but the building had been positioned so that the side windows, which were now fully open, caught the afternoon breeze. As was their custom, they held hands around the table for a moment of silent prayer.

"Okay," Ron began, "I'll be away four or five days, and I'll leave the station in both of your hands. Are you happy you have everything you need to keep things running smoothly here while I'm gone?"

He looked up at Joseph and Hallie, who both nodded.

"Do you have that list of medicines?"

"Yes I do." Joseph passed him over a piece of paper. "There is nothing wrong with what we have, we just need more. The surgery is so popular we struggle to meet demand."

"More popular than some of our services," said Ron.

"They need the medicines," said Joseph. "Especially with the children, it can be a matter of saving their sight."

Ron looked at him sharply. "They also need spiritual salvation. That's what we're here for, after all."

"Is the one dependent on the other?" interjected Hallie.

"Not necessarily," Ron countered evasively. "We are here with a mission, to bring God's will and the good news of Jesus Christ's salvation to these people. Our mission takes many forms, some of them physical, like the clinic, others intellectual like the literacy classes, while others are spiritual, like our services and bible studies. The important point to remember is it's a unified approach, just as we have the Father, the

Son and the Holy Spirit. If people reject the salvation we are bringing, that's their concern. But we can't have them playing pick'n'mix like they're standing in line at some candy counter. Yes, I'll have your medicines, thank you very much, but I'll carry on my sinful ways if you don't mind. No, I don't want to know about Jesus, but could you spare me another bottle of penicillin for that dose of gonorrhoea? If we're not careful, we'll not only end up being totally ineffective against evil, we'll be contributing to it."

"We always make sure they understand this is a Christian mission run on Christian principles," countered Hallie with a convivtion Ron didn't find entirely persuasive. "But it's all about winning hearts and minds."

"You make it sound like we're in Vietnam," Ron retorted.

"There are definite parallels, I think most people would agree with that. If we're on a mission here, shouldn't we use all the tools God has placed at our disposal? At the moment the most effective have to be our clinics and our literacy classes. They draw the villagers in like nothing else. They bring their sick children because they would probably die if we didn't treat them, and they come to the classes because they want to learn English so they can get jobs with the oil companies. Once they're here, we're in a much stronger position to spread the good news of the Gospels, but if we can't reach them we don't have a chance."

"So, how is that different to what I'm saying, Hallie?"

"It's just a question of emphasis, Ron, that's all. This way they can tell their friends and relatives in the village they're using us for the medicines and knowledge we have to offer, so it takes the pressure off them. They then find themselves immersed in a Christian environment, which hopefully rubs off on them. It's a slow burn kind of thing, rather than dramatic conversions in the river. It's in the examples we use in the classes, it's in the blessings we give them when we treat them, it's all around us."

"If that's the case," replied Ron feeling decidedly outmanoeuvred, "we need to be absolutely sure that's exactly the environment they do find themselves in when they step inside this mission station." He leant back and looked first at Hallie then at Joseph, who had begun to blush.

Hallie, though, was prepared to face him out. "What do you mean by that?" she asked.

"I think you both know what I'm referring to."

There was no Joseph to rescue her now; her paramour was staring down at his feet, his hands firmly placed in his lap below the table.

"I'm sorry, I'm still not with you."

How the girl reminded him of Sue-Ann, daring him to utter the unutterable, name the unmentionable. He had to force himself to remain calm, she wasn't his daughter and giving her a sound slap around the face most certainly wasn't the answer. Quickly, he sent up a silent prayer for restraint, took a deep breath and trusted in the words that came out.

"Since you force me to be specific, I am referring to your relationship with Joseph." He glanced across at the object of her affections, who was now trying to drill a circle through the floorboards with his eyes down which he could disappear.

"Joseph and I work very closely together. We rely heavily on each other. He depends on my medical knowledge, such as it is, and I need him to communicate with the local people. We've learnt a lot from each other, and yes we have become good friends."

"You appeared to be a great deal more than that the day I arrived."

"I don't think that's any of your business."

"It certainly is my business!" Ron felt himself edging towards anger before remembering his prayer. "May I remind you, you are employed by the First Pentecostal Church of Oklahoma and technically you report to me. And may I also remind you, your contract specifies that you conduct yourself on the mission station at all times in a manner consistent with Christian values and behaviour. Now, I don't want it to come to that, but it's quite clear to me your relationship with Joseph, who is also employed by the Church, amounts to more than mere friendship. I don't necessarily have a problem with that, it's also clear to me you make a good team, but I think we have to establish a few ground rules here."

"Like what?"

"First, you both agree to keeping your relationship chaste while you remain outside of marriage." He looked across at Joseph, who was finally able to meet his gaze. "Agreed?"

Joseph mumbled something that sounded close enough to assent for Ron's satisfaction.

"Hallie?"

Grudgingly Hallie nodded. "I still think you're treading into areas that aren't your concern."

"Let me be the judge of that."

"You said a few ground rules. What else is there?"

"The other thing I insist on is nothing that happens between you can be allowed to interfere with the mission's work."

"Naturally," replied Hallie.

"It's easy to say that now, but if things change between you, you must remain professional about your working relationship. Is that absolutely clear?"

Like naughty schoolchildren caught smoking behind the bicycle sheds, they offered him their assurances.

"Of course, if you ever reached a point where you wanted to make that deeper commitment to each other, I'd be delighted to help make that happen."

He noticed Joseph breathe a huge sigh of relief as he broke the tension with the suggestive remark, deliberately delivered with a warm smile. There was nothing to be gained by alienating his team; his point made, he could ease up on them before leaving them alone for a few days. Neither of them looked about to take up his offer, which seemed to have embarrassed them more than any of his accusations, so he decided to drop the matter there.

"Shall we move on, then?" he continued cheerfully.

"Of course," replied Joseph, relieved to change the subject. "What you say about salvation in very important Ron, but we still have to tread carefully. Many of these people live in great fear."

"They have nothing to fear from us."

"I am not talking about us. They live in fear of dangerous people in their communities, people who have also brought their education and medicines and building projects with them in the past, and who detest everything we stand for."

"I've yet to encounter any opposition like that in the villages. Wherever we've gone, I've been welcomed, or at the very least accepted."

"They wouldn't dare oppose you openly, for that would give them away to the authorities, who would move in and arrest them."

"For being hostile to Christians? Isn't this meant to be a Muslim country?"

"For being communists. When Sukarno was overthrown many of his supporters fled into the jungle. Thousands of them were killed, along with many more thousands of completely innocent people who had nothing to do with Sukarno or the PKI, but some of them escaped. They are spread all over the country, living quietly, but patiently waiting for the day when they might return."

"Are you saying they are putting pressure on the local people to stay away from us?"

"It's not so much the communists the people are afraid of," explained Joseph, "but the trouble they might bring."

"Yet still the communists dare oppose us?"

"It's not what they do that matters but what people think they are capable of."

"Let me get this straight," said Ron, struggling to keep up, now they were well out of the terrain covered by the Sierra Club Guide to Indonesia he had read before his departure from the States. "You're saying that we should give up on our efforts to evangelise this community on account of people's fears about what a few old communists might think?"

"A few of the elders have asked that we leave, yes. But there are others who value what we are bringing and want us to stay. They cannot agree amongst themselves. So we should tread carefully. People here have suffered greatly in the past, all they want is to be left alone in peace."

"You can tell them that I for one am not about to walk away from the mission God has called me to. I've come too far to be put off by a few shadows in the bush."

"Just be careful, Ron."

"You forget, Joseph, God is protecting us. We are doing his work, not ours. We will be fine, and I will see you back here on Monday."

The following afternoon Ron took his siesta in an air-conditioned company guest apartment overlooking the Constar club. It had been a surreal experience to be plucked out of the jungle and plopped down in another world less than an hour later; a world with hot showers, hamburgers as good as the ones at home and a Bears game on the video screen. How he relished such comforts after the austerity of Katapulu. He couldn't quite decide whether this constituted a weakness and therefore a sin on his behalf, or whether feeling guilty about it was the sin in that these too were God's gifts which he had placed in front of him. They were good Christian men running Constar, and they had been more than generous in their hospitality and support. He was looking forward to holding a Sunday service in their clubhouse and telling them all about his adventures in the jungle. Whilst it lay on their doorstep, for most of them it might as well be on a different continent. From nothing more than a name and a contact number in Jakarta, he'd been adopted as some kind of spiritual mascot. Ron conceded his progress would have been considerably tougher and slower without Constar's logistic support, but he also knew that many of the problems he'd encountered in the jungle – the alcoholism, the gambling on illegal cock-fighting bouts, the thefts, even a murder following a feud over a motorcycle – were recent phenomena brought about as a direct consequence of flushing villagers who had lived for centuries in unchanged primitive societies with oil wages. Perhaps this was Constar's way of atoning for some of the wreckage strewn in their path, and he for one would not be hesitant in hinting at the parallel, although one had to be careful when talking to Benny Surikano, with whom he now conducted most of his dealings. But it did show that material progress had to be aligned with spiritual development, and in that respect he could see he was every bit as critical to the future of this country as the geologists and production crews lining its national coffers. A good theme too, he thought, as he strolled out onto the terrace holding a glass of Tab filled with – luxury of luxuries – ice cubes, for his next newsletter back to his sponsors.

He sat down on a chair and looked out to the three-quarter sized Olympic swimming pool, where a small group of mostly white women were sunbathing on recliners. He thought he recognised the young helicopter pilot who'd flown him out of the clearing earlier in the day. Yes, it was definitely Eddie, there was no mistaking the self-contained, distant manner in which he held himself, even when relaxing over a cool drink and a book. They'd barely exchanged more than a dozen sentences over the intercom, but it had been sufficient for Ron to diagnose a wanderer in the wilderness. Is that how he would have had Ron Jr turn out, emotionally frozen and spiritually bereft? None of it had gone according to plan, and whilst he still liked to say the war in South East Asia had been lost inside the Beltway, now he'd spent a little time here he wasn't quite so sure. Maybe his son had been right after all, maybe they should all just leave these people alone to work out their problems themselves; maybe the Katapulu village elders who wanted him to pack up his mission station and go back to Oklahoma knew what they were talking about. Yet his every instinct compelled him to stay. He was just having a wobbly moment. He needed to pray harder, to be firmer in his faith. His church back home believed in what he was doing, and he had a duty not to let them down. Besides, if they gave in to their fears and left a spiritual vacuum, who knew what dark forces would enter into the hearts of these people to replace the love he had to offer.

Later that evening, showered, shaved, his pressed slacks and shirt barely recognisable from a trip to the club laundry,

Ron presented himself at the Cole's front door. In one hand he held a bottle of Paul Masson rosé, purchased that afternoon from the commissary, in the other a tin of Bath Oliver biscuits, also purchased from the commissary and whose sell by date had passed into history some nine months ago. It wasn't a big deal. People round here were used to mouldy delicacies, they thought nothing of munching greying Hershey bars and floppy Doritos, and most of them would have chosen the stale but familiar over the fresh but exotic local produce on offer down in the market. He would have to trust to their indulgence and the vacuum packing, and hope that when the tin was opened a family of weevils didn't spill out.

He pressed the buzzer, then stepped back so he was neatly in line with the spy hole set into the hardwood door. From within he heard the recognisable sound of high heels on tile approach, move back, pause, then move towards him again. The door opened, and he stood face to face with a tall, attractive woman in her early forties. His first impression was how unsuited her complexion was to the humid equatorial climate. In her native England she would have retained that characteristic porcelain quality which was about the only payoff he could think of for the depressing grey weather he knew enough of from Michigan winters not to need to experience first hand. Out here the sun had given her a tan but exacted a leathery hue as its price, now unsuccessfully concealed behind a mask of foundation and rouge. But it was the eyes that struck Ron. Long experience counselling humans in distress and sorrow had left him with an uncanny ability to diagnose what he called deep soul sickness, that fundamental existential despair brought about by living year upon year bereft of any spiritual axis. Boy, did this woman have it bad. She looked like a drinker with it, and probably a pill-popper to boot. "Lord, make me an instrument of your peace," he prayed as he passed the tin of biscuits over to the hand gripping the neck of the bottle of wine, and extended his right hand in greeting. And here he was thinking all along that God had brought him here to deliver salvation to the jungle.

"Hi, I'm Ron Milliner."

"Barbara Cole, pleased to meet you. Do come in." Her grip was strong but slightly clammy. She released his hand quickly and then led him inside, into the air conditioned hallway. "Are those for me? Oh, thank you, you shouldn't have gone to the trouble," she added taking them anyway. "Come on through, and let me get you something to drink. You're the first to arrive, Dennis will be through in a minute, he's just putting on a fresh shirt. What can I get you?"

"A coke would be great, thank you."

"Just a coke?" She seemed disappointed.

"With a bit of ice would be perfect."

"Are you sure I can't tempt you with anything stronger? A beer, a scotch, a glass of wine?"

"No, that'll do me just fine."

"Francesca!" she called out, and a few moments later a local girl dressed in a batik cotton sarong shuffled in, only meekly raising her eyes to look them in the face when she stood directly in front of Barbara. Ron estimated she couldn't have been more than fifteen or sixteen, yet already she wore the beaten, submissive aura of some housewife with decades of domestic violence behind her. Underneath the mask of pain, and perhaps its source in this misogynist heathen country, lay an exquisite gentle beauty that was somehow slightly different from the girls he was used to seeing in Katapulu. He felt like he was staring at an incarnation of the suffering Jesus, an impression he discarded as ridiculous until he caught sight of the small silver crucifix strung around her throat.

"One Coca-Cola, plenty of ice, one gin and tonic, you know how I have it. Thank you." Barbara barked out the order as if she were a drill sergeant standing on the parade ground, while Francesca quickly retreated towards the kitchen.

"Come and sit down," she continued, seamlessly shifting back to her normal voice, a soft English accent his American ears found impossible to place. "Would you like some peanuts?"

"Thank you," replied Ron, helping himself to a handful of nuts before positioning himself at one end of a long three seat sofa. Barbara came round behind him, placed his offerings on a side table, and sat down herself on an armchair at right angles to him.

"Dennis tells me you've been working in the jungle."

"Yes, we have a mission station not too far from your operations in Gunpura."

"It must be fascinating," she said in that typically English way that made it quite clear she didn't want its chronicled history recited chapter and verse.

"It's certainly different from anything I've undertaken before," he agreed.

"Do you find it incredibly uncomfortable?" she asked, leaning forward. "I mean, you must miss all the comforts of civilization."

"I certainly see them through fresh eyes when I come back somewhere like here. You wouldn't believe how soft a freshly ironed shirt can feel, or a hot shower. It keeps you from taking these things for granted."

"Rather you than me," she said, looking across to where Francesca was approaching with a wicker tray on which rested their drinks. "You must really believe in what you do to choose to live somewhere like that."

Ron waited for the servant to hand over their glasses before looking straight at Barbara, who had already left a lipstick imprint around the rim of her drink. "Yes, I do believe passionately in my work, but as for choosing it, well, I think it chose me. In my experience, that tends to be the way things happen when you allow yourself to be a channel for God's will and direction."

"It must be strange to have such a strong sense of destiny," she mused dreamily.

"For me, what's strange is the idea someone can go through life without any faith or sense there's any meaning or purpose to it all. What's always puzzled me is how someone like that can force themselves to get out of bed in the morning."

"I guess they do it because they have to," she replied, swallowing a large slug of gin. "Isn't life simply a matter of survival for most people on this planet?"

"I grew up poor too, you know."

It was as if he'd slapped her round the face. "How do you know I grew up poor?"

"Someone who was brought up surrounded by privilege could never say something like that. They lack that hunger, that keen awareness of how little stands between themselves and destitution. They may feel unfulfilled in other areas of their life, they probably do, but not that one."

"I've been hungry my whole life," she replied, "ever since I could remember. Not just for food, there was always enough to eat, even though we were constantly being told there wasn't."

"I know what you mean," he said softly, taking a sip from his coke. "And has this," he gesticulated to the well furnished surroundings "satisfied that hunger? As you say, it's more than most people on this planet could ever aspire to."

"Nothing can ever satisfy that hunger. It's something you're born with, and something you die with."

"I believe we're all born with it in some form or other, but as for it being something nothing can satisfy, you should know enough about why I'm here to understand I couldn't possibly agree with that. It's my mission, the task God has called me to, to help satisfy the hunger that can only be satisfied through the salvation offered by Jesus Christ."

"Why you are here in this country, or here in my living room?"

Ron shrugged his shoulders. "I just go wherever the Lord sends me."

"Well, you're here tonight, and I can see you're being looked after," said Dennis, who had quietly slipped into the room.

Instinctively, Ron stood up to greet his host. The first thing that struck him was the urbane aura, expressed perfectly in Dennis's loose silk shirt and leather loafers. He exuded such self-confidence even Ron found himself wanting to believe in him. What would this man have achieved, Ron asked himself as he did whenever they met, had he followed his natural gift for selling?

Dennis, for his part, was more concerned about Barbara's gin consumption and the possibility of his wife making an exhibition of herself in front of his boss than with the opinions of this tedious American missionary he had been instructed to entertain. He couldn't for the life of him fathom Harry's interest in the man, it had to be the latest passing fancy of Angie, who'd probably heard of him through some group she attended. What a dull evening yawned ahead, so unlike the sparkling parties they were famous for, where the wit flowed with the wine, and worldly guests sang for their supper with arias involving the most exotic people and places.

A puritan stiff like Harry Bird would never have been invited to sit at such a table, never mind the Reverend Ron Milliner from God knows which church in the arse end of the United States. He had a flash of yearning for the good old days in Bahrein, when Barbara and he were still in love and the world seemed such a bright, hopeful place. Though Bandakan was a superior gig in every way, more money, more freedom, more opportunities for a bit of action on the side, something had happened to his wife, something profound that threatened to strike at the heart of their enviable expatriate life. He believed their placelessness, which didn't actually unduly bother him, was the source of the malaise. There was no going back home for either of them, as they were reminded with a jolt each time they were unwise enough to spend any of their annual leave in the UK, but equally there was no chance of putting down roots here. It wouldn't take the Indonesians forever to figure out how to run this show, despite all the racist ranting in the club bar to the contrary, whereupon they would all be unceremoniously tossed out of the country, working permits invalidated, like any other piece of obsolescent junk. And then where would they go? Another gig, another brutal dictatorship blessed by geophysical providence in the market for some western know-how to facilitate the process whereby its leaders lined their offshore bank accounts at the expense of the ordinary people, who remained just as poor as they ever were?

For all her revulsion of her provincial roots and for all the exotic visas stamped in her passport, Barbara was at heart a small-town girl. It was Dennis' belief that many of her problems in settling, and almost all of her rage, stemmed from her inability to see the Indonesians as people, human beings equipped with the same intellectual powers and driven by the same motives as anyone else. It had been the same with the Indians in Arabia, and before them the Nigerians. Seen through her West Yorkshire eyes they were little more than savages, damned by their darker skin as incapable of higher emotions or anything but the most base cunning. Dennis, who dealt with these people every day, had no such difficulty. It was one of the gifts he was most proud of, and one of his greatest assets to any employer, this ability, so lacking in his wife, to talk to everyone in the same equal fashion, regardless of status or nationality. It wasn't a virtue he had to work at either, it arose quite spontaneously out of his natural curiosity in people and his belief in their fundamental sameness. How, he asked himself, could he have married such a narrow-minded prude, for essentially that was what she was? How could he have known? Back then it was all hope for the future and escape from a world that shut the likes of them out. Increasingly, he found himself cringing at her bigoted views and apologising for her more outrageous episodes of behaviour. It wasn't just him, it had got worse, along with the drinking. Seeing her glass was filled up to within an inch of the brim, he didn't bother asking if she wanted a refill. He just hoped she didn't choose tonight for one of her benders when she told everyone exactly what was what. Not wanting to bother Francesca, he turned and helped himself to a beer from the drinks cabinet before placing himself down on the sofa next to Ron.

"Are the girls going to be joining us?" he asked his wife.

"They're still getting ready." She turned to Ron with a smile. "You know, teenagers."

"Oh, I know only too well," Ron replied with a chuckle, "I've had two myself."

"Though only one of the girls is ours, that's Amanda. Melanie is her school friend, who's come out to spend a few weeks with us."

"You have another boy, don't you?"

"Yes, James. I think he's still in his room, reading. He'll be along, though he'll only stay for the meal."

It was one of the consequences of the drift in their marriage that Dennis now found himself experiencing long periods when he had just his own thoughts for company. As their dialogue diminished, so the monologues in his head expanded, thoughts that no longer had to be censored by propriety because they were thoughts that would never have to be shared with anyone who could label him criminal or insane. One of the more disturbing of late, and which he knew to be loaded with potential disaster, was the realisation that the young Lady Melanie had begun to flirt with him, at first on the odd occasion in such a subtle fashion he couldn't be sure whether it was merely a bout of overactive middle-aged imagination on his behalf, lately with such increasingly obvious gestures he wanted to yell at her not to be so unsubtle; here a touch, there a look, somewhere else a hand laid on his that fraction of a second too long. Even more dangerous, he realised, was the effect her behaviour was having on him. He knew he hadn't proffered a single remark or act that could be interpreted in any way as encouragement, but he could no longer look at her without undressing her inside his head. He couldn't think of a single individual alive in whom he could confide these thoughts. The only man he knew who he thought would understand, strangely enough, was Benny Surikano, the last person with whom anyone should entrust incriminating information. He wondered how the missionary sitting to his left would take such a confession. The square looked as if he'd led a pretty sheltered life in some small town, USA, where the worst things that ever happened were a few hot rodders burning up rubber on a Friday night or the occasional football jock who approached him for a shotgun wedding after going too far with his cheerleader girlfriend in the back of his daddy's Chevvy.

"So, how are you finding the jungle?" he asked with a smile.

Ron turned to him with a piercing look Dennis found unnerving. "You know, Dennis, I feel like I'm right in my element, which is kinda surprising when you consider where I've come from. Of course, I have you guys to thank for a lot of that. I don't think you realise how much of a difference the support you've given me has made."

"It can be a pretty hostile environment," Dennis conceded. "If you're going to survive you need all the help you can get."

"I'd agree with you there," Ron said, quickly glancing up at the ceiling to make his point.

"Well, we're delighted to be of any assistance we can."

Dennis was spared having to make any further small talk or delve into the precise nature of the help Ron was receiving from Constar or anywhere else by the double chime of the doorbell.

"That must be Harry and Angie," he said, placing his glass on a side table and standing up.

One look at Angie's face dispelled any notion Harry had asked him to stage this evening at her request. She couldn't have looked more the bored corporate wife dutifully lending her dignity to some dreary reception. She offered him her hand as if he were some mid-ranking official whose benevolence her husband temporarily required, a stance Dennis found moderately insulting. A cold, self-righteous, uptight bitch, Barbara referred to her behind her back, and whilst Dennis didn't quite share his wife's hostile feelings towards his boss's spouse, which he knew to be warped by Angie's publicly acknowledged status as a recovering alcoholic, he knew what she was driving at. There was a certain smug aura about her, as if somehow, through superior intelligence and richer experience, she had cracked the coda to life's meaning, while all around her less evolved mortals hopelessly batted about like so many bit players in a game of blind man's bluff.

"Delighted you could make it, do come in, hey Harry, you're looking great." It was a blatant lie, Harry looked as if he hadn't slept in a week, but Dennis had been with Constar long enough to know how well Americans of a certain age and background responded to such positive affirmations, and he now deployed them unthinkingly whenever the opportunity presented itself. "Ron's already here, and I think we might be able to winkle the girls out of their room."

"We're not too late, are we?" asked Harry in a voice that implied it didn't matter if they were.

"No, no, not at all. Perfect timing, what can I get you? You'll have a beer, Harry, won't you?"

"Oh, I could probably manage just the one."

"Club soda, Angie?"

"I think I'd prefer a tomato juice with some ice and a dash of Worcester sauce."

"Coming up." Ever the genial host, Dennis steered his guests towards the seated area of their open plan reception room. Ron seemed genuinely gratified to be in such elevated company, while Barbara retreated into her cold English shell while she made polite conversation with Angie, who seemed to find the effort equally unpalatable. Long periods of silence followed monosyllabic replies, after which someone would interject with a complimentary remark about a piece of furniture, followed by an exposition of its purchase (such a bargain, very authentic, not like the rubbish they knock out for the tourists, you have to know where to look). They couldn't possibly keep this up for three hours, Dennis had to think of some way to relax them off their guard. As a start, he could at least get them round the table.

"Barbara, do you want to fetch the girls and James, I think we could probably sit down now. I don't know about you guys, but I'm starving."

Clearly relieved to be spared Angie's tortuous conversation, Barbara broke off to walk over to the other side of the house, while Dennis escorted their guests to the dining table. In front of each seat rested a large open glass containing peeled tiger prawns dressed in a cocktail sauce, sitting on a bed of shredded lettuce.

The younger generation arrived in tow, to be briefly introduced and shown to the remaining places. Dennis opened his arms towards his guests.

"Let's dig in, then," he said cheerily in an attempt to relax the surrounding company.

"Would you like me to say a blessing first?" Ron's voice sounded hurt, and Dennis cursed himself for his oversight as Barbara shot him a filthy look from the other end of the table. There was a silence, punctuated by the sound of Harry's fork, complete with speared tiger prawn, dropping noisily onto his plate. Dennis tried to ignore the stifled giggles both Melanie and Amanda were failing miserably to suppress.

"Of course, that's very kind of you to offer." Dennis fought to recover the situation with the English self-deprecating bluster he'd learnt from observing public school types caught in a tight spot. "I'm terribly sorry, how silly of me, it's just we're not used to being honoured by having a man of the cloth in our presence."

"You don't need to be a minister to say thank you." Dennis could tell from his face Ron had spoken without thinking and immediately regretted the sharpness of his remark.

"Absolutely," he replied, toning down the Bertie Wooster in an effort to smooth away everyone's discomfort. "We forget ourselves sometimes. Please, go ahead."

Ron joined his hands and closed his eyes. Dennis thought how much more comfortable the man seemed in the company of his maker than the fellow humans around him. "Lord," Ron began in what Dennis feared might become a five minute petition to the Almighty, "we thank you for this food you have placed in front of us, and for your infinite blessings. We thank you also for bringing us together, for Barbara and Dennis's generous hospitality, and as we eat may we feel the joy of your spirit fill our hearts and our minds as your physical gifts fill our bodies. Amen."

"Amen," mumbled the voices assembled around the table. Dennis breathed a sigh of relief as the tricky moment passed. Never had a prawn cocktail (what had got into Barbara, serving prawn cocktail for God's sake!) looked quite so appetising. Francesca, he noticed, had emerged from the kitchen with a bottle of chilled white wine, the label deliberately masked by a starched cotton napkin. Having selected it himself the previous day, Dennis knew it to be a Château nothing particularly special, in fact pretty damn ordinary from one of those industrial Californian vineyards, best served as cold to zero centigrade as possible without actually freezing it. He nodded her cue to go round the table. While he held eye contact with her, he discreetly pointed his finger in the direction of first Ron and then Angie, before making a brief cutting motion with his hand to signify who she should pass over. He had Angie to his left and Melanie to his right, with Barbara looking after Ron and Harry down at the other end of the table, while their own children formed a buffer in the middle like a sandwich filling. He resolved to keep his attention firmly on Angie. The last thing he needed was to encourage Melanie any further, especially in full view of his boss's wife, whose powers of intuition he doubted not the slightest.

Of all Constar's managers, Dennis Cole was the one in whose company Angie felt most at ease. There was something about his reluctance to judge, so at odds with his classic English dress sense and mannerisms, that she found deeply reassuring. It was only in the past year she'd felt strong enough within herself to accompany Harry to any corporate function. It was the chore in her marriage she enjoyed the least, but if she had to do it, Dennis was better company than most. Unlike so many well intentioned hosts, he didn't make a huge performance out of finding a suitable non-alcoholic drink for her, and he actually listened to what she had to say, treating her like a human being with a mind of her own.

She'd never meant to hurt Harry or damage his high flying career when she'd taken to the bottle, all she'd ever wanted was to be heard above the fray of naked self-interest fighting to the top of the corporate pole. Harry, for all his clean cut homespun charm, was as tough as any of them, and she hadn't had to push him too far before he intervened, offering her the stark choice of a stint at a drying out farm and his unswerving loyalty or a sharp divorce in which he'd be represented by one of the nastiest attorneys practising in the state of Texas.

She'd chosen well, primarily for David's sake, and Bandakan had been their reward. However, Harry's ultimatum had coincided with darker forces working through her life, and it was these, if she was honest, that had led her to step out of character and accept Harry's offer with gratitude rather than telling him where to stick it. It was the blackouts that had finally got her attention, coming to at three o'clock in the afternoon behind the wheel of their Jeep, a lane of traffic to either side of her and not the slightest idea of where she was travelling at sixty five miles per hour, or how she had got there. She'd trotted each episode out to her fellow patients in the group therapy sessions, noting their heads nodding in identification, bar one, the one that had really driven her into Harry's arms for help, the one she'd saved for her fifth step confessional prior to graduation.

Only then, in the company of Marlene, a senior counsellor who'd seen and heard it all, did she try to piece together three lost hours during a Constar cocktail reception in Houston when she'd wandered off from the party, past the security gatehouse at the neighbouring refinery to end up in the tanker drivers' rec room. Still, two years later, there was no chronological sequence of events she could piece together to make sense of what had happened, just horrific fragments: her hand touching the groin of a uniformed security guard, a penis bursting out of an oily pair of overalls to explode across her face, and the agonising shockwave ripping through her body as she was pierced from behind by a third anonymous figure.

If Angie had expected a modicum of sympathy from Marlene when she mustered all the courage at her command to recount the events of that terrible evening as she could remember them, she was sorely mistaken. Marlene had simply fixed her with a stony stare and told her quite plainly in her gravely midwestern voice that this was the place her illness had taken her. Any notion of justice was out of the question, even if she could have secured convictions (somewhat unlikely in the state of Texas), against whom would they have been made? She couldn't even remember how many men had been in the room, perhaps eight, maybe more, the only face she could recall was that of some unshaven hick with a weak chin in a Dallas Cowboys cap who'd tickled her splayed legs with a pool cue to the vengeful laughter of his mates as the snotty bitch got what was coming to her.

Then there would have been the unbearable cost to her, to Harry and most important of all, to David. So she buried it, pretending it had never happened, that she had imagined it, read about it, seen it in a movie, or heard about it from someone else, anything, dredging the bitter fragments up only, as Marlene suggested, if a cut crystal glass of vodka winked at her from the other side of the room. Sometimes she wondered what the demure wives of the Indonesian foremen and junior managers she was obliged to entertain from time to time, or the innocent looking servant passing round the wine, would have thought if they could have seen her spread-eagled in that hideous room. Out here she was as remote and dignified a figure as a governor or congressman's wife: decorous, proper, sheltered from the seamier side of life and the squalid compromises her husband's underlings were forced to make on a daily basis.

Across the table from Angie sat Amanda, the object of so much adolescent angst in her David. A glance was all Angie needed to know the girl was bad news. She possessed a doll-like prettiness with perfectly shaped features that reminded Angie of herself as a young girl. How cruel it was to know in your heart that your own son was someone you wouldn't have looked at twice when you were of a similar age. She would no more have responded to David's awkward advances than Amanda looked likely to nurture any interest in what he thought now.

The same had been true of Harry. When she looked at pictures of him as a teenager, it was hard to reconcile the lanky dork staring intently into the lens with the self-confident achiever people naturally marked out as someone going places. Her heart breaking, she recalled the way David had tried to adopt an offhand manner when earlier that afternoon he'd asked her who was going to be at the dinner party. He'd wanted to know of course if Amanda was going to be at the table, and if she was (which Angie hadn't been in a position to establish one way or the other) why he too hadn't been invited. It's not that sort of party, she'd replied, trying desperately to protect his feelings. Just some dull missionary Daddy wants to meet. She'd wanted to add that if he was so interested in Amanda Cole he should just pluck up the courage and ask her out, be done with it one way or the other once and for all. But you couldn't do that any more than you could take on board the pain they had to bear as part of growing up. Still, it irked her how her son pined in such misery over what was clearly such a hopeless and, yes, worthless cause.

Around her the talk droned on, oil politics mostly, the favourite topic of conversation on the ridge whenever a table felt obliged to elevate themselves from the titillating gossip that was their standard fare. Ron had begun pumping Harry for information, and her husband had reverted to an edited version of the introductory political briefing he gave to new managers coming out here for the first time, the one in which he warned them not to step into a car off the ridge without a company driver, consort with local prostitutes or get involved in business dealings with Indonesians. If something delicate needed doing, the systems were already set up and all they had to do was turn to tonight's host, the versatile Dennis Cole who would brief the enigmatic Benny Surikano appropriately. Angie had heard it all a thousand times before, but she could see that Ron was shocked by the extent of corporate complicity in institutionalised corruption.

"I don't much like it either," she heard Harry tell Ron, "but quite frankly it's often the only way you'd ever get anything done."

"So you actually have a guy on your payroll whose sole job is to bribe officials and pay people off?"

"It's not his sole job," replied Harry, starting to struggle. Normally new hires simply sat there and listened, trying to take it all in before they retired with their shattered illusions to digest the new reality. "Help me here, Dennis," he called across the table, "what else does Benny do?"

"Apart from what?" Dennis cocked an ear to break into the conversation.

"Apart from bribing corrupt officials," interjected Ron helpfully.

"Oh, he does all sorts of things," replied Dennis cheerily.

Harry pressed him. "Like what?"

"Well, he knows the best place down town to have shirts made. If either of you gentlemen need any more, I'm sure he could get you an excellent price."

They all laughed gratefully, following Harry's lead. "But Dennis has a serious point," added Harry when the titters had died down. "Working and living here is so different to what we're used to back home, we sometimes need a local pair of hands to guide us."

"What do you make of the government here?"

Harry paused, as he tried to decide how frank he could be in front of such an audience. Those two girls couldn't be trusted to remain tight-lipped, for a start. Anything controversial that came from his mouth would be all over the ridge by lunchtime the next day. But Ron, he was beginning to realise, was more perceptive and intelligent than he had initially realised. He would have to choose his words carefully.

"The thing to remember," he began, Carl's voice echoing in his ear, "is this is not our government, elected by the American people to represent American values. It is the Indonesian people's government, and we are guests in their country. It's really not up to us to dictate how they run their affairs."

"But you must have a view on it," persisted Ron.

"Certainly, I have a view on many things, and there are decisions I might take differently if I were in their shoes, the same as I would with any politician back home."

"Do you think you have any power to influence things here?"

"What do you mean by that?"

"What I mean is you represent a rich and powerful company operating in what is quite an undeveloped country. Are there ways in which you feel you can become a force for good? What you're doing and the way you're going about it, is it the right thing to do?"

"It's not really what we're about," replied Harry, "but in so far as we are here, I am committed to acting with as much integrity as possible, and perhaps setting an example through our behaviour of a successful role model. I'm not sure what else we can achieve. We create local jobs, we provide the Indonesian economy with valuable oil revenues, and whilst we're not a charity and we have shareholders back home to satisfy, I personally believe in conducting ourselves with as much benevolence as is possible within those constraints."

"What about the communists?"

"What about them?"

"Do you believe they pose a serious threat to the stability of this country?"

This was not the way Harry had planned the evening to go. Wasn't he the one who was meant to be asking the questions? He was glad Carl wasn't sitting at the table with them to witness the ease with which Ron had seized the initiative to set the agenda. Furthermore, he didn't like the implication of some of Ron's questions, and the light in which they cast him and his employers, hand in glove with a bunch of thugs all greedily thrusting their hands into the cookie jar, every so often tossing down a crumb or so to the mob below in order to preserve the social stability they needed to continue their plunder.

"No, in all honesty I don't," Harry replied. "Why, do you?"

"I believe the godless life as expressed through the teachings of Karl Marx is a serious threat to anyone wherever they live. And in South East Asia I think people have even less reason to be complacent than anywhere else."

"And why is that?" Harry asked.

"Just take a look at what's happening in China, in Vietnam, in Cambodia, in North Korea. If that spreads down through Thailand and Malaysia, this country could have a serious problem on its hands."

"I don't think the Thais have much of a taste for the workers' paradise," said Dennis, joining the conversation from the other end of the table. "Nor the Malays, for that matter."

"You could have said that about the Vietnamese," replied Ron. "We did say it, we went to war over it, but we underestimated the forces pitted against us."

"And do you think we're doing the same thing here?" asked Harry.

"It's always a danger."

"Have you seen anything, apart from what you've read in the press back home, to suggest it might be?"

"You don't see these people, that's not how they operate. This stuff spreads like a virus, and the one thing they feed on more than anything else is corrupt leadership."

"Barbara, this fish is really delicious," interrupted Dennis in an attempt to change the subject. "Where did it come from?"

"The sea," Barbara replied. Everyone laughed, even Harry, though he wasn't sure whether it was at her deadpan tone or the domestic situation Dennis thought he had under control. He'd seen too much during the latter days of Angie's drinking not to realise the Coles had a serious problem on their hands. She was hiding it well, but Harry could tell Barbara was well and truly blasted, just as he'd always known when Angie had been at it. Dennis hadn't an inkling of the nightmarish ride ahead of him, the extent of the misery her illness would introduce into their home if he didn't do something about it. It had been rough at the time, but carrying out that intervention and seeing through with it had been amongst the best advice he'd acted upon.

Harry was spot on, for standing up to sort out the dessert course Barbara realised she was indeed quite unsteady on her feet. Thankfully, Francesca seemed to have everything under control. Barbara stood at the doorway for a minute, watching the waif like figure stand over the enormous iron pan, in which half a dozen bananas sliced lengthways were sizzling away in a pool of Courvoisier VSOP.

Oh shit, she thought, why hadn't she thought of it?

"Francesca, you're going to have to fry another two of those in oil, for Mrs Bird and the Reverend Milliner." Francesca turned and looked up at her as if for an explanation. "They don't drink. Just drizzle some maple syrup over the top and serve it up with vanilla ice cream like the others. But make sure you give them the right ones. Here, I'll have a drop of that."

She reached for the Courvoisier and a tumbler from a cupboard, unscrewed the top, poured out a good three quarters of an inch and took a slug.

"Want one?"

Francesca shook her head. "No thank you, ma'am."

"Suit yourself. But don't burn those bananas. They're meant to be a crispy brown, not charcoaled like the ace of spades."

Barbara leant against the counter nursing her brandy, while Francesca found a smaller pan, some cooking oil and two fresh bananas from the fruit bowl. Feeling like a performer who has momentarily stepped into the wings after four gruelling acts on centre stage, she let her forced smile and bright eyed interest drop to daze lazily at the golden liquid in her hand. Sensing her face fall like that made her resolve once again to check out that Lebanese doctor who was said to do first rate eye jobs next time she was in Singapore. Everything seemed under control with her guests, if she cocked an ear she could hear the conversation had turned towards seafood. She had to admit, Suki had chosen well and grilled the fish to perfection; it was one of the best she'd ever tasted.

"Is there anything I can do to help?" She looked up and there he was, standing right behind her. Guiltily, she slipped her glass behind her back onto the counter and slid it away from her towards the wall.

"Sorry, you made me jump. I didn't hear you come in."

"I apologise, I didn't mean to alarm you."

"No, it's fine, I'm just sorting out an alcohol free banana fritter for you and Angie. I didn't think, otherwise I'd have served something else."

"Alcohol-free banana fritter sounds perfect to me." He turned towards Francesca. To her alarm, Barbara realised she was jealous, wanting him to probe further, to ask more. Yet he suddenly seemed fascinated by this insignificant maid.

"Who are you?" he asked.

"My name is Francesca," she replied softly, not daring to meet his gaze.

Ron pointed to the silver crucifix hanging from the thin silver chain around her neck. "I see you're also a Christian."

"Yes, I was."

"You were?"

"In my old life I was a Catholic. Now," she paused and shrugged her shoulders, "I am nothing."

"You cannot be nothing, each one of us is a child of God, precious in his eyes. Where are you from, anyway?"

"You wouldn't know it."

"Try me."

"I come from a place called Dili. It doesn't matter, it doesn't exist any more."

"Dili? You're right, I don't think I know Dili. Where exactly is Dili?"

"Dili is the capital of East Timor." She said it simply, quietly, then turned away to slice the banana in her hand.

But Ron wasn't about to be put off. "Timor," he repeated, rolling the word around his mouth before pereating it. "Why do I know about Timor? Wasn't there a bit of trouble there recently?"

Barbara interrupted before she could reply. "Francesca, make sure you don't wash up the glasses in the same water as the plates from the fish."

"Of course not, Mrs Cole."

"Barbara!" Barbara looked round to see Dennis standing in the doorway. "Have you any idea where those Bendix mints are? You know, the ones you brought back from Singapore in the cold bag."

"They're in my closet in the bedroom. I put them there to stop anyone swiping them."

"Great. Thanks."

"No, it's okay, I'll get them. You'll never find them." She turned to Ron and pointed at the banana fritters, handing him the spatula. "You couldn't keep an eye on these for a moment, could you?"

"Sure, no problem." Ron waited for Barbara to leave, then turned to Francesca. "I used to cook these for my kids when they were young. Do you have family?"

"My family are gone."

"What do you mean, gone? Have you run away or something? If you have, I'm sure they'd love to know you're safe. You don't have to tell them where you are, just that you're alive and well."

"When I say gone, I mean they are no longer here. In this world. Indonesian soldiers, they kill them all."

"Oh, my God!" exclaimed Ron, momentarily forgetting himself. "And this was in Timor, right?"

Francesca nodded.

"They just killed them, for no reason?"

"Just like that."

"I am so sorry, Francesca, I don't know what to say."

"There is nothing to say. And please, you say nothing to Mrs Cole or anyone else. If people know what I have seen, it might not be so safe for me."

"Of course, I won't breathe a word," promised Ron. "But can I pray for you?"

"If you like. But it will not bring them back. Nothing can bring them back."

"I will certainly pray for you tonight, Francesca. I will pray that God looks over you, that he comforts you in your sorrow, that he gives you the strength to continue."

"I continue not because I have the strength, but because I do not have the choice."

9

It was one of Rollo Surikano's greatest pleasures, in a life dedicated to the pursuit of pleasure in its multifarious forms, to eye up the bikini clad daughters of his father's western masters as they splashed about in the club swimming pool. Strategically positioned beneath an umbrella at the far corner of the astroturfed deck, wandering eyes masked by a pair of Ray Bans, he let his imagination canter through a riot of sexual possibilities, encounters that deep in his heart he knew were condemned forever to remain fantasies by the unspoken apartheid prevalent on the ridge. Occasionally he took a sip from the ice-cold Coca-Cola at his side, discreetly jazzed up with a generous shot of Bacardi by Achmed the barman, who owed his job and therefore his whole livelihood, to Rollo's family. Not that anyone was going to give him a hard time for drinking liquor, certainly not up here of all places, but long ago he had learnt the wisdom of not flaunting his good fortune. There were too many hungry mouths down there wallowing in the stench of the cess-filled kampongs, too many outstretched hands all too eager to grab whatever slither of the good life was dangled in front of them. It was a hunger you couldn't reason with, neither did it respect the laws that made the country work. As his father had drummed into him so often, you could only keep it at bay with the butt of a rifle.

He flipped open the pack of State Express resting beside his glass and lit a cigarette from the Zippo he'd found slipped down the back of one of the company limos. Of the countless pearls of wisdom his father had chosen to share with him, the advice to slide his hands along the back seat of any taxi he climbed into was one of the few fruitful tips he'd adopted, along with never allowing himself to be heard badmouthing the government. Over the years it had yielded an impressive haul of wallets, money clips, keys, cigarette packs and the Zippo, which he knew from his ongoing studies into American popular culture was far more of an impressive icon than the ridiculous electronic gadget his father sported.

While he was sitting up, Rollo took the opportunity to adjust the lounger slightly to keep his body in the shade. He'd never really acquired this western taste for sunbathing, although it was good to rest his sore muscles. He'd certainly earned it. After two years and nine months of purgatory he never wanted to see another barrack block, feel the coarse khaki against his skin, lug another forty-pound pack through the harsh sun as the edges dug into his ribs, or eat that filthy food ever again. But he'd done it, he'd honoured his side of the bargain, made the contacts his father insisted were so critical to his future, established himself as an insider, as part of the machine that ran the show. Now it was payback time, but before that, he was long overdue some fun.

If it was his curse to have been born an Indonesian, at least it was his blessing to have been born a wealthy, well connected Indonesian. He was acutely conscious of straddling two worlds, at home in neither. Perhaps this was where he really belonged, up here on the long sandy ridge that looked down on the sprawling town dominated by the oil refinery. The camp they called Little America, territorially Indonesian but spiritually part of some fictional state in the Midwest, a state within a state carved out of the jungle as a testimony to what was possible given enough willpower and oil dollars. The seven hundred acre complex certainly looked like the America he was familiar with from the movies: the floodlit softball pitch, the tennis courts, the club with its four lane bowling alley, pool tables, juke box and air hockey machines, the commissary stocked with goodies unobtainable anywhere else in Asia outside a PX store. Oh, the delight of sinking one's teeth into a Hershey bar grey from six months intense refrigeration, the soft crunch of a bowl of stale Fruit Loops, so exquisite after all those peasant breakfasts of sticky rice and sweet tea. Best of all was the air conditioning. It didn't just cool one's body and keep it from breaking out into an undignified sweat, it obliterated the world beyond, the world of poverty with its particular smells and sounds he found not just humiliating, but terrifying too.

It was so tantalisingly close, this little piece of ersatz America, close enough to touch, yet still he remained an outsider. It didn't matter that his father practically ran the place; when you stripped matters to their essentials, he was just another Indonesian, a necessary evil that had to be tolerated, possibly indulged even in his case, as part of the broader scheme of things. Whilst they sat on billions of barrels of oil they had a use. Take that away and they were totally expendable. Another of his father's cynical mantras. Don't expect anything of them, don't expect them to care about you as a person because they not only don't care about you as a person, they don't see you as a person. To them you're just another brown face upon whom nature has mistakenly bestowed her precious resources, an oversight they will spare no effort to correct. So screw them for as much as you can for as long as you can, because it won't last. In the end they always get whatever they want, regardless of how dirty they have to play to get it. The chasm you couldn't cross.

But that was his father's generation, Rollo protested in his more optimistic moments. They were different, they'd been brought up in the kampongs with rags for clothes, fought against the Dutch, wrestled whatever was theirs by force from the reluctant white man. Different rules applied. Wealth didn't come naturally to them, they settled into western ways with the residual unease of someone who speaks a foreign language fluently but still accentuated by his native tongue. Whereas he had been born to this. The prospect of living in a hut on stilts surrounded by mangy chickens and open sewers filled him with just as much revulsion as it would for any one of those pretty white girls frolicking around at the shallow end of the pool. His father and his ilk, they could return if they had to. They might not like it, but at least they would recognise the landscape, and there would be comforting childhood resonances to ameliorate the discomfort. For Rollo, like the other senior officers' kids he grew up with, there was no going back.

Like the whites, he defined the months by European and American calendars created around seasons thousands of miles and tens of latitudes away. So it was summer and winter, rather than dry and monsoon. Christ – yes, him too – they'd even sprayed fake snow from an aerosol can across their windows upstairs, and only this morning he'd heard his father cursing at his annual chore of dressing up in a red suit, donning a white cotton wool beard and dispensing good will and candy to the Yankee kids. Ho, ho, fucking ho! He was glad someone found it funny. What Rollo needed was to set himself a goal, a challenge to fill those empty days until he was able to stop being a fake American in a fake America, and start being a real one in the real thing.

Take that pretty girl on the lounger over by the shallow end, the one being eyed up by the American helicopter pilot sitting on the lounger across from her. Dennis Cole's daughter, with her dark blonde hair and fine pale features, she epitomised the idyllic English rose. She exuded a childlike innocence, though he'd heard she'd just been kicked out of some expensive boarding school. If she was so keen on breaking rules, perhaps she'd be up for a bit of living on the wild side. Rollo could certainly show her a thing or two, nothing too heavy, he did have his father's position to consider, just a little fun before they returned to the destinies which had been respectively mapped out for them. It was a stupid idea, but then again no more outrageous than many of the antics that went on round here. What the hell, he thought, rousing himself from his torpor, nothing ventured, nothing gained.

She was called Amanda and seemed completely untouched by a world in whose jaded squalor Eddie had languished for too long. Her eyes lacked that prophylactic coating of cynical nihilism he'd found even in the youngest pre-pubescent hookers turning tricks in Saigon for a couple of bucks a time. It was an innocence Eddie simultaneously yearned to protect and possess, and the contradiction only served to make her appeal more alluring. More than any single physical feature in her appearance, it was her freshness that struck him with the greatest force. Somehow the aura of her innocence allowed him momentarily to shed those two tours of Vietnam, so even if it wasn't as if they had never happened, it was almost as if they had happened to someone else, an alter Eddie he could bury in the defoliated jungle. How could someone so young yield so much power? It had to be unconscious; there was no way she could begin to understand what he had seen, what he had been through, what he had been a part of. Mesmerised by her pale skin and soft English accent, he couldn't stop staring at her. He yearned to take that innocence of hers, not like some lecherous serviceman snatching it on a brief bit of R&R, but in an all-consuming manner that would rush through his veins and flush out all the shit that had contaminated him ever since he embarked upon this crazy adventure.

Part of him knew he was making a fool of himself – after all she was no more than a stupid kid kicking her heels while she worked out what to do with her life – but another, deeper part sensed that she represented a lifeline, a last chance to return from the moral abyss that had kept him rattling around Asia with neither purpose nor ambition, looking ahead no further than the next binge in Bali or Manila. What a pathetic creature he had become! If he wasn't careful, he'd end up like Shaky Mick, reduced to compiling pilot rosters because he was too addled to fly. The thought struck him that she might agree with his damning verdict of himself. It came as something of a shock, for he was used to women being drawn to him, then being locked in by their urge to crack him and heal the demons tormenting his soul. Of course they never did, and Eddie had become an old hand at the dichotomy of intense physical intimacy combined with utter emotional disengagement. Sometimes he was the one who ran away, more often it was the women who finally decamped in despair at their inability to penetrate the chilly wall surrounding his heart.

Then again, what right did he have to unburden all that garbage onto her? It wasn't her fault he'd got himself fucked up over Vietnam, just as it wasn't her responsibility to make it alright again. No one could do that. The stuff he'd witnessed through his visor was simply too much. He didn't deserve to live when so many around him hadn't, let alone flourish through the intoxicating aura of her youth and beauty. Have another drink, smoke another Camel, screw another whore, take what comfort you can, and fuck everyone else. Retire gracefully from the fray with a loaded pistol, point the barrel against your head and pull the trigger. Oblivion.

He sensed a movement from behind his shoulder, and he looked up to be faced by a young Indonesian man of slight build, dressed in a pair of baggy swimming trunks and brown leather sandals, along with the twin status symbols that let no one mistake him for a waiter or a gatecrasher, a stainless steel Rolex (a real one, Eddie noted) and a pair of Ray Ban sunglasses (again, real) carefully parked in his gelled, swept back hair.

"Who the fuck are you?" Eddie wanted to say but didn't. He'd been around Bandakan long enough to realise only an Indonesian brat with heavyweight connections could ever be decked out like that. Instead, he satisfied himself with a restrained "Yes?"

"Would you mind if I ordered a drink for this beautiful young lady you are with? And for yourself, of course."

Eddie looked at the kid, who was at least six inches shorter than him, then turned to Amanda, whose eyes pleaded "Rescue me!". He was wary of taking a stance on her behalf, and it was certainly dangerous to blow the boy off before first finding out who he was. For all Eddie knew, the little prick could be directly related to Suharto himself. The last thing he needed was to be accosted down some dark alley by half a dozen off-duty soldiers out for a bit of freelance work.

"Sure, you can ask her," he eventually replied.

The boy, whom Eddie estimated to be in his early to mid-twenties, now stared directly at Amanda, their eyes level. "What would you like?"

"I'll have a Seven Up, thank you, Rollo," she answered without any apparent enthusiasm.

"And yourself, sir?"

"I'm fine, thanks."

Rollo signalled to the barman, who came scurrying down the steps to take their order. Trying to muster as much dignity as he could, Eddie sat back in his chair and reached for his cigarettes. Rollo. Who the fuck was Rollo? He was pretty sure Suharto didn't have a son called Rollo, not that that meant anything in itself. Since the oil and timber industries had moved into full swing, the place was crawling with retired generals and their offspring shoving their snouts into the gravy trough. And Amanda knew him, though thankfully she didn't seem pleased to see him. Fighting his jealousy, he stood up and wandered over to the bar, where he ordered a fresh beer. From there he stood watching Rollo engage her in stiff conversation, while Amanda impersonated the glassy-eyed expatriate ritually performing some tedious colonial duty. Fortunately, she didn't seem interested, and he was happy to sit it out on the sidelines while Rollo dug his own grave. Rollo was animated now, gesturing with both hands, pointing towards downtown. Amanda seemed uncomfortable in her posture, she had sat up and become defensive, holding her towel in front of her, looking round towards the table where he'd left his sunglasses and book, some trashy thriller lifted from the library in the ops room.

He watched Rollo waltz back to his lounger with a wave, waiting until he was out of earshot before returning himself.

"What was that all about?" he asked.

"Why didn't you rescue me?"

"I didn't know you needed rescuing," he replied, sitting back down beside her. "Who is he?"

"His father works for mine."

"What did he want?"

"He wanted to take me out for dinner."

Eddie felt the jealousy tighten his chest, even though he'd known her less than an hour. "What did you say?" he asked in an unconcerned a voice as he could muster.

"Oh, I said yes, but just so he would leave me alone."

"Are you going to?"

"What?"

"Go out for dinner with him."

"Of course not." She looked at him as if she were astonished he could even contemplate such a notion. "I'll think of some excuse closer to the time if he presses me for an actual date."

"Is that what you would do if I asked you out?"

She gave him a smile. "Guess there's only one way to find out."

"I'm not interested in being blown off because you've decided you need to wash your hair."

"Who said anything about washing my hair, Eddie?"

"So, would you?"

"Would I what?"

"Like to go out sometime?"

Again, she gave him that demure English look which held a mirror to the great well of loneliness within his soul. "Thank you, I would love to."

"You're not just being polite?"

"Would you rather I was rude?"

"No, I just want to be sure you mean it."

"I mean it."

"Rollo over there thinks you mean to go out with him," Eddie pointed out.

"That's different. If I didn't want to go out with you, I'd just say so. You can't do that with Indonesians, you always have to find a way for them to save face, otherwise they start getting nasty. It's one of the reasons my father is so good at working with them. He never backs them into a corner, he's always told me you won't get them to do anything that way. Whenever you want them to do something, the trick is to make them think it was their idea in the first place."

"Sounds like a smart guy."

"Sometimes I think he's the most perceptive man in the world. And at other times, I wonder whether he ever sees anything at all."

"Does he see you?"

"Not really. I mean, deep down he loves me, but I don't think he has much of a clue as to what's going on inside my head."

"Does anyone ever?"

"I don't know." She paused, looking up at him while she considered this. "I would like to think someday someone could. Otherwise what's the point of any of it?"

"But have they?"

"Not yet. You like to ask a lot of questions, Eddie."

"Does that bother you? I'm sorry," he laughed, "I'm doing it again."

She smiled back at him. "No, I don't mind. In fact, I find it refreshing. Most of the guys I've known have only ever been interested in one thing, and it certainly isn't my ability to answer questions about the meaning of life."

"That's because you're young and beautiful."

"I'm not beautiful."

"Don't say that." His voice was serious now. "Don't ever say that."

"Why not?"

"Reason number one, it isn't true."

She blushed, but he could tell she liked the compliment. "And reason number two?"

"I can't think of reason number two, but number one is enough on its own."

"I suppose it's because people always assume if you look a certain way you can't be intelligent. Or at least, that's been my experience."

"You don't have to be ugly to be smart," he replied. "There's no justice in the way nature bestows her gifts. She doesn't act like some ledger clerk with a balance sheet, handing you an IQ of a hundred and forty then deciding she'd better distort the shape of your face to compensate for it."

"She seems to have dealt you a pretty good hand."

"Maybe. When I look at my life and the lives of people around me, I certainly can't complain. But it's not just about that. What I'm saying is, if you're surrounded by a pile of crap, if you'll pardon the expression, it's no less a pile of crap simply because you're sitting on the top layer."

"Sometimes I think all this is a pile of crap." She spread her arm to point at the clubhouse and apartments beyond.

"Would you rather live downtown in a wooden shack with a tin roof and no plumbing?"

"Of course not."

"Me neither. So we put up with the pile of crap, hoping the wind will blow in the right direction and we won't have to smell it."

"Have you always been this cynical?"

"I don't think I'm cynical, Amanda. A cynic always believes the worst in people. I may see the bad, but I also believe in the good. Or at least, I'd like to."

"But you don't."

He smiled. "Put it this way, I struggle with it."

"You were in Vietnam, weren't you?"

"How do you know that?"

"My father told me. He said all the best Constar pilots learnt to fly in Vietnam."

"It taught you how to handle a helicopter, I guess that much is true. At least it's true for those of us who are still alive."

"Did you lose many friends?"

"Some," he replied, before pausing. "But not as many as you might think. In fact, the odds of surviving a tour as a pilot were generally stacked in your favour. The three things most likely to get you were human error, mechanical failure and enemy fire. The human error you dealt with as best you could by keeping your mind on the job and staying off the weed; mechanically the Huey's a pretty reliable ship, and as for enemy fire, although it can be terrifying having a rocket suddenly come at you from nowhere, for the most part the VC weren't very good shots. They could never get their heads round the idea you have to lead on a moving target if you want to hit it. I guess it's because they were peasants, they didn't grow up duck hunting. It meant we were always taking hits in the tail, which makes everything shake and rattle a lot, but unless you're very unlucky doesn't do a great deal of harm. It's the other stuff that gets you."

"Like what?"

"Oh, I don't know. Well, I do, but I don't really feel like talking about it now. Some other time."

"Saving it for our date, are you?"

He smiled. "Something like that."

"I can't wait."

"Neither can I," he replied softly. "Neither can I."

10

Huddled between a threadbare blanket and a thin cotton rollup mattress laid out in a corner of the cement floored cooking and eating area that constituted her living quarters, Francesca eyed the large mechanical alarm clock ticking away on the edge of the melamine topped table set against the far wall. The luminous hands caught the moonlight shining through the barred window slots above her head to allow her to read off the time: twenty to five. Another twenty minutes with her own thoughts for company, twenty precious minutes that belonged just to her, before her working day began. First it was breakfast for the three of them; Francesca, Suki and Hamid, Suki's ineffectual husband who liked to spend the entire day glued to a wicker armchair in whatever portion of the carport was catching the most shade, smoking one roll-up after the next, occasionally switching to Djarums if Suki had had a good day, gazing into the middle distance where a crew of construction workers were adding an extension to the main administrative office block.

This morning they had some pork to go with their rice. Last night Francesca had prepared some chops for the following day; mindful of Mrs Cole's obsessive phobia about fat she had trimmed the edges liberally enough with the kitchen scissors to provide a good meal for the three of them once she had thrown in the unused peas and carrots from the tureen. Spiced up with a bit of saté paste, she was confident it would offend neither Suki's crotchety taste buds nor her loose Islamic principles, allowing her to move on without further criticism to scrub the amahs' quarters from top to bottom.

Fortunately, there were only two rooms; three if you counted the small lavatory and washbasin with its single cold tap. During the day the servants lived in the space where she now lay, which was why her mattress had to be bundled up and tucked behind the small wooden box containing her entire worldly possessions before breakfast could begin. The other room was Suki's private bedroom, furnished with a table and two chairs, a wooden dresser cast off from somewhere, and an iron single bed into which Suki and Hamid spooned themselves together when their day was said and done. Only then could Francesca move into the house proper to begin her official working day, the one for which she was paid the grand total of sixteen thousand rupiah a month (reduced to eight thousand rupiah once Suki had taken her clip for food and accommodation), with the preparation of Mr Cole's breakfast. He was easy to please, so long as she never varied from the full percolator of strong black coffee, large glass of chilled orange juice, two pieces of buttered toast with a dish of marmalade on the side, and a fresh packet of Peter Stuyvesant with the cellophane wrapper removed. He consumed this resuscitation – you could hardly call it a meal – alone on the balcony in quiet contemplation. Mrs Cole, whose whims were altogether more complex and volatile, ate later, usually taking a tray in bed, while the others drifted in and out throughout the morning to pick away at bowls of cereal and plates of toast until around eleven, when she could start clearing the table for lunch.

Her day, though long, was not necessarily onerous. One person could have managed it quite easily, and there were long periods between preparing and cleaning up meals when her sole requirement was to be on hand should any of the family need her. By the standards of the ridge Mrs Cole was considered a harsh taskmistress, demanding high standards of polishing and dusting, but the presence of servants in her home made her uncomfortable and one or both of them were frequently dismissed to their quarters in the middle of a job simply because she wanted to be alone. Later, long after she had retired to her room, Francesca would tip-toe around, discreetly clearing out the empty vodka bottle and tins of tomato juice carelessly shoved to one end of the sideboard.

"It mostly happens when Miss Amanda is away at school," Suki had warned her.

"What does Mr Cole think of it?" she asked.

"Often he's away when it happens. But she never gets violent and she doesn't hurt anyone except herself, so he pretends it doesn't happen. Usually he comes home and finds her passed out in her bed. She tells him she's tired or not feeling well, and he believes it because he wants to believe it."

It was a mystery to Francesca how someone who had so much could be so unhappy. Mr Cole wasn't a brutal man, if anything he leant the other way. So far he had treated Francesca well, and he was certainly indulgent towards Suki. He had to know about her entrepreneurial sidelines, but so long as someone appeared at the kitchen door when the cry went out for assistance he seemed happy to overlook it. You wouldn't have been able to say that about many masters on the ridge, especially the Americans.

The entrepreneurial activities were the main reason – other than that labour was so dirt cheap it was considered a social duty to put another mouth on the payroll – why it took two servants to manage the Cole household, a single level home equipped with a washing machine, vacuum cleaner, tumble dryer and dishwasher. For how could you cook and serve up a curried stew to twenty or more construction workers, take their money, replenish their enamel mugs with tea, and generally keep an eye on things if you were constantly being interrupted to iron a special shirt for the evening or make someone a peanut butter and jelly sandwich? During the day, the deal was that Francesca was on call for any demands to emanate from the house. Between chores, she could help with the washing up or preparing more food, for which she was rewarded with a few hundred rupiah if Suki was feeling in a generous mood.

Once her bedroll had been stowed away in its box, it was made quite plain to Francesca that she had no space within the amahs' quarters she could mark out and claim as her own. If she tried to stake out a corner, Suki immediately honed in on it and shuffled her along, keeping her on the move until she tired of shifting her weight from one leg to the other in the middle of the floor space and retreated outside into the carport, where she could sit down next to Hamid in one of a pair of ancient rattan chairs peeling away at the arms. Only then could she be relatively confident of finding a temporary peace. The evenings, between vegetable chopping and returning to the house for the wash up, were when she was made most unwelcome, and it didn't take long to figure out why.

The two of them, Francesca and Hamid, were sitting side by side, looking out towards the front lawn shortly after sunset. The Coles had all gone off to the club for a drinks party and had indicated they would probably not need supper. Hamid was dressed in his usual pair of pyjama bottoms topped out with a Hash House Harriers T-shirt, smoking while he examined various bits of grime underneath his toenails. Francesca sat primly beside him, her hands resting on her lap. They had been sitting this way, barely a word passing between them, when one of the construction workers, a foreman Francesca recognised from slopping out stew duty, pulled up on a Vespa and walked towards them. He'd smartened himself up markedly and even donned a light blue batik shirt, which contrasted against a pair of cream slacks and brown leather loafers. All that detracted from the otherwise dapper demeanour was a nasty oil stain towards the bottom of his calf.

Hamid nodded a greeting. "I'm afraid you've wasted your journey, Suki's out."

"You think I got all dressed up like this for her?" the foreman replied with a short laugh. "No offence, it's this little orchid bud I'm interested in," and he gestured towards Francesca.

Hamid looked straight ahead so he wasn't making eye contact with either Francesca or the foreman. "I'm afraid you're out of luck," he said slowly. "She's not for hire."

"Says who?" demanded the foreman.

"Benny Surikano," replied Hamid. "He was quite specific, she works here, but no tricks."

"What's so special about her? Apart from the obvious, that is?"

Hamid shrugged his shoulders. "I don't know."

"Is she Benny's new girlfriend?"

"Benny doesn't have a girlfriend."

"In that case, what's the problem? Benny owes me, he won't mind."

"Then you take it up with him. If Benny tells me it's okay, then you can do what you like, I don't care. But until he gives Suki and I the word, no dice."

The foreman turned to face Francesca. "I came all this way specially for you, my lovely," he continued in a syrupy voice that sent a chill down her spine. "Don't worry, if it's the idea of being paid you're worried about, we can always have a good time for free! Go for a little ride on the bike, find a nice secluded spot somewhere, get to know each other a bit; surely you haven't got a problem with that, Hamid?"

"So long as she's up in time to cook breakfast she's free to do what she likes," replied the jaded figure to her side.

"So, what do you say Francesca? It is Francesca, isn't it? An unusual name for these parts, I might say."

"What I say is you can go to hell."

The foreman didn't seem the slightest put out by her vehemence, which only served to make Francesca realise the sheer powerlessness of her situation. "That's not what you said to the captain of that shit bucket which brought you here," he countered back at her with a laugh. "From what I heard, you couldn't have been more obliging."

Francesca remained expressionless as she fought to maintain her composure against the wave of terror shooting through her body in jolting, stabbing motions. Any notion she had any autonomy over anything at all was a complete fiction, a sick joke to enable her to be tormented all the more. Yet this time she wasn't going down without a fight. Suddenly she no longer cared what it cost her, she couldn't go through with any more compliance. Let them do their worst.

"That's a lie!" She spat the words out at him as she stood up and turned back towards the amahs' quarters.

The foreman didn't try to pursue her; instead he turned to rail at Hamid. "Are you going to sit there and let her talk to me like that?"

"Like I said, it's her choice." Hamid shrugged his shoulders as Francesca opened the door to the amahs' quarters and slammed it shut behind her.

"I tell you one thing now, Hamid, I wouldn't want to be in your shoes when Benny hears of this conversation. He owes me big time and he is not going to be happy when he finds out how you let that stuck-up little madam behave. If you're smart, you'll get off your arse right now and spell out a few facts of life to her before things start looking uncomfortable for Abdul as well."

"If you think anyone here gives a fuck about Abdul, you've come to the wrong place. He brought his problems on himself."

"I don't think Suki sees it that way."

"As I said, you mind your own business and let me worry about Suki and Benny."

"Fighting talk, Hamid, fighting talk. Most unlike you, I must say. If I didn't know better, I'd say someone had put a little fire in your belly."

From behind the door Francesca could hear every word, every breath. She pressed her full weight against the wooden slats, shuddering at the lecherous chuckle. "Been giving her one yourself, have you? Is that why you can't bear to think of me inside her? I can't say I blame you Hamid, she's a cute little thing, despite the mouth on her."

Collapsing into a heap, Francesca heard the Vespa kick start into life. For the umpteenth time she cursed the overwhelming will to live that was imbued within every fibre of her being, over which she seemed to have no more power that she did over the faces whose satiated leers would forever haunt and torment her. She had been a fool to ever set foot on that boat, she should have lined up in the square with the rest of them. At least then she would be with them, wherever they were, and that surely had to be better than this lonely living hell of a half-life.

Suki flicked the feather duster across the shelf containing family photographs commemorating the Coles at different milestones in their lives with an irritated tic. She had a way of running things, and for the past three days events had conspired to upset the careful rhythm of her life. With so many different interests within her orbit competing for her attention, there just wasn't room for any one element to roam outside its carefully delineated box. Yet this was precisely what was happening all around her.

A foul mood had descended over the big house. The girls, who had been grounded for the weekend following their antics at a party they'd sneaked down to at Base Camp, had sullenly retreated to their room, which they had proceeded to turn into a pigsty, strewing clothes, empty cassette cases, magazines, candy wrappers, drinks cans and cigarette butts all over the place. Francesca could barely get in to clean, and to make matters worse they had been given permission to take some of their meals in there too. Meanwhile Mrs Cole had worked herself into a terrible state over a dinner party she had been ordered to host in honour of a group of senior managers who'd just made an unannounced visit from the United States. The menu had changed at least three times in the past twenty four hours. First snapper, then lobster, then chicken, now back to snapper again. Suki just hoped they had some good ones at the market. The last thing she needed was to give them all a bout of food poisoning. Whatever the state of indecision, tomorrow she would get up early and have Hamid ride her down to the market on his moped. If they opted against snapper at the last minute she could always sell it off to the construction workers (it was far too dear to eat themselves). At least that way she was guaranteed a good supply of some fresh fish even Mrs Cole could make palatable.

She couldn't entrust the mission to Francesca. Well-intentioned and hard-working though the girl had turned out to be, she would end up paying way too much so there'd be nothing left over from the stash of rupiah handed over by Mrs Cole. More importantly, she didn't know what to look for. The gills were the giveaway. That and the eyes. A cloudy stare, like that of some blind beggar hopefully tapping his stick for change, and chances were it was yesterday's catch cunningly slipped on top of the fresh pile, ready to fool the unwary. It was funny how you could tell so much through the eyes. Take Francesca, for instance. There was something impenetrable there, an all too familiar veil masking a deep pain Suki could only guess at. The girl had showed up on these shores like some shipwrecked piece of flotsam, complete with her inexplicable grasp of the English language. One day she would wake up and figure out how to exploit this knowledge along with her good looks, and that would be the last they would see of her. Until then they should all just enjoy the good fortune that had come their way.

Mrs Cole rarely spoke to Suki these days. The new arrangement, whereby instructions were relayed to Francesca in English and then translated into Bahasa back in the amahs' quarters was infinitely preferable to Mrs Cole hammering away in a Pidgin English peppered with a few Indonesian words that had permeated even her resistant brain, accompanied by crude sign language usually revolving around chopping or sweeping motions. Suki's abiding memory of Barbara Cole would forever consist of the two of them standing in the western equipped kitchen, Barbara wielding an imaginary machete over a large fish, responding to Suki's incomprehension with ever more violent arm movements as she repeated the same few foreign words over and over again in an increasingly loud voice. Yes, it was better on all parties to be spared that. The only drawback was it had given the girl an inkling of her indispensability. Ever since she had turned down that damned pest from over the road, she had walked around with if not quite a superior air, an aura of serene detachment. It wasn't as if she relished the power her linguistic skills afforded her (Suki could have killed Hamid for ramming home the point so effectively), it was more the defiance of the condemned prisoner crouched in his cell, from whom everything has been taken, including hope, and who no longer has anything to gain by feigning amenable compliance.

Images of bars and cells turned her thoughts to Abdul, rotting his youth away as he had done for the past eight years in Bandakan jail on the strength of nothing more than a bit of innuendo and a childhood grudge from a classroom contemporary, now in the junior echelons of the secret police. There had never been any charges to refute; if ever anyone pressed his case, as a few ill-advised lawyers she had hired at great expense in the early days had done before being warned to back off, they were told he has being held for routine questioning about possible subversive activities. Suki wondered, as she frequently did, whether Benny really was powerless to intervene beyond marginally improving the conditions in which her brother festered, introducing the odd piece of chicken into his rice and ensuring he received the occasional cold shower and change of clothes. Suki suspected his protests that the whole thing was over his head and out of his control had more to do with the level of inconvenience he was prepared to put himself to on her behalf than any limit on his level of influence. After all, it was said the man even knew President Suharto personally, having been responsible for keeping his forces in supplies during the long insurrection against Sukarno. Surely a man like that, given the run of Bandakan as his reward for such critical and well-timed loyalty, could do more than improve Abdul's food and restrain the guards from their savage beatings. If it was his own pampered son Rollo who'd found himself in a similar fix, or one of the American kids, he'd have found a way to sort it out.

Angry as she was at the few scraps Surikano chose to toss her way, they were better than the alternative, which was to leave poor Abdul unshielded against the brutality and torture perpetrated by the prison guards on a daily basis, more as a form of entertainment than a means of extracting any information that might be relevant to their political and military masters. The stories aside, she had heard the blood-chilling screams from across the courtyard during her own monthly visits. You didn't ask questions, not unless you wanted to join the poor soul in torment from who knew what, you didn't even exchange a knowing look across the table, you simply continued your own conversation under the watchful eyes of four guards, the pair of you mustering every last drop of will to ignore the only sound that made any sense in such a place. If the best Benny was willing to do for her was spare her Abdul from that, so she didn't have to lie in her own bed at night imagining him strung up in some dark blood-stained cell, the plaything of a group of mindless sadists, she was willing to accept it and pay his price if not willingly, then at least with an element of gratitude. So it was with some concern she viewed the offence Francesca had caused Sayeed by making him lose face in front of Hamid. At the very least he would have to try and make good his threat, but whatever favours Surikano owed the foreman and his gang, they would count for nothing against his continued good standing in the eyes of the Coles. Try as she might, Suki hadn't been able to find it within herself to be as angry at the girl as she felt the situation warranted. There was something admirable about Francesca's defiance, such a refreshing change from Ida's sullen acceptance of her lot, that made Suki want to forgive and even embrace her. Her reaction surprised her, for Francesca had potentially placed them all in jeopardy, and one of the qualities Suki prided herself on was her lack of sentimentality. She knew just how precarious their perch up here was on the ridge, how many hundreds of able-bodied good-looking girls down town would jump at the chance to elevate themselves to these lofty heights for a fraction of the paltry wages she was forced to supplement in ever more ingenious ways. So while she had admonished Francesca sharply for her stance and come up with half a dozen domestic chores that didn't really need doing, as well as assigning her to the job of disposing of the rats caught in the sticky traps they set each evening, usually Hamid's task, her anger had lacked sufficient conviction for it to be anything more than a passing squall.

It left Suki with a problem, though. Traditionally the appointment of the junior servant was left to her to present a candidate to Mrs Cole for approval, or find another one until her mistress pronounced herself satisfied. In these instances, Suki would have made damn sure to establish that the candidate understood the full extent of the role beforehand. After all, what girl in her right mind expected full board and lodging and to be paid eight thousand rupiah a month in return for a little light cleaning and cooking? That was just the starting point. The real money, and work, came later, after hours and between chores, serving the physical appetites of the construction gangs, hawkers and anyone else who dropped by.

With Ida, as with Ida's predecessors, she had had someone to bear the brunt of the work, leaving Suki free to concentrate on a few favoured clients, including Benny Surikano. (Not that Benny did anything as undignified as line up outside her door next to the rice canteen and tea urn; their weekly assignations took place in a private room above the Atomic restaurant on her supposed day off.) With Ida gone, and Francesca unwilling to follow in her footsteps, the sheer workload presented by the new extension to the company's main offices over the road, which were at least six months away from completion, was overwhelming. Even if Suki had been willing to accommodate the crude labourers with their cement stained hands that left her with such painful rashes and their sour body odours, her body just wouldn't take it. She was already twenty five, and whilst she reckoned she had another four or five years in her before the better customers ceased finding her attractive, she was simply too exhausted to meet all the demands placed upon her.

What she would probably have to do was find some willing girl downtown to come up to the ridge for evening work, and just keep her out of sight of the Coles. Benny would have to be prevailed upon again, to speak to the guards at the main gate, and yet more rupiah would undoubtedly have to change hands. But if there was one valuable lesson her years in business had taught Suki, it was the knowledge of when you had to spend. People like Benny mattered, and it was important to make sure they were properly looked after. She'd remember that when she stepped away from all this and started to live her own life. She estimated she was probably a third of the way there, if you took all her savings deposited at the Bank of Bandakan. She'd have been considerably further down the line if she wasn't always having to buy favours off Benny, but she had to admit he was a more than valuable contact, certainly worth cultivating into her new life. He could prevent her being ripped off by equipment suppliers, and smooth the way with all the government clerks who demanded such a greedy cut of anything going it was a wonder any business got done at all. He could also help with finding suitable premises; a good location was critical, she knew.

She hadn't quite decided whether to have some girls working for her or just focus on the restaurant. Girls meant hassle and even more palms to be greased, but they certainly pulled in the punters. The trouble was, Suki found it hard to imagine how she would be able to make a decent return without them. When you considered the profit on a bowl of fish curry against the clip she could take from ten minutes boom boom in a back room, it was crazy not to have the girls. That was the sting in this line of work, it ruined you for anything else, and not just in the obvious ways. Because part of the reason, indeed the most important reason, for doing this was to break with the past, to sever her dependence upon the largesse and goodwill of the Americans, upon Dennis Cole's willingness to turn a blind eye to her commercial activities, and most important of all upon the men continuing to find her attractive. Of all the urges driving her forward, the strongest of all was the desire to be her own woman. Even if she declined to serve any customers herself, eventually passing Benny too on to a younger girl, some of the aura of what she did would stick to her. You couldn't wash it out with the sheets. Whilst she was for the most part immune to what people said about or thought of her, she didn't particularly want to be known as a brothel keeper.

What she really wanted was a place like the Atomic, where westerners would come when they were feeling adventurous and had tired of the stale fare on offer at their clubs. Of course, she would tone the experience down, provide knives and forks alongside the chopsticks, as well as plenty of chilled beer. One lesson her experience on the ridge had taught her was how far you could push the unfamiliar and the exotic onto westerners. For instance, they liked the spices, especially when added to cuts of meat or fish they recognised, but they loathed squatting on their haunches and they were especially adverse for a so called civilized people to the notion of removing one's shoes before walking indoors. Many of them had already worked in the Middle East, so anything that didn't permit alcohol had them running a mile. Suki knew all this, which is why she knew her restaurant would succeed where so many other establishments set up downtown to lure in a slice of the oil bonanza had failed.

Who knows, the day might eventually come when people would seek out Bandakan simply to experience it as a place, rather than somewhere that had to be tolerated in the pursuit of a dollar, though when you looked at the sprawling shanty town from the heights of Little America, it was hard to see it.

11

Sitting at the desk in his small office set off from the staff room, Peter Adisono enjoyed a grandstand view of the tennis courts, where Rollo Surikano was busy thrashing it out with the club pro while Peter struggled to come up with a suitable theme for the Constar 50th Anniversary pageant he'd been instructed to put on for the entertainment of the company's managers and their wives, together with anyone else who happened to be passing by and couldn't take another *Hawaii Five O* rerun. It was a signal of the esteem in which he was held by the parents of the children to whom he taught Indonesian history and culture, as well as the basic smatterings of the language, that Harry Bird had, against the advice of Benny Surikano, appointed Peter master of ceremonies, along with a cheerful and probably equally ill-advised request to put on something a bit livelier this time round. For Peter, it was a rare opportunity for truth to crawl out from under the tombstone in which it had been interred, if only for an hour or so. Which reminded him of Harry's parting edict not to make the whole thing too darn long. That was fine by Peter, there was plenty he could say, or rather have his troupe act out, in his allotted time frame. Rehearsals were due to start in a day or so, but before they could begin he had to have a script, or at the very least a theme.

What could one say about the fledgling history of his country after they had finally kicked out the Dutch? That it had been a massive disappointment, that the early promise of a non-aligned, genuinely independent, vibrant young nation had given way to cynicism, corruption and army sponsored cronyism? That the leaders entrusted with guiding their nation's faltering steps into an uncertain future had robbed it blind, siphoning precious natural resources into self-serving business scams and private Swiss bank accounts? No, that wasn't what the assembled audience of dignitaries had come to hear at all. Take that useless scion of the Suharto regime slugging it out on the tennis court, pathetically trying to recast himself as some American preppy. Thanks to his father he had all the accessories and all the connections, but none of it could evade the fundamental injustice upon which his privileged position was founded. For a moment Peter relished the image of a caricatured Rollo lampooned on the stage, complete with oversized Rolex, gold neck chain and sunglasses, before dismissing the idea. He would have to be subtler, his barbs insidious, his message oblique.

Not for the first time Peter asked himself what he was doing here at all, using his gifts to entertain the privileged white kids of Constar like some court jester, when there were children in the kampongs who could barely read and write. Like some paid up member of the Communist Party with a second car and a weekend bolthole in the country, his life continued in a comfortable state of ongoing moral crisis. What sickened Peter most of all was he owed it all to the father of that fat oaf on the tennis court. It was Benny Surikano who had fixed it for him, the job that paid three times the salary of an equivalent post in a local school, the company apartment, access to the Constar club (even though he rarely set foot in the place), and most of all a life free from the fear of bumping into a couple of plain clothes cops or receiving that chilling knock on the door in the small hours, to be hauled off to some cell where the nightmare could begin in earnest. Yes, good old Uncle Benny had fixed it, just as he fixed everything round here. In return, Peter had to kowtow to him and pretend to be grateful. Grateful for what? For the privilege of being able to lead a life few Indonesians outside the higher ranks of the army and its closely allied business circles could dream of, or the honour of despising himself every time he looked in the mirror or thought about where he had come from?

What would Rudi Adisono, that illustrious intellectual powerhouse of the PKI, have made of Peter's shabby compromise with the forces of corruption? Would he have expressed his disappointment in his only son blatantly, or would he have kept his views to himself, as Peter was compelled to do these days? It was different now, Peter rationalised, times had changed. It was one thing to be a communist or a socialist in his father's era, but that had been before the great purges of 1965. These days, if you leant to the left, you made sure you kept damn quiet about it. When the pangs of conscience became too hard to bear, Peter would find himself angrily wondering just how vocal Rudi the orator, Rudi the martyr, Rudi the giant of the party with the pygmy of a son, would have been in today's harsher climate. That was the convenient thing about having been shot dead during a raid on the party's newspaper offices, you weren't around any more to field the hard questions left for your inadequate son to deal with.

Rudi Adisono had been one of the last prominent socialists to have been murdered by the incoming Suharto regime, despite his many provocative speeches and essays, and broad following in the countryside. The only reason this thorn in the side of the generals had been tolerated for so long was due to an astute marriage to the rebellious daughter of one of Suharto's most loyal generals, a match Peter could attest was driven by love. Time after time, the family had tried to rein Rudi in, imploring him, even if he couldn't change his views, to at least moderate the more inflammatory calls to action that were inciting impressionable young hotheads to cause serious problems for the new regime. Their words had fallen on stony ground, and eventually they too washed their hands of him, quietly informing certain shadowy parties that he no longer stood under the umbrella of their protection. How Peter's mother had railed against her own father after Rudi's inevitable death, screaming at him in a most un-Indonesian manner, calling him a bastard and a murderer to his face, and much worse besides. And whilst she had never forgiven him for sanctioning the assassination of her husband, not even when he lay in agony on his death bed riddled with bone cancer, for the sake of the impressionable nineteen-year-old Peter, she had eventually allowed the family, now headed by her sister's husband to come to their assistance. Eight years on, there wasn't an aspect of their lives that wasn't owed to Uncle Benny.

Relations between Peter and Benny were delineated by formality and a healthy dose of suspicion on both sides. Though no one had ever directly linked Benny to Rudi's death, there was no doubt he was a trusted insider in the machine that had brought it about. Peter had a theory that much of Benny's generosity, which on occasions had far exceeded the requirements of familial duty, arose out of a sense of guilt. He also suspected that Benny was terrified of Peter turning out like his father, which was why he had done everything possible to dull any raging sense of social injustice in his protégé by inundating Peter with as many trappings as possible of the good life. And

Peter, like the weakling he was, had unquestioningly accepted the lot, gritting his teeth and choking back the bitterness as he thanked Uncle Benny profusely for another string pulled, another favour bestowed.

Rollo, on the other hand, he owed nothing. Being five years older than his benefactor's only son, Peter had watched the spoilt brat grow up with a mixture of envy and disgust. Envy because he had a father who clearly adored him and would do whatever it took to ensure he received only the very best. Disgust at Rollo's unquestioning acceptance of these dubious riches as no more than his birthright, and his utter indifference to the plight of millions of his fellow citizens. If he really wanted to despair of his country's future, all Peter had to do was imagine it being run by a junta made up of Rollos. The notion of social justice was totally lost on his cousin; all he saw was a world full of things for him to covet, goodies that would only go to someone else if he didn't get hold of them first. For as long as Peter could remember, whenever a new gadget, toy or accessory was introduced, you could count on Rollo having it before anyone else. But recently father and son had expanded their horizons with a conceptual leap that left Peter speechless in their wake. The two of them, so the rumour went, were cooking up a plan whereby Constar would actually pay to put Rollo through Harvard Business School. Rollo's complete lack of aptitude for the rigors of academia aside (you could hardly count a couple of years fooling around at the University of Jakarta), the sheer audaciousness of it was beyond anything Peter had seen on the ridge, a genuine masterstroke in the long corrupt career of Backhand Benny. And the astonishing part of it was, if the gossip he'd heard was accurate, Constar were looking like going for it: tuition fees, air fares, living allowance, expenses, miscellaneous sundries, the lot. It was enough to make an honest man want to vomit. Such was the stranglehold Colonel Surikano exerted on so many necessary components of doing business here, a hard edged US corporation which viewed all Indonesians as cheap, expendable labour, was prepared to go to these lengths to keep him sweet. For whilst Uncle Benny couldn't halt the inevitable exploitation of Indonesia's oil reserves by foreign companies, he could make life for any particular one amongst them exceedingly difficult. The Americans weren't the fools some of Peter's more radical friends made them out to be, they just shrugged their shoulders and wrote it off as another cost of doing business.

Outside, the object of these envious musings was approaching the end of his workout. They had stopped playing, and now stood under the awning separating two of the courts, where the pro was drawing attention to a facet of Rollo's grip while his student leant against the water cooler.

Rollo wiped his brow with a towel, plucked a couple of strings around the sweet spot on his racquet, which Peter noticed was one of the new graphite models, and gathered up his balls in a string bag. Off to the club now, no doubt, for a long cool drink and a lazy session by the pool. Not that Peter's afternoons were particularly onerous, now he thought of it, more often than not the hours between two and three found him in his office with the blinds drawn taking a little nap on the wicker chaise longue. His lessons were all done by midday, the afternoon sessions being handled by the American teachers, giving him plenty of time to mark assignments, prepare topics, organise corporate anniversary pageants and worry about the general state of the world.

Inspiration was eluding him, so he decided to lock up his office for the day and attend to the other small matter on his conscience. Walking out of the school buildings, he decided to leave his motorbike parked where it was. Although it was still hot, it was less than a ten minute walk away and he could use the time to gather his thoughts. Not that he had anything new to impart, just the usual platitudes. He wondered why he bothered, and realised it was the guilt, his constant companion, calling him again.

He arrived to find Hamid sitting in his usual wicker arm-chair, staring into the middle distance as he did whenever his wife was busy indoors. Not a good time to call, he realised, but he was here now and could hardly walk on by as if nothing was happening.

There wasn't an etiquette guide in the world, or at least one Peter knew of, that described the correct protocol for enquiring after a man's wife while she was servicing a client. Hamid, though, seemed to have attained a level of acceptance beyond the reach of most men and merely nodded at Peter without getting up, before gesturing him to take the chair beside him.

"Suki will be out in a few minutes," was all he said.

Taking the offered seat, Peter tried to ignore the male grunts coming from the other side of the single skinned concrete block wall. And whilst intellectually he had turned away from the teachings of Islam years ago, he could not help finding the ways Hamid and Suki made ends meet offensive. What kind of man, thought Peter, lived off the immoral earnings of his wife while spending the entire day lolling in an armchair smoking one cigarette after another, watching his life drift by in an apathetic trance? Disapprove of him as he did, it was still hard to dislike Hamid, and Peter shook his hand before settling into the seat beside him.

"Shouldn't be too long now. Guy she's with is a regular, but he can never keep it going more than a few minutes."

Peter wished Hamid would spare him the details. Had the man no shame?

"How are you keeping?" he asked in a desperate attempt to change the subject.

"Oh, not so bad, can't complain," Hamid replied, rolling himself a fresh cigarette. "Things are a lot easier round here now we've got the new girl."

"Where did she come from?"

"East Timor of all places. Apparently, she turned up in one of your Uncle Benny's boats along with a load of motorbikes and coffee beans. But she's the answer to Mrs Cole's prayers, as she can actually speak English. Bit of a miracle when you come to think of it. As you can imagine, Mrs Cole is now deeply in Colonel Surikano's debt."

"So, what's the new girl like?" he asked.

"Doesn't say much, keeps to herself mostly. But she's helpful enough and Mrs Cole is delighted with her, which is the main thing. Only problem is," Hamid grinned, "we can no longer use the language barrier as an excuse for not doing things we don't want to do. Now Mrs Cole goes straight to Francesca and we're expected to have it done. Such is life. You win some, you lose some. Suki sure lost out if she was hoping for someone to take the pressure off her client commitments."

"A woman of integrity?"

Hamid smiled. "Are you suggesting my wife isn't?"

Peter blushed at his blunder. "I guess we all just do what we've got to do. I'm not in any position to judge anyone."

"That's for sure."

Peter looked at Hamid sharply. "What do you mean by that?"

"Nothing. Only you're a lot closer to the people running this place than the likes of us." Hamid pulled on his cigarette, inhaled and then stared straight ahead as he blew out a neat cloud of smoke.

Peter squirmed in his chair, stung by Hamid's insouciance. "I'm just here to see if there's anything I can do to help."

"I doubt it," replied Hamid, still not looking at Peter. "Though Suki always likes to see you. I think she's done now, she'll be out in a moment."

As if on cue, the door opened and a shifty looking construction worker emerged, adjusting the belt around his trousers and glancing from side to side to check he'd not been observed. Shutting the door softly behind him he walked past Peter and Hamid without acknowledging either one of them, back to the site office portakabin.

"Another two thousand rupes down the hatch," muttered Hamid once the punter was out of earshot. "Don't know what we'll do when all that building work is finished."

A moment later the door opened again, and this time Suki walked out, prim in her self-containment, her sarong neat and smooth as if it had just been pressed. Unlike her husband, she appeared rattled by Peter's presence, her face taking on a guilty look.

"What brings you over here?"

"What kind of a way is that to greet an old friend?" replied Peter in an effort to put her at her ease.

"Do you have any news?"

"About Abdul?"

Suki looked at him expectantly, and he shook his head. "Sorry."

"Oh well." She shrugged her shoulders, momentarily turning her face away from his. "I wasn't really expecting anything. Would you like some tea?"

"Sure."

Suki turned to Hamid. "Where's Francesca?"

"In the house, I think."

"Is she still doing that ironing?"

"I've no idea," her husband replied.

Suki crossed the carport and softly opened the door to the Cole's kitchen.

"Francesca," she called quietly.

A few moments later Peter saw a shadow move into the doorway, followed by a slight figure dressed in a blouse and full length western skirt. The girl nodded deferentially at Suki, who directed her to the amahs' quarters. Peter managed a quick glimpse as she crossed the carport, during which the girl kept her gaze firmly ahead of her, acknowledging neither him nor Hamid. There was dignity in her deference, and although she had scraped her hair back into an unflattering bun held in place with a long wooden pin, there was no disguising her beauty or the defiant sense of self she carried with her. Peter found himself intrigued by this exotic refugee from the Timor annexation who understood three languages and chose to speak in none of them. She was certainly a refreshing change from sulky old Ida, well worth hanging around over a cup of tea for.

"I heard things got pretty rough in Timor."

"So they say," replied Hamid.

Peter turned to Suki. "Was she caught up in it?"

"The whole country was caught up in it."

"What I mean is, she must have lost things, her family, her home, to have ended up here."

Suki shrugged her shoulders. "I don't know. She didn't say."

"Didn't you ask?"

"Why should I do that? It's none of my business where she came from. I've enough problems of my own without taking on hers. So long as she does her job and minds her manners around the house, I'm not about to pry."

"It's still a strange place for a Timorese refugee to end up," persisted Peter.

"Who said anything about a refugee?" retorted Suki.

Peter was prevented from pressing any further by the sound of Francesca emerging from the amahs' quarters with a tray on which were balanced two long glasses of dark tea alongside a bowl of white sugar cubes, courtesy of Barbara Cole's kitchen. She placed the tray down on the side table between the two chairs, first quickly glancing at Hamid for permission to move his pack of rolling tobacco. No one indeed may have said anything about refugees, but it was not hard for Peter to discern the once proud and now shattered spirit reminiscent of so many of his father's contemporaries. It was there in the eyes, in the reflexive flinch when Hamid unexpectedly moved to pick up his lighter, in the defensive, hunched posture designed to keep everyone, including well wishers, at bay.

Peter looked up and smiled at her, forcing her to hold eye contact with him, if only for half a second.

"That's very kind of you," he said.

She nodded, then shrank back into the carport.

Peter stood up and reached forward towards her. "I'm Peter, by the way."

Francesca nodded once, but didn't offer any reciprocal introduction.

Peter then thrust out his hand. "And you are Francesca, I am told?"

Francesca shrunk back further, ignoring the proffered hand, giving only the faintest acknowledgement to Peter's question.

"Well, I'm very pleased to meet you," Peter pressed on, as Francesca retreated inside.

Hamid snorted as Peter returned to his seat. "I can see our little Francesca's charms aren't lost on you, Peter."

"I don't know what you mean," replied Peter, blushing heavily.

"Oh, come now!" laughed Hamid. "Since when did you pay such attention to a lowly amah?"

"I was just being polite," Peter said, aware his words lacked any conviction. "I mean, it seems as if she could use someone being nice to her, a friend perhaps."

"I think what she could really use is being left alone," replied Hamid. "What do you think, Suki?"

"I don't care either way."

Hamid smiled with the satisfaction of a scientist laying out a new theory he was confident to be irrefutable. "She's good looking, Peter, I'll give you that." He reached for his tobacco pouch, then looked up again at Peter. "So, it looks like we might be seeing a bit more of you. It's about time you got out of that head of yours and started to feel something for a change."

"Are you suggesting I'm cold-hearted, Hamid?"

"I don't think you have a cold heart, it just hasn't had much practice, that's all. You might want to start out on something a little more straightforward, though."

"You know straightforward has never appealed to me. Just ask my mother."

Hamid took a sip from his tea and began the intricate process of rolling a cigarette one handed. "Sometimes I wonder what it must be like to have life so easy you have to make things difficult for yourself." Having shaped the cigarette to his satisfaction, he ran the paper along his tongue, sealing it into its roll. "It must be very strange," he continued, "very strange indeed."

12

The day after Eddie met Amanda, Mick sprung a week long assignment on him to fly up country and ferry supplies between Gunpura and some new exploration sites freshly cut out of the jungle. Eddie protested but Mick, whose hangover was so bad he wasn't even bothering to conceal the can of Tiger at his desk, was in no shape to recompile the rosters.

"Can't Derek do it?" Eddie asked, standing in the ops room doorway.

"No, Derek can't do it, I need someone who can park a Huey in a tight clearing without slicing the fucking tail rotor off. I swear those lazy bastards keep felling fewer trees with each new well they drill. They see what you fellas can do in a tight spot and don't bother giving us any room to breathe."

"Can't you have a word with someone about that?"

"Believe me, Eddie, I've tried, but no one wants to know. All they see is another day's exploration lost and another twenty thousand dollars down the drain. It's going to take a fully gassed up Huey exploding in their fucking faces to wake those dozy cunts up. So be careful, take her in nice and slow and don't try any flash stuff." Mick reached for his beer and took a long swig, followed by a loud belch. Eddie glanced up at the clock on the wall: ten to eight in the morning.

He tried another tack. "In that case, can I at least fly back here at the end of each day?"

Mick shot him a perplexed look. "What's so exciting about Bandakan nightlife all of a sudden? The beers are just as cold in the Gunpura Rec room." A smile spread across his face as he made the connection. "It's that bird you were hanging out with up at the club, isn't it? I heard all about it."

Eddie blushed, and shuffled his weight from one leg to the other. "News travels fast."

A deep chuckle emanated from the recesses of Mick's throat. "Guess those years in 'Nam left you with a taste for them young."

"Age has nothing to do with it," retorted Eddie primly.

"Let's hope Dennis Cole sees it the same way," replied Mick. "Though somehow, I can't see it myself."

"Well, can I?"

"Can you what?"

"Can I fly back here at the end of each day?"

"Of course you can't, I've never heard of such a dumb fuck idea."

"Oh, come on Mick, have a heart."

"Don't come on Mick me like that. Besides, they need you out there on call." Mick's tone softened. "Tell you what, do the week out of Gunpura and I'll base you out of here next week, doing short hops to the sea platforms. Who knows, I might even get overcome by an attack of goodwill and roster you a day off."

"That's real kind of you, Mick. I appreciate it."

"You know that underneath this gruff Australian shell lies a sentimental old fool!" Mick flashed Eddie a smile. "Besides, it'll do you good to be away for a week or so. Keep her nice and keen, and what's more give Dennis time to come round to the idea."

"Whatever you say."

"Just remember what I said about those tight landings."

Eddie retired back to his quarters, which consisted of one half of a portakabin, to throw a few clothes, some toiletries and a couple of paperbacks into a grip bag. The week-long tour, normally half welcomed as an opportunity to treat both his liver and his bank account to a respite from the routine après fly shenanigans, now stretched out in a desert of tedium. As his mind filled with self-loathing at the futility of his life, he felt cheap at the ease with which he had awed Amanda through his supposed glamour and sophistication. The burnt-out Vietnam chopper pilot, what a fucking cliché. Her purity and her unscarred heart were what drew him to her, which made it all the worse to fall back on the tried and tested seduction lines, and why he so resented Mick's cracks. If Amanda was to mean anything, he had to make himself more like her rather than introduce her to his squalid bachelor world. Both of them needed to step out of their familiar realms. He had the urge to protect her from the cynical banter of the Base Camp bar, but he could not return to her world of adolescent concerns and pretend to squeeze himself into it as if the past ten years had never happened.

He spent the next seven days flying, sleeping, eating, reading and thinking of her. When he finally returned to Base Camp he quickly took a shower and jumped on his motorbike to head up to the ridge. The bike was an old Yamaha 125 he'd bought for too much money from a Bouraq pilot, but to Eddie the freedom it gave him made it more than worth it.

He didn't share the phobias most expats had of being lynched by a mob following a road accident in which the white man was invariably held to be at fault (after all, the logic went, if he hadn't been in their country in the first place the accident couldn't have happened), and there was a limit to the harm he could cause with an underpowered motorcycle.

Eddie wasn't an especially familiar face at the Constar club. It reminded him all too much of a cross between a midwestern country club, the sort of place his grandparents would summon the family for Sunday brunch when they needed to use up their monthly minimum, and a sleepy supper club where the same grandparents would retire for a staid dinner to celebrate the passing of yet another year in each other's company.

All that had changed now, he thought as he slipped his watch off his wrist and placed it in his pocket for the ride through downtown Bandakan. He could use a bit of swimming to get himself back in shape, fifty laps two or three times a week should restore the washboard stomach he had been so proud of in high school. He was acutely sensitive of the age difference between them, and Mick's jibes had stung. He was also worried about what Dennis Cole would make of it all, and determined to cast himself in as clean a light as possible. He'd always fancied himself as a somewhat louche, jaded character from the pages of a Graham Greene novel, prematurely debauched with eyes weary from over-exposure to the world's wicked ways, seeking temporary solace from the bleakness in opium dens, booze and prostitutes. All that would have to be swept aside. He wasn't quite ready to become some clean cut college jock patriot who personified J. Edgar Hoover's ideal of American youth, but he certainly needed to straighten out his act and curtail some of the habits he'd acquired during his years in Asia.

He kept an eye out for her as he drove along the ridge, but it was still mid-afternoon and hardly anyone was out and about.

Those who weren't at work preferred to take their afternoon rest in the air conditioned comfort of their homes. He parked the bike outside the club and sauntered in, making straight for the terrace and down a flight of concrete steps to the pool deck, again empty bar three expat wives lazily sizzling their tans. The obsession the women on this social peak of Bandakan had with their pigmentation both fascinated and amused him. While the wealthier Indonesians doused themselves in skin lighteners and kept out of the sun at all costs in an attempt to make themselves look as western as possible, the expats went the other way, frying themselves in coconut oil, with the net result that they all met at the same indistinguishable rich tan.

The clear blue water looked inviting, and so he bagged an umbrella stand and placed the shoulder bag containing his towel, wallet and keys on the table. He unbuttoned his cut-off Levi's and stripped down to the trunks underneath, relishing the gentle breeze on his body. He laid his T-shirt out across a metal chair so the sun could dry out the sweat stains around the armpits. Instinctively he looked around for any locals who might be watching and waiting for him to dive underwater before sidling in to filch his wallet, and even though he knew he should be safe enough in this rarefied environment, experience had taught him to take nothing for granted. He clipped his watch back on his wrist, glanced at the time, and then walked around the edge of the pool to the deep end. The pool itself was L-shaped, with the toe of the L forming an added diving area where a one-metre springboard was set beside a three metre diving board. He clambered up the springboard, paced it with his eye, and took five quick steps, a jump, then launched himself into the air.

The cool water washed off any mid afternoon torpor, leaving the sweat and the heat of the day in his trail. He took a few breast strokes underwater then broke the surface, turning back quickly to check on his belongings. He was sorry there was no sign of Amanda, but he was glad to have come here if only for a swim. He wondered whether he dared phone her from the club. It was a risk. Dennis would still be at work, but there was every chance Barbara would reach the phone first, and he wasn't quite ready to declare his hand in that quarter yet. It was so ridiculous, this importance people attached to chronology. He and Amanda were destined for each other, he knew it with a certainty he'd felt for nothing else in his life. And just because they'd been born on this planet a few years apart, which was a blink of an eyelid in the broader movements of the universe, their match was deemed inappropriate and smutty, exploitative even. Why couldn't they just celebrate the purity of their love, rare enough in today's world, rather than casting him as an ageing lecher and her as naïve victim? This wasn't about selfish gratification, he thought angrily as he thrashed up and down the pool, it was the coming together of two kindred spirits, spirits that were ageless in their compatibility. For the first time in his life he felt the possibility of being heard and understood by someone, of being fully known by another human being, in a relationship where all that had happened in the past mattered not one jot. How could that be when they had spent no more than an hour or two together? Yet as with their respective ages, time had nothing to do with it either. What had occurred was two souls recognising their mate in each other, and they both knew it. Eddie suspected Amanda in her inexperience might not appreciate just how rare such an occurrence could be, that one could go a whole lifetime without happening on it again, and that it was a crime against one's essential being to turn away from that love when it showed itself, regardless of the circumstances and the consequences. He could always try getting a note to her – Indonesian servants were easily bribed

– but if he was found out, it would be tantamount to admitting he was trying on something underhand. The other thing he could do was leave a message with the reception desk at the club, letting her know he would be there at a specific time and asking her to join him. Such an approach combined the directness his heart demanded with the discretion his head counselled, and he resolved to act upon it the moment he'd dried off from his swim. For now he was content to feel the cool water on his body, celebrate being alive by exercising his muscles, and think of a future in which he could close the door forever on the bitter loneliness that had shadowed him for as long as he could remember.

Eddie didn't have to resort to notes and subterfuge, for Amanda wandered out on to the pool deck some twenty minutes later. An intuition she couldn't explain had compelled her to leave the video room, where a scratchy episode of *Charlie's Angels* was playing for the umpteenth time, to step outside on the pretext of fetching a soda and a cup of popcorn. Like a well-lit fire, a week with Melanie and her own thoughts for company had done nothing but intensify the heat of her desire for Eddie, and she almost tripped over her flip-flops when she saw him ploughing up and down the pool in an intense crawl. The sight of his physique sent a thrill through her body; tall, lean and strong, pulling against the water as he propelled himself forwards. She checked her impulse to dive in and embrace him, choosing to draw out her pleasure and simply watch him while he remained unaware of her presence. She yearned to be held by him, to be possessed by him, to be infused with his being. At the same time she felt wholly inadequate to the task. Against his worldliness she was so inexperienced, her ignorance so great, her views so unformed. Since their conversation a week ago she had made a determined effort to keep more on top of current affairs, working through back issues of Time Magazine. It had certainly been an education, if only in the extent of the gaps in her knowledge. Vietnam, Cambodia, Laos, the VC, the NVA, the ARVN, it was hard enough working out who was fighting who, let alone why, and as for trying to isolate the root causes of the conflict, she'd given up and for now resorted to accepting the prevailing domino theory so beloved of her father and his friends. She wanted to ask him about it so badly, but first she needed to learn a little more herself so she didn't humiliate herself with some stupid question that would simply spotlight the embarrassing reality she had been seven years old when the war started, and that lately, while more serious minds had been digesting the violent nightly news footage, her thoughts had been given over to movements up and down the pop charts.

Another question she wanted to ask, but hadn't yet found the courage or the appropriate words, was whether he had killed many people. It had occurred to her first when he brushed his finger against her cheek as they parted, and since then she hadn't been able to dispel the image of those sensitive hands twitching a trigger or knifing some stranger in the chest. There was a sense of heightened danger, excitement almost, of being held by a pair of hands that had taken a human life. It made everything so real, so intense, and she knew then she would never be able to take another callow schoolboy seriously again.

She walked around the edge of the pool over to the table where he'd left his clothes, sat down on the metal chair padded out in foam and orange faux leather, and waited. She'd stay here as long as necessary, breathing in his presence. She wanted to pick up his shirt and press it into her face so she could drink in his smell, and would have done so were it not for the condescending looks of the three old lizards sunning themselves nearby. Instead, she reached over to his bag and helped herself to one of his cigarettes. She loved the petrol aroma from his Zippo and the rich smoky orange flame it gave off.

Whatever it took, she was going to give herself to this man. Already she had endured several lectures from her mother on the promiscuity and undesirability of helicopter pilots in general and Constar pilots in particular, monologues in which the age difference between them had loomed large in the list of reasons as to the unsuitability of the match. She had fought back valiantly until she realised no one was actually listening to her, whereupon she stopped listening herself and resolved to do what she was going to do without telling anyone, and to hell with the consequences. If they had to keep their love secret, it added another layer of excitement to the thrill of the relationship. It was strange, she noticed, how she had already taken their intimacy as a given, almost as if it were a long established fact, even though they had spent but part of one afternoon together. An hour or so of conversation, it was nothing when you thought about it, but she really didn't need to know any more before committing herself wholly to him.

She leant back in her chair, crossed her legs and watched him once more. He had a wonderful physique, and not too muscular either, unlike those dreary hearties who were obsessed with themselves and their sporting prowess, in that order. She had been upset he hadn't attempted to contact her since that afternoon a week ago to firm up their date; after five days of hearing nothing she had begun to doubt herself. Maybe she was missing some vital piece of information, perhaps her mother was right after all, maybe there was something wrong with him but she hadn't spotted it even though it was right in front of her. Round and round her head these thoughts rattled to torment her until she could stand it no more, and when no one was looking she had jumped into the car and demanded to be driven down to Base Camp. Once there, a mechanic put her mind at rest with the news Eddie had been up country all week and wasn't expected back until the day after tomorrow.

Now she knew he was back in town, her instincts told her to come here, and she was pleased they had served her well. She'd hoped he wouldn't risk trying to contact her at home; every time the phone had rung these past few days her mother had pounced on the receiver before Amanda could get anywhere near. No, thankfully Eddie was smarter than that. It was as if they already read each other's thoughts. She wanted so much to cross the pool deck and stand at the end of his lane, but decided once again to sit it out until he saw her. A few strokes later it happened. Eddie stood up in the shallow end, swept back his hair, wiped the water from his eyes and glanced over towards his table. She gave him a huge smile and thrilled to her heart at the reflexive response of joy in his face. There was no lying in that split second first reaction, and she knew then he felt as she did. She had to grip the chair with both hands to stop herself running towards him as he waded across to the steps, hauled himself out of the pool and made his way towards her.

"Hey, you!" she smiled when he finally reached their table.

He leant over, kissed her briefly on the cheek then rested his hand on her forearm. "Hey, you too."

"Long time no see."

"I know." He grabbed his towel and quickly dried himself off before pulling up another chair and sitting down beside her. "I'm sorry, I wanted to get in touch but I've been stuck out in the jungle the whole week."

"I know."

"You do?"

"I went down to the airport to look for you."

"I'm sorry about that. There was nothing I could do about it."

"It's not your fault."

"I know. But I didn't want you to think I'd dropped off the face of the earth. Fancy a drink?"

"Sure."

A waiter delivering a tray of snacks to the lounger lizards caught Eddie's eye, and he summoned him over. As soon as he was gone with their order Eddie turned back to Amanda.

"I thought about you a lot when I was gone."

"Me too." Her gaze wandered up and down his chest, where droplets of water were drying off on the soft pale brown hairs. "I mean, I thought a lot about you, not about me," she added clumsily with an embarrassed laugh.

"I know what you mean."

There was a momentary pause, during which neither one of them seemed to know where to look or what to say.

It was Eddie who finally broke the silence. "You know this makes no sense," he said reaching for his cigarettes.

"That I'm some silly schoolgirl out for a fling, you mean?"

"No, that's not what I mean at all. It's just our worlds are so different."

"That doesn't matter to me," replied Amanda softly but with a firm edge to her voice.

"It matters to a lot of people."

"I don't care what people think."

"Nor do I, but there are people round here who could make things difficult for us."

"My parents?"

"For starters. Look at those women over there."

"Those shrivelled prunes?"

"They've not stopped gossiping about us since we saw each other. I bet they can't wait to get back to their husbands and their friends and tell them what scandalous goings-on they witnessed at the pool. By tonight it will be all over the ridge."

"Only because they haven't anything better to do with their lives."

"The net result is still the same."

"Let's face it, Eddie, it's not us coming from different worlds that bothers you, it's the difference in our age."

"It doesn't bother me in itself, it means nothing to me, it's just the conclusions people draw from it."

"So how old are you?"

Eddie laughed. "Really! What kind of question is that?"

"One that needs an answer. Come on, you're the one who brought up the subject, spit it out. You can't be more than forty five."

"Thanks a lot!" He picked up his pack of cigarettes and flung it at her. "Put it this way, I'm still in my twenties. Though not for much longer," he added after a pause.

"Well that's okay then. My mother said you were at least thirty five. Old enough to be your father, she kept repeating endlessly."

"I guess in some of the southern states I would be!"

"It's not funny, Eddie. People still see me as a child. You're different, you work here, you're your own person. I don't have that, I'm just someone's daughter, a dependent. It's even stamped on my visa."

"I don't see you that way."

"I know you don't."

"So tell me who you really are. Now we've established you're not some silly little schoolgirl out here on vacation with her parents."

Amanda sighed. "I guess that's what I am really."

"No you're not."

"Well, I do still go to school. Or I did until a few weeks ago."

"What did you think of it?"

"Not a lot. It's a rigid place stuck in the middle of the last century. It's not like anything you'd ever have in America."

"You'd be surprised," said Eddie with a chuckle. "It's probably not a whole lot different from where I grew up."

"Where was that?"

"Illinois."

"I've only ever seen America through TV and films. It looks pretty cool, though."

"Yeah, I guess you could see it that way." His voice trailed off and she saw his focus drift away from her.

"How do you see it?"

"I'm still a little too pissed off, as you British say, at my country to be able to give you a fair appraisal. But even if I wasn't, you can't define it in a few words. It's too big, everything is there. Good, bad, heroic, tawdry, majestic, trashy, in twenty six flavours, it's whatever you want it to be. The minute you point to something that encapsulates the pure essence of the United States, something else pops up that proves the exact opposite. It's what makes it such a wonderful and such an awful place at the same time."

"Whereas England is just damp, grey and boring."

"You have great history."

"That's half the problem, all people think about is the past. They spend their whole time trying to hang onto something that disappeared a long time ago, they can't face up to the fact they live in a crappy third-rate country where nothing works any more."

"I've always wanted to go there."

"Why?"

"I guess it's that sense of history you complain about, all those beautiful castles and gardens. It blows my mind, the idea of being surrounded by things that are hundreds of years old, that have been used and added to by generation after generation."

"The weight of it can crush you."

"Do you feel crushed?"

She nodded, and he extended his hand to reach her fingertips. The touch of her flesh on his sent a thrill up his arm and through his body. He yearned to reach over and embrace her, knowing if he did she would not repel him, but managed to restrain himself. His emotions were unstable explosive, liable to detonate in an uncontrollable eruption if handled carelessly.

"We must be careful." He spoke the words softly, almost in a whisper.

"I know."

"Do you want to know how I feel, Amanda?"

"Tell me."

"I feel there's this whole routine people go through when they meet, of finding out about each other, exchanging information, I like peanut butter ice cream, you prefer vanilla, I went to school here, did this, this and this, you did whatever you did, and somehow it all feels totally superfluous. It's as if I can communicate with you on some deeper level, that there's an understanding between us, that we connect in some powerful and primal way. Oh God, what am I saying, I've barely met you. But that's the whole point. You must think I'm completely crazy."

"No, I don't think that, Eddie. I know exactly what you mean. I feel the same myself."

"You do?"

"Yes, I do. I feel like I've spent my whole life as this isolated person full of all these mad thoughts rattling around inside my head, that if I told people what was really going on they'd lock me away."

"To be honest," said Eddie, "I've never really understood how most people carry on, given the lives they lead."

"Do you think anyone would say anything if I kissed you?"

"I think it would be all over the ridge in half an hour."

"Is there anywhere we can go?"

"I've got the bike out the front."

She smiled, then started to gather up his clothes and stuff them into his bag. "Come on, what are we waiting for?"

Half an hour later they pulled in to a sandy car park by the sea. As Eddie brought the bike to a standstill, she reluctantly released her delicious grip around his waist and climbed off the back. The ride through town had been heaven. The security guards at the ridge gates had noted her departure, but no one had tried to stop her, and so long as she was back by nightfall, there was no reason to suppose her absence would be reported. After chauffeur-driven air-conditioned cars, the freedom of the bike was exhilarating, and she thrilled at the warm afternoon air rushing through her hair. There were catcalls and whistles at the sight of the scantily dressed blonde girl bombing past the mosque while the devout lined up for afternoon prayers, but they encountered no hostility along the way, just envious glances.

Hand in hand, they walked up to the entrance of the French beach club, where Eddie signed them both in. They then walked through the clubhouse, which was in fact no more than a large wooden floor covered by a pitched rush ceiling, open to the elements at all sides. They ignored the bamboo furniture dotted around the bar and went straight to the steps at the far end leading down to the beach, where a dozen or so teak sun loungers had bleached to a pale grey.

Although the local staff spoke English, French was the language of the club, and it had become every bit as much an annexe of metropolitan France as the ridge had been turned into an idealised slice of small-town America. No one seemed scandalised by their presence together, they were just another attractive young couple enjoying the best part of the day in each other's company. For now she was unaware of the need amongst the French community, whose colonial history in the region predated the Americans by more than a century, to counter the cultural hegemony imposed by Constar's economic muscle. If the French decided to establish a racy club where women could sunbathe topless without raising eyebrows and no one challenged your right to be with the man holding your arm or questioned your age, she was happy to enjoy the benefits it had to offer.

They bagged a couple of loungers and Eddie went back to the bar to order some drinks. While he was away, Amanda tried to settle down on her lounger and shut her eyes, but she was far too alert to contemplate dozing off or doing anything so passive as soaking up the sun's rays.

"Here you are," Eddie said as he handed her a glass filled with liquids of several hues, some ice and a paper umbrella.

"What's this?"

"A Batakan Bateau. BB for short."

"What's in it?"

Eddie shrugged his shoulders and smiled. "What isn't? Go on, try it."

Gingerly she sipped at the rim. The cocktail tasted smooth and sweet, with a hint of coconut, but even her inexperienced palate could discern the undertow powering it. "Mmm. Not bad. Tastes a bit like cool-aid."

"I saw the barman layer at least three white spirits in the bottom. That's the trouble with cocktails. They slip down so easily you think there's nothing to them, then all of a sudden they rear up and bite you in the butt. Next thing you know you're passed out on the floor."

"Are you trying to get me drunk?"

"Not at all. Just a little something to help us relax a bit. This whole thing that's happening between us is so mind-blowing, I need to step back a moment and take it all in."

"Eddie, I want you to teach me everything you know."

He laughed. "The trouble is, the older I get the more I realise how little I know."

"Well, I'd better get in now before all that wisdom disappears forever."

"When I was eighteen I thought I had life cracked," he said, stretching out and taking a long sip from his drink. "People were innately good, and all you had to do to create an ideal world was establish the right conditions and everything else would follow."

"The trouble is," she replied, "there's always someone like me who'd rather make their own arrangements. Who doesn't want to fit in with everyone else's perfect world."

He looked up at her sharply. "How did you know that?"

"I don't know, just looking around." She spoke hesitantly, as if she had said something wrong. "It just seems to me that's how people are," she added apologetically.

"Jesus, Amanda, it took me ten years and being at the centre of one of the most destructive wars in modern history to work out what you know as a matter of course."

"I mean, I could be totally wrong."

"No, Amanda, you're not wrong, you're dead right. That's exactly how people are, and if you try to make them into anything else, it's a recipe for disaster. And you want me to teach you everything I know?" He laughed. "I thing it should be the other way round!"

"There's plenty you can teach me, Eddie." She leant up on one elbow and took another sip from her cocktail. The sight of her reclined there, gazing up at him, was too intense for any verbal response, so he reached down to brush her lips with his own. She placed her glass to one side and wrapped her arms around his neck, then opened her mouth to touch his tongue with hers. He was vaguely aware of a glass being knocked on its side into the sand as he climbed onto her lounger to lie beside her, running his hands up and down her back, just a thin T-shirt and a bra strap between their flesh. In his hands she felt so warm, so alive. He hadn't intended to go so far and so fast as this, his plan had been to move cautiously, to get to know her better, but the frisson between them had been too intense for the restraint experience warned him was wise. So much for experience, he thought, and whilst he knew he was condemned to be judged harshly for their match, his heart told him it wasn't like that at all, and he was putty in her hands. She could ask anything of him and he would find a way to do it. He was sure she was oblivious to the power she held over him, which only strengthened his desire. For now, he let himself fall into her, sink, sink, sink into the cocoon of her arms, that for the first time in conscious memory made him feel whole.

Eventually she broke off for air, turning her head so she was breathing gently in his ear. He could feel her rib cage moving up and down in time to her breath, when she whispered into his ear.

"You could take me right now, Eddie, and I wouldn't do a thing to try and stop you."

Somehow he managed to bring himself to his senses. "I don't think even the French are quite ready for that," he said with a smile, gently kissing her lips before sitting up.

"Think of something, Eddie."

"Think of what?"

"A time, a place." She leant forward towards him again, her voice so low he could barely hear her. "I mean what I say."

"My God," was all he managed to whisper in reply.

"Do you not want that?"

"Of course I want that, Amanda! It's what I want more than anything in the world right now. It's just, well, you've blown my mind. I can't think straight, that's all." He grinned. "I'll be okay in a minute, I promise you I will."

She continued in her intense, low tone. "Make it happen, Eddie. I'm going to leave it up to you. Just do it. Think of a way, a time, a place. I'll follow you."

"I'd better take you back to the ridge before people start to miss you."

"Yes, you'd better." He noticed a calculating edge to her voice, born of a new singleness of purpose, which both awed and frightened him. She stood up to readjust her clothing and he noticed the damp patch spreading from the crotch of her cut off jeans, matching the erection he was doing his utmost to hide. "But make it soon," she continued, her voice now urgent. "I can't wait much longer."

13

It was the third rehearsal and still everything was an unconvincing shambles. Even Peter, who could see the whole scene so vividly in his imagination, was having trouble picturing the team of club waiters as Dutch soldiers. In their black trousers, white shirts, name badges and bow ties they sensed trouble, and it was clear from their body language they couldn't wait to return to the safety of the restaurant.

Once again Peter took them through the script, which now seemed to him as creaky as the acting was wooden. Peter had sought out Brecht for inspiration, but the result looked like alienating everybody including the cleaning staff, huddled around a makeshift hut waiting for the Indonesian freedom fighters, in the shape of the bar staff, to valiantly take on the superior armed colonials and save the day.

It would have been a tricky enough feat to pull off with skilled actors; with this reluctant crew he'd shanghaied from their duties it was proving to be downright impossible. Increasingly, Peter was pinning his hopes on the dance troupe he'd hired downtown to pad the story out with some traditional singing and dancing. The way things were going, he might have to scrap the drama altogether and serve up the predictable routine any tourist could see for a couple of hundred rupiah in a Bali resort. Beer and circuses, he thought bitterly, as the limitations of his talent and the material he had to work with resonated back to him with their clunky rhetoric. Why not just give them what they want, watch their bored faces and polite handclaps from the wings, let off a few fireworks and get on with the serious eating and drinking?

On came the Dutch, who proceeded to rough up the villagers with the butts of their pretend rifles in accordance with the script. The villagers, lacking the urgency of any real threat, failed to respond, leaving the soldiers little option but to stand around grinning, looking as if they were waiting to catch a bus. From his vantage point at the back of the auditorium Peter sighed in despair. He sat back onto the table he'd been leaning against, as he did so inadvertently sliding off the large circular cage used on Sunday evenings to dispense bingo balls. The cage hit the ground with a monumental crash, whereupon its hatch flew open to eject brightly coloured balls across the highly polished wood laminate floor. The noise immediately silenced the dispirited proceedings at the other end of the hall, and Peter was confronted by titters and smiles from his entire cast. Here at last, he could feel them think, some entertainment worthy of the name.

The sniggers were quickly replaced by looks of concern as balls rolled under stacks of chairs and into corners. One thing you didn't mess with, they all knew, was the Americans' bingo. The prospect of ball number 47 catching the eye of some 280 pound Ohio production engineer's wife from a dusty corner when it had eluded her card the entire evening was too awful to contemplate. As this realisation sunk in, aloof Dutch soldiers metamorphosed back into waiters jumping in to avert potential catastrophe.

The cage had to be emptied and every ball laid out in order and accounted for before it could be refilled. Leaping on any excuse to be liberated from the yoke of Brechtian political consciousness, all hands turned to the task. Maybe they should just play hunt the bingo ball. Number 33 proved to be a problem, and 26 took a further fifteen minutes to track down, but eventually the full set was laid out in front of them for Peter to replace in the cage before fifteen witnesses.

"Okay, let's call it a day for now, you can return to your duties," he called out in Bahasa to the relief of his cast. "Next rehearsal is Tuesday afternoon, same time, don't be late." Sullen eyes evaded his as men and women returned to their stations, each no doubt wondering whether their presence would be missed if they failed to show up.

Left alone in the auditorium, which was really a large rectangular room with a stage set up at one end, Peter pulled himself up a chair and reflected upon his position. What was he hoping to achieve anyway? The image of the white man beating the native into submission before plundering his resources was as strong as it was timeless, and Peter was beginning to doubt the wisdom of ramming such a spectacle down the throats of their employers, who remained for the most part under the illusion they were bestowing the benefits of progress, wealth and civilization upon the community in which they found themselves.

In Peter's eyes, no one had let themselves down more than the Indonesians themselves. It wasn't the Americans' fault, they were just doing what anyone would do in their position; you could hardly accuse them of exploiting naïve natives. For every oil dollar Constar pumped out of the ground, using their people, their money, their technology, their equipment and their expertise, the Indonesian government took eighty five cents. On the face of it, it seemed perfectly reasonable, a fifteen per cent clip for making everything possible. The problem, as Peter was at pains to point out to anyone who would listen, was what happened to that eighty five per cent? Was it used to fund health programmes, to extend literacy, to improve the basic welfare of the people under whose land and in whose seas the oil lay? Only a fool would believe such nonsense. Most of it was siphoned off by Suharto and his cronies in Jakarta to fund their jet-set lifestyles and maintain the infrastructure of a military dictatorship, using the army they'd bought off to keep their boots firmly placed against the throat of anyone who might presume to want to elevate themselves from the miserable subsistence that constituted most of his fellow countrymen's day to day reality.

Now they were at it again, extending their reach into East Timor, using sheer numbers and western weaponry to crush any resistance. Peter couldn't imagine what there could possibly be in the tiny former Portuguese colony worth all the trouble the army were going to, beyond the paranoia rampant amongst the senior generals surrounding the President about any neighbouring territory being used as a base from which displaced communists could undermine their junta. A few reports of the so called annexation had leaked out and made their way on to the Australian radio bulletins Peter listened to most evenings. Here in Indonesia the press had for the most part ignored what was going on, occasionally glossing over the violent invasion with words like "integration" and references to "our Indonesian brethren".

From these fragments and his own knowledge of how these things worked, Peter understood the situation to have been bloody. He wanted to ask Francesca about it, but in the five visits he had so far paid to Hamid and Suki's quarters it was only on the most recent two she had even deigned to speak to him. Still, progress was progress, and however slow it might be, at least he was moving in the right direction, which was more than could be said for his little drama. The time, though, had come for some more decisive act on his behalf if he wasn't to make himself a laughing stock. Perhaps suggesting a gentle walk on her afternoon off, something innocent enough not to frighten her but sufficiently bold to at least declare his interest, a bridgehead from which he could launch his campaign proper. He found it ironic to be thinking in military metaphors, when armed forces had caused such heartache to both of them, and he reminded himself once again of the need to proceed gently. She'd not told anyone so far as he knew, not Suki nor Hamid nor Benny, anything of what she had seen or had happened to her, but everything about her manner suggested it was bad. He wondered how it would leave her. There was a quality to her presence that hinted at the potential to transcend the circumstances of her enslavement, which drew Peter towards her and compelled him patiently to stay the course when progress looked so unpromising. Because if Francesca could do it, perhaps there was hope they could all do it, and if that was the case then everything he held dear was not necessarily the idealistic fantasy scorned with such contempt by the likes of dear Uncle Benny Surikano.

Peter was in luck, for Hamid was taking a rare nap with Suki, and Francesca was sweeping the carport when he turned up the following afternoon to pay court. She sensed his aura almost before she glanced up to catch sight of his nervous presence, and smiled. It really was too absurd, this wealthy young Indonesian, related by marriage to the powerful Benny Surikano, nervous in her company. Did he not realise who she was? Had no one told him she was a nothing person, a unit of labour to be used at the convenience of the people who really mattered, those with lives and feelings and hopes, whose dreams were deemed worthy of being heard and answered by whatever chaotic force arranged such matters? So convinced was she of her fundamental worthlessness and the unlikelihood of the situation, she hadn't taken seriously the teasing and suggestive remarks from Hamid and Suki that followed each visit. Both had come out in favour of the match, for entirely selfish reasons, but so far Francesca had refused to accept their speculation as anything more than idle banter to pass the time and amuse themselves at her expense. Yet here he was again, standing at the carport entrance, shuffling in that nervous way of his. She stopped sweeping, leant the broom against the wall, and crossed over to greet him.

"Have you come to see Hamid? I'm afraid he's resting."

"No, I have come to see you."

"Me?"

"Yes, you. Is that so very strange?"

"It's just I don't normally have visitors. I don't really know anyone here, apart from Suki and Hamid."

"Then it is time you did."

"Would you like to sit down?" She gestured towards the wicker chairs. "I can make you some tea if you would like."

"That would be very nice." He smiled at her and sat down in one of the chairs. "But will you join me?"

"I am meant to be working."

"You are working. You're entertaining me."

"I'm not one of Suki's girls, if that is what you mean," she snapped at him sharply.

"Of course not, I'm terribly sorry, I didn't mean that at all." She could sense he was sincere, that he had tied himself in knots out of nerves.

"All I want is for you to sit down and share a pot of tea with me," he continued apologetically.

"In that case, maybe I can spare ten minutes before I have to return to work."

Softly, so as not to wake Suki or Hamid, she opened the door to the amahs' quarters and tiptoed across to the stove. She slid the still warm kettle back onto the heat and reached up for the two best cups on the little shelf alongside the tinned milk and bag of sugar. She hadn't even asked him how he liked to take it. And did she dare sneak into Mrs Cole's pantry and help herself to a couple of biscuits from the tin? She knew servants had been summarily dismissed for similar offences, sent packing with a single grip bag to face an uncertain future downtown. She was confident Amanda wouldn't say anything if she saw, and when she last went through the house twenty minutes earlier to stack some laundry she'd ironed, Mrs Cole was passed out on her bed, gently snoring. Never had there been a better opportunity to escape detection. What clinched it, though, in her mind, was the chance to act out a decision she herself had taken. Just this tiny sliver of autonomy represented in two stale digestive biscuits gave her back a glimpse of her old self, a delicious taste of a free world in which she made choices to suit herself. Yes, Peter should have his biscuits, and she would watch him politely eat them, reading his mind as he, too, wondered why westerners held such affection for the strangest of delicacies. Who knew, perhaps he actually liked them too?

The kettle boiled, and she let the tea brew while she stepped outside again. He was sitting at the chair where she had left him. What struck her most was his vulnerability and sense of unease. He looked up expectantly when he heard her softly glide towards him.

"I have decided one thing," she said. "I wish it that we speak to each other in English. That is okay with you?"

"That is fine with me," he replied, his voice edged with pleasure and surprise.

"Good. Would you like with your tea milk and sugar?"

"Milk and sugar would be perfect."

"And perhaps a biscuit?"

"A biscuit would be great too."

"Very good. Wait here. I fetch."

She prepared the tray with finesse, elegantly bearing it out to set down on the small table between the two chairs. Peter rose as she did so, in itself another novelty. No one stood up for servants, it was part of their invisible nature. Try as she might, she was unable to suppress the thrill that charged through her body when she took the seat he so graciously pulled back for her.

"Would you like me to pour?" she asked.

"Thank you."

She lifted the pot, poured the tea first into his cup and then into her own, before gesturing to the sugar bowl and small milk jug, also on temporary loan from Mrs Cole's kitchen.

"Please, have yourself to some milk and sugar." She was aware of the mechanical lilt to her voice, as if she were practising imperative verbs back in the English classes that were proving so useful in ways she had never been able to imagine. But although her Bahasa had improved immensely these past few weeks, to a point where she could almost pass herself off as a native, it was important for her to meet this man on linguistically neutral ground. She wasn't prepared to be courted by any man using the oppressor's tongue. "Hamid tells me you work in the school."

"That is right. I teach Indonesian to the American children. Unfortunately, most of them do not think it is a language worth the effort to learn."

"There is no school today?"

"School is finished for the day." He took a sip from his tea, broke a section off a crumbling biscuit and popped it into his mouth which was studded, she noticed, like his uncle's with two gold fillings around the molars.

"I liked my school," she said simply. "I thought maybe one day I should like to be a teacher." She shrugged her shoulders and smiled. "Now I am this."

"You can still train to be a teacher if that is what you wish to do."

"It is not so simple."

"I understand."

"I do not think you do."

"My father was killed by this regime. They said he was a communist."

"I am not a communist."

"I know that."

"My family were not communists either."

"I am sure they weren't."

She heard a stirring from the servants' quarters, followed by the familiar sound of Hamid clearing his throat. Immediately she stood up, whisking away the plate of biscuits as she did.

"I must go," she said, flustered. "I am sorry. It was kind of you to call. Thank you, goodbye."

He stood up, pushing his chair back so he could turn to face her. "Do you have a day off?"

"Sunday afternoons I am sometimes free."

"That is excellent. Would you like to take a walk with me?"

"Afternoon is very hot here."

"It is cooler a little later. Say four o'clock?"

"This Sunday?"

"If you are free, this Sunday would be very good."

"I am free this Sunday."

"I will come at four." He smiled again, then offered her his hand, which she shook gently. "Thank you for the tea."

"I am sorry you could not stay to enjoy it more."

"I enjoyed it just fine." He slunk backwards away from the carport, almost tripping over a cat dozing in the sunshine, until he gave a half-wave and was gone.

She stood frozen on the spot for a moment, then remembered the plate of biscuits. Quickly she grabbed the creamer from the table, shot into the kitchen and tossed the biscuits into the bin, taking care to cover them with some carrot peelings. She poured the remainder of the milk down the sink, washed up the jug and replaced it in the cupboard where it belonged. Feeling the relief pass over her, she returned outside and cleared up the rest of the tea tray, carefully washing and drying each piece of crockery. She stacked Suki's cups and saucers to one side, then secreted them in the folds of her sarong for the short trip across the carport. It would be good to replace them before either Hamid or Suki rose from their siesta, if only to avoid the inevitable teasing. As if it wasn't bad enough complicating her life by accepting Peter's advances, she had no desire to spend the next four days as fodder for their amusement.

What was she thinking? Hamid had told her who Peter was, and those gold fillings in his teeth revealed more about his position in Indonesian society than any words could. He didn't strike her as a playboy, but if his intentions were sincere that was almost more dangerous than if he'd been some bored scion of the military machine looking for someone to fool around with. So far she had survived by freezing her feelings, continuing to move forward automatically without regard for her emotions, which she held so firmly in check they might as well not have existed. Now the frozen lump was being exposed to the harsh sun, and as her position on the ridge, albeit a lowly one, settled down, she could feel the edges of her heart begin to melt. Her mind screamed at her to resist it, to slam the lid back on the ice chest she had willed herself to become, but resistance in the face of an overwhelming force was, as she knew only too well, utterly futile. It would have its way in the end. That was the inevitability of her life, the only experience she knew.

14

When they were at home together, the Surikanos were in the habit of taking dinner on their large balcony overlooking the clubhouse, surrounded by paraffin lamps and mosquito coils, from where they could look down on the floodlit swimming pool and flickering lights illuminating the coconut-thatched terrace bar. Their view, extending as it did to the harbour below and beyond, was one of the more desirable on the ridge, far superior to anything enjoyed by the Indonesian elite, and on a par with the senior western managers. It was only natural that Benny, amongst whose responsibilities included allocating accommodation, should have bagged it for himself when the work permit of the previous occupant had been mysteriously revoked at short notice. No one who knew Benny would have expected anything less.

Benny knew that it rankled amongst some, especially the wives of the more junior expats, stuck in poky apartments or the smaller houses on the far end of the ridge until promotion graced itself upon their husbands' shoulders, that a greasy-palmed Indo and his family should occupy such a prestigious residence, and he relished their rancour every bit as much as he savoured Harry Bird or one of his acolytes meekly approaching him with some ghastly problem only he could solve. The more unsavoury the fix, the more squalid the details, the more unedifying the light in which it displayed the supplicant, the more Benny liked it. Each time it happened only served to strengthen the leverage he held over these nincompoops who affected to despise him for the colour of his skin.

These thoughts returned to Benny as he watched his son across the table. His wife had retired, as she tended to do, to the bedroom where she could watch the latest episode of *Magnum PI* on their video cassette recorder, ostensibly pre-screening it for suitability before Benny could allow it to be released at the club, as she did with every tape in the weekly consignment from Houston. Benny waited for the amah to clear their plates away and bring out a bottle of brandy and two balloon glasses before he broached the delicate subject that hung between them like the stenched corpse of a kampong dog.

Eventually he broke the silence. "Son, I know what you're up to."

"What are you talking about?"

"That English girl, Dennis Cole's daughter."

"I don't know what you mean."

Benny could tell from his son's blushes his instincts had not been awry. "Come on Rollo, you can't bullshit me, I've seen the way you eye her up at the club."

"I've hardly spoken a word to her."

"You don't have to." Benny brushed a hand against his son's forearm, trying to ignore the hurt he felt when Rollo flinched. "Sometimes, often in fact, what we don't say reveals far more about our intentions than what we do. I learnt that lesson the hard way at the poker tables."

"I haven't done anything wrong, Dad."

"I know that. So why don't you tell me what's going on?"

"Nothing's going on," Rollo protested.

"Son, how many more times do I have to tell you, I'm on your side. You are the most precious gift I have, you are the future of this family. I was blessed with just one child, and my blessing was it was you. You mean everything to me. All this shit," here Benny gesticulated behind him to the living room through the glass sliding doors with its opulent fabrics and ornate Chinese carvings, "all this shit can come and go, but you, yes, you are all I really have."

"So why are you giving me such a hard time?"

"I'm not. I'm your father. I have an interest in your happiness. I want what's best for you. And I know that girl is nothing but trouble."

"She's only a kid, Dad."

"Precisely. And she's stupid with it. Which is what makes her so dangerous. Let me tell you something about women. The times they hurt men the most is when they're not even thinking of them."

"You don't think she thinks of me?"

"I doubt she notices you exist."

"Because I'm Indonesian?"

"Because she's an ignorant, ill-educated white bitch just like her mother."

"Aren't you being just as prejudiced as you accuse her of being?"

"No, Rollo, I'm simply pointing out some facts. I'm not saying an Indonesian can't find happiness with a white woman. But I am saying it can't happen in a place like this."

"But this is our country," protested Rollo. "These people are only here because we say they can be."

"Son, it's not that simple." Benny raised his brandy glass, sniffed the rich alcohol and took a sip. He flipped open his pack of Dunhill, extracted a cigarette and slid the packet across the table to Rollo. "We need the Americans every bit as much as they need us. Unless, that is, we want those fucking PKI bastards moving in and taking over. And if that happened, we really could kiss goodbye to all this."

"Well, I've done my bit in the battle against communism."

"I know you have, and no one's asking you to go back."

"Dad, some really bad shit went down when we were over there."

"I'm sure it did." Benny lit his cigarette, inhaled deeply and then let the smoke seep slowly out of his nostrils. "Never mind how it looks in the movies, these things are never pretty."

"No, Dad, I mean really bad."

"Son, you don't have to explain. I was in the army too, you know."

"But it was different then. You were fighting a guerrilla army, men who were trying to kill you. We were killing civilians, old men, women, children, whoever got in our way."

Benny held up his hand to silence his son. "Rollo, it's only the passage of time that sanitises war, that makes it look like a neat struggle of good against evil, strong against weak. If you think it was a clean fight against Sukarno's boys, think again. A lot of innocent people got caught in the crossfire of that, too. Not to mention some not so innocent ones. It happens, that's what war is like."

"I keep having nightmares, where I'm back there again. I was just so unprepared for the sheer brutality of it."

"I know, son. You can't explain it to someone who's never been in that situation. But I know what you're talking about."

"Then other times, especially since I came back and slipped into life here, it's almost as if that stuff never happened. When I'm lying by the pool with a drink at my side, it's like I imagined the whole thing. It doesn't seem real any more."

"It's best to keep it that way, believe me. There's a whole world out there, Rollo. You've got to put that stuff behind you and set your sights beyond this ridge. You did what your country asked of you, no one can ever accuse you of using your contacts to shirk your duty. Now it's time to start living and enjoy the fruits of your success."

"Success?"

"You're alive, aren't you? All in one piece? No one shot your balls off!" Benny let out a laugh at his son's discomfort. "I'd call that success. Ask any decorated veteran being pushed about in a wheelchair and he'll tell you it's all that matters."

"But when I try to enjoy myself you tell me to keep my eyes off the white girls."

"Only because I know it will bring you nothing but trouble," replied Benny. "Besides, if that's what you really fancy, save it for when you go to America."

"When's that going to be?" asked Rollo slightly nervously.

"I don't know, I'm still working on it. They're trying to fob us off with some correspondence course crap run out of East Texas University, wherever the hell that is, but I told them it's Harvard Business School or nothing."

"You'll get the company to pay for me to go to Harvard?"

"Sure."

"But that'll cost thousands of dollars."

"What's your problem, think you're not worth it? That it's too good for an Indonesian?"

"No... but..." Rollo stammered.

"It's chickenfeed." Benny waved his brandy glass in a manner to suggest he blew such sums daily. "The geophysicists can burn that much and more on one bad hunch. Besides, they owe us. They wouldn't be able to do half the things they do if it weren't for me. No, an MBA from Harvard is what you need to set yourself up in tomorrow's Indonesia. With that and my connections no one will be able to stop you. And so long as you keep an eye on your studies, you can chase all the Yankee skirt you like."

Rollo smiled.

"Just so long as you come back home when it's time and marry a nice well brought-up Indonesian girl. Preferably one whose father's a general."

"This is my home, Dad," replied Rollo in such a manner Benny wasn't sure whether he was being sentimental for a lost childhood or plying him with platitudes he thought his father, now the gatekeeper to the American dream, wanted to hear.

15

Although he'd lived less than a hundred miles south of the equator for close on a year, Eddie had never quite adjusted to the way the sun popped up and down at six o'clock either side of the day, month in month out. The sunrises and sunsets were more spectacular than anything he'd known back home in the flat Midwest, but he was still learning to grab them as a transitory visual feast rather than the backdrop to a long lazy evening. So whilst it was pitch-dark when he emerged from his portakabin to kick start his motorbike, the airport perimeter lights twinkling in the distance, he knew he would arrive at his destination just the other side of town in bright daylight. In the meantime, he would relish the quickly grabbed cup of coffee fresh on his taste buds, the sea air in his nostrils, the prospect of a blissful day ahead on his mind. Riding out along the Kendalakkan bypass, kicking the bike into fourth, he felt glad to be alive. It was the same feeling he'd experienced after returning in one piece from a successful mission, a freedom he feared he might never know again.

If he worried about anything, it was the weight of the burden he was placing upon her immature shoulders, but try as he might, he found it impossible to play cool and casual with her. He was in too deep, and they both knew it. Instinctively, they had resorted to animal cunning to foil any arbiters of moral decency who might try to come between them. Eddie no longer cared what any of them thought, his heart was pure and he would take whatever steps were necessary to preserve what he had found. Most observers, he thought with a wry smile, would assume it was he, the jaded flyboy, who was the strong one playing with her fragile emotions, whereas the opposite was the case. If their passion blew up in their faces, he knew it would be Amanda, the unwitting innocent, who would walk away unscathed, while he could look forward to a lonely and bitter middle age sharing a barstool with the likes of Shaky Mick.

A carton of Camel smoothed his path through the ridge gatehouse, promising to seal the lips of the night shift at least. Now his enthusiastic champions, they cheerily gave him the thumbs up while he accelerated towards the commissary.

He'd been fully prepared for her to stand him up, not through lack of desire on her part but from having her plans foiled by others. But when he turned the corner to bring the commissary into view there she was, leaning against a lamp post, her canvas bag slung over her shoulder. She looked up when she heard the bike, and he was rewarded with an intimate wave and the sight of a face lit up by love. Her hair was pulled back from her face with a tortoiseshell clip, and she was dressed in a pair of tight white jeans that flared from the knees down, and a thin pink cotton T-shirt. On her feet she had a pair of pale khaki Keds.

He drew up beside her and let the engine idle while he flipped down the kickstand with the heel of his shoe. Stepping off the bike, he stood straight in front of her and savoured her pure beauty for a few precious seconds before she flung herself around him. They kissed, and he tasted the toothpaste fresh on her lips. His nostrils sucked in the delicious scent of her hair and perfume, while his hands took possession of her body, pressing her chest into his so he could feel the contours of the thin bra underneath.

"Hi there!" he grinned when they finally broke off. "Ready to fly?"

"Oh, yes!"

He returned to the bike and flipped down the passenger toggles. "Let's get out of here before anyone sees us."

She climbed on the pillion and wrapped her arms around his waist. With her face nuzzled into his, they could hear each other talk as they nosed their way out.

"No problem skipping out, then?"

"None."

"Good." He braked as they approached the gatehouse, waving once again as they signalled him through, before accelerating away from the compound. Downtown, which they hit a few minutes later, was coming to life with the early birds already picking over the market stalls for the freshest fish and best vegetables. They made an unfamiliar sight, and their progress was marked by catcalls and cheers. With her warm body pressed against his, he felt the luckiest man alive. When they stopped at the town's sole set of traffic lights, several bikes drew up alongside them, each driven by young dudes who stared enraptured at Amanda, then burnt them off with a whine of two-stroke and a cloud of dust when the light turned green. With nothing to prove, Eddie kept their progress smooth and gentle, laughing at his good fortune.

When they arrived at the airport, he showed her to one of the armchairs in the veranda bar and fetched her a coffee while he collected his paperwork from the crew room. A number of pilots were up and about, swilling cups of coffee and chatting amongst themselves. She could tell they were trying not to stare at her, as their expressions questioned what she was doing here, and she realised they probably assumed she had spent the night in Eddie's portakabin. With as much poise as she could muster, she studiously ignored them, sipped her coffee, and looked out at the apron, where the first helicopter was turning over its engine. Nearby a couple of larger machines were being refuelled, seasoning the salty air with an intoxicating whiff of kerosene.

When Eddie returned, he had changed into a formal pair of shorts and a uniformed shirt, along with white socks pulled up to his knees and a pair of rubber soled black shoes. The effect was to make him look both intimidating and faintly ridiculous. She stood up as he approached but kept a respectful, formal distance from his side, the uniform at once repelling intimacy.

He smiled. "You ready?"

"Where are we going?"

"Come with me."

She followed him out onto the apron, where his helicopter sat at the far end. By now the sun was well into its morning arc, and she could feel the asphalt stick against her shoes. Meanwhile, the first helicopter had reached full throttle. The engine noise made any conversation impossible, but when they were halfway across the pilot tweaked the pitch and the machine lifted off, briefly hovered some fifteen feet above their heads, then dropped its nose and headed off towards the jungle.

"Mail run," said Eddie as the Gazelle disappeared into the distance.

"Where to?"

"There are a whole series of wells they're drilling out in the jungle about fifty miles to the north."

"Is that what we're doing?"

"Not quite. We're nipping up to Gunpura to drop off some replacement parts for one of the generators and pick up a few drilling reports. Hopefully there won't be anyone wanting a ride back."

They reached Eddie's ship just as the tender finished fuelling her up. Eddie exchanged a couple of words with the driver, then nodded a brusque greeting to the porters, who took his arrival as a cue to break off for a cigarette behind one of the hangers. Once they had dispersed Eddie began his walk round, checking locks and caps were tight, fingering the rear blade, checking lubrication points and tugging against the communications antennae protruding from the metal skin, satisfying himself there was nothing loose that could drop off mid-flight. It was superficial, as much superstition as anything else, for like all helicopter pilots he knew that any mechanical failure destined to kill him was likely to originate from deep within the engine or gearbox, hidden from the perfunctory once-over of a visual inspection. He opened the cockpit door and peered inside, noting the yellow sticker on the landing lights switch, still awaiting the spare bulb from the States. Whilst the mechanics weren't bad, considerably more competent and resourceful than he'd feared when he'd joined Constar, there was no way their workmanship was up to US Army standards. From time to time this worried Eddie, until he remembered it had to be set against the distinct advantage that in this role people weren't taking pot shots at him with rockets and machine guns.

Amanda noticed his attention completely switch away from her while he performed his checks, returning only when he opened the passenger door and helped her up into her seat. He showed her how the seatbelt worked, then handed her a headset.

"'Fraid they're a bit sweaty. If you press the button here you can talk to me. You'll never hear me otherwise over the engine noise."

She adjusted herself in her seat, headset over her ears, while he slammed her door shut and joined her from round the other side. Once comfortably seated himself, he switched on the ignition, and she felt the headset come to life along with the cockpit dials.

"Everything alright?"

She nodded. Having his voice so close to her ears was reassuring, and she realised she was excited to place her body so completely in his hands. She watched him flick on switch after switch, each movement stirring yet another function to life, culminating in the gradual whoop-whoop of the rotor blade above her head.

Once the engine was running, the helicopter took on a life of its own, the blade evaporating into a shadow of buffeted air while the vibration and noise sealed a mechanical wall against any sounds from outside. They sat on the apron for what seemed an age, the engine screaming at full revs, while Eddie scanned the dials, making the odd adjustment, then repeating the process. Finally, he looked across at her with a smile.

"Ready to go?" his voice came over the headset.

She nodded, and he pulled up the stick by his thigh. All of a sudden, she felt like a puppet whose strings had suddenly been jerked from above. The blades bit into the air, snatching the helicopter's weight from the skids to lift them off the tarmac. They may have only been a few feet off the ground, but they were flying, they were out there on their own, they were free.

She felt her stomach flip over as they quickly shot up seventy feet, until she had a view of the entire apron and the Base Camp roof. Eddie turned the helicopter round on its axis, dropped the nose and suddenly they were shooting forward, out towards the sea, bent down but rising with every second. They whizzed over the beach by the French club, out above the gentle waves breaking on the shore, rising all the while until Eddie turned them in a gentle arc and they headed back inland to take a northerly bearing.

"You okay?" Again, his reassuring voice through the headset.

Again she nodded.

"You like it?"

She pressed the button dangling down by her shoulder. "I love it, Eddie. It's amazing. I want to fly with you every day."

He seemed pleased, and his face set in a contented smile as their eyes met. Below she could see the wake from a small fishing boat making its way out to sea, while to her left the last kampongs surrounding Bandakan were giving way to jungle unscarred by human progress bar a single narrow road snaking its way north in the direction they were heading. Behind her seat, the passenger bay had been cleared out to make room for half a dozen boxes, which were strapped to the floor with webbing belts.

They levelled off at three and a half thousand feet. Eddie did have a map on his lap with some crosses marked at different points, but he wasn't really looking at it, and to Amanda it seemed as if they were simply following the coastline. Staring at the jungle beneath her feet, she was struck by the enormity of it when set against the tiny ribbon at the edge colonised by the forces of civilization, the minute fraction of this huge island she thought of as home. Of course, she had flown across the Borneo interior many times, but she had always been up high, thirty thousand feet or more, in a pressurised cabin that turned the jungle beneath into a monotonous green carpet broken up only by the occasional river snaking through it. This was different, she could feel the jungle breathe with the swaying of the trees, she could sense the life contained within. Like most of the westerners up on the ridge, she was frightened of the jungle, and her occasional forays into it had been both hesitant and brief, surrounded by the protective shell of a Land Rover or the hull of a river boat equipped with a refrigerator and a VHF radio. The jungle was not a place you chose to loiter in, you went there because you had to, because that was where the money was to be made, and you headed out the moment your work was done.

She knew whole communities sustained themselves from the jungle, but she had no real urge to understand how they accomplished this astonishing feat. There was nothing unusual about her lack of curiosity, and whilst she may have rebelled against the constricting fence delineating her cosseted life, when presented with the reality outside, she knew she would take the little piece of America carved out of the scrub by the Constar engineers any day.

Was she really no different from her contemporaries whose complacency she so despised? Suddenly she doubted herself, wondering what a man as complex and experienced as Eddie could see in her. What could she offer him in a relationship that he wouldn't find utterly trite? She could hardly talk to him about the intrigues amongst her school friends, it would bore him to death. Her opinions were so unformed, despite her valiant efforts with Time Magazine, her world so narrow.

She felt a sudden anger at the way she had allowed everyone around her, her mother, her friends, her teachers even, to dumb her down with their assumptions of who she was and how she should think. She realised it was not the physical manifestation of Constar's colonization she hated, but the accompanying mental laziness. Her world was founded on a set of assumptions: that western goods were superior to anything obtainable locally, that a six-month-old frozen TV dinner was preferable to a piece of fish hauled out of the sea that morning, that Indonesians were by nature slothful and incompetent, that a white life was intrinsically worth more than an Asian one. If you dared question any of these assumptions, you might as well step outside and make your own way in the jungle.

She heard the click in her headset and looked up to meet his eyes. "Welcome to the northern hemisphere."

"I beg your pardon?"

"We've just crossed the equator. Not that you can see anything, I just know where it is."

"So we're nearly there?"

"A few minutes away." As he spoke, his right hand tilted the joystick and they banked out to sea. At the same time he rolled off the power and they began to lose height. She could see Gunpura ahead, a cluster of tin roofs reflecting the harsh mid morning sun, surrounded by neat rows of large silver oil tanks. A couple of dirt tracks extended out from either side of this small community, which was delineated from the jungle by a short airstrip. Behind the buildings a long jetty ran out to sea, where a tanker lay at anchor. She kept quiet while Eddie flew the helicopter towards the pad, a miniscule figure H that reassuringly grew in line with their approach.

He placed the Huey neatly on the ground and closed down the engine, waiting for the blades to stop rotating before signalling to two porters who were waiting patiently in the shade of the airport shed to approach. The porters were accompanied by a large moustachioed Australian, who strolled up behind them, flicking a clipboard against his thigh.

"What news do you bring from sunny Bandakan?" he asked with mock bonhomie as Eddie flung open the door.

"Just a message from Ming that if you don't clear your tab by payday, he's going to bar you from the mess."

"Cheeky sod. Tell him I'll settle up when I'm down next week. Are those the parts we ordered for the air con unit?"

"It's all there, or at least that's what they told me," Eddie replied.

"Bloody well hope so, it's like a sauna in that map room. Excuse my French," he added, glancing at Amanda. "You fellers had some breakfast?"

Eddie and Amanda looked at each other, then shook their heads.

"Go help yourself to something in the mess hall. I'd get in quick though, the early shift will be taking their break in about ten minutes."

They thanked the Australian and made their way to a triple portakabin. From the outside it wouldn't have looked out of place on any construction site in the world, inside it had been decked out to resemble an American diner. An Abba tape was playing softly through a pair of large wooden speakers suspended from the ceiling and covered in a film of grease. The blinds were all drawn against the harsh sun, the whole place illuminated by fluorescent overhead strip lights. Closing the door quickly behind them to keep in the air conditioning, the sense of placelessness was complete. Along one end two Indonesian chefs tended to a buffet, which was lavish both in its choice and quantities on offer. Staring up and down the long, starched cloth covered trestle tables, it was impossible to tell whether it was breakfast, lunch or dinner. Eddie helped himself to a small sirloin steak and some fries, while Amanda satisfied herself with a bowl of Corn Flakes, a glass of orange juice and a bowl of ice cream.

"Guess what?" said Eddie once they had found a table. They sat opposite one another, divided by a selection of condiments ranging from mustard and ketchup to Tabasco and chilli pepper sauces.

"What?"

"Don't look round, but there are about ten guys sitting in here, and I swear there isn't a single one who has taken his eyes off you since we walked in."

Amanda blushed. "Don't be ridiculous!"

"It's true."

"This place is weird."

"Food's good, though. Hard to imagine we're surrounded by nothing but jungle for hundreds of miles."

They ate in silence, Eddie tucking in with gusto, Amanda picking at her cereal and trying not to make eye contact with any of the gazes coming at her from all sides.

"You know, Eddie," she said when he had finally cleared his plate, "everyone goes on about how we should respect native cultures and not destroy them with our progress, but if their lives are so wonderful, how come they all want jobs with the oil companies?"

"I sometimes think these people would be better off if none of us had ever set foot on these islands."

"Do you really believe that?"

"Not really," replied Eddie, pushing aside his plate and reaching for his cigarettes. "Westerners have been coming to these islands for hundreds of years. Some of the stuff we've brought has been good, some not. Take what's going on here, for instance. Are we bringing good to the Indonesian people, or are we just helping ourselves to their oil to fuel our comfortable lifestyles?"

"I don't know."

"Nor do I. The truth is, it could be either. We extract oil on their terms, and the government does very well out of it. Our hands are clean. Or are they? We all know what Suharto's like, and we also know the oil we pump out of the ground helps him buy the weaponry he needs to keep the people in their place. So do we say, no we're not going to drill for oil here, even though that's the business we're in, because we don't like the look of your government and we think you should be spending your oil reserves more responsibly? Sounds a bit like colonialism to me."

"So do we leave them alone?"

"For the French to move in?"

"At least we're clean. What they do is up to them."

"So turning a blind eye suddenly makes you into a saint?"

"You're not adding to the problem."

"Maybe you are, maybe you aren't. It's not always so easy to tell. And what they've had on their own hasn't always been so wonderful. Did we leave South Vietnam a better place for ten years of war? We helped some people, we hurt a whole load of others, but I sure feel bad about leaving the South Vietnamese to face the Viet Cong."

"Why?"

"We made a lot of promises to them, but when the crunch came, we turned our backs and walked away. And it's not as if we didn't know what they were in for. Let me give you an example." Eddie stubbed his cigarette butt into the ashtray and continued. "We got a call once from a company who'd gone through a village where they'd just flushed out some VC. They needed a medivac ship fast. I was the only pilot they could spare, so I hightailed it over and they loaded up this girl in the back, she can't have been much older than you. She was a teacher, and although she was bleeding heavily around the mouth you could see she was a pretty girl. The medics had jacked her up with morphine but still she was in a terrible state of shock. Why? The VC had cut out her tongue. Literally, they'd sliced it off with a knife just like this." He made a neat slashing gesture with his steak knife.

"Oh, my God," said Amanda softly.

"For what?" demanded Eddie, the anger in his body language now seeping through into his voice. "Indoctrinating the village children in false consciousness? Spreading capitalist ideology? I don't know and quite frankly, Amanda, I don't fucking care. Barbarism is barbarism, and I know we did our fair share of bad shit out there, but when I see pictures of some movie star cooing all over those evil fuckers I just want to show her that teacher."

"I don't think I can eat any more," said Amanda pushing aside her plate.

"But would any of it have happened if we hadn't interfered in the first place? Who knows?" continued Eddie without waiting for her reply. "Saigon still fell. Maybe the best thing, the course of action that will lead to the greatest good, or at least result in the minimum harm, is to be here, accept you're going to get your hands dirty from time to time, and try to act as a force for good through your own example."

"Is that why you're here?" asked Amanda.

"Good God, no!" Eddie laughed. "I'm here for the same reason as everyone else. I can't stand living in my own country right now, and I'm just trying to make a bit for myself."

"At least you're honest about it."

"In the end, it's the only thing that has any chance of saving you. I'm sorry, I'm ranting away now, I didn't bring you here for that."

"You can talk all you want."

"That's one of the things I love about you."

"What?"

"You actually listen."

Blushing, Amanda reached over to Eddie's cigarettes. "May I?"

"Of course, help yourself." He slid the pack towards her and their hands touched, her delicate ringless fingers caressing his palm as he turned his hand face open. She let it rest there, using her other hand to extract a cigarette, which he leant over and lit.

"You're right about those guys, Eddie," she said softly after they had sat quietly for several minutes drinking in each other's presence. "I'm tired of being stared at. Is there somewhere we can go?"

"Sure." He pushed back his chair. "Come on, let's get out of here."

She followed him outside, looking dead ahead to ignore the stares. He opened the door for her and she stepped outside, squinting in the face of the late morning sun.

"Here, have these." He handed her his sunglasses.

"Don't you need them to see where you're flying?"

"There's a spare pair on board."

The helipad was a short walk away, set off from the freshly bulldozed runway strip that could just accommodate a twin prop aircraft. A lone Skyvan was parked nearby; otherwise Gunpura airport was a study in idleness. Eddie fished out a couple of sweaty hundred rupiah notes from his pocket and handed them to the porter who'd volunteered to mind the Huey while they ate. He helped Amanda into her seat and slammed the door behind her.

"Be back in a minute," and he set off towards the airport shed in a gentle jog.

She could get used to this, she thought, trying to make some sense out of the array of dials, switches and levers in front of her. It was certainly a step up from being squired around the ridge on a bicycle by some horny teenager.

A few minutes later Eddie returned with a huge grin spread across his face. "I just spoke to the Control Room in Bandakan. They're not expecting us back until half one."

"How long does it take to fly back?"

"Oh, less than forty minutes."

She looked across at his watch. "That gives us three hours before anyone will miss us."

"Exactly." His eyes were ablaze.

"Where shall we go?"

"I've a place in mind." Just as the rotor began to turn for the second time that morning he leant over and kissed her briefly but fully on the mouth.

"Let's go for it, Amanda."

The island was too small to feature as more than a dot on the map spread across Eddie's knees, but he located it without any difficulty, flying over it once at two hundred feet before turning round for a return pass. It was less than half a mile long and just a few hundred yards wide, thickly covered in trees bar a narrow strip of sand rising to a hillock at one end and a flat rocky outcrop at the other.

"It's paradise," Amanda said into the headset as Eddie flared the ship down towards a firm plateau on the rock outcrop large enough to take them.

"The best thing about it is you can't navigate anything in. That ring of coral you see surrounding the island would take the bottom off anything bigger than a rowing boat. There's no natural harbour either, just coral giving way to sand."

He sat the helicopter down so gently she barely felt the skids touch the ground, then quickly shut off the engine.

"It always makes me feel a little nervous closing her down somewhere like this," he said once the engine whine had been replaced by the gentle sound of waves lapping onto sand.

"In case we can't start up again?"

"There's a battery in the nose but as you can see, there's no one round to plug in a generator and give you a kick start if it decides to pack up."

"We'd be stuck here?"

"I'm sure I could get the radio working, and there are always some flares in the back. But you have to admit, it would be pretty embarrassing!"

"I'll say." He returned her smile, and she reached over to kiss him firmly on the mouth. "Here, Eddie, now," she said when their lips finally broke off from each other."

"Are you sure?" His voice was soft, whispering into her ear.

"I've never been more sure about anything."

"Let's go for a little swim first."

They stripped down to their underwear and picked their way down to the shoreline, the dormant helicopter behind them their sole link to the century and the world they had left behind. The clear shallow water was so warm it lacked even that momentary chilly tingle, and they paddled in until it came up to their waists, Eddie keeping one eye open for sea urchins or stonefish. Amanda seemed to have no such reservations and dove straight in, swimming several strokes underwater, her hair trailing down her back. She popped up half a dozen paces from him, ran her fingers through her hair and laughed. He smiled sheepishly at her, taking in her mermaid-like beauty. As he stood there, she cupped some water in her hands and flung it at him. "Come and get me!"

She shrieked as he dove in and swam towards her, grabbing her by the waist and nuzzling his face into her buttocks. She gave in to him and he stood up beside her, turning her as he pulled her in towards him to kiss her long and deep on the lips.

"You can take me back in now," she whispered softly when they finally broke off.

They made love in the shadow cast by the Huey, an old tarpaulin hauled out from the back spread beneath them for a blanket. When it finally happened she let out a sharp cry, digging her nails deep into his back in an attempt to channel the pain out from her body back to its source. There was no escaping it, he was inside her now, deeper inside than she could have imagined it possible to be. For a while he remained still, and she looked up to see him examining her with a mixture of desire and concern.

"Are you okay?" he whispered.

She nodded, biting her lip, not trusting herself to talk.

"Did I hurt you?"

Again she nodded, feeling a single tear slip from the corner of her eye to roll down her cheek.

"Do you want me to stop? Say if it's too much."

She shook her head. "No, don't stop, Eddie," the words coming out between shallow laboured breaths. "Just go easy."

Using his elbows he raised himself above her so that he was able to make the slightest shifts within her. These movements, too small to rip her flesh, were discernible enough to dispel some of the pain and overlay what remained with the most intense buzzing pleasure she had ever known. At one point he tried to pull himself away from her but she wouldn't let him, pulling him back inside her in a thrust that was excruciating yet delicious in its agony. She felt his hot wet warmth as he came inside her, and she begged him to stay, to keep going until she too could join him in his bliss. It was so close she could feel its edges lapping up around her, but at the last moment when she was sure it would overwhelm her it eluded her grasp, and she realised with a twinge of sadness that the ultimate expression of her joy would have to wait for another time. Their movements had taken on a mechanical dimension, and he was beginning to hurt her. He must have sensed this, for he slowed down and gently pulled from her, flopping down beside her with his arm laid across her chest.

They lay side by side under the helicopter in a pool of shadow as the midday sun beat down on the rocks around them. Amanda closed her eyes and fell into a dreamy doze that was located in neither place nor time, but in which she felt cocooned and safe for the first time ever. When she opened her eyes, aroused by a parched throat, Eddie was beside her, leaning up on one elbow smoking a cigarette, his eyes fixed upon her.

She smiled up at him. "How long have I been asleep?"

"Half an hour or so."

"Have you been watching me the whole time?"

"More or less."

"Did I look happy?"

"You had a smile on your face."

"I am happy. Sore and thirsty, but happy. Do we have any water?"

In response he passed over a large plastic bottle from which he'd taken the top third. She leant up, taking care not to bump her head against the helicopter's underbelly, unscrewed the cap and drank. The water was lukewarm but she was so thirsty she didn't care. Meanwhile Eddie retrieved their clothes and dressed himself.

"Do we have to go back now?"

Eddie looked at his watch, which he was in the process of clipping onto his wrist. "We should probably be on our way soon. You can take a shower at Base Camp."

"I don't want to go back to that world."

"Me neither. But we can hardly stay here." He stood up and opened the passenger door for her. "Come on, we've got some flying to do."

16

Christmas had come and gone, its jarring Nordic traditions making it seem more irrelevant than ever, whilst the much anticipated New Year celebrations had been an anticlimactic squib. Eddie had been sent up country again for the week, leaving Amanda to while away the empty days until he returned on a pool lounger at the club. A drink and her cigarettes rested at her side next to a tatty paperback borrowed from the club library. Beside her Melanie sunned herself in a similar repose. Neither had spoken a word for the past half hour, and it hadn't been long after that Amanda abandoned her novel, a three generation family period saga. The euphoria of her day out with Eddie had now been replaced by a keen sense of irritation at anything and anyone around her that wasn't him. Nothing could please her. Her cigarettes felt stale and raw against her throat, she could taste the chlorine in the ice cubes, the characters in her novel had become tiresome bores. Meanwhile, a wall had gone up between her and Melanie, whose foundations had been cemented the evening she returned, flush faced, on the back of Eddie's motorbike to face a barrage of questions from her mother, followed by a more subtle and probing inquisition from her friend.

Handling Melanie's inquisitiveness had proved somewhat harder. The minute they retired to their room she demanded to know everything, believing a blow by blow account in which no detail was too intimate to be spared the light of her prurience was the least she was owed for covering for Amanda.

"So, did you?" The glee in Melanie's voice made Amanda want to slap her.

"Did I what?"

"Come on Mandy, don't play dumb."

"Don't ever call me that, my name is Amanda."

"Okay Amanda, did you screw him?"

Still high on the wave of Eddie's love, Amanda saw Melanie clearly for the first time, and decided the fortnight until she was due to fly back home couldn't come quickly enough. This insight, however, still left the original problem of how much to tell. Her heart wanted to keep it all to herself, not let one moment be sullied by the tacky slut with the title and the posh voice. But she also knew she had to tread carefully; she had encountered Melanie's jealous streak before and knew her capacity for spite that went alongside the wit which had attracted Amanda to her in the first place. What should she give her? Perhaps the best course was a general admission followed by a refusal to elaborate. If she held back on that, Melanie would simply badger her until it was forthcoming.

"We made love," she said softly.

"Way to go!" cried Melanie with a whoop.

"Shhh!"

"Well done, girl! I can't wait to hear all about it. Tell me, has he got a huge one? I bet it's a whopper, it always is with those tall slim guys."

"I don't want to talk about it."

"Don't be ridiculous," Melanie dismissed her. "I'm dying to hear all the gory details. Where did it happen?"

"On an island."

"Where?"

"I don't know exactly. Somewhere a few miles off the coast. It's deserted, we saw it from the air and landed at one end."

"You lost your virginity on your very own desert island! God, you lucky girl! I had to make do with the boys' locker room at St Edward's, surrounded by stale socks and smelly jockstraps."

"I'll never forget the smell of the sea air mixed in with the aviation fuel," mused Amanda.

"Never mind the aviation fuel, what was he like?"

"He's the most amazing man I've ever met. I plan to spend the rest of my life with him."

"Yes, but what did he do? Was he hard on you, did he hurt?"

"I just love him, that's all," replied Amanda dreamily, inadvertently stumbling upon a tactic favoured by politicians of responding to unwelcome enquiries by answering the question they would have liked their inquisitor to have asked rather than the one they actually did. It had the desired effect, and eventually Melanie gave up in frustration to flop down on her bed and flick through an old copy of *Vogue*.

Since then a coolness had descended upon their friendship, so that while they still went places together, they no longer shared what was on their minds. Conversation was stilted, and the time hung heavy upon them. In their awkwardness they had become, Amanda realised, the epitome of the bored expat dependents they affected so to despise. She looked at her now, eyes closed, skin glistening with coconut oil, dark hair fanning down from the headrest of her lounger. She had always considered Melanie the more beautiful of the two of them, and it didn't surprise her she had had so many boyfriends. Lately, however, it was Amanda the men sought out, leaving Melanie in the cold. It made Amanda fearful, for if Melanie turned against her, who knew what mischief she might wreak in her nascent relationship with Eddie?

As she tried to work away through the problem, she gradually became aware that she was being watched. Looking up she spotted Rollo Surikano, fresh from a game of tennis, sipping a drink on the balcony above the pool deck. She'd not seen him since he'd cut in on Eddie when they first met. They made eye contact, he smiled and raised his glass at her. She smiled back, thinking her polite little wave would be the end of it, but he stood up and began to walk towards her, clutching one of those effeminate Louis Vuitton men's handbags that had started to appear in the Singapore department stores. She was just wondering how she could fob him off when it occurred to her that here could be the solution she was seeking. Melanie was into notching up new experiences, and she certainly had a taste for the exotic. While the unwritten social codes of the ridge most definitely precluded any relationship between an Indonesian man and the daughter of a white manager, Melanie's temporary status could be said to exempt her from the sexual rules prevalent within their little community.

Amanda nudged her friend. "Hey, Mel."

"What?" grunted Melanie.

"Approaching us from the steps."

"Who is it?" Slowly Melanie opened her eyes and looked round. "It's that Indo who was hitting on you the other day."

"I know, Rollo. He's coming our way."

"So?"

"So, maybe there could be some interest."

"He's interested in you, Amanda, not me."

"He could be persuaded."

"I don't need your cast-offs, thank you very much."

"Shh, he'll hear us." Both girls shut their eyes as Rollo approached, his muscles and brow still glistening from the rigours of the tennis court.

"Good afternoon, ladies," he announced himself. "A perfect afternoon to take to the poolside."

So far as Amanda was concerned, it was no different to any other afternoon in Borneo this time of year, extremely hot with the humidity made bearable only by virtue of their elevated position which caught what little sea breeze there was. However she said nothing and simply smiled, content to let this pampered oaf do all the work.

Undeterred, Rollo continued. "Do you mind if I join you?"

Amanda was on the verge of telling him it was a free country, but since it was so clearly anything but, she contented herself with a tart "Feel free."

Rollo smiled and pulled up a metal chair. "Can I order you some drinks?"

Amanda looked down at the dregs of her glass, now a small pool of melted ice. "Another Seven Up would be fine."

"And you? I'm sorry, I didn't catch your name the other day when we met."

"Melanie."

"Melanie, can I order you something from the bar?"

"I'll have a Bacardi and Coke, thank you."

Rollo snapped his fingers at a barman, who just happened to be standing on the balcony looking out in their direction, before turning back to face the girls. "I'm Rollo, by the way," he said to Melanie, offering out his hand.

Still lying on her front, Melanie reached out to shake his hand, forcing Rollo to lean down from his seat.

"Have you been swimming?" he continued.

"A bit," replied Amanda sleepily.

"I love a cool dip, especially after some hard exercise."

Neither girl replied, and Rollo was only saved further embarrassment by the arrival of the barman. He barked out an order in Bahasa, then dismissed the barman with a contemptuous wave of his hand.

"Did you enjoy the party the other day?" he asked once the barman had gone.

"It was okay," replied Amanda, momentarily taking pity on him.

"I love parties. Do you like parties, Amanda?"

"Sometimes," she replied, her voice devoid of all enthusiasm. At this point Melanie closed her eyes and resumed concentrating on sunbathing, giving Rollo the excuse he needed to focus on Amanda.

"Parties are good. Sometimes it can get a little quiet up here, especially at night. Do you find that so?"

"It can be," conceded Amanda.

"We should go out sometime. There are some good places downtown I know."

"Like where?"

"There are some restaurants that serve excellent seafood, and there's always the nightclub at the Hotel Bandakan. They play some good disco."

"I've not been there."

"Would you like to?"

"Sure."

"How about next Thursday?"

Amanda shrugged her shoulders. "Why not?"

"Do you like Indonesian food?"

"Some."

"This place I know serves the best saté sticks you have ever tasted."

"What do you do, Rollo?" interjected Melanie, suddenly opening her eyes and leaning forward.

"Me? I am presently waiting to start my further studies."

"Oh yes?" Even Amanda winced at the supercilious tone in Melanie's voice. "What are you studying?"

"I am hoping to study for an MBA at Harvard Business School."

"As in Harvard, America?"

"Yes, Harvard, Massachussettes." Although his tongue struggled with the pronunciation of the state, his voice was full of pride.

"So what do you make of the Indonesian economy?" continued Melanie.

"It has its problems, to be sure." Rollo shrugged his shoulders. "But there are many natural resources, there is great wealth in the forests and in the oil fields, so I think we will be fine." He smiled, causing Amanda to note how he wasn't intimidated by the assumed superiority of the white memsahib.

The barman arrived with their drinks, whereupon Rollo produced a gold-nibbed pen from his handbag to sign the proffered chit with a flourish. They made a little more small talk for a few minutes, then Rollo downed his drink and announced he had to be going.

"Until next Thursday," he said, rising from his chair.

"See you then," replied Amanda breezily.

"Seven o'clock?"

"Sounds fine."

Melanie turned on Amanda the moment he was out of earshot. "Have you gone mad?"

"What are you talking about?"

"Going out with him! I thought you just told me you were madly in love with Eddie."

"I am."

"So why are you going out with that slimy creep?"

"I'm not."

"But you just agreed to go on a date with him next Thursday. I heard you."

"Oh, that," Amanda said airily, "I only said that so he'd leave us alone. I'll think of some excuse closer to the time."

"Is he really going to Harvard?"

"Apparently so. Dad was complaining about it the other day. The company's paying for the whole lot. He said it comes to more than thirty thousand dollars a year."

"But why?"

"It's just part of doing business here. They're calling it a scholarship to promote cultural awareness, but really it's no more than a huge bribe. His father's an influential man, he can make a lot of things happen round here. Or not. You saw how he got David Bird out of that trouble with customs."

"Is that the kind of guy you want to mess around?"

"Oh, Rollo's harmless enough, he'd never hurt anyone."

"Whatever you say, Amanda. You're the one who's going to have to deal with him. But if you ask me, he looks as if he's got a real mean streak to him."

17

On Sunday afternoon Peter presented himself in front of Suki's door at four o'clock on the dot, having parked his motorcycle in the bay across the road normally used by the administration workers in the neighbouring office block. He tapped on the wood, almost immediately he heard the distinctive shuffle of flip flops on the cement screed floor. The handle turned, and the door opened to reveal Francesca's shy face in the crack. She was dressed in a simple western skirt and blouse and her hair, instead of being pinned up in an efficient bun, now fell across her shoulders and down the upper half of her back. The effect was to make her appear simultaneously more beautiful and childlike, causing him momentarily to step back and question the wisdom of what he was opening up. Suddenly the bachelor within him was overwhelmed by a sense of her neediness, engulfed by the urge to run, to make his apologies, to admit he'd made a mistake. He forced himself to stand his ground, and smiled at her. She blushed, smiled back then lowered her eyes towards their feet, where his leather loafers and her rubber flip flops only served to emphasise the gulf between them.

"Are you ready?" he asked.

She nodded, then slipped through the doorway without a word, softly shutting the door behind her. She followed him out of the carport, where they had to pick their way past a large blue Datsun. He led her across the road, turning to face her when he reached his motorbike, an ancient 100cc Honda which had once been red, but whose petrol tank was now a sun bleached light pink.

"Are we still to speak in English?" he asked.

"Of course," she replied coyly.

"This is my motorbike here. Would you like to walk here for a bit or take the bike and walk somewhere else?"

"I think I would wish to take the motorbike."

"I would like that too. Where would you like to go?"

"You decide. Maybe somewhere near the water."

"Okay." He straddled the bike, put the key in the ignition and flipped up the kickstand. "Have you ever ridden on the back of one of these?"

She smiled. "Many times."

"So you know what to do." To his relief the engine caught on the second kick, and he held it idling in neutral while she climbed up on the pillion and placed her hands around his waist. He was glad she wasn't attempting the ridiculous and dangerous side saddle preferred by some of the more traditional women downtown, as he dropped the bike into gear and pulled away towards the gatehouse.

It felt good to be out of the white man's world, this fifty-first state of America, as the expats sometimes jokingly referred to their compound. Perhaps she sensed how he could hardly have taken her to the club, and you never knew who you would bump into walking the carefully fashioned cul-de-sacs. Besides, it was a pleasure to feel her warm body pressed against his back as the imperatives of gravity and balance forced them to adopt a premature intimacy.

He took her down the hill towards Pasar Saru, then headed right at Jalang Sudiman to take the coastal road all the way round the bay, past the Pertamina oil complex with its neat rows of huge tanks glistening in the late afternoon sun, towards the harbour, where he brought the bike to a halt.

"Is this alright for you?" he asked.

"This is fine." Expertly, she climbed off the bike, adjusted her skirt and ran her fingers through her hair while he found a streetpost around which he could chain the bike with the stainless steel cord he kept in the small compartment under the seat.

He offered her his arm, and to his pleasant surprise she took it, allowing him to lead her along the harbour promenade. It was a popular spot for courting couples, and they slipped in easily enough amongst the young men and women dressed in their Sunday best. Peter felt a rising sense of elation at the rewards of his decisiveness; here she was, on his arm, exactly as he had planned. Now all he had to do was think of something to say to her.

"What do you think of Bandakan?" he offered as an opening gambit.

Francesca shrugged her shoulders. "It is big, it is noisy, it is okay."

Conducting themselves in a second language lent a formality to their exchange that Peter, to his surprise, found rather comforting.

"Do you like it here?" he continued.

"I am alive here," she replied.

"I heard things were bad in Dili."

"They were bad."

"For you?"

"For everyone."

"Did you lose many people?"

She didn't reply, and when he looked down at her he saw a tear running down the side of her face. Her facial muscles were quivering, suggesting to him a supreme act of self-control.

"I'm sorry, Francesca, I didn't mean to pry into your business. But you are safe here."

"I am safe, yes." There was bitterness in her voice. "Others were not so lucky."

"I am sure that is true. It is a terrible thing that happened to your people."

"It was done by your people."

"I know, and I am very sorry for what happened. Truly sorry."

"You did not do it, why do you have to say sorry?"

"There are some bad people running this country. Most Indonesian people are not like that. It is the generals in the army who order such dreadful happenings, not the ordinary people. We are peaceful people."

"It wasn't generals who, who…" she paused, seeming to run out of words.

"You are right," he said quickly, "it is not for me to apologise to you for anything that happened. Or is still happening."

"What do you mean?"

"Your Fretilin friends aren't taking their integration into Indonesia lying down. You may not read about it in the newspapers here, but the Indonesian army is facing stiff resistance. They are tying down thousands of soldiers in the mountains."

"How do you know all this?"

"I listen to the radio broadcasts from Australia. I am sure it is not the full picture, but I think it is more reliable than anything they are saying in Jakarta."

"It doesn't matter," she said in a deadpan voice. "It is not my country any more, it is finished. They are right, we are all part of Indonesia now."

"We are both in the same boat."

She looked at him sharply. "I do not think so."

"It's true."

"How can you say such a thing? I am a nothing here, not even a refugee. Officially I don't even exist, I am a mistake. You... you are connected to these people, the people you say carry out these things. Colonel Benny is your uncle!" She spat out the words, as she did wrenching her arm out of his.

"Only by marriage!" protested Peter. "His wife is my mother's sister, he has nothing to do with me. I had no control over who she chose as a husband." He stopped, grabbed her arm and forced her to face him. "Listen, Francesca..."

"Don't you ever touch me like that!"

Horrified, he immediately released her from his grip. "I'm sorry, I'm really sorry, I didn't mean to hurt you."

"You're no different from any other Indonesian man I've met."

"That's not true!"

"I want to go back now, please." She turned round, and started to march towards his motorbike. Peter chased after her, and when he caught up with her he gently grabbed her waist, but she shook him off and continued striding towards the bike. Around them couples pointed and stared, clearly entertained by what they perceived to be a lovers' tiff. When she finally reached the bike she turned to face him, daring him not to do her bidding.

"Please, Francesca, listen to me."

"I listen to people like you every day. I think I am allowed to have some peace on my day off."

He reached down to unlock the steel cord twisted around the front wheel, in the hope it would take some of the heat out of her anger. She stood over him, arms crossed while he gathered up the cord and placed it under the seat.

"I am not who you think I am," he continued, confident he had her attention for a few more minutes at least. "You think I'm some spoilt playboy son of the regime throwing his weight around the ridge with the western men, a bit like Rollo."

"Who's Rollo?"

"He's Benny's son. He spends his whole time playing tennis and sitting around the swimming pool staring at the white girls. He is especially fond of your boss's daughter."

"I have not seen this Rollo, I don't know who you are talking about."

"Never mind, you're not missing much. He is an unimpressive person in every way. The point is, you think I am like him, but I am the total opposite."

"How can I think you are like him when I don't even know who he is?"

"It doesn't matter who he is! He is not important. Put it another way, who do you think I am?"

"I do not know who you are, and I am not sure I care."

"I am not like them!" Peter cried out in frustration. "I may have been born into a rich and powerful family, but I am not one of those lazy, spoilt sons who doesn't care that their wealth has come from robbing the people of this country, who doesn't want to see or know anything so long as their privileged existence can carry on as normal. I am not like that! Neither was my father like that, and that is why he was murdered."

"Your father was murdered?"

"They called it resisting arrest during a routine security operation, but it amounts to the same thing. He was killed by the same people who trampled all over your country, and he was killed because he dared to stand up and say that what he saw was wrong."

"What did you do about it?"

"What could I do? I was in no more position to do anything than you. I just had to stand by and watch. If I were to draw attention to myself, they would have just thrown me in jail to rot away for the rest of my days. They don't need to prove anything, they don't need to charge me with anything, it is enough that I am suspected of being a subversive threat to national security. So what do I do? I live quietly, I keep my mouth shut, and I wait."

"For what do you wait?"

"I wait for the day when I am free to say what is on my mind, I wait for the day when this country finally learns to speak the truth about itself, I wait for the day when the generals who have robbed its wealth rot in their own corruption. So you see, we are not that different, you and me. Welcome to Indonesia, aren't you glad you joined us?"

"I am not glad for anything."

"Not even to be alive? After what you have been through?"

"You have no idea what I have been through."

"That is true, Francesca, I have not, and I do not presume to know what it was like apart from that it must have been awful."

"No one can understand who wasn't there."

"It was that bad?"

She nodded. "Yes, it was that bad," she whispered. "Now, will you please take me back?"

"Of course." He stood the motorbike up and straddled it. "But can I see you again?"

"Why?"

"It is simple. Because I like you."

"What do you want from me?"

"Francesca, I don't want anything from you apart from your company."

She looked at him in disbelief, then seemed to accept what he was saying. "Okay, you can come and see me again some-time."

"Next Sunday?"

"Next Sunday is fine."

She climbed up on the pillion and he kick-started the engine, relishing the reassuring touch of her delicate hands around his middle. He would show her he was different, what-ever it took to prove that would become his mission. For the first time in as long as he could remember, he found himself filled with a sense of purpose, a goal that was not only within his grasp but actually worthy of pursuit.

18

Rollo stood in front of the three-quarter-length mirror in his bedroom and tried to decide, as he had been doing for the past half hour, what shirt to wear. There was more to it than a simple choice between a blue batik silk number he'd had knocked up for him by a Chinese tailor in Bali and a short sleeved western style cream shirt, again hand tailored in silk. The batik was the superior garment, but did it make him look too Indonesian? Whereas the western one could all too easily make him look like some over-promoted office supervisor going round to the boss's house to be patronised with soft drinks and small talk. The other option, of course, was to go completely informal – flared Levi's topped out with an Expressions Dynamic T-shirt, perhaps the one embossed with the slogan *I'm allergic to work*, that so infuriated his father. Too close to the bone, Rollo thought, too similar to what all too many people thought of him for comfort. Given the current situation, he should probably bury that one deep in his wardrobe. The jeans were good though, and he was particularly fond of the flares that burst out from below the knees, ending almost at the tip of his leather loafers.

That was some progress, he thought. He'd return to the shirt later, he had his hair to attend to. Thankfully it was starting to grow back, again much to the chagrin of his father, to a point where he now at least had options – to slick it back with gel, or blow dry it and go for the wavy bouffant look favoured by the stars on the American cop shows. That was easy, he thought, as he applied some mousse and reached for the hair dryer hidden away in his locked bedside drawer along with all the other items he preferred to keep away from the prying eyes of his mother, including a stash of girlie mags purchased from Captain Durijarian, some foil wrapped rubbers, a .38 police revolver and a small box of ammunition he'd somehow forgotten to hand in with the rest of his kit.

He cast his eye along the shelf containing his collection of aftershaves. After some early experiments with cheap aerosol sprays, a session with the sales girl in the duty free lounge at Jakarta International had initiated him into the world of proper, sophisticated scents and he now possessed an ample supply of his two firm favourites, Eau Sauvage and Givenchy Gentleman. This evening was definitely a Givenchy night, he thought, with its sweeter, more intimate aroma; the Eau Sauvage, so suggestive of a gin and tonic, being better suited to the large, set piece occasion.

Hair dried and styled into a reasonable approximation of Tom Sellick (he would have to work on the moustache), Rollo returned to the vexing question of the shirt. He slid open his wardrobe and picked through the garments hung along the rail. There was the orange short sleeved cotton one, but unfortunately he'd already worn that several times at the club. He didn't want to be thought of as someone who could only afford one going out outfit. In the end it was so simple he kicked himself for not having thought of it earlier. A plain white T-shirt, tucked into his jeans so that it emphasised the silver eagle buckle on his brown leather belt. It was also the perfect backdrop to the gold shark pendant hanging around his neck, and the copper bracelet he wore on his right wrist to balance the Rolex on his left.

Finally ready, he picked up his set of housekeys and the silver money clip into which he'd earlier folded a thick wedge of 10,000 rupiah notes. Giving himself a last once over in the mirror, he blew himself a good luck kiss and strode out into the hallway through to the living room, where he'd left his handbag. Unfortunately, there was no avoiding his father, who was sprawled out on his La-Z-Boy recliner, watching the early evening news on a fuzzy black and white TV, a scotch and soda in one hand, an ashtray and lighter in the other.

"Where are you off to?" Benny demanded without looking around.

"Just out."

"I can see that, out where?"

"Just out."

"Are you taking the car?"

"You said I could."

"I said you could use it with my permission."

"You're not going anywhere, are you?"

"That's not the point. It's my car and my driver. If you want to use it, you ask me."

"Okay, may I borrow your car tonight please, Dad?"

"Where do you want to go?"

"Just to the Hotel Bandakan for dinner."

"We've dinner here. Your mother bought some steaks from the commissary."

"I didn't know that. I'm sorry. Keep mine in the fridge, I'll have it tomorrow."

Benny shrugged his shoulders. "Suit yourself. Who are you going with?"

"I'm just meeting up with some friends."

"Friends? You don't have any friends here."

"Yes I do."

"Such as?"

"Just a few people who hang out there."

"The Hotel Bandakan isn't a place where people go to hang out. It's where you go to take a girl."

"Dad, I held a commission in the Indonesian army in case you've forgotten. I didn't think I still had to ask your permission to go out in the evening."

"I haven't forgotten, and neither have I forgotten that you are living in my house and wanting to use my car and my driver. Who are you taking out?"

Rollo knew better than to lie to his father over something that could be so easily checked. "Amanda Cole agreed to accompany me this evening," he mumbled.

"Amanda Cole!" Benny barked. "I thought we talked about messing around with white girls."

"She seemed friendly, and when I asked she said yes."

"She's going to make a fool of you."

"I can look after myself, Dad."

"You know she's hanging around with that American helicopter pilot."

"What pilot?"

"Eddie someone. He flies one of the Hueys. She's all over him, she's disgraced her family with her behaviour."

"If that's true, why did she agree to go out with me?"

"I have no idea, but I do know she is bad news."

"Can I take the car?"

"No."

"Dad!" pleaded Rollo. "She is expecting me in ten minutes. What am I going to say? What will she think of me then? She'll assume I'm just another useless Indo who can't deliver what he promises."

"Maybe you should have thought of that before you decided to take my car without asking."

"But you said I could use it."

"Yes, and I also said you should ask me first."

"I am asking you."

"And I say no."

"Dad!"

"That girl is no good for you. She will cause nothing but trouble."

"You can't stop me seeing her."

"I'm trying to stop you making a fool of yourself."

"Then why won't you let me borrow the car? If I turn up on two feet, or with my motorbike, then I really will be making a fool of myself. What's more, the only place I will be able to take her is the club, where all your American friends will see us."

Benny sighed. "Does her father know about this?"

"I don't know."

"You'd better not forget he is my boss."

"I won't do anything to embarrass you, Dad."

"You'd better not."

"Can I have the car, then?"

"Go on. I think Stephen is still out there with Ah Ming."

"I can drive it if he's gone home."

"Stephen can take you," Benny replied firmly. "And if I get an earful from Dennis Cole when I go into work tomorrow morning, I promise you there will be big trouble."

"Don't worry, Dad, I won't cause you any problems. And thanks." Rollo crossed the room and clumsily embraced Benny's shoulders.

"Go on," said Benny, squirming at this physical display of affection, "get out of here before I change my mind. And be careful."

"I will," replied Rollo, slipping out of the house before his father had a chance to regret his indulgence.

Stephen was dozing in the driver's seat gently snoring, his stomach digesting Ah Ming's sweet potato and lemongrass curry. When Rollo opened the passenger door, the smell of sweat and stale breath assaulted his nostrils to conjure up the most humiliating associations. This was more like being in an army locker room than a luxurious limo on the way to a romantic evening. A couple of turns around the block with the windows wide open were called for before they could turn up at the Cole's residence. The last thing he wanted to stir in Amanda was any impression that by going out with him she was going native.

The Hotel Bandakan was a bit chancy, but westerners did like to eat there, and it was the only alternative he could think of to the club. He knew only too well how its stultifying atmosphere reduced her to a spoilt little expat brat, crushing the fine woman she had the potential to be. Downtown he could throw his weight around and the staff would flatter him unreservedly, in the full expectation of a generous tip. He could hold forth on his country, while at the same time somehow rising above it, flaunting his new status as a graduate student at Harvard Business School.

It was wonderful finally to be able to talk about it properly, now that Constar had given the green light to the financing. That morning his papers had been filed at the US embassy in Jakarta, and a message had been relayed back via his father that no problems were anticipated in obtaining the necessary visa to study in the United States. He really felt as if he was going now, and what better way to celebrate his new life than to seduce the daughter of his father's English boss. He could understand why his father remained unenthusiastic about the relationship, but he would come round in time. It was a generational issue, Rollo concluded sagely; the problem with his father and his cronies was they remained stuck in the whole issue of post independence Indonesian identity. The new Indonesian elite, of whom Rollo could now justifiably consider himself a part, would be more international in their outlook, less parochial in their customs, more open to outside influences and fully capable of plucking the sweetest and finest fruits from the tree of western affluence. And if that included their women, it was only fair after two centuries of colonials treating their counterparts like prostitutes.

It was an ebullient and confident Rollo who pulled up in front of the Cole residence after the requisite drive around the ridge to air the car and let the air conditioning cool down the cabin. He had commandeered the rear seat to create more of a limousine feel, and he instructed Stephen to wait with the engine idling while he collected Amanda. Walking the short path to her front door, he realised he had forgotten to bring her flowers, and he kicked himself for the oversight. Nothing fancy was called for, but a single orchid would have been a nice touch, something to sit in isolation for her to remember him by. Never mind, he could make it up over dinner, and it offered the chance to send something over in the morning.

Rollo reached the door, stood straight and quickly ran his fingers through his moussed hair. From around the side of the house he could hear the amahs washing up in the kitchen, while the smell of their own supper wafted into the early evening air. He suffered a momentary loss of nerve as he recalled the scents of childhood. He very much doubted the Cole family were dining on Nase Goreng, which Mrs Cole probably dismissed, like so many of the ignorant expats he'd encountered, as "nasty goring".

He pulled himself together and forced himself to concentrate on the task at hand. Really, it was nothing compared to leading his men into battle, how stupid to feel that same awful churning inside his guts. There was a spyglass set in the door, and he wondered if anyone was peeping through it right now, laughing at his indecisiveness. He put his eye up to it but all he could see was a distorted light and some wooden parquetry from the hallway.

Enough of this. He pressed the doorbell, holding his finger on the button until he heard the double chime, then stepped back and waited. Aware of possible eyes at the spyglass, he tried to compose his face into a suitable expression and refrain from running his fingers once again through his hair.

Silence. He wondered whether anyone had heard the bell, or if the family was even at home. He was on the verge of pressing the buzzer again when he heard soft footsteps approach the door from inside the hallway. A hand unclipped the chain, and a moment later turned the knob, to reveal Suki's face in the doorway.

"Good evening, sir, how may I help you?" she asked politely.

"I have come to see Amanda," he replied reluctantly in his own tongue. "Is she in?"

"Let me see."

She disappeared, leaving the door ajar with Rollo standing in the entryway, his feet still the street side of the threshold. He strained to hear anything, and was rewarded by the sound of tapping on a door, Amanda's presumably. He pictured her in front of her mirror, applying a final touch of lipstick before taking an approving glance at herself. Like him, she would have spent the afternoon agonising over what to wear, perhaps finally settling on something elegant but understated. His guts were churning almost uncontrollably now, and he desperately suppressed a fart lest she should arrive at that very moment.

He heard the door creak open, followed by whispering voices. Some kind of counsel was going on, but strain as he might he couldn't make out any of the words. He knew Suki didn't speak English, so she was probably trying to announce his arrival in sign language. No matter, Amanda would be out in a few seconds and they could laugh over it later.

After a minute or so, he heard Suki's bare feet against the flooring followed by her reappearance at the doorway.

"Is she expecting you?"

Immediately he knew there was a problem. Had he got the wrong day? Had she thought he meant tomorrow? Worse, had she been waiting for him yesterday? No, he was sure he'd said Thursday, just as he was sure she had agreed.

"Yes, she is expecting me," he replied, trying to keep the wobble out of his voice.

"One minute please." Again she disappeared, and again there was more pidgin English whispering. Silence, then footsteps again, this time the click clack of heels on wood. Closer they came, until suddenly he saw Amanda turn the corner and face him head on.

Any impression he had of her industriously beautifying herself in honour of the occasion was shattered the instant he saw her. The heels, which had obviously been slipped on at the last moment to lend a little authority and extra height, gave way to a grey tracksuit bottom and a sloppy oversized T-shirt. Her hair was pulled back into a pony tail, and her face devoid of any make up. She looked every inch the slobby teenager set for an evening in munching popcorn and listening to records with her girlfriends.

"Oh my God, Rollo," she announced in her distinctive English accent.

"Amanda."

"Oh my God."

"Weren't we…" he let the question hang in the air.

"I am so sorry," she continued, laying emphasis on each word.

"You forgot?"

"I meant to call you yesterday. Something came up."

"You can't come out then?"

"No, I mean, no, I mean I'm so sorry, I should have called you, I meant to but it completely slipped my mind."

Rollo couldn't take much more of this. "It doesn't matter," he said simply.

"Rollo, I am so sorry, you must think I'm awful."

"It's okay," he said, withdrawing a step and a half. "Maybe some other time."

"Yes, definitely," she replied, clearly seizing on the lifeline he'd offered her. "We'll do that. God, I'm sorry, I'm so embarrassed," and she slapped her head with her hand in mock castigation.

"I'll see you later, then."

"Yes. Absolutely. Look, I'm really sorry about this, it's totally my fault."

"It doesn't matter. It's fine, Amanda. Some other time."

He turned, not even waiting for her to close the door, and retreated to the car where Stephen, who had witnessed the entire encounter, was waiting, expressionless, letting the engine idle as instructed. Rollo opened the rear door and climbed in, slamming it behind him. He felt numb, but he had to move, keep moving. He was going to get drunk, not just a little tipsy, but completely, utterly plastered. He'd find a bar, or more likely a succession of bars, in which to drown the pain he knew would take over his whole being once the initial shock had passed over. He'd stay well away from the ridge or any other place off duty oil men hung out, and keep company with his own kind. It was a terrible thing, he knew, to have no choice but to seek comfort amongst the people he despised.

"Drive on," he ordered curtly.

"Where to?"

"Just drive downtown. I'll tell you where when we get there."

"Okay, boss."

"I'm not your boss."

"Sure thing."

"Just drive."

Smoothly shifting the engine into gear, Stephen gently pulled away with his passenger for what he sensed was going to be a long night.

From the main kitchen, where she had been busy peeling and chopping vegetables, Francesca heard the entire exchange. She looked down at her hands; the one holding the small, sharp paring knife visibly shook in her grip, as suddenly everything fitted into place. She considered running out round the side of the carport and plunging it hard in his back. She was confident enough of finding a vital organ and being able to wreak sufficient damage to kill him before he or someone else managed to restrain her. It would be a tiny, symbolic gesture of retribution for all that had happened, and to hell with the consequences. She would suffer them willingly, whatever they decided to do to her. Just one tiny consideration restrained her hand, tipping her back into the realm of cunning and reason.

She had been curled up on her mattress against the wall nearest the stove, a position earnt by virtue of her willingness to prepare and clean up after meals, when the first shells exploded at two o'clock in the morning, dramatically proving her father's optimistic predictions wrong. Although the first salvo landed over a mile away, it was the loudest and most forceful sound she had ever heard. The shock wave seemed to split the planks from the beams, causing the four-inch nails holding the frame of the house in place to rattle like so many rotten pegs in an old peasant woman's mouth. At the same time, its brittle force pierced the warm bubble of her dream, a sequence unbound by the constraints of linear logic or cause and effect, in which she and Miguel walked along the beach and played half-naked in the river. There was a sensuous quality to the dream that had she been true in her devoutness would have left her feeling ashamed and impure. As it was, her first thought was to resent this rude interruption for wrenching her away from such a delicious paradise, a thought quickly followed by the knowledge that the world had come to an end.

The first explosion was quickly followed by five more, followed by a pause long enough for her to wonder whether she had imagined the whole thing and it was a continuation of her dream with Miguel, the divine conclusion punishing her for her sins of the flesh. Then another salvo came, this time closer. By now the entire household was up, shouting above the squawk of chickens and the barking from chained dogs. Her father stumbled into the room, his pyjamas silhouetted in the doorway seeming only to heighten his aura of vulnerability. At that moment she knew, before she even caught his dazed expression, that he would not be able to protect them as up until now he always had; that this phenomenal terror closing in on them was something his fragile body was powerless to resist.

Although there had been much talk about the prospect of invasion, for Francesca it had always been an abstract concept, something upon which you adopted a position or took bets as to the likelihood of happening. Never had she taken the time to try to imagine what an invasion might actually look, sound or feel like, or how it would affect their lives. In those few moments punctuated by barrages of exploding shells it became a living and monstrous outrage. How dare the Indonesians do this to them? As another shell landed, this time closer than any before, shaking the house so that it became a blur before her eyes, she was overwhelmed by the fundamental wrongness of it all. Who were these people who had decided to attack them for no reason? For it was quite clear they had not the slightest chance of resistance. Each explosion sent shockwaves that reverberated through her, jarring vital organs of whose existence she was only now becoming fully conscious, so that on top of the deafening noise that made any kind of thought or intellectual response completely impossible, there was a sense of physical violation that assaulted, overwhelmed and shattered her most private being. It wasn't possible to stand up to this barrage, all you could do was seek out the nearest corner or hole and cover your head with your arms. So this was what people meant when they talked about being softened up, or reduced to quivering jelly.

"They're coming, aren't they?" she said to her father once the noise from the latest explosion had abated.

"Yes, they're coming." His voice was deadpan, resigned in its shock at his failure to anticipate this turn of events and make good their escape to the hills. They all knew without anyone having to mention it that he of all people should have correctly predicted what course of action the Indonesian army would take. Meanwhile, her two brothers were up and about, dragging on items of clothing in a fit of panic.

"We've got to get out of here!" yelled Antonio.

"No!" her father barked back at him sharply. "Stay here!"

"You're crazy!" shouted Antonio. "Can't you hear those shells? They're coming in closer all the time."

"Of course I can hear them. Do you think we're going to be any safer from them out there in the street? Unless we receive a direct hit we're better off inside. The walls will protect us from shrapnel blast. In a while the shelling will stop and then the town will be crawling with soldiers. The last thing we want is to be out and about when that happens. Now, everyone get under the table and let's pray none of those guns manage to find our roof."

"I can't stay here," said Antonio, not quite so loud this time but still in a voice shot through with panic.

"Do as you're told!" Francesca had never seen her father so decisive, so firm. It was as if, having let them down once with his wavering, he was determined to hold them together with his last reserves of resolve.

Antonio backed down, and together they pulled the table into the centre of the room, directly underneath the two largest beams, and covered it with blankets to shield them against flying glass. They stacked the sides with furniture to create something that to Francesca's eyes resembled a child's den. Her mother held the baby in her chest with one hand, comforting Marco with the other as they all clambered in to huddle together in their makeshift shelter. Around them the shelling continued. It moved perilously closer so that Francesca thought it was only a matter of minutes before the blast waves whipped the flimsy walls and roof from around them to leave them naked to the street, and then it gradually moved away again. She knew that meant someone else was receiving a pounding and she was sorry for them, but all she really felt was a sense of relief that the barrage was no longer directly above their heads.

The baby, who up until then had done nothing more than shiver and whimper in her mother's arms, now began to howl. Her mother offered her her breast, but Angelica was too distraught to latch on properly. In the end her mother rocked her back to sleep with a gentle lullaby, which somehow also managed to soothe the rest of the family. Then the shelling diminished to the odd explosion in the distance, until it ceased altogether.

No one knew quite what to do. With the threat from artillery fire averted, temporarily at least, it seemed silly to remain under the table like children playing some party game. Francesca was curious to look outside, to see if any of the landmarks she knew so well had been destroyed. She wondered how her friends had fared, and Miguel too. Had their homes come under fire? Were they too, like themselves, crouched under some table terrified for their lives, or had they decided to run for it? Francesca wasn't entirely convinced as to the wisdom of her father's decision to stay put – her own instinct, like that of Antonio, was to grab what few essentials they could carry and make a dash for the countryside.

The lull, during which what was left of the night was given over to barking dogs and cockerels fenced in under hundreds of houses similar to theirs, didn't last long. They were out from under the table and beginning to ask themselves what they should do next when they heard the sound of aircraft approaching from the direction of the sea. First one or two, then dozens of them, droning so low overhead it seemed they would land on their rooftop.

"We've got to get out of here, father!" Antonio protested yet again. "They're coming in, they'll kill us all."

"No! The streets are far too dangerous. Anyone who's about will be shot for sure. We have to stay put."

"And do what?"

"Nothing. Just wait."

"For them to come here and take us away?"

"No, just wait for them to pass through. They're not interested in individual houses, it's the government buildings and radio station they'll want to secure. We can't do anything that risks getting in their way or we'll be dead for sure."

"I want to go," Antonio continued.

"And leave your family here?" Francesca watched her brother hesitate in the face of her father's words. "No, we're staying together through this as a family."

Antonio stood up and walked across to the front door, which he cracked open so he could peer through the narrow gap into the moonlight outside. Quickly he slammed it shut again, locking the door with the flimsy metal bolt.

"They're everywhere," he whispered, the blood draining from his face.

"Who?" asked her father.

"Parachutists. They're falling from the sky in thousands. That's what all those aeroplanes are doing."

"Oh, my God," her father said simply. "God help us now."

"We should have run when we had the chance." Antonio looked accusingly at their father, and from the way he evaded his son's gaze Francesca knew that he knew Antonio was right.

"Let me see," said Francesca all of a sudden, and before anyone could stop her she had crossed the room to the front window and lifted the blind to peep outside. All above, the sky was full of them, dotted figures like little toy soldiers dangling from the large circular parachutes by the neat, symmetrically arranged cords. She could just make out the rifles strapped tightly to each soldier's back, and the rope stretched from their legs to a large bag some ten feet below. Each time a paratrooper landed, the bag hitting the ground to announce his arrival a half second before the soldier kicked up a pile of dirt, rolled over and stood up again, running around into the wind to collapse the parachute, he was replaced by another two or three more spewing out of the open rear doorway of the large four-propeller aircraft. They were flying so low overhead she could make out the figure standing in the doorway giving out orders and throwing his charges into the void. The sky was full of them, too many to count. Already the first troops were on the ground, and in the distance she heard the rat-a-tat-tat of small arms fire. After the artillery barrage it seemed almost harmless, chocolate gunfire from chocolate soldiers until it swung around in an arc to fly directly over their rooftop, where the deadly crack-crack-crack once again started up the chickens and the dogs.

Francesca dropped the blind back in place and rushed over to the bosom of her family, now huddled once again around the table. Her father was right, there really was no place for them to run now. All they could do was hope these soldiers from the sky were looking for something more significant than their little lives and would pass them by. She looked up at her mother, desperately trying to keep Angelica from crying. Francesca wished she would just shut up, she would draw attention to life inside their house. She wanted to put her hand over the baby girl's mouth, and momentarily she wondered that if it came to it, if they had to hide from the Indonesians as a family, would she be prepared to suffocate the baby to prevent her giving them all away? As if her mother could read her guilty thoughts, she pulled the infant closer still into her breast, where thankfully the crying receded into a whimper, for the time being at least.

While Antonio's fear was still shot through with rage at their father for keeping them in the house when they might have had a chance to make good their escape, Marco's terror was undiluted. He kept looking back and forth from one parent to the other, then to Francesca, on to his elder brother, even once to the baby. Gradually, the realisation was dawning upon him – and Francesca's heart went out to him in the peeling-away of his innocence – that none of them could help him. How they had protected Marco, until recently the baby of the family himself, doing his homework, reassuring his nervous disposition, not letting him out of the house alone until a few short years ago… Here, now, when he really needed it, there was nothing any of them could do.

From outside she could hear commands being barked out in Bahasa, interspersed with the sound of heavily laden boots clumping up and down the streets, together with more bursts of gunfire. There was some more to-ing and fro-ing, presumably as the parachutists regrouped after jumping in on them, then all of a sudden a horrible splintering sound, which Francesca guessed was a rifle butt smashing down a door, followed by a hideous scream she recognised as coming from the mouth of Mrs Ho, who lived three doors down and ran a rice export business with her husband and two sons. Half a dozen shots rang out in quick succession, then silence, then an order shouted out in Bahasa. Francesca tried to make out what the soldier was saying, but there were too many other noises from all around – gunfire, screams, chickens, dogs, a few remaining aircraft droning overhead – for her to be able to make any sense of his words.

The soldiers were close now – she could hear them gather round the house directly opposite theirs on the other side of the road, which Francesca knew to be empty. The owner, Mr Mattu, was a big time Fretilin activist and had left with his family for the hills several weeks ago, presumably better informed than her father, she thought bitterly. Another crack of splintering wood, followed by footsteps crashing up the wooden steps into the house. More shouting, more crashing, it sounded like rifle butts smashing into rickety furniture, a short burst of gunfire, then more shouting. This time Francesca could just about discern what they were saying; it seemed they were arguing over Mr Mattu's television set. If that was all they wanted, she wasn't going to be like the grasping Mrs Ho, they could have the TV, the radio, the furniture, anything – just so long as they went away and left them in peace. She fingered the silver crucifix around her neck and prayed. God, please help us now, she silently pleaded, please keep us safe from these soldiers, please help us, help us, just help us. God please, Jesus look after us, Mummy and Daddy and Antonio and Marco and baby Angelica, and me of course, please just keep us all safe, they can have whatever they want, just keep us safe from these terrible things happening outside.

The nuns at St Xavier's had done a good job and her faith until then had been strong, but it evaporated in a crash of splintering wood, as the flimsy bolt on their own front door gave way to a vicious blow from a rifle butt. Her first thought was to wonder why her God had forsaken her, followed quickly by the realisation that she had been conned by the nuns, and there was no God at all. Their reality was reduced to the four grinning Javanese soldiers now standing in their front room, rifles raised and pointing towards them.

The four soldiers were quickly joined by two more, one of whom wore sergeant's stripes. As soon as he entered, the others deferred to him, pointing to the radio as if its presence somehow explained everything. A few gruff words were exchanged between them.

"What are they saying?" whispered Antonio out of the side of his mouth.

"I can't tell," replied Francesca, trying not to move her lips.

"Quiet," whispered her father.

The soldiers gestured towards the back wall with their rifles, motioning the family to move over there which they did, still holding onto each other as best they could. Francesca felt Marco squeeze her palm and she tried to reassure him while keeping her own terror under control. Instinctively she knew not to make any sudden moves; close up these soldiers were no more than kids really, overgrown oafs handed a rifle, heads full of crass indoctrination, and all the more dangerous for it. She knew that to plead for mercy with such people was to enter into their game on their terms and surrender oneself to their power, now magnified to lethal proportions by the might of the Indonesian army. She knew too, that if you removed their weapons, their uniforms and their comrades, took them out of their barracks and returned them to their kampongs, they wouldn't raise a murmur in protest at their mothers' contemptuous slaps.

More words were quietly exchanged between the sergeant and the soldiers. Taking care not to walk between the soldiers' rifles, still raised, and the family, the sergeant picked his way around the room towards the radio.

"What's this?" he barked in Bahasa.

Francesca's father, the only other family member to understand the neighbouring dialect, replied softly. "Just a radio. You can take it if you want."

The sergeant flashed a menacing smile. "Radio, eh?" he continued in Bahasa. "So you can listen to Fretilin broadcasts?"

Pulling the family close in towards him, her father shook his head. "Just a radio. You know, music, *boom-boom*. You take it. Please."

Continuing to smile, the sergeant glanced down at the radio and switched it on. There was a crackle of static, through which a panicked voice emerged. "They're all around us now, they are attacking, thousands of them…"

The sergeant clicked off the radio. "No music," he said, as if that were the end of the argument. "Fretilin." Then he looked along the rest of the shelf where, to his delight, lay several half-full spools of studio audio tape.

"More Fretilin!" he announced with a flourish, picking up the spools, examining them briefly and placing them down. Suddenly his eye caught something and he crossed over towards them, first checking he wasn't in any line of fire. Francesca wondered what had attracted his attention, and then to her horror she realised that, gripped between Baby Angelica's fingers was an eighteen inch ribbon of brown quarter inch tape.

The sergeant was right up to them now, and Francesca noticed that he wasn't armed, apart from a pistol clipped into a holster on his belt. He reached out his fingers, which to her surprise were actually quite delicate, the sort of fingers that might even play a piano, and tugged on to the other end of the tape, while Francesca's mother tried to pull Angelica into her body as tightly as possible. Thinking this was some new game, Angelica gave the sergeant a full smile and gripped her end of the tape. Any hope that his delicacy suggested a more merciful disposition evaporated with his next remark.

"Junior Fretilin!" he exclaimed, to titters of laughter from the soldiers in the room. He then turned to Francesca's father.

"You! Outside!" The grin had snapped from his face in an instant, while the soldiers, relishing some real action after this piece of puppet play, enthusiastically moved round to grab her father, one at each arm.

"Leave him alone!" It was Antonio, and although the soldiers couldn't understand his words, the sentiment was clear enough.

"No, Antonio, don't!" her father urged him, but Antonio continued to pull at the soldier's sleeve. Two of the remaining soldiers rushed forward and grabbed him, prising him away. Expertly, as though they had done this a hundred times before, one kicked Antonio in the groin, causing her brother to stumble and fall into a corner. Thus down, the other raised his rifle butt and brought it down with full force onto Antonio's head. Francesca flinched at the last moment so she didn't see the impact itself, but there was no avoiding the thick dull thud followed by the involuntary exhalation from her brother. She forced herself to look around, where Antonio's head lay split open, blood gushing from a huge wound between his ear and his eyes.

Her father offered himself forward, sacrificing himself in a last ditch attempt to save the rest of them. The sergeant looked him up and down then, standing stock still in front of him, glanced first at the body of Antonio, resting in a pool of blood in the corner of the room, then at the remaining members of the family. Francesca saw her father cross himself before addressing the sergeant in a soft, low voice.

"Shall we go outside and get this over with? Then you can leave my family alone."

Outside, the gunfire and troop movements continued, interspersed with shouts and screams from all directions, but mostly, Francesca discerned, from the harbour.

"I've changed my mind," replied the sergeant, the grin returning to his face. "Before we go anywhere, I have a little show I want you to watch." He unclipped his pistol from his holster and drew it up to her father's face, where he jutted the muzzle painfully into his nostril. "Now you listen to me," he began menacingly, "you may be a communist troublemaker, but I just noticed you have one very pretty daughter."

"You leave her alone!" her father protested, his voice rising in panic.

"Yes, she's very pretty. She could be a movie star or a singer. Very pretty!" He leered over at Francesca, who felt sick to the core of her stomach. "So, what you say Mr Fretilin, I go boom boom fucky fucky, and you stand back and watch? I'll give you a real good show, I promise. I'm good at this, I've had plenty practice."

He laughed out loud, to be joined by another chorus of titters from his men. Francesca felt her body freeze. If she gave in to him, could she save her father? She was worth more to them alive than dead, and so long as this sergeant wanted to play his sick games with them, so was her Daddy. She couldn't look him in the eye, but she knew she had to follow his example and offer herself forward to save the rest of them. Momentarily she thought of the nuns at St Xaviers and their devout emphasis on chastity. Where was Jesus now, she thought bitterly, when they really needed him? Her father could cross himself all he liked, it wasn't going to make one bit of difference to their plight. They were on their own now.

She looked up at the sergeant. She was dead as a girl, she knew it, and would be stigmatised forever as a woman. Of course, she had never done such a thing, and whilst naturally she had imagined it, it had always been sacred in its beauty, with her husband on her wedding night, surrounded by gentleness and love, her surrender both willing and voluntary. How she had been cheated, she thought; none of that would now be for her. Even if Miguel was still alive, she would never manage to look at him after this. Forcing herself to shut out such thoughts, she cauterised her humanity and stepped forward like her father had before her.

"Don't do it!" her father exclaimed through gritted teeth. The sergeant turned on him and in one movement smashed his nose with the butt of his pistol. Her father crumpled to the ground where he lay in a heap, clutching his nose which was now gushing with blood.

"You shut up and watch!" he barked out at her poor father. "I don't want to hear another squeak out of you or I'll have one of my boys take you up the bum with his rifle!" He then turned to Francesca. "As for you, my pretty little one, let's have a closer look at you." He reached forward and with one hand ripped away the thin cotton top she had hastily put on when the shelling started.

"Oh my, oh my," he leered, taking in her budding breasts and smooth belly. "You are something special."

Francesca said nothing. Already she'd decided to absent herself from whatever was about to happen to her body. She wouldn't be giving her body over to this ghastly murderer with his crooked nicotine-stained teeth and foul breath, she would be giving it back to the family who had raised and nurtured her.

And then he was on to her. He passed his pistol to one of the soldiers, muttering with a chuckle "I don't want the bitch grabbing it and shooting my balls off!" then faced her square on. Moving towards her he shoved her roughly in the chest, causing her to stumble and bang her head against the wall as she fell. Now she was looking directly up at him. He was close on her now, leaning down. She felt his strong fingers around her waist as he ripped her skirt off and greed-ily pulled at the thin pair of cotton pants beneath. Momen-tarily she looked past him to see an audience of cheering, jeering soldiers, before zoning her focus somewhere into the middle distance. What was left of her family had retreated to the far corner, unable to watch her humiliation, where her mother tried to tend to her father's wounds while Marco held the baby.

"Go on, Sarge, give her one!" cried one of the soldiers.

"Man, is that some sweet looking pussy," called another.

"Shit, these Fretilin chicks are hot," joshed a third. "I'm in the wrong army."

"Shut up!" barked the sergeant. He turned to face Francesca. "You ever done this with anyone before?"

Francesca remained silent, looking through him with glazed eyes. The sergeant slapped her round the face, catching her cheekbone with a ring on his fourth finger.

"I said, have you ever done this with anyone before!"

"Hundreds of times." If there was any small satisfaction she could deny him she would do so, regardless of the cost. She didn't dare look round to her family to see how they responded.

"Somehow I don't think so," the sergeant leered back at her. "But we'll soon find out, I'm something of an expert in these matters." With that he unclipped his webbing belt buckle and opened up the zipper on his fatigue trousers to reveal a pair of black underpants decorated around the waistband with little white bunny rabbits. She looked away while he peeled off the underpants with one hand and pinned her to the ground by the throat with the other. He moved the hand around her throat up towards her chin and jerked her head so that she was forced to look directly into his dark eyes. For the first time in her life she felt in the intimate presence of evil.

"You make this good for me, and maybe I let your family live." He spoke softly so that only she could hear. "Now, I'm going to ask you one more time, am I the first?"

She pushed her head against his hand and nodded briefly.

"That's what I like to hear," he replied. "I don't want any little slut giving me a dose of something nasty." With that, he shuffled his body onto her so she could feel that thing of his move between her thighs as it tried to seek out what remained of her intimacy. It was time, she knew, to absent herself again, to reach out for that dreamworld from which she'd been so abruptly awoken, to be anywhere but here and now. She forced herself to leave her body, to be some kind of third party coldly witnessing this scene of horror but not really part of it. It worked for a moment, until he found her and shoved himself forward into her with such force she felt she was being ripped in two. Involuntarily, despite having sworn to remain silent throughout, she emitted a high-pitched scream. From the corner of one eye she saw her father rise to help her, quickly pulled back down by her mother.

He thrust himself in and out of her, each agonising stroke ripping her flesh so she felt like a pig being disembowelled while still alive. Not that he seemed to care, in fact she sensed her pain only enhanced the sick pleasure he was deriving, a realisation that made her more determined than ever not to show how she was feeling. The only mercy was the end came relatively quickly. Just as she thought she would be pinned down forever in this hell, he pulled that slimy thing of his from her with a last rip, and stood up with a smile. She stole a glance, only to see him wiping off a thin film of blood with the remnants of her skirt before tucking himself away and turning to his men.

"Okay boys, your turn now. Rank before beauty." He leant down towards Francesca and grinned. "Now I've shown you how it's done, my pretty one, maybe you can put on a good show for me."

From her vantage point sprawled across the floor, she saw the sergeant retrieve his pistol from the soldier who'd been holding it for him, then lift it towards Marco's mouth. She could see her little brother shaking with terror as the sergeant cocked the mechanism and jammed the weapon up against Marco's teeth.

He turned to her mother. "Don't think I forgot about you either. Here, let me hold the baby for you. Double act, eh?" he tittered.

He then pulled the pistol back from Marco and reached down towards little Angelica. Francesca's mother couldn't understand his words but the meaning was all too clear. Gripping the baby tight, she emitted a wild, primal scream. The sergeant pulled at her arms, trying to prise the infant from her grasp. Marco rushed over to her side and pulled at the sergeant's wrist. Suddenly, a single shot rang out. In the confines of the house it had a shattering effect, obliterating all conversation or thought. When the noise stopped ringing in her ears Francesca looked up. The remains of her little brother's brains were splattered across the back wall and Marco lay slumped on the floor within arm's reach of Francesca, his face punctuated by the entry point of a single bullet just below his right cheek. In the silence that followed, Angelica began to cry once again.

"I'm sorry, Sarge." It was the tallest of the four soldiers, out of whose raised rifle emitted a whisper of cordite. "He was going for your gun, I thought he might grab it."

The sergeant waved the soldier away, as if the act was of no more consequence than swatting a fly. With this second murder all strength seemed to leave Francesca's mother, and the sergeant was able to prise the baby from her grip. He picked Angelica up and looked her up and down, cooing ever so softly to her. The baby responded with a blank stare, while the sergeant, losing interest, turned to the soldiers.

"Well boys, they're all yours." Still holding Angelica, he wandered over to the front door and peered outside. Apparently satisfied, he returned over to her father's armchair and sat down. He crossed his legs, and jogging the baby up and down with one hand, lit a cigarette with the other.

The soldiers came at them, in ones and twos and threes, tearing the two women apart as if their bodies were so many pieces of barbecued chicken. Francesca couldn't bear to look over to her mother, but she could imagine from the desperate groans and shrieks the indignities the person who had given her life was suffering. Above it all Baby Angelica watched on, seeing nothing yet seeing it all, while the sergeant, his cigarette between his lips, consulted a map he'd pulled out of a side pocket.

"Quickly now," he called without looking up. "Anyone who hasn't had a turn at these communist bitches had better get a move on, we need to hit the RV in ten."

Energised by his ultimatum, the soldiers redoubled their efforts with schoolboy-like enthusiasm. Their trousers were all around their knees now, rifles laid out on the table, cocks poking out from greying underpants. She lost count of the number of times they raped her, all she could focus on was that moment when they squirted out at her, went floppy and lost the ability to hurt her any more.

Just as the last one was thrusting into her, the door opened and a young Indonesian officer stepped inside. Francesca couldn't see his face, but from the way the soldiers rushed to dress themselves and reach for their weapons it was clear he was a figure of authority.

"What the fuck's going on in here?" the officer demanded.

The sergeant looked up, but didn't rise from the armchair. "We encountered a little bit of resistance, sir. Boys are seeing to it now."

"Well, get a fucking move on, then." The officer seemed irritated. "The rest of the platoon's been at the RV for twenty minutes waiting for you lot."

The sergeant seemed unimpressed. Still holding the baby, he pointed to the radio and the spools of tape, one of which had unwound itself and now lay unravelled over the floor. "I think this place was being used as a Fretilin safe house."

The officer looked over at the bodies of Antonio and Marco. "And did you manage to extract any useful intelligence out of them?"

"I'm afraid not, sir. They were resisting arrest, we had to shoot them."

"What about over here?" The officer gestured towards Francesca, now crouched naked in a ball.

"Just a bit of light relief for the boys. They've had a hard fight."

"Hard, my arse! We're the ones who've done all the work. Well, you'd better finish them off before you leave." He then seemed to notice the baby for the first time. "And what the hell's this?"

The sergeant lifted Angelica and stared into her uncomprehending face. "They had a baby with them."

"What are you going to do with it?"

"I don't know, sir. Any suggestions?"

"You can't leave it here. We're professional soldiers, not child murderers. These people are fellow Indonesians, remember, we've come to liberate them – not annihilate them."

A radio clipped to the officer's belt suddenly it squawked – an indecipherable burst of Bahasa surrounded by static. The officer reached for it and spoke a few words into the mouthpiece. He then turned back to the sergeant.

"Okay, we need to get going. I'm off to the RV now, I want you there in five. Do what you've got to do and send a runner over when you're in position."

"The baby, sir? Our little fellow Indonesian?"

"Send one of the men back to Company HQ and tell them to put it in the First Aid tent. They can sort it out later. What is it anyway, boy or girl?"

"Girl, I think."

The officer made a humph sound, turned on his heels and left. Sighing, the sergeant roused himself from the armchair and aimed his pistol at Francesca's father.

"Time to take our final bow," he said simply. "Hope you enjoyed the show." He was standing less than six feet from her father, and as Francesca looked up she saw his index finger gently squeeze against the trigger.

The shot was well aimed, entering her father in the centre of his skull, just above the eyes. Francesca turned away and flattened her face against the floor, awaiting her turn. The sergeant moved over towards her side of the room, when the door was flung open once again, and an irate voice shouted through the doorway. "Get a fucking move on, the platoon's come under fire at the RV! We need to mount a counter attack!"

"We're just finishing off in here," called back the sergeant.

"We haven't got time for that!" shouted the voice. "Just get out of there, there's work to be done."

One by one the soldiers piled out of the house, running to the fresh orders.

"What the fuck's that?" she heard.

"It's a baby," replied the sergeant.

"I can see that. What are you doing with it?"

"The platoon commander told me to take it back to the First Aid tent at Company HQ."

"And what are they going to do with it?"

The last thing Francesca saw before she buried her face in the floorboards was the sergeant, babe in arms, shrugging his shoulders before being pushed aside by the figure dishing out the new orders.

"Where do they find these officers?" he asked at no one in particular before emptying his M16 into the house.

All around her bits of wall and furniture were reduced to matchwood. With her head pressed against the floor, Francesca felt a line of bullets rake her precious mother, naked and bloody beside her. The tremendous echo of the automatic rifle reverberated around the house, and then there was silence.

She placed the paring knife back on the chopping board and tried to take a couple of slow, deep breaths. Think, girl, think, she urged herself. Where could she turn for help? Immediately she thought of Peter, but that would involve telling him the whole story, of exposing her shame to her suitor's eyes. But if he could help her, even if all he could do was point her in the right direction to look, she really didn't care what he thought of her. She would speak to him when he called on Sunday. Thank goodness she hadn't dismissed him entirely when he upset her last week. Picking up the knife again, she turned its blade back to the benign task of slicing the remaining pile of carrots, becoming aware for the first time since the invasion of a feeling she thought she had lost forever, the warm feeling of hope.

19

Amanda had been in her bedroom reading when Rollo called by to take her out. Having dispensed with the adventures of Pip, she had found herself dissatisfied with interegenerational sagas and moved on to the altogether more fertile and sensuous ground occupied by Anna Karenina. In her current state of mind she felt nothing but sympathy for Anna's decision to follow her heart. Her mother's tedious carping about Eddie's unsuitability as a lover had left her in no mood to have any truck with concepts like familial duty, and as for sacrificing your heart's imperative out of some sense of social obligation, it seemed absurd to countenance such a thing. Tolstoy's choice of motif for the flyleaf left her in no doubt as to where the author's sympathies lay and the kind of fate he had in store for his heroine who refused to live by a patriarchal society's rules, and she hated him for it. *Vengeance is mine, and I will repay.* It sent a chill through her heart.

She felt guilty about Rollo. She hadn't intended to stand him up like that, it was just in the excitement of all that had happened with Eddie, she'd forgotten she'd even agreed to go out with him. Maybe she should send him a note in the morning, apologising for her absent-mindedness. She'd have to be careful how she worded it, though – the last thing she wanted to do was encourage him to shoot for a repeat performance.

She placed her book down on the bedside table, stood up and walked over to the air conditioning unit set into the window. Opening the fascia, her mother's harsh words of warning rang in her ear. "Are you on the pill?" Barbara had demanded the day after Amanda returned from her flight into the interior.

"You know I'm not," Amanda countered defensively.

"I don't know what you've been up to or managed to get hold of lately. Besides, Dr Betts wouldn't tell me anything. I know, because I asked. Patient confidentiality, he said. What about a mother's right to know about her daughter, I said."

"Well, I haven't been to see him."

"Then I suggest you do."

"What for?"

"To sort you out with something. If you're going to gaddy about like some little gutter slut, you should at least take some precautions. Get yourself a Dutch cap if you don't like the idea of the pill. Dr Betts or one of the nurses will advise you. The last thing I need is to have to sneak you out to Singapore for a scrape."

Amanda had been appalled at her mother's coarseness, but she had taken her advice and made an appointment to see one of the Indonesian nurses in Dr Betts' clinic. In an excruciatingly embarrassing and uncomfortable session, she had been fitted out with a diaphragm that now nestled in its plastic box along with a tube of revolting-smelling gel and an instruction leaflet outlining the correct procedure for insertion, removal, cleaning and maintenance, each step accompanied by a crude line drawing.

Opening the box, she fingered the flattened rubber hemisphere, wondering how long she would have to wait before she got a chance to use it. It was silly to hide it away like this, what was she so ashamed of? As she tried to work it out, she heard footsteps in the hallway. Quickly, she snapped the box shut and stuffed it into her tracksuit pocket before returning to flop down on the bed.

There was a gentle tap on the door.

"Yes?" Amanda said softly. God forbid it was Rollo again, demanding she honour her word and get dressed to go out.

The door opened to reveal Francesca, half hidden beneath a pile of freshly laundered clothes.

"I am sorry, I can come back later if you are busy," she began timidly.

Amanda waved her hesitation aside. "For goodness sake, I'm not doing anything. Come on in."

Francesca stepped inside the room and set the pile down on the chest of drawers, where she proceeded to sort the garments by category. There was a dignity to the way she worked that made Amanda feel slovenly and ungrateful. If she was honest, she was uncomfortable being waited on to such an extent.

"Don't worry about that, Francesca. I can put those away."

"Please?" She could tell the girl thought she had done something wrong.

"Sit down."

Nervously eyeing the dressing table chair as if it might bite her, Francesca did as she was bid.

"That man who came to see me, Rollo, the one Suki answered the door to, is he still there?"

"No, I think he is gone."

"Are you sure?"

"I heard his car drive away."

"Thank God for that. It's not that there's anything wrong with him, it's just I forgot I was meant to be going out with him."

"You like him?" Francesca asked simply.

"Not really. I mean, I neither like nor dislike him. I'm sure he's a perfectly nice guy, just not my type."

"Because he is Indonesian?"

"Because I'm in love with someone else."

In response, Francesca looked down at her lap, where her fingers nervously fidgeted against one another.

"Francesca, can I ask you something?"

"Of course," Francesca replied without enthusiasm.

"Do you have a boyfriend?"

Francesca shook her head. "No, I have not."

"What about Peter Adisono? I hear he comes round all the time."

"He is friendly with Suki."

"Not that friendly. He never used to come and visit us before you arrived."

Francesca shrugged her shoulders. "He is just someone who comes to visit."

"Have you ever had a boyfriend? I'm sorry," Amanda checked herself. "What am I doing grilling you with all these personal questions? It's none of my business, tell me to shut up, I will."

"It's okay, you don't have to shut up. There used to be someone, he was called Miguel."

"What happened to him?"

"He died."

"I'm sorry." She paused, before her curiosity got the better of her. "Was it sudden?"

"Yes. It was sudden."

"That must have been hard."

"I try not to think of it, Miss Amanda. That part of my life is over, it can never come back."

"Still, it must be awfully hard, especially if you loved him."

"We were more what you like to call good friends, but yes, it was hard. Very hard."

"My mother would kill me for saying this, but you could do so much more with your life than stay here working for us."

"I am happy here," Francesca replied, her voice deadpan.

"What about your family?"

"I have no family."

"None?"

"I left them behind when I came here."

"Where are you from, Francesca? I mean, really from? And where did you learn to speak English so well?"

"I grew up in Timor. I learnt English from the nuns in my school."

"East Timor?"

Francesca nodded.

"Where the Indonesians have just invaded?"

"Yes. Where the Indonesians have just invaded."

"Crikey. So, how did you end up here?"

"Some people helped me along the way. One of them was a man who worked for Colonel Surikano."

"Is there nothing that man doesn't have his fingers in?"

"What do you mean?" Francesca demanded sharply.

"God, I didn't mean to imply anything like that. He seems to know everyone and everything that's going on. I'm sure he'll find out how I stood up Rollo soon enough. Did you know Peter is his nephew?"

Francesca shrugged her shoulders, while Amanda raised herself from her bed and walked over to the closet. "Whatever you say, I still think he's a nice guy. You could do a whole lot worse." Amanda slid open the closet door and reached up to the top shelf. "Here," she said, pulling out a brown leather shoulder bag. "This is for you."

"For me?"

"Yes, it's brand new, I've never used it. Have it." She thrust the bag towards Francesca, who took it suspiciously, holding it as if it were an unexploded bomb. She looked it over, waiting, Amanda could see, for the trap. "It's Hermès, a real one too, it came from CK Tang in Singapore. I think the price tag's still inside."

"What do you want with it?" Francesca seemed perplexed, upset even.

"I want you to have it. It's no use to me, gathering dust up there on that shelf. If you don't like it, sell it. I won't be offended, I promise you."

"No, I do not think I will sell it." For the first time, Amanda saw a small smile spread across Francesca's face. "Are you sure you want me to have it?"

"Quite sure. A girl needs a bag, especially if she's going to go out. And if you want to use any perfume or make up, feel free to help yourself. You know where it is."

"You are very kind to me."

"Not really, I just want to see you make something of your life. You're so beautiful and obviously intelligent, it seems such a waste for you to be hanging around here."

"Your mother treats me well, I have no reason to complain."

"You know what I mean, Francesca. There are plenty of men who'd be interested in you if you don't fancy Peter. Take Rollo, for instance. He may not be much of an intellectual, but seems a decent enough person."

"You are very good to me, Miss Amanda, but I do not think this Rollo is right for me."

"Suit yourself. But he's certainly got prospects now I hear he's off to Harvard."

Francesca shouldered the bag and started to shuffle towards the door.

"Francesca, can I ask you something else?"

Francesca shrugged her shoulders.

"It's kind of personal. You don't have to answer if you don't want to." She paused while Francesca waited in silence. "Have you ever slept with a man?"

Amanda watched Francesca's eyes drop towards the floor, studying for any telltale gesture.

"I'm sorry, you're right, it's none of my business. It's just... it's just it's the most delicious feeling in the world, and I wondered if you had experienced that too. But it has to be the right man, of course. It's no good if it's just anybody."

"Maybe when you are somebody, somebody like you, that is true. Me, I am nobody."

"You're not nobody, Francesca. Don't let anyone tell you that. Come back here, I want us to take a look at some more of these dresses in the closet. With a few alterations, I reckon we could put together another couple of nice outfits for you."

When Peter turned up on Sunday to take Francesca out, not only was she wearing a new pale blue dress with a set of coral buttons running down the front, she'd also slung a rather smart brown leather bag over her shoulder. To top it off, she gave him a smile so warm he thought at first he had got the wrong house.

"Where do you want to go?" he asked once she was on the back of his motorbike.

"Anywhere, just away from here."

Happy to oblige, he steered the bike past the gatehouse, down the hill and out towards the airport road. He planned to park at Base Camp, and from there take a little pathway round the side of the French beach club where they could walk on the sand adjoining that owned by the exclusive establishment.

As they rode, he tried to work out what lay behind her apparent enthusiasm for his company. It wasn't just the way she had greeted him, he was sure she was gripping him tighter than before.

"How much do you know about what happened in my country?" she asked once they were walking along the strip of public beach between the club and the airport perimeter fence.

Peter shrugged his shoulders. "Not as much as I should," he admitted. "But I do know the resistance continues to be much heavier than the army expected. I think they thought they'd just roll up, stroll in and take over."

"There can be no forgiving what they did."

"I am sure that is true."

"I'm not talking about the fighting. I mean what they did to the people, people who weren't involved. People just trying to get on with their lives."

"It was like that in sixty-five. It's always the people caught in the middle who suffer the most."

"What is wrong with these people?" Francesca asked in exasperation. "Did their mothers teach them nothing? How did they turn out this way?"

"It's the army," Peter replied. "The army does it to them. It takes them when they're still impressionable boys and brutalises them until they are no more than mechanical beasts, automatons set loose by their officers to carry out their wicked desires."

"It is an officer I need to ask you about." Francesca stopped walking, turned and faced the sea. "How much do you know about your cousin, Rollo?"

"He's not my cousin!" protested Peter.

"He is the son of your mother's sister. That makes him your cousin."

"He has nothing to do with me. In my eyes Rollo represents everything that is wrong with this country."

"Do you know if Rollo was in Timor?"

"It's possible, but I do not know for sure. He spent a couple of years in the army before he came out here, but I don't know where he was posted. We're not exactly friends."

"He was there." She said it with finality, daring him to dispute her.

"Did you see him?"

"No, but I heard him. On Thursday he came over to the house, hoping to take Amanda out. It was then I recognised his voice."

"Are you sure about that?"

"His voice is one I would never forget, not if I live to be a hundred."

"What was he saying?"

"Oh, nothing much," Francesca said airily, her upper lip quivering as she tried to keep her voice from breaking. "He just stood by while his soldiers murdered what was left of my family when they'd finished beating us and raping me and my mother."

"My God!" Peter felt the blood drain from his face. Around them the waves continued to crash onto the shore, oblivious to the revelations being spilt out on the beach above. "Rollo presided over that?"

"He wasn't there when it happened, he turned up near the end."

"So how did you survive?"

"Somehow none of the bullets hit me when they started shooting. I pretended to be dead, the soldiers were in a hurry to move on to their next massacre, they left without checking whether I was still alive."

"Would Rollo recognise you?" Peter asked once he had had a chance to digest this information.

"I am certain he does not. It was dark, I was huddled in the far corner of the room, and he was standing in the doorway. He didn't see me, or any of us, as human beings. We were just a problem he had to dispose of."

"You are absolutely sure it was him?"

"I am sure. But I would like you to check for me. If you will."

"Of course, I'll do anything I can to help."

"Just find out what unit he served with and if they took part in the invasion. That would be enough proof for me."

"I can do that."

"Thank you. I appreciate it."

"Those other things you mentioned," Peter began hesitantly. "Did that all happen?"

"You are a kind man, Peter, too sensitive to say the words, so I will have to say them for you. Yes, they raped me. Six or seven of them, I cannot remember. They took turns and did the most horrid, disgusting things to me, things I thought it was not possible for one human being to do to another. But they did them all the same. I guess I did not know anything about life before that day. So you see, I am not who you thought I was. Are you sure you still want to take me out for a walk on a Sunday afternoon? I won't be surprised if you don't. Just find out about Rollo will be enough for me, and maybe if you could find it in your heart not to mention my shame to anyone else, I would be very thankful."

"Francesca, how could you say such a thing?" He moved closer to her and placed his arm around her shoulders, ignoring her half-hearted attempt to shrug it off. "I'll kill him," he continued, "I'll stab the bastard in his sleep, I'll pay someone to have him knifed in the street."

"No!" she said sharply.

"He doesn't deserve to live."

"I know that, and I've thought of doing the same thing myself. When I recognised his voice, I was working in the kitchen, preparing vegetables. I was holding a sharp knife in my hand, and I wanted to rush outside and sink it into his back before he knew what hit him. But I couldn't. Because there's more."

"More?"

"Yes, more. We had a baby, my little sister, Angelica. She was eight months old at the time. The soldiers took her away."

"Why?"

"Your cousin ordered them to. He said they weren't child murderers, and they should take her to the First Aid tent. But I have no idea whether they did or not."

"So she could still be alive?"

"That is what I also want you to find out. If that officer was Rollo, of course I would like to see him suffer the most painful death imaginable, but how does that help me if he takes the knowledge of what happened to Angelica with him? It is more important I find her, if she is still alive, than I have my revenge."

"I can't promise anything, Francesca, but I will do my very best. Finding out if Rollo was in Timor will be easy enough. The other thing will be more difficult, and may require delicate handling."

"I can't thank you enough, Peter."

"It is the least I can do. What happened to your people makes me ashamed to be an Indonesian."

"All I want is to find out what happened to my baby sister, and if she is still alive to try to help her. Do you know, when the soldiers were in our house she reached out to play with one of them?"

"It makes me sick to think of it." Peter spat out the words. "I'll get the truth out of Rollo if I have to wring his neck like a chicken."

"Tread carefully," Francesca warned him. "I have seen with my own eyes what these people are capable of doing."

"Don't worry, I won't do anything rash. I'll think hard about the best way to go about it."

"Peter, this means everything to me. When I left Timor, which I had to do after what happened, I knew I was leaving everything behind. I had just the clothes on my back and half a loaf of bread. I had no idea where I was going, and I thought the only way I could survive at all was if I became a completely new person. Then maybe I could exist in some faraway place somehow. It is Angelica who has destroyed that possibility. While there is the faintest chance her precious little heart is still beating, I cannot completely leave that part of me behind. I have to pursue it, even if it means I am humiliated in this place where I have begun to make a new life."

"You won't be humiliated, I promise you that," said Peter, taking her hand. "If anyone deserves to be disgraced it is Rollo."

"Rollo is from a rich and powerful family. I know these things matter. He will always be protected."

"I too am from a rich and powerful family," Peter said, "and I will protect you. Until now I have protested against injustice in this country and fought for change, but my cries were feeble because they had no focus. People looked at me, the hopeless idealist, and they laughed. But they won't laugh at this."

"Peter, I just want to find out what happened to my baby sister. I don't want to pick a fight with the whole Indonesian government."

"I know that. Don't worry, I won't do anything to put you or her in any danger."

"Do you think she is still alive? Tell me the truth, what you really believe, not what you think I want to hear."

"I think there is a good possibility. I know there is an orphanage outside Jakarta where some children of Fretilin soldiers killed in the fighting have been placed. It's a start."

"It is very kind of you to agree to help me," she said once again.

"It is my pleasure." He paused a moment, cleared his throat, then spoke. "Francesca, there is one other thing."

She stopped and looked directly into his eyes. "What's that?" she asked sharply.

"It cannot have escaped your notice that I am drawn to you."

Coyly she looked away, but Peter continued, trying not to stutter on his words. "I would like to take you out, I would like our friendship to continue, and maybe one day become more than just a friendship."

"Even after I told you about what happened in Dili?"

He nodded. "Even after everything you have gone through. It doesn't change anything about how I feel for you. But if we are to be friends, it must be because you want to be with me, and not simply because I may be in a position to help you find your baby sister."

"But I do enjoy being with you. You are a bit stiff," she laughed, "but I can tell you are a good man, you have a good heart. That is more important than anything."

"What I am saying is I want to help you, whether you accept my advances or not. My assistance doesn't have a price."

"Everything has a price, Peter. It's how the world works."

"Not this time, Francesca." He took her hand, which she had let drop, and they continued walking as the watery horizon moved closer and closer to kiss the setting sun, now a huge rich orange ball in the sky. Eventually the beach gave way to a narrow estuary where they stopped and turned to face out to sea. There they stood, hand in hand, looking first at the waves brought in on the high tide, then at each other. Their eyes met, they smiled briefly, then moved to return to where he had parked the bike.

20

It was a tight squeeze, but somehow Amanda managed to shift from underneath Eddie and navigate herself between his body and the wall so she could rest on his chest. As he rolled over to make space for her, she felt another rivulet dribble out from deep within, down the inside of her thigh onto the sheet below. Part of her wanted to reach for a tissue, but she quashed the urge and allowed herself to enjoy the wicked thrill of what had just happened between them. The one point in favour of the horrid, uncomfortable single metal bed squeezed into the corner of Eddie's portakabin was that it forced intimacy upon them. For Eddie had been intimate with her in ways she had not believed possible, leaving her feeling as raw as if someone had peeled away a layer of her skin. She felt she knew now what it meant to be possessed utterly by another soul, to willingly give herself up to another human being. Nothing, she thought, could shock her now. For this and more, she would be forever grateful to the man in whose chest she now buried her face.

Around them all was quiet bar the hum from the air conditioning unit. The curtain let in enough light from the electric bulbs gaily strung out between the rafter beams outside for her to be able to make out the utilitarian furniture filling out this most bachelor-like of crash pads. Outside a mosquito coil burnt away, its unmistakable citron aroma seeping through the air conditioning intake, a smell she would forever associate with thrilling, illicit sex. On the table a bottle of red wine, two thirds empty, sat next to a pair of empty glasses, drained to the tiny sediment grains scattered about the bottom. A packet of Camel lay on the bedside table next to Eddie's lighter and a small lamp. For now she was content to rest where she lay and gently twirl his soft fair hairs with her fingers. She needed to rest a while and let her body recover. They lay together like that, naked and half-sleeping but still conscious of their togetherness, for half an hour or more while the air conditioning cooled their bodies down.

It was Eddie who moved first, sliding his arm from under her to the pack of cigarettes on the bedside table.

"Would you like one?" he asked as he illuminated the room with his petrol lighter.

"I'll share yours."

She heard the crackle as the tobacco caught, then raised herself to sit up against the wall so she could see him properly. The air conditioning was beginning to give her a chill, so she pulled the single wool blanket up around her chin to resemble a Bedouin crouched around the dying embers of his fire.

"Tell me about Vietnam," she said as he passed his cigarette from his lips to hers.

"What do you want to know?"

"All of it. I want to know everything about you, I want to know everything you've done."

"God, I wouldn't know where to begin."

"How about at the beginning? Were you drafted?"

"No, I volunteered. Not that that means much – I would have been called up once I graduated from university. It was back in sixty-eight, I was just about to finish my degree and I'd heard about this programme the Army were running for helicopter pilots. I mean, I knew I was headed for 'Nam, but being in a helicopter sounded like more fun than ending up as a grunt on the ground, which was what I'd have been if I'd waited for them to come for me. So I applied. I knew nothing about flying, I'd only been in an airplane a couple of times, but I passed some aptitude tests and got in. In those days they were desperate for pilots. Most of the guys I trained with were straight out of high school, hadn't even been to college."

"What was it like?"

"The flying itself was fun, I liked it. And you could do stuff over there you would never get away with anywhere else. You learnt fast and became good at your job pretty quick. But at the end of the day, you were participating in a war, and most of the time you were just focused on getting through your tour in one piece."

"Did you ever get shot down?"

Eddie stubbed out his cigarette and ran his fingers gently across her belly. "Came close a couple of times, especially during my second tour when the VC had cottoned on to the idea of putting up walls of lead for us to fly through."

"Did you kill many people?"

"Directly, no. But that doesn't mean anything."

"What do you mean?"

"Well, I didn't kill anyone with my bare hands, and I didn't shoot anyone either. But that's only because it wasn't my job. I was just as much a part of the war machine as anyone. My flying skills put soldiers where they needed to be, and without them the things that happened couldn't have happened, or at least not in the same way. That's the point about modern warfare, everyone is implicated. No one gets off with a clear conscience, not even some fat-assed jerk handing out uniforms and blankets. It's just some people are closer to the reality of what the machine is doing than others, so it becomes more real, leaves more of an impression upon them."

"Do you mind me asking you about it?"

"No," he replied, but she could tell he was lying.

"You can always tell me to shut up. I won't mind."

"Amanda, I'll never tell you to shut up." He bent his head down and pulled her towards him, kissing her on the fore-head.

"It still haunts you, doesn't it?"

"Of course it still haunts me, it'll be with me until the day I die. You don't serve two tours of Vietnam and then go home and forget about it like you've been to a ball game. It was the children that got to me the most. I have a couple of nieces, they're four and six. Sometimes I'd go over to my sister's place after I got back and read to them, then watch over them while she and her husband went out. I'd creep up to their bedroom and just stare at them sleeping, those beautiful little girls fresh from a bath in their pyjamas, smelling of soap, innocently gripping their teddy bears as they dreamt their sweet dreams, and I'd think of what we did to children just like them, and of the parents who would have loved those children just like we loved ours. It makes me want to cry, it makes me terrified to ever have children of my own, it makes me loathe myself for allowing myself to be sucked into it in the first place."

"Is that why you came here?"

"Partly. The thing to remember, Amanda, is a lot of people were lied to over Vietnam in a lot of different ways, including the people who were there. For instance, we were told we had a career in the Army as pilots ahead of us if we wanted it, but that simply wasn't true. Round the time I joined up they were passing out around a hundred and fifty new pilots a month. Some died along the way, but a lot didn't, and by seventy-two when the war was beginning to wind down, at least for us, they simply didn't need us any more, and we found ourselves out on the street. I didn't feel too good about my country anyway, but that was the final straw. I cared about the guys I'd fought alongside, but the rest of them could go hang themselves so far as I was concerned. So when the only flying job I could find was out here, it wasn't the hardest decision to make. And the one positive thing Vietnam gave me was a love of Asia. I like the people, the food, the way you can just be yourself and no one seems to mind. It's easy to forget here – the money's good, the living's easy and if you're running from someone or something, you can put a hell of a lot more distance between you and whatever that is in a place like this than you can back home. Still catches up with you in the end, one way or another."

"When I'm with you, Eddie, everything seems so clear. I feel strong with you by my side. Do you promise you'll never leave me?"

"Leave you, Amanda? You've got to be joking!"

"Not even for something a bit more exotic? After all, this part of the world you so like is full of it."

"I've been waiting my whole life for you to turn up. Where have you been all these years?"

"Growing up, getting ready for you."

"We're here now, together, and that's not about to change. Though I'd probably better take you back to the ridge before your father gets half the Indonesian army out of bed looking for us."

"I know, it's horrible isn't it? Whatever we do just makes me crave for more. When we first went out, all I could think about was you having me, now I want nothing more than to sleep in your arms and wake up beside you."

"Then what will you want?"

"Oh, to have your babies and grow old with you at my side. You deserve to have children, Eddie, you don't need to punish yourself any more. I can't think of a better father than you. I can see us sitting side by side on our rockers on a wooden porch, the early evening breeze on our faces, a grandchild or two playing inside, holding each other's gnarled hands."

"Blink and we'll be there," replied Eddie. "Come on," he said, raising himself up onto his elbows. "I'd better get you back."

"Just once more, Eddie," she begged, pulling him back down on her. "Quickly, before we go."

"You're wearing me out, Amanda Cole!"

"I know, and you're doing the same to me, but we've all day tomorrow to recover."

"How can I say no?" he laughed. "Just looking at you makes me want to stay in the moment forever."

It was pushing eleven when, showered and dressed, they stepped out of the portakabin and picked their way down the wooden steps, taking care not to step on the chit-chits scurrying to and fro between the wooden stilts, towards Eddie's motorbike. The air was still warm, the saltiness from the nearby sea lingering to embrace them in its liberating balm. Two pilots sat at a table drinking from frosted bottles of Anchor. As they passed, one raised his towards Eddie with a knowing wink. Eddie briefly smiled back, more so as not to provoke any suggestive banter than to share in male camaraderie, then turned his attention to guiding Amanda towards his bike. Coming from his little air-conditioned box it felt good to be outside, and he found himself looking forward to the twenty-minute journey. He didn't need another glance at his watch to tell him there would be hell to pay at the other end, but it really had been her choice. Try as he had numerous times to suggest he ought to be getting her back, she had refused to budge, each time pinning him down with her body or another question. How he loved her for it.

He straddled his bike and lifted it off its kickstand, smiling at her as he made room for her to join him on the pillion. Once he had the engine running, she jumped up behind him with the ease borne of utter trust and frequent practice, wedging the little bag containing her fold-up hairbrush, diaphragm gel, spare pair of panties, toothbrush and lipstick between her belly and his back, before wrapping her arms around his waist and interlocking her fingers across his navel.

The guard waved them through with a grin that managed to remind Eddie it was time for another carton of Camel, and he made a mental note to pick one up when he next came over. He pulled up outside Amanda's house, braking gently and putting his left foot out to take their weight when their forward momentum died. Reluctantly, she prised her hands from his body and hopped off. Eddie was about to kill the engine when he saw a hall light flick on.

"I'd better go now," he said in a low voice, nodding towards the incriminating illumination.

She reached up to kiss him firmly on the lips, then broke off. "Ride carefully, my knight in shining armour."

"I wish I could take what's facing you behind that door for you."

"Oh, don't worry about that," she replied with an airy confidence he could tell was fake. "I can handle Mummy and Daddy."

"I'll see you the day after tomorrow."

"You'll be at the club?"

"Usual place, two o'clock."

"I'm counting down the minutes already."

"I won't come to the door."

"No, don't. Say good night now."

"Good night, Amanda. I love you."

"Good night, Eddie. I love you too." They kissed again and she was off down the short concrete pathway, leaving him to taste the bitterness of sudden solitude. He waited in the shadows of the streetlamps while she reached for her key, opened the door and disappeared inside, then pulled away with as little noise as possible. A middle-aged Indonesian was sitting in a rattan chair in the carport smoking a clove cigarette, but everyone else seemed safely tucked up in bed, the epitome of the respectable small American town they had done such a perfect job replicating. The Indonesian nodded at Eddie, briefly the two men's eyes met, then Eddie was off, back to his spartan camp bed now scented with the memories of his precious Amanda. Oh yes, he felt blessed indeed.

They were waiting for him just inside the Base Camp entrance, six of them armed with baseball bats and police truncheons. Two of them stood in front of his path, forcing him to slow the bike to a walking pace, while the others jumped him, wrenching him away from the bike, which fell to the ground, spluttered and went silent. Outnumbered and caught by surprise, Eddie was powerless to fight back to any effect, so he curled himself into a ball, shielding his head as best he could with his hands and arms while they laid into him. The first three or four blows stunned him so hard he barely felt the pain from the others as he tensed his body and tried to shield his vital organs from their blows. Down on the ground, his face pressed into the sandy track, the dirt filled his mouth and his nostrils, making it almost impossible for him to breathe.

Blow after blow rained down upon him, interspersed with kicks from feet shod in cheap training shoes. In the end he was saved by the two pilots who had saluted him with their beers less than an hour ago. Hearing a noise, they staggered out into the darkness to investigate, whereupon one of the gang barked an order in Bahasa. Immediately the others broke off and ran away from the untended Camp entrance into the night. Drawn towards him by his low groans, the pilots almost tripped over the motorbike before stumbling across him.

"Jesus Christ, it's Eddie!" exclaimed one in a drunken slur.

"Hey, are you okay, mate?" asked the other, leaning down towards his face.

Incapable of movement, Eddie lay there while they entered into a dialogue devoid in its drunkenness of all urgency.

"He looks pretty bad."

"Is he alive?"

"I don't know. Hey, Eddie! Can you hear me?"

Eddie moaned softly and moved his fingers.

"Yeah, there's movement there."

"Better get the doc up."

"You want to wait here or shall I?"

"I'll go call him. We'd better not move him until he arrives."

"Jesus, what a mess." The pilot leant down towards Eddie's face, close enough for Eddie to smell the warm beer on his breath. "Hang on in there, mate, we'll have you sorted out in no time."

"Looks like he was mugged," said his colleague.

"Whoever it was did a pretty shit job of it," replied the other. "They didn't even take his watch."

21

The club had been instructed to reserve an extra seat, and so when Harry turned up two minutes before the show began, there were four empty places in the middle of an otherwise fully taken front row, behind which sat a packed house. Harry quickly glanced at his watch as he showed first Carl, then Angie to their seats either side of him, leaving a single space for David next to his mother. Seven twenty-eight, perfect timing. He knew the festivities couldn't begin until his party was settled, and he could hear his mother's Episcopalian voice in his ear, chiding him for his lack of consideration for all those good people around him, reminding him that punctuality was the courtesy of kings. As they sat down, Harry turned to Carl with a smile.

"I told them to keep it as short as decently possible."

"Don't worry about me," replied Carl. "A career in the foreign service has hardened me to pretty much anything in the entertainment department. Last one of these I went to was in Bali, it lasted four and a half hours."

"I can promise we won't inflict that on you here."

"In fact, it was quite interesting, for the first forty-five minutes, that is. Then it became, how can you say it, a touch repetitive. Is that Reverend Ron back there?"

"Where?"

"Leaning up against that pillar. Tall, slim guy."

Harry tried to glance back without drawing attention to himself. "No, he's one of our finance guys."

"It must be the shirt. Same kind of shirt all the squares at college wore. You know, with the pens lined up in the breast pocket."

"Yeah, I know the type, I've got a whole closet full of them at home."

"I've never seen you wear one."

"I'm pulling your leg. I don't see Ron anywhere, but I know he's somewhere around. He flew down last night."

"Courtesy of Air Constar?"

"You said you wanted to see him. Shall I send you the check?"

"Save it for your tax return. Either way Uncle Sam picks up the tab."

They looked at each other in what felt to Harry like mutual understanding for the first time in their relationship. It was only a moment, for the house lights dimmed and Carl looked round towards the stage, which now resembled a jungle clearing with the yard to a small hut spotlit in the centre. The audience quietened at their cue and Harry turned to face the entertainment, adopting the tuned-out look of studied seriousness he deployed for such occasions. Neither traditional Indonesian music nor its counterpart in dance were his chosen forms of entertainment, and he fully anticipated ninety minutes of polite boredom during which he could escape into the kind of contemplative meditation that was all too elusive given his schedule of corporate and civic commitments.

Instead, he was treated to a crude political diatribe whose intent seemed solely to offend. Ostensibly the story of Indonesian independence, the parallels between Dutch political occupation and American economic colonialism were spelt out and rammed down the audience's throats through a series of gross caricatures and heavy handed skits. When a fat Indonesian, whom Harry vaguely recognised as one of the club kitchen porters, dressed as a Dutch soldier complete with pale pink make-up, began to batter a demure villager taking temporary leave from her station as a waitress in the restaurant bar, he felt the mood around him chill. Who the hell did these people think they were, he could sense the audience demanding, biting the hand that fed them so generously? He heard a chair pushed back half a dozen rows behind him, and out of the corner of his eye he saw Jack Sweeney, Operations Manager, and his wife ostentatiously pick their way to the aisle and march out the front exit, heads fixed forward. Mr Sweeney was followed by several of the more bullish expats, while the actors, clearly aware of the impact their re-enactment was having on their masters, continued to plough through their drama with a lack of enthusiasm that was discernible to the most casual viewer.

Suddenly, Harry felt the focus of the auditorium shift like a roving spotlight onto him. Everyone knew what was happening on stage; what they wanted to find out now was how he was taking it. If he joined the boycotters, it would effectively bring the show to an end; there would be vicious post mortems in the bars and public spaces, and who could tell, possible reprisals against the staff who had made up the acting troupe. Whatever the inflammatory content of the entertainment they were being treated to, that was not a desirable state of affairs. Funnily enough, although part of Harry thought he should be offended, the well of justified outrage was dry and he could only look upon the scene with detached curiosity. Who was it who felt like this, they needed to stage such a scene?

So he sat there, adopting the face of an unamused Queen Victoria as the show continued, acutely aware of Carl beside him silently weighing up every nuance. His decision to stay did achieve its purpose in stemming the tide of outraged departures, leaving the players free to resume their agitprop. Mercifully, the story quickly ground to its bleak conclusion whereupon the stage was recaptured by the dancers and musicians. Angie slid her hand over to Harry's and gave him a discreet but comforting squeeze. He let it rest there a while and turned to smile at her, grateful for her reassurance and support against the loneliness of his position.

"Do I detect a certain amount of hostility out there to what we're doing?" asked Carl once everyone had dispersed to various refreshment spots.

"I shouldn't read too much into it," replied Harry nonchalantly, reaching for a handful of peanuts.

Carl shrugged his shoulders. "Whoever staged that thing didn't leave any room for misinterpretation. At least there was no danger of me nodding off and embarrassing you."

"That's for sure," said Harry, relieved Carl seemed happy to laugh the episode off.

"Angie, that dress looks just great against your skin. Where did you get it?"

"Oh, it's something I picked up in Singapore."

"Jimmy Chan?"

"It's unusual for a man to know something like that. Harry couldn't name a single designer on Orchard Road, could you, dear?"

Harry grunted. "I may not recognise the names, but I know the prices."

"It's beautiful."

"Why, thank you, Carl. Harry, has anyone seen David?"

"I think he's over there with that Cole girl," replied Harry glancing around the three quarters full bar. Interestingly, no one seemed keen to talk to him, perhaps for fear he might grill them over their knowledge of or involvement in or opinion of the tasteless little drama they had just been treated to, and which everyone seemed keen to forget had ever happened. The author and director was certainly maintaining a low profile, for whilst Harry had been keeping an eye out for Peter, so far there had been so sign of him anywhere in the vicinity of the club public rooms. Waiters and bar staff had rapidly dispensed with their costumes, as if the garments were contaminated with radioactive waste, and assumed their club uniforms. Gradually they all moved out towards the balcony to watch the obligatory fireworks. Harry inhaled the warm evening air and listened to the sound of the crickets from the bushes nearby. It would be okay, he realised. The stupid play was already receding in people's memories like a loud embarrassing drunk who'd gatecrashed a polite cocktail party. Constar had brought the good life to too many people here for any upstart to unsettle it with a few inflammatory remarks. He'd have Benny take Peter aside and have a word with him, then forget about the whole thing.

As he leant against the railing he felt Angie nuzzle up to him. "You okay, darling?"

"Yes, I'm fine."

"I love you."

"I love you too."

"I'm proud of you too. You handled that real well."

"Thank you."

"Ignoring it was the right thing to do."

"I hope so."

"Anything else would have just played into their hands."

"That's what I was thinking. Where's Carl?"

"At the bar."

"You okay for something?"

"Yes, I'm fine. I think I'm ready to go home soon."

"Me too. We don't have to stay much longer, Carl can look after himself. I'll tell him you're tired."

Harry turned, taking his wife's waist in his arm, and led her through the crowd that opened before his procession, towards the front entrance where their car would be waiting. It felt good to have his feet firmly on the ground.

The meeting had been scheduled for eight o'clock the following morning in Harry's office, which took up almost a quarter of the top floor of the administration block. The office itself, which had been designed by a firm of architects in Houston, included a mini-bar, a leather sofa suite that wouldn't fit in most of his managers' living rooms, a shower room and even a single bed set up in an adjoining room. The first of many eye-openers as to how well Constar's top executives looked after each other, its excess offended Harry's puritan spirit and frequently caused him to wonder what actually went on in the higher echelons of the company back in the States.

Ron arrived promptly at two minutes to eight, but by eight fifteen there was still no sign of Carl. Harry, who had cleared his desk of any pressing correspondence a good half hour ago, was tired of moving papers around his desk and buzzed through to his senior secretary to have Ron shown in.

Harry was shocked to see the change a few short weeks in the jungle had wrought on Ron. Gone was that fresh-faced eagerness, burnt out of his skin along with that formidable aura of rectitude that Harry was sure he wasn't alone in finding irritating. When they'd first met Harry had felt the urge to apologise for the opulence of his surroundings. Now he just took his hand, showed the missionary to the leather sofas and offered him a coffee from the percolator just completing a fresh brew of the Sumatran mountain blend he'd acquired a taste for since it had been introduced to him by an obsequious Benny Surikano.

"I can never get over the great views you've got here, Harry," said Ron, admiring the vista that extended down their cordoned off compound all the way to the harbour.

"Yes, it makes a pleasant relief from some of the other things you have to look at from this position," Harry replied enigmatically. "Do you take cream with your coffee?"

"Is it UHT?"

"I'm afraid so. Not even we can obtain it fresh. It's the one luxury I really miss from back home."

"I'll take it black. Two sugars, please."

Harry poured two coffees and handed one across to Ron. "No sign of Carl yet, I see."

"Exactly who is this Carl?" asked Ron, taking a sip from his cup. "My, this coffee truly is excellent."

"It's good, isn't it? Carl works with the embassy in Jakarta. He does a lot of political analysis, research, that kind of stuff."

"You mean he's with the CIA."

"He's never introduced himself as such, but you get the general picture."

"What does he want from me?"

"I don't know, but I'm sure he'll tell you when he turns up."

"Do you deal with these guys a lot?"

"Some. They can be a useful source of information. At the end of the day we're all on the same side. We help each other where we can."

"You've certainly helped me, but I'm not sure how I can be of assistance to you, or to Carl."

"Nor am I, but he seemed keen to meet you. It's probably just more background stuff he's after – to fill out one of the endless briefings he has to write to continue justifying his existence to some sub-committee in Congress."

Ron shrugged his shoulders. "I'll do what I can. And while I'm here, I'd just like to say again how much all of us at the mission station appreciate the logistical support you guys have given us."

"Oh, you're very welcome, Ron. It's a pleasure to be able to support your work in a small way."

"Believe me, your contribution is not small."

"We're glad to help."

"You should come out some time yourself, and take a look at what we're doing."

"I'd love to," replied Harry non-commitedly, breathing a sigh of relief at a gentle tap on the door. "Ah, that sounds like Carl. Come in!" he called.

The junior of the two secretaries showed Carl in before bowing deferentially and retreating to her desk, softly shutting the door behind her. Harry stood up and crossed the room to greet him. Carl had the look of a man who had overslept and then dressed himself in a rush. His hair was still wet from the shower, and there was a small blob of gel above his lip where he'd nicked himself shaving.

"Hey, Carl, nice to see you," he said cheerily, offering his hand.

"Sorry I'm late, Harry, damn alarm clock didn't go off. It's one of those electric ones, if the current wavers during the night it slows down."

"No problem, no problem," replied Harry, brushing his irritation aside. "Can I get you a coffee?"

"You sure can. Black, straight up, two sugars please."

"You look as if you could use a tall glass of orange juice with it," said Harry, reaching for the fridge.

"Harry, you must be able to read my mind."

"Yeah, you'd better watch out with all those dirty secrets you've got stashed away at the back of it. Good night, was it?"

"I don't know about that," replied Carl, shuddering. "I met up with some of your pilots in the bar and ended up getting into a huge argument over Vietnam."

"Sounds familiar to me," said Ron. "My son's still in Canada, we've barely spoken for three years."

"These weren't draft dodgers, these were guys who actually fought there. Between these walls, I have to admit some of the things they were saying really did make me question the whole thing."

"Terrible things happened, I know," agreed Ron, "but we've got to remember when we went in there it was with the best of intentions. We didn't go there to destroy a country or kill its children, we did it to save the region from communism. At the time it seemed like the right thing to do. People forget that. All they do is focus on how badly it all turned out."

"All I can say is thank God we finally did get out. But talking of the spectre of communism, Ron, brings me very neatly to the purpose of this morning's little gathering." Carl helped himself to a couple of sachets of sugar, stirred the contents into his coffee, then gulped down the entire glass of orange juice in one go. "As you know," he continued, "when Suharto came to power eleven years ago he did a pretty effective job of suppressing the PKI. It may not have been very pleasant, but to the best of our knowledge no serious communist threat has ever been able to gain momentum in Indonesia during his time as president. As you can imagine, with Vietnam gone, we're especially keen to keep it that way. Now, Congress has dictated a whole bunch of stupid rules as to what we can and cannot do to help in this country, and all I can say on that subject is the deployment of US forces in any way, covertly or otherwise, is most definitely out of the question. But we can assist our Indonesian hosts in their part of the struggle to stem the scourge of global communism by using our intelligence and network of contacts to identify areas of concern they might then choose to investigate on their own. It's a question of resources really. With three thousand islands and a population of more than a hundred million people, it can be hard to know where to start looking."

"You think there's communist activity round where I'm working?"

"I don't know, Ron, that's what I'm asking you. What we do know is the PKI tends to stay away from the towns and cities, preferring to concentrate on villages where it can both indoctrinate a less well-educated population and evaporate into the jungle if government forces come their way."

"I don't have anything that would stand up as evidence in a court of law," Ron began hesitantly.

"We're not talking about proof here," Carl reassured him. "This is the intelligence gathering community. It's all about detecting patterns and understanding methods of operation, so we can begin to devise ways to counter those threats. The kind of tests you'd have to pass to satisfy a jury simply don't apply."

"I'm still not sure it's my place to get involved in all this," said Ron guardedly. "I came here as part of a mission to spread the good news of Jesus Christ to the people of these islands. I'm not sure it's appropriate to start fighting wars on behalf of the Indonesian government, which, between the three of us, seems about as close to a military dictatorship as it's possible to get."

"Let's not get too carried away here, Ron." Carl stood up to help himself to more coffee. "First of all," he continued, the coffee jug in his left hand, "we all know the Suharto government isn't perfect. Let's face it, it's a long way short of perfect. No argument there. But if you look at the problems they're facing, and the very real threats they have to deal with, you have to accept it's hardly fair to hold them to the same standards we'd expect of our own leaders. Look at it this way, if we tore Suharto down the way we destroyed Nixon, we've no idea who would replace him or whether there'd be another election in this country ever again. Second, you say it's not your place to start fighting wars here, Ron, but isn't that exactly what you chose to do when you decided to leave comfortable Oklahoma and come out here? You chose to engage in a Christian mission, to your credit I might say, and if that means anything to me, it's all about engaging in the battle between good and evil. And if communism isn't the manifestation of a godless evil on this earth, then I don't know what is. You're already involved, Ron, by being here, whether you like it or not, and if you think otherwise then all your mission amounts to is a huge exercise in personal vanity."

Harry watched from the sidelines as Ron absorbed Carl's assault, noting the missionary's face first relax then crack into an ironic smile.

"Gee, Carl," Ron replied after a moment's pause during which he took a large swig of coffee, "I sure wish my son was here to hear you accuse me of being soft on communism."

"You can laugh," Carl came back at him, "but it's a very real threat that Chinese, and now Vietnamese-sponsored activity could tip this sensitive and finely balanced country into the wrong hands. And you don't need me to tell you what they make of the good news of Jesus Christ in those places. So what's your problem?"

"My problem," Ron said slowly, "is I don't want to bring some kind of guerrilla war to the villages where I'm working.

I've got to know these people, I'm beginning to win their trust, and I'm making real progress in demonstrating just how rich and rewarding a life can be when you invite Jesus into it. These people aren't communists, quite the opposite, they're terrified of the communists."

"So there are communists operating in the region."

"I don't follow you, Carl."

"You said the people you work with are terrified of the communists. It follows there must be communists around for them to be terrified of."

"Certainly they're afraid of something," conceded Ron.

"Do you have any idea what that might be? Specifically, I mean."

"It's hard to tell. Most of what I hear amounts to no more than rumour or hearsay."

"Have you ever encountered any communists while working in and around Katapulu?"

"Personally?"

"Yes."

"No, I haven't. But that doesn't mean they're not around."

Carl looked up towards the ceiling. "It fits the pattern."

"Carl, what exactly are you proposing to do with this information?"

Carl shrugged his shoulders. "On its own, Ron, not a great deal. What it does is help build up a broader picture of what's going on across the country."

"That's not what I meant. Who will it be passed on to?"

"Oh, the usual government channels," Carl replied airily.

"What about the Indonesians?"

"We share certain bits of information," Carl said, this time more guardedly, "where we judge it to be in both our interests."

"Which this clearly would be."

"I couldn't say."

"No."

Harry felt it was time to intervene. "Listen Ron, all Carl is trying to say is if there is anything you know, anything you've picked up, that could help us piece together this picture of subversive activity across the region, it would be real helpful to all of us. This isn't some witch hunt, we're not asking you to write a list of names on a piece of paper, are we Carl?"

Carl shook his head vehemently. "No, no, not at all. This is nothing like that."

"Ron, we're all on the same side here," continued Harry. "Every time a country falls to the hammer and sickle, it increases the threat to the free world. A communist uprising, even if it wasn't successful, here in Indonesia would be bad news for all of us. It would be bad for you, it would be bad for me and my company, and it would be bad for the United States, whose interests Carl represents and to whom ultimately we all owe allegiance."

"Ultimately we all owe our allegiance to God," replied Ron.

"Well, it would be bad for him too," added Harry with a satisfied flourish.

Carl spoke up. "Ron, I've had a lot of experience in these matters, and I appreciate you don't want to invite trouble into your area. But pretending the problem's not there isn't going to make it go away. Believe me, these things are far better nipped in the bud before they mushroom into something none of us can control."

Ron took a deep breath, paused and then exhaled. "So, what do you want to know?"

"Just whatever you've heard or seen. It doesn't matter if it's hearsay or whatever, we'll filter out the trash and do any corroborating that's required."

"Where do you want me to begin?"

"At the beginning." Carl looked across at Harry. "Harry, do you have a jotter I could use?"

"Sure," replied Harry, crossing over to his desk to pick up a legal pad.

"Okay, Ron," said Carl taking the pad and clicking a stainless steel biro he'd removed from his shirt pocket, "let's shoot."

22

Peter was in his office after school had ended catching up with some paperwork when Benny finally caught up with him. He heard the familiar click from the steel tips of his uncle's cowboy boots on the concrete floor, incongruous against the silence after a morning of thirty children running, shrieking and shouting. Benny didn't bother even to knock, but simply barged in and slammed the door behind him.

"I thought I might find you here," he began.

Peter forced himself to remain firm. "It is where I work."

"You've been avoiding me."

"I've been busy."

"With this Mickey Mouse part-time job you call your profession?" Benny let out a sarcastic laugh. "I don't think so."

"Would you like to sit down?"

Benny tossed the chair beside him back and plonked himself down on it. He sat, legs spread apart, arms folded. Although Peter was supposedly in the commanding position, shielded behind his desk in his territory, he still felt the errant schoolboy.

Benny began by going straight to the point. "I think you have some explaining to do."

"About what?"

"You know damn well about what. That childish stunt you pulled the other day."

"Oh, that," Peter replied. "Oh, I forgot to ask, can I get you some tea?"

"No, you cannot, instead you can start by giving me an explanation for your behaviour." Benny looked hard at Peter, then extracted a pack of Dunhill from his breast pocket while Peter struggled for a reply. He realised then Benny had waited so long to pounce that Peter had let down his guard; now he struggled to think of anything to justify the fiasco. He'd wanted to force them to pause and think, to question what forces of exploitation propped up their privileged lives, but all he'd done was piss them off and harden their prejudices. He'd fully expected to lose his job, but even that political martyrdom was denied him, and instead he had to face the silent disapproval of his masters. To top it off, Harry Bird, whose disappointment Peter had so clumsily aroused, was actually a decent man whom Peter respected for his fairness and integrity. It had been a wearing few days. He wouldn't be doing it again, especially now he needed to enlist Uncle Benny's help on behalf of Francesca.

Peter watched Benny light his cigarette, fold his right boot over his left thigh and lean back, then flick a tiny piece of ash onto the floor. It was the kind of gesture an interrogator might make before going to work on a suspect. Though it annoyed Peter more than frightened him, he thought the better of drawing attention to it.

"I thought it might be an interesting idea to show people a view of our history a little bit different from the one they're accustomed to."

"Bullshit!" exploded Benny. "You took a captive audience of Americans and rubbed their noses in it, depicting white men as nothing more than a bunch of greedy thieving thugs."

"Actually, I was attempting to draw some parallels between our colonial past and how it was reflected in our present foreign policy."

"Don't you start playing the fucking clever dick with me!" Benny screamed directly into Peter's face. "We both know exactly what you were doing, you subversive little shit. You were stirring up trouble and drawing attention to yourself. No more, no less. Just like your father, and if you don't watch it you'll end up the same way."

"You leave my father out of this."

"Your behaviour has caused me huge embarrassment. I can hear them snigger, there goes poor old Colonel Surikano, he's the one with the mouthy nephew he can't control, who he has to keep out of trouble."

"You don't have to feel responsible for what I do," Peter said.

"Don't be so childish," snapped back Benny. "If it weren't for me, you wouldn't be here lording it over all the locals in the first place. You'd be an out-of-work schoolteacher who couldn't get a post as a janitor because you were considered a security risk."

"What do you care?"

"Personally, nothing. I despise you and everything you stand for. The only reason I do anything for you is out of consideration for my wife's feelings of pity for your poor mother."

"So it seems we are stuck with each other."

"Don't push me, I warn you. Family loyalty only goes so far."

"I'm well aware how far it goes," said Peter pointedly.

"What do you mean by that?"

"I think you know exactly what I mean."

"Then you'll also know it's not a good idea to cross me."

Peter's intuition told him to change tack. Benny was right, a head to head confrontation would leave one winner, and it wouldn't be him.

"Uncle Benny," he said, noticing Benny's mouth tighten in suspicion at his softened tone, "I am genuinely sorry my pageant caused you embarrassment. I didn't think through carefully enough how it would be taken, and I apologise for that."

"Are you making fun of me?"

"Absolutely not. Since it happened, I have had time to reflect on what I did, and I now realise it achieved nothing apart from upsetting a lot of important people and endangering a whole group of innocent little people. It was a stupid, thoughtless act, and I promise you now it won't ever happen again."

"You're damn right it won't happen again. You won't be given another chance to do something like that again."

"I'm not just talking about pageants," replied Peter patiently. "I'm talking about my whole attitude to life. Some things have changed in me."

"And may I ask what astonishing force has brought you to your senses?" Benny asked, his voice dripping with sarcasm.

Peter blushed, trying to keep his thoughts ahead of his words, which were revealing more than he had intended. Yet somehow he knew it all had to come out if he was to persuade Benny to help him. Uncle Benny, as had happened so often in the past, had to be let in on the secret. It was the only way to bring out the best in him.

"I've met someone," he began simply.

"Well, your mother will be relieved at least, she was beginning to worry you'd turn out to be a fucking homo. So who is the lucky lady who's captured the heart of the biggest loser in Kalimantan?"

Peter ignored the jibe. "She's the girl who came over from Timor on one of your boats. Francesca, she works in Dennis Cole's house."

"I know who she is," snapped Benny, who then smiled, shook his head several times before smacking his forehead with the palm of his hand. "Dear God, is there no end to the torment you are willing to put your poor mother through? Maybe it would have been better if you'd turned out to be a homo after all. If it isn't enough to keep her up all night fretting over when your communist sympathies are going to get you tossed in jail, now you tell me you're courting an amah!"

"First, I am not a communist, and second, she is from a perfectly respectable family."

"She's not even Indonesian!"

"Oh, really," replied Peter, his adversorial instincts momentarily giving his resolve for caution the slip. "I was under the impression the whole justification for the invasion and massacre your friends oversaw was based on the premise of reuniting our brethren from the twenty-seventh province with the motherland."

"You say you understand politics," growled Benny. "You don't need me to point out certain strategic realities our country faces."

"One of which is that, for better or worse, Francesca can well and truly consider herself an Indonesian citizen."

"That may be the case," conceded Benny, "but why her? I mean, she's a pretty girl, I can understand a man wanting to have a bit of fun with her, but marriage? There are dozens of eligible girls from good families, powerful families, who would be prepared to overlook your youthful indiscretions and set you on your feet again. What's wrong with them?"

"Nothing's wrong with them, Uncle Benny. It's just I'm looking for a partner to share my life with, not some political or business alliance to help further my career. It so happens I'm in love with her."

"You've always been naïve, Peter."

"That may be true, Uncle, but it's who I am."

"And is this Francesca behind your sudden desire to desist from being a complete pain in the arse?"

"Indirectly, I would say she is."

Benny grunted. "I guess she can't be all bad, then."

"She is a very fine woman, a woman of pride and integrity, who has suffered greatly at the hands of our forces."

"Haven't we all."

"Uncle, I need to ask you a favour."

"I was wondering when that was coming."

"I promise to change the way I conduct myself. No more sniping, no more protests, no more criticising the government or doing anything to cause you embarrassment. I plan to live quietly, work hard at my job and keep my head down."

"And in turn, what am I expected to do?"

"I need you to find something out for me."

"What's that?"

"When our army invaded Dili, they did some dreadful things to the people of that town."

"What of it? War is dreadful, that's the whole point. If you'd had the balls to serve your country, you'd understand that."

Peter forced himself to ignore Benny's contempt and continue. "Francesca's family suffered terribly, and most of them did not survive. They weren't Fretilin supporters or combatants, just innocent civilians caught in the crossfire."

"That's unfortunate, but it happens. There's nothing I can do about it."

"Rollo was involved."

Benny balled his hand into a fist and slammed it on the table so fast and hard it made Peter jump. "You keep Rollo out of this!"

"I can't, he was directly involved. He was there."

"I knew it! Yes, I knew it, it was too good to be true, the idea you'd somehow grown up and grasped an awareness of your responsibilities. I can see it now, it was no more than a ploy to dig even deeper in the dirt and spread your shit all over the place!"

"No, Uncle, that's not my intention at all," protested Peter. "I'm not trying to implicate Rollo in anything – he's the one person who emerges from the whole sorry tale with any degree of honour."

Benny looked suspiciously across the table at Peter, who continued after a moment's pause. "He was there, wasn't he?"

"Unlike some people, Rollo did his bit for Indonesia, and you know as well as I do he had the honour of serving as an officer in the Strategic Reserve Command. I have nothing but pride in his military achievements."

"His brigade was there, wasn't it?"

"Why don't you check for yourself?"

"I could, easily, but why don't you just tell me?"

"He was there, yes," admitted Benny grudgingly, before adding firmly, "doing his patriotic duty as a soldier."

"I'm not disputing that," Peter said. "Unfortunately, some men under his command didn't quite share Rollo's sense of honour, and engaged in atrocious acts against innocent people during the invasion."

"Now, if you're suggesting…" Benny's voice rose again in anger until Peter held up his hand to quieten him.

"I'm not suggesting anything of the sort. Apparently Rollo wasn't there when these acts occurred, Francesca is adamant about that. But he did turn up later, and this is where I need your help."

"I don't see how I can help you. I wasn't there, I retired from the army years ago."

"We both know you never retire from the Indonesian army, you just get promoted to its business wing."

"I still don't see what I can do. If this girl's family suffered during the Timor integration I'm very sorry about that, but you'd have to apply to the appropriate authorities."

"I'm not interested in applying to anyone. It's not compensation or even justice I'm after."

"Then what do you want?"

Peter spoke deliberately, holding the table edge with both hands in an attempt to moderate the rage he felt welling up inside. "Rollo turned up at Francesca's house when members of his platoon were in the process of murdering her family."

"This was a war, Peter."

"Uncle, it was murder. Nothing less. But that is not my point. Rollo interrupted this massacre, and when he did, he noticed there was a baby in the house. A baby girl, eight months old at the time, Francesca's little sister, her only surviving relative, if indeed she is still alive. Whatever else he may have done, to his eternal credit Rollo ordered the baby to be taken to an army First Aid tent."

"And was she?"

"This is what I am asking you to find out. Rollo was ordered away from the house to another position which had come under fire just as he gave that order. The baby was taken away; she was alive when she left, but Francesca has no idea what happened to her or where she went."

"What is the baby's name?"

"She is called Angelica, but no one would know that."

"Hmmm."

"What about that orphanage near Jakarta, the one Tien Harto is patron of?"

"The one taking in the victims of the Fretilin terror?"

"That's one way of putting it."

"I thought you'd agreed to drop the sarcasm."

"I'm sorry, Uncle, you are right. It's just I read somewhere some children who had been orphaned in Timor were placed there."

"It's possible. I'll see what I can do."

"Thank you. I appreciate it very much, and so does Francesca."

"I'm not doing it for you. Or her, come to think of it."

"I don't mind who you're doing it for, so long as we find out the truth."

"She may not have survived, or she may have survived and already been adopted. In which case there's not a whole lot I can do. So don't get your hopes up too high."

"Whatever you can do, I'll be grateful for."

"I am going to Jakarta early next week for some business. I will try and call in on Tien. She will see me if she is in town – she still remembers how I helped keep her husband's battalions supplied when he was taking on Sukarno, even if he seems to have forgotten."

"Uncle, may I ask you something?"

"You can ask, I don't promise to answer."

"How close were you to the President? I've heard the stories, but I've never dared to ask."

Benny breathed out deeply, stretching his frame while he seemed to gather his thoughts from amidst the numerous memories swirling around his head.

"There was a time we were quite close," he began, "but it was always a political alliance, based on a shared vision we held for our country. We worked well together, and we trusted each other, but somehow we could never relax in each other's company. Maybe it was the situation, maybe just our personalities. So it never became a true friendship in the way it did with some of the other old-timers he surrounded himself with."

"What's he like?"

"Suharto?"

Peter nodded.

"He's unknowable. People say they know what he's really like, or they understand what makes him tick, but all they see is the face he decides to show them that minute. He's spent so long juggling factions all around him I doubt anyone ever gets to see what he's like inside, who the real man is. Maybe Tien Harto does, then again maybe there are areas even she can't penetrate."

"Do you ever wish you'd stayed in Jakarta? You'd probably be a general by now."

"What is this, confession hour? I came here to ask you some questions, not have you interrogate me!"

"I'm sorry, Uncle, I didn't mean to be rude. I was just curious, I don't know anyone else who is that close to the centre of power."

"I don't have any regrets about the choices I have made," Benny replied primly, pushing his chair back to stand up. "I have to go now. I will make what enquiries I can, and in return I don't expect to have to reprimand you again for your behaviour."

"Uncle, I am very grateful for your help, and I promise you, you will not hear another squeak out of me. I intend to live out my days as a humble schoolteacher in peaceful obscurity."

"A wise decision," said Benny as he moved towards the door. He turned to face Peter, and flashed him a smile. "A very wise decision. There are plenty of worse ways to live, I can assure you. Maybe you are actually a little bit smarter than I thought."

"I hope so."

"Well, if you are, I know which side of the family it came from," he said and then left, softly closing the door behind him before Peter had a chance to think of a reply.

He listened for the familiar click of his uncle's boots to fade away, then leant back in his chair to consider what he had just done. He had abased himself in front of a man he had spent his entire life despising, for the sake of the woman he loved. He had abandoned every political principle he'd ever held to intervene in the fate of a baby he'd never met and wasn't even sure was still alive. It was irrational, it made no sense in the belief system he had grown up in and taken on as his own, it was an intellectual betrayal on every level. Still, as he searched his soul for some new ballast, he found himself incapable of mustering the self-loathing he believed should naturally follow such an act. Instead, he felt light-headed and centred, focused for the first time in his life on some greater purpose that actually meant something to him as a person, rather than an abstraction aimed at the greater good. He couldn't explain it to himself any better than that.

23

Benny was waiting for Rollo when he sauntered in later that evening after an afternoon preening his athletically toned body at the club. The two of them hadn't spoken properly since Rollo had been stood up by Amanda; they had danced around each other, nodding in the hallway or taking their meals in front of the television where the steady diet of dubbed American cop shows precluded the necessity for anything as uncomfortable as meaningful conversation. Naturally, Benny had had a full account of the disastrous evening from Stephen, and he had deliberately avoided raising the subject. He felt his son's humiliation as keenly as if it had been his own, and he would have loved nothing more than to have gone round and given that Cole brat a good hard slap. Worst of all, so far as Benny was concerned, was the predictability of the whole episode. He had no wish to shame his son further by lecturing him on how he had told him so, but how he wished Rollo hadn't had to learn the hard way. His privileged upbringing had shielded him from the squalid fact that trumped all others; no matter that Rollo was rich, good looking and well connected, a girl like Amanda would never see past the colour of his skin. Poisoned since birth by her crass mother, she would forever consider anyone of non-Caucasian birth to be a fundamentally inferior form of human being. Benny could afford to laugh at such basic ignorance, but he knew Rollo could not. He was still too insecure in the white man's world, despite Benny's conscious efforts to groom him in western ways and shower him with their toys.

"Hey, Rollo," he called from his Lay-Z-Boy when he heard the door open and his son attempt to slink through to his room. "Come here a moment, will you?"

"What is it Dad?"

Benny looked his son up and down as Rollo cautiously picked his way past the furniture into the living room. He needed a damn good haircut, but other than that Benny had to concede Rollo was shaping up well. He wore the Rolex Benny had presented him on his successful return from Timor with just the right insouciance, and his physique managed to add a tough edge to an outfit that could make a weaker man look like a spoilt playboy fop. Benny was keen to see the change Harvard would bring; hopefully, it would open his eyes so wide the likes of Amanda Cole would be all but forgotten by the end of his first week.

"Sit down, son," he said, gesturing to the twin Lay-Z-Boy beside him. "First fix yourself a drink."

"I think I'll have a scotch, Dad."

"Great idea. You can get me one too." He watched Rollo flinch as he passed him on his way to the drinks cabinet. He waited until Rollo had added some ice and a dash of soda to their glasses, then continued. "Son, I have a little job for you."

"What sort of job?" Rollo replied guardedly, passing a glass to his father before sitting down himself.

"Nothing too complex, just a little recce mission."

"Oh yes?"

"I want you to fly up to Gunpura and take a look round a Christian mission station being run by an American priest."

"What for?"

"There have been a few reports of possible communist activity in some of the villages in the area. Have a sniff round, ask a few questions, see what you can find out."

"Who wants to know?"

"I shouldn't worry about that, just do it for me, will you?"

Rollo shrugged his shoulders. "Sure. If that's what you want."

"I'd appreciate it."

"No problem. How will I get up there?"

"Take one of the company choppers. I've okayed it with Base Camp, just let them know when you plan to go."

"What's my cover?"

"If anyone asks, just say one of the churches in Java is thinking of setting up a similar operation and they want to see how it's done."

"But I'm a Muslim."

"They won't know that. Praise their work and all that shit, then gently lead them round to the challenges they face, including communist resistance, and see where it leads you."

"Sure thing, Dad."

"Quite frankly Rollo, the whole thing's a bit of a waste of time. There probably are a few reds hiding out there in the bush, but I doubt they're any real threat to anyone. I don't expect you'll find much, so you'll just have to take what you get and pad it out in your report. I'll dig out some general background stuff you can use, it's only low grade intelligence, probably ten years out of date by now, but you can lift some figures and tweak them a bit. It's just I've been asked a favour, and I don't want to go back empty-handed, especially as this came through today." Benny pointed to a large manila envelope resting on a side table.

"From Harvard?" Benny thrilled to hear the excitement in his son's voice, to see his face light up in pure joy.

"Confirmation of admission, US student visa, accommodation details, an open return from Singapore to Boston via San Francisco." Benny smiled. "Harry Bird handed it to me this afternoon."

"It's really happening!" Rollo pulled at the open ended envelope and tipped it up, excitedly spreading its contents over the carpet. "I hardly dared believe in it, but it's here, isn't it? They won't take it away now, will they?"

"It's here, all right," confirmed Benny. He reached down and patted his son on the shoulder. "No one's going to take it away from you. It's yours, I've seen to that, and what's more you deserve it."

"Thank you, Dad." Rollo looked up to meet his father's loving look. "This means everything to me."

"Son, you don't understand the half of what this means to you, and to me, too. But that's okay, in time you will."

"How can I ever repay you for this, Dad?"

"The best way you can repay me is by having the time of your life at Harvard, getting yourself a first class MBA, then coming back to play an important part in running the future of this country. The opportunities will be there, don't worry, I'll see to that as well."

"I promise you, father, I'll make you proud of me."

"I am already proud of you, my son." Benny reached down again and this time placed his arm all the way around Rollo's shoulder. As he did, he was overcome with love for the strength and vulnerability contained within that young but fully formed frame. It seemed only yesterday he had held him as a baby in his arms. Benny allowed himself to relish his son's physical being a moment longer, then released his grip and fell back into his chair. "There is, though, just one thing I need to ask you about."

A look of guilt clouded Rollo's joyful face like a tropical squall, causing Benny to feel a dreadful sense of foreboding for what he was about to hear.

"What's that, Dad?" The warm bond between them had evaporated; Rollo now sat before him, suddenly defensive and evasive.

"It's no big deal, son, nothing to worry about. It's just something that happened while you were over in Timor."

"You look fucking terrible."

"Thanks, Mick. You look pretty good too."

"How you feeling, mate?"

"I have to say, I've been better."

"Any closer to finding out who did it?"

Eddie shook his head. "Not really, other than it was a professional job. I've a few ideas, but nothing I can prove."

Mick swung his ancient, ash and coffee stained swivel chair towards Eddie and tutted as he smiled. "'Fraid that's what happens, mate, when you play around with jail bait."

"She's not jail bait," Eddie snapped back irritably.

"I can't think of any other reason. You don't owe anyone round here money, do you?"

"No."

"And you haven't had some fun with some local good-time girl who turns out to be the Chief of Police's only daughter?"

"Of course I haven't."

"Nah," conceded Mick, "you wouldn't have crawled away to tell the tale if you had. I reckon her old man set it up."

"Dennis Cole? Surely he wouldn't do that!"

"He might, if he was pissed off enough at you. One thing's for sure, he knows all the right people to arrange for it to happen."

"I don't think Dennis would do that. Besides, I'm not doing anything wrong. Amanda's eighteen," adding after a pause, "almost."

Mick raised an index finger and smiled triumphantly. "Well, Eddie, it would be my guess it's the almost bit that's bothering Dennis."

"He never said anything to me."

"Why should he? He has Benny Surikano and his boys to do all the talking he needs for him. Speaking of which, a little job's come in from him for you."

"For me?"

"For someone, but you're the one who's going to do it. He wants us to fly his kid up to that clearing we cut west of Gunpura. You know, the one near where that jackass bible thumper has his outfit."

"Rollo wants to go there?"

"Apparently so. I guess no one told him Club Med decided not to set up a resort there after all."

"Can't someone else do it?"

"Not today they can't," snapped back Mick. "You've been back flying three days now, what's your problem?"

"I'm still trying to ease myself back into it."

"What do you think this is?" exclaimed Mick, throwing his hands up to the pilot roster. "I can't make it much gentler. It's not as if I'm asking you to make a foul weather landing on a supply ship rocking around in a force eight!"

"I know that, Mick, and I appreciate it. It's just Rollo, that's all."

"You don't have to talk to him. Just drop him off and go back to pick him up a bit later on."

"Sure, Mick," replied Eddie gruffly. "Has the ship been gassed up yet?"

"On the pad, gassed up and ready to go. Once you've had your walk round, you can go get yourself some breakfast."

"Is he here yet?"

Mick shook his head. "Haven't seen him. Benny said he'd be here for nine, which gives you forty five minutes to sort yourself out."

Eddie strolled out to the apron, donning his sunglasses to shade his eyes, one of which still bore a purple bruise, from the early morning glare. The heat bounced straight off the apron, while the humidity embraced him like a hot wet blanket. It was going to be a warm one, even by Bandakan standards, and he could already feel his rubber-soled flying shoes picking up globules of molten asphalt. Over by his Huey four men in overalls loaded a pallet of cardboard and plywood boxes into the rear compartment with a lethargy so refined it could only have been conditioned in an environment of equatorial temperatures and eighty-five per cent unemployment.

Satisfied with his walk round, he shuffled back to the Base Camp portakabins, still limping slightly from the bruising on his left leg. A fortnight on, most of the swelling had receded, and in the past few days he had begun to feel like himself again. For a week he had lain in bed recovering while his body mended itself and his mind tried to work out whether he was a victim of circumstance, the wrong person in the wrong place at the wrong time, or the object of some deeper grudge. Those long days spent flat on his back in the darkened portakabin had been relieved only by Amanda's daily visits, when she brought little treats and the radiance of her sunny presence. She would sit at the end of the bed, smiling at him as she stroked those parts of his body she could touch without causing him to wince in pain. Every so often, she would break off to add some tiny feminine dimension to the room – a small jug of flowers, an embroidered cushion she'd brought from home – which Eddie could stare at for hours on end when she was gone. The bastards had hit him hard, but by some miracle he'd escaped without any broken bones. Doc Betts had given him some painkillers, which Eddie was trying to use as sparingly as possible, but other than that it had been a case of resting up and letting nature do its repair work. A week ago he'd emerged from his lair, and two days ago he'd flown for the first time since the attack, a short hop around the bay with another pilot alongside him. Both had concluded, to Eddie's great relief, that his reactions and confidence in the air didn't seem to have been adversely affected.

He was no closer to identifying the culprit or culprits, and he was beginning to accept the mystery might never be solved. That was Bandakan for you. If indeed Dennis had been behind it, which Eddie doubted, his strategy had backfired badly, for Amanda was even more devoted and single-minded in her love now that she was nursing him.

He lined up with the other pilots, transients and hangers-on in the canteen, taking a tray and loading it up with bacon, eggs, tomatoes and a couple of pieces of toast, together with a large glass of orange juice and a cup of strong black coffee. He found a table in the corner of the canteen, hoping to remain undisturbed, and tucked into his breakfast while he mulled over some of the options that lay ahead. Foremost in his mind was Amanda. Perhaps the mugging was a sign to move on, to begin a new life where they would be known as a couple from the outset, free from the sniggers and taunts. There were plenty of flying gigs around for someone with his experience and contacts, and it shouldn't be too difficult to set something up in the Philippines or Malaysia. Of one thing he was now certain; wherever they chose to go, she would follow him.

He ate his breakfast in silence, and was just finishing off with the first cigarette of the day when he saw Rollo approach his table, a small leather bag slung around one wrist, his other hand twiddling a pair of expensive Polaroid sunglasses.

"Yes?" he asked frostily.

"You're flying me out to Gunpura," Rollo replied, the arrogance oozing through his voice.

Eddie crushed his butt in the ashtray and stood up. "I'll see you outside in five minutes."

"Where are you going?"

"To the bathroom. Why, do you want to hold my dick while I take a piss?"

Rollo ignored the jibe, turned on his heels and strutted out of the canteen, while Eddie picked up his empty coffee cup and replenished it from the filter machine. He returned to his table and lingered over it while he smoked another cigarette. Finally, he stubbed that one out too, pushed the remains of his coffee aside and walked across to his portakabin where he brushed his teeth, before collecting his maps and flight plan.

Rollo was waiting for him on the veranda, sprawled back in a wicker chair, one leg crossed over the other, his feet fully stretched out so there was no missing the leather cowboy boots protruding from the flared Wrangler jeans.

"Come along, sunshine," said Eddie, "it's time we were off."

Rollo stood up and haughtily followed Eddie out onto the apron, where Eddie slipped on his shades.

"You ever flown in a helicopter before?"

"Of course."

"How long do you need to be there?"

"Six hours should be enough."

"There's not a whole lot to see."

Rollo ignored the invitation to elaborate on the purpose of his trip, and they walked in silence across the rest of the apron to the now fully laden helicopter. Eddie opened the co-pilot's door for Rollo, pointed to a headset, then stood back as Rollo awkwardly climbed in and tried to make sense of the seatbelt. Eddie slammed the door shut behind him, walked once more around the tail of the ship to check for any trash or debris, then climbed in on the pilot's side. Donning his own headset, he switched on electrical power and looked over to Rollo.

"Can you hear me?"

Rollo nodded.

"Press that button there if you want to talk."

"Like this?"

"You got it. Now sit back, don't touch anything and enjoy the ride." Eddie turned to face the familiar dials and tried to expel his passenger from his thoughts while he went through the start up sequence. The engine fired and above them the blades began to cut through the sticky morning atmosphere, at first heavy and reluctant, then firm and decisive, rotating faster and faster, until Eddie tilted the pitch and they shot upwards. Quickly he took them up to five hundred feet, turned out to sea and climbed another fifteen hundred feet before turning back in a gentle arc towards the coastline and the jungle, where he climbed another two thousand feet before levelling out to head north-east, keeping the sea to his right and the huge mass of land to his left. From above it seemed vast and endless, but even in the twelve months Eddie had been flying these skies he'd seen the area succumbed to the bulldozer almost double in size to feed the insatiable Japanese timber market. Soon the whole coastline would be opened up with kampongs and clearings, as more people made their way across the sea from the overcrowded islands of Java and Sumatra to seek out the opportunities in this new Wild West.

Eddie glanced across at his passenger, noticing the way Rollo gripped the door handle and kept his eyes fixed on the horizon. He smiled at the telltale signs of the nervous flyer, then smiled again as he kicked the ship sharply to the right and waited for the predictable look of shock to spread across Rollo's face.

"How you doin', Rollo boy?" he crooned into the intercom, putting on a cowboy accent.

Rollo scowled at him, but said nothing.

"Hey look, no hands!" Momentarily Eddie lifted both hands from the controls and waved to his passenger. This time Rollo's fingers scrambled for the intercom button.

"What the fuck you doing, man? Are you crazy?"

"You know how to fly a Huey, Rollo?"

"Get your hands back on the stick!" he shouted.

"I'm the captain, I give the orders round here," replied Eddie with a grin. "I think it's time to play Let's Remember. You ever played that game?"

Rollo looked confused, then relieved as Eddie reached forward to take back the controls.

"I don't know what you're talking about," Rollo snarled. "Just fly the goddam helicopter."

"Not so fast, Rollo boy, not so fast. Your Daddy's not sitting here with us now. I guess you never have played Let's Remember. It's very simple, really. You remember the truth, then I remember how to fly this helicopter." And to Rollo's horror Eddie rolled the throttle towards him, pushing down the collective as he did, and folded his arms as he turned towards Rollo like a dogged interviewer who's finally managed to pin down an evasive politician with a question he can't wriggle out of.

Immediately the machine began to drop as the engine revs died and the blades auto-rotated against the weight of the fuselage, braking its descent but no longer pulling the ship forward. The noise around them withered away too, making it impossible to ignore the extent to which they were alone with each other. Rollo reached again for the intercom button; Eddie could see he was struggling to control his fear.

"Man, are you crazy?"

"Oh, I'm certifiable. Didn't they tell you?"

"Start this thing up at once!"

"No problem, just as soon as you tell me who paid to have those goons beat me up."

"What are you talking about?"

"Think hard, Rollo, you haven't got that long to remember. I want the truth now, did you set that up?"

"You're crazy, man!" Eddie could see Rollo was beginning to panic, fighting the urge to reach for the controls himself.

"You know how to start one of these birds up again?" Eddie asked genially. "Didn't think so. So, the truth please. Think hard, dig deep into your memory, just look down at those trees getting larger every second if you need some help. You've all the time in the world. In fact, that's a lie, I reckon you've got about another forty-five seconds."

"I didn't do it, man, I swear! I wasn't there! Now, start that fucking engine!"

Eddie made an exaggerated play of rubbing his chin as if to ponder this answer, while keeping one eye on the altimeter, which had passed through two thousand feet into the fifteen hundreds.

"You were behind it."

"Yes! Yes! I'm sorry, it was me!"

"Why?"

"I don't know."

"Why?" Eddie was shouting now, relishing each drop of sweat pouring from Rollo's petrified face.

"Start the engine, please, I'm begging you!"

"It was because of Amanda, wasn't it? You were jealous."

Miserably, Rollo nodded.

"So what did you think having me beaten up would achieve?"

"I don't know."

"Not good enough, Rollo. Come on, we're playing 'Let's Remember', in case you've forgotten. Concentrate, focus your thoughts on those trees. They're getting bigger and bigger. Can you make out the branches?"

"You start that engine up and I'll tell you everything you want to know. Come on, man, we're going to crash."

With the altimeter in the five hundreds, Eddie was reaching the limits of his bluff, so he satisfied himself with this partial confession and rolled the throttle back to his left.

Nothing.

He rolled off the throttle and tried again, still the engine didn't take.

Forcing himself to remain calm, he waited a full five seconds, then tried again.

"What the fuck are you doing, man?" screamed Rollo, not bothering with the intercom. "I told you what you wanted to know. Now start up the engine again!"

"Shut up!" snapped back Eddie.

"You can't do it, can you?"

"I said, shut the fuck up!" They were at two hundred feet now, the ground was approaching fast and Eddie could make out a lot more detail in the trees than he would ever have wished. Again he tried to reignite the engine, and again he failed. Was it flooded or had the humidity flared it out? Not that it mattered, they were going to pancake straight into the trees, and he hadn't even bothered to scout a possible crash landing site. He pulled back on the stick to slow the aircraft, at the same time pulling up the collective to put some pitch back into the blades and slow their descent. They were sinking, and with no power from the engine, the fuselage was straining to turn with the blades, so he gave the right pedal a quick kick to bring them in straight. He cursed himself for his stupidity; three and a half thousand hours and over four hundred combat missions without so much as a scratch, and he had to humbug out pulling a dumb-fuck stunt like this. It was so cruel, just when he had no much to live for, just when he should have known better, just when he should have taken more care of himself. Too late, the engine reignited a moment before the first branch clipped the left skid, knocking the ship onto its side and causing the main rotor to slash into the jungle like a massive circular saw, chopping off the blades three feet at a time. One of them must have hit a large branch because it suddenly wrenched itself away from the transmission, jerking the fuselage around and upside down in a whiplash movement that banged Eddie's head into the metal door frame. He was dazed but still conscious when the airframe crashed through the foliage to hit the ground and roll on its side. His last image was Rollo's perplexed expression mouthing a simple "Why?" before the fuel tank behind them exploded, enveloping them in orange and black flame. The heat seared conscious thought from him, giving him time only to conjure up one final picture of Amanda, acknowledge the beauty of what might have been, and regret what never would.

Later that day, when the last of the flames had ebbed away, the first scouts hired from the kampong ten miles to the south picked their way towards the scorched clearing where the wreckage of the helicopter lay in two charred pieces. Stumbling across the open cockpit, a still recognisable frame of twisted metal, they saw two bodies strapped to the remains of the seats. They had been told one was Indonesian, the other white, but both were so badly burnt it wasn't possible for them to make out which was which.

24

News that a Constar helicopter had gone down somewhere over the jungle spread fast through the expat communities, and Amanda heard about the crash a few hours before she was able to confirm Eddie had been in it. Dennis had been the first to know, through the company radio network, and he had hesitated from mentioning the incident over lunch for fear of needlessly worrying his daughter. But Amanda soon found out. Everyone on the ridge was talking about it, only no one knew the identity of the crew, or if there had been any survivors.

Constar operated four Bell Hueys but there were double the number of pilots, so if you discounted Shaky Mick, there was only a one-in-seven chance that Eddie was involved. Besides, he was one of the best pilots in the business, and if anyone was likely to crash, it wouldn't be him. Try as she did to reassure herself that the laws of probability suggested Eddie was at this very moment perched on a stool in the Base Camp bar analysing the possible cause of the crash with his fellow pilots, she could not avoid the intuition which delivered a single, powerful, chilling message. He had been taken from her.

Crazed with anxiety, she demanded to be driven down to Base Camp, so she could find out for herself, touch him, hear his reassuring voice. Dennis refused to let her have the car, and made a point of walking round to the servants' quarters with her tagging alongside and forbidding anyone from taking her anywhere, on the grounds the flight crews had enough to worry about without a hysterical teenager getting in everyone's way. Amanda swore to her father she would never forgive him his cruelty, and promptly began planning another way of getting down to the airport. She found a club waiter coming off shift who was prepared to take her on the back of his bike for 500 rupiah, but Dennis had already alerted the guards on the main gate, who feared for their jobs more than the wrath of a frustrated young woman.

In despair, Amanda returned home, then walked across the road to the company office, where she apologised to her father for her behaviour and begged him to share any news he might have. By now Dennis had had an hour to make further enquiries, and it was with a heavy heart he stood up from his desk, crossed the room to the door and softly pushed it shut.

"You know, don't you?" Amanda began, her voice cracking.

Dennis put his arm around his daughter. "I'm afraid so, my darling."

"It was Eddie." There was a numb, atonal quality to her words, and Dennis knew she was going to take it even harder than he'd feared.

"Yes." He paused a moment. "It was Eddie."

"Did he manage to survive?" She looked up at him in desperation, willing him to change the ending to this particular story, just as he had amended the fairy tales he'd told her as a child to be more to her liking. But this time there was nothing he could do to protect her from the pain he would have done anything to take on for her if he could.

"No, he didn't. They were both killed. The only mercy was it was instant."

"Who was the other person?" Amanda asked without knowing why.

"Rollo Surikano, Benny's son."

"Poor Rollo," she said flatly. "Is Benny alright? That's a silly question."

"He's devastated," replied Dennis. "Rollo was his only son, he adored him."

"And I adored Eddie."

"I know you did, my little petal," and he hugged her tight as she broke down, howling hysterically and banging her fists against his back. Dennis, who had never really held anything against Eddie, now cursed him for whatever carelessness it was that had caused his helicopter to crash and bereave his daughter like this. Then he thought momentarily of Benny, and felt a pang of guilt at his relief it had been Rollo and not Amanda at Eddie's side when the chopper went down. This, he could handle; that, he wasn't sure of his ability to survive. What agonies must be going on in the Surikano home right now? Dennis tried to picture the scene: curtains drawn, Benny bleary-eyed and beaten, Mrs Surikano (Dennis realised he didn't even know her first name) stoic and upright, ready to fall apart the moment anyone touched her. What despair would emerge from behind those walls, what reason to carry on living would they be able to come up with? Guiltily, Dennis thought of the Harvard scholarship Benny had pressured them into funding, and how he was now spared the headache of justifying it to an aggressive audit team from Houston. He felt shitty at his relief, for he genuinely liked Benny, and didn't begrudge the old rogue for simply trying to do the best he could for his boy.

In his arms Amanda continued to sob, and he continued to hold her, gently stroking her shoulders and back with his hand. The front of his shirt was now blotted with her tears. He led her round to the corner of the room and placed her down on the leather sofa, sitting down beside her with his arm around her shoulder. She continued to weep, until the first wave of grief passed through her, and her body forced her to take a respite. He watched her shift into a state of calm lucidity, as if she was now staring in silence at the abyss and its awful loneliness, facing the terrible knowledge that in the end we must all journey wherever we are headed alone, that the people we surround ourselves with and call our loved ones will not stay once their allotted time is up, as Eddie's now was. And what do we leave behind, he wondered? The puny accomplishments of our ego, so soon forgotten and eclipsed, and, if we are fortunate, the children who outlive us? Dennis thought of Eddie's parents, wherever they were, going about their business, oblivious to the body blow about to be delivered from halfway around the world. It was so fleeting, all of it, he should cherish Amanda and keep her near him while he could.

"Daddy, there's nothing you can do to make it better, is there?"

"No, my precious one, there isn't. It's going to hurt like hell, but you will get through it. You're young and you're strong, you will recover."

"I'll never get over it, I'll never recover."

"You will, I promise you."

"I won't, I promise you. I don't even want to."

"I know."

"Getting over it means accepting it's okay he's no longer here. And that will never be alright with me."

"Nothing can make it all right, but in time you will learn how to live with it being all wrong."

"Have they found his body?"

"I don't know if they've recovered him yet," Dennis said softly. "They've located the spot where he went down, but it could take them a while to gain access to it. It's thick jungle out there."

"Was he burnt to death?"

"Sweetheart, I don't know, but whatever happened it would have been quick. He was probably killed by the force of the helicopter hitting the ground."

"But it exploded, didn't it? David Bird told me it exploded when it hit the trees."

"David Bird doesn't know what he's talking about," said Dennis angrily.

"But did it explode? Daddy, I have to know."

"No! I mean, I don't know, I think so, but whatever happened it doesn't make any difference. It was instant, merciful in that respect."

"It makes a difference to me, Daddy. I want to see his body, I need to know if there's anything there."

"My darling, that's out of the question."

"Why?"

"It just is."

"But why?"

"I'm telling you, it just is. Now, don't ask me again!"

"You're hiding something from me. I can tell."

"No, I'm not."

"Then why won't you tell me?"

"I won't tell you for the very simple reason I don't know myself. There was evidence of an explosion, but whether that happened before or after the helicopter hit the ground it's too early to tell. As for that other thing, remember Eddie as you knew him, don't try and seek out all that gruesome stuff over his body."

"I need to see what happened to him."

"No, you don't."

"It will help me."

"It will do the opposite, I promise you. Right now you have your memories of Eddie, as he was, and you can draw upon those memories in your mind to comfort you whenever you want to be with him. If you see what's left of him now, after he's already departed, that's what will stay with you, and it won't be pretty. You don't want that, do you?"

"No, but…"

"No, but nothing! I don't want to sound harsh, but take comfort from the fact that he died quickly, that he died loving you and knowing you loved him. Don't contaminate that with all that rubbish about needing to see him to grieve."

"Daddy, do you believe in life after death?"

"No, poppet, I don't."

"Me neither."

"But there are plenty of people who do, and who's to say they're not right."

"Like that American missionary?"

"Exactly. Maybe you should talk to him."

"I don't think so."

"Come here," and he pulled her towards him. "I know you loved him, and I know he loved you. I may not have been thrilled about it, but that's only because I'm your father, and it's my job to disapprove of your boyfriends. It doesn't mean any more than that. He was a good man and what you had in a few short weeks was more than many people are fortunate enough to experience in a lifetime."

"I'm not yet eighteen and my life is over already," Amanda wailed.

"No it isn't, it isn't over at all, it's just beginning."

"If God exists, he's a cruel bastard and I fucking hate him."

"That's my girl," comforted Dennis. "Let him have it. If the old sod's out there, I'm sure he can take it. That's nice, give me a smile through those tears."

"Daddy, I don't want to smile, I never want to laugh again."

"I know, poppet, but you will, I promise you that. Not now, maybe, not for a long time perhaps. But you will. You're my girl."

"I was Eddie's girl."

"I know you were, and he was a very lucky man to have known you for the short time he did."

"It was too short."

"Yes," he replied with a sigh, pausing for a moment while he held her tightly in his arms, "it always is."

Francesca had been expecting Peter, but at the last minute before he was due to arrive Suki had triumphantly presented her with a monumental pile of ironing which she insisted Francesca attend to before she went anywhere. Convinced though she was that Suki was acting out of spite, Francesca had little choice but to smile gracefully and walk through the house dressed as she was to go out, to the laundry room set off the back of the kitchen. There she set up the ironing board, plugged in the steam iron and waited for it to heat up while she removed clothes from the drying rack and piled them up on the table in the corner of the room.

She liked ironing. The hiss of the steam and the slow movements had a meditative quality to them, and if she allowed herself to ignore the size of the mountain stacked up beside her and focus on each garment laid out on the board in front of her the time passed almost without her knowing it, invariably leaving her with a sense of calm and accomplishment. She was seldom disturbed while ironing, and the process held her in a safe cocoon from the nightmares and the memories that were still her frequent, unwelcome companions.

Peter would wait. Although she didn't really understand why someone of his high status, with all those eligible girls within his grasp, should choose to devote his energies pursuing her, she had at least begun to accept his advances towards her were genuine, neither some practical joke he'd been put up to by his friends (he didn't seem to have any), nor a passing fancy driven by the endless quest for physical gratification that seemed so important to men. She found herself looking forward to his visits, while her nature kept compelling her to open up towards this man she was beginning to trust. Suki may have been trying to foil any joy that entered into her life, but all she had done was enhance the day with blissful anticipation. Peter would be waiting for her when she had finished, sitting quietly outside, perhaps sharing a pot of tea with Hamid.

After the helicopter crash that had taken the life of her nemesis, she was quickly returning to the idea that perhaps there was a loving, just God after all. The news may have plunged her master's household into mourning, but Francesca herself had woken the following morning with a lightness to her body she hadn't experienced since before the invasion. Exploded on impact was what they said. Was it too much to pray for that Rollo had managed to survive the helicopter hitting the ground so he could have remained conscious while he burnt to death in his seat? She was sorry the American pilot had had to die with him, especially for the pain it had caused Amanda, but they did say he'd fought in the Vietnam war. As she ironed a pair of Amanda's white Levi's that probably cost about four months wages, she allowed herself to indulge in fantasies of equally unpleasant demises for the other soldiers who had brutalised her. Each one had it coming to him in some divine way or other, she decided, and the best part of it was that there was no need for her to become personally involved. The good Lord would do it for her far more effectively than anything her feeble efforts could accomplish. She fingered the cross hanging around her neck, grateful she'd not ripped it off and cast it aside during those dark days when her faith had abandoned her utterly. It was a lot easier to obey Jesus' dictum to love your enemies when you knew God had something really unpleasant lined up for them. She still wasn't ready to go to confession and tell a man about all those terrible things that had happened to her, and her own murderous thoughts arising from them, but maybe even that day too would eventually come.

Peter was waiting for her as she had expected. He stood up to face her as soon as he heard her; in the moment their gaze met she saw the essential goodness in his heart. Waiting for her, just patiently waiting, he reminded her of her father, a man who would be true to her and never let her down. Having reached the conclusion she could never trust another human being again, she was finding exception after exception to the rule she had created to protect herself. After all, she reasoned, if the world in all its barbarity could throw up good men like her father and her brothers, it was possible for it to leave some mark of benevolence elsewhere. Despite her initial indifference, her rudeness, her flashes of anger, Peter had remained constant. He came when he said he would come, he delivered what he promised, he'd never yet let her down. She wondered, as she had on more than one occasion since accepting his courtship, how she would fare were they eventually to get married. Her insides were still frozen, and the thought of being invaded ever again in that way made her want to reach for a carving knife. Peter was a good man, and he professed to understand, but he was still a man with perceived rights and expectations. How would he react if she clammed up when the critical moment came, unable to banish the joking devils waving their appendages around the recesses of her brain? Only a supreme act of will or a miracle would see her through it, she knew that. Perhaps if Peter was able to put aside the fact that she was no demure virgin but shoddy shop soiled goods, that he was eighth in line after a platoon of filthy soldiers, she in turn had to put all that behind her and accept him for the man he was. It was another fire to walk through, and perhaps in the walk she would find that part of her begin to be cleansed.

He walked towards her, and she savoured the look of joy on his face when for the first time she offered forward her cheek for him to plant a gentle kiss. Blushing, he obliged, then stepped back, somehow retaining a gentle hold of her hand.

"Good news," he said with a smile.

"Rollo?"

"No."

"Angelica?" she asked, her voice rising with her hopes.

"We hit the jackpot!" he said triumphantly.

"She's alive?"

"Alive and in good health. I spoke to Benny yesterday, apparently Rollo told him everything before he died. I was right, she was placed in that orphanage I mentioned. They gave her a new name, but Benny managed to work out who she was from the ages and where she was picked up. Fortunately, no one's taken her yet."

Oblivious to Hamid's startled expression and her own guarded inhibitions, Francesca threw herself around him, catching Peter by almost as much surprise as she had herself.

"You did it! I can't believe it, you found her for me!"

Peter smiled.

"We need to fetch her," Francesca continued, her voice bubbling with excitement, "Quickly, before someone takes her."

"Finding her was the easy part," he said, and she steeled herself for the sting. "Come with me. We need to talk."

She followed him out of the carport, but instead of leading her to his motorbike, he headed for a bench under the shade of a palm tree near the office block entrance.

"Please, sit," and she did his bidding, looking into his eyes for signs of what was to come.

"You can't just waltz into an orphanage, especially one as well known as this, point to a baby and say I'm taking her home with me."

"But she's my sister! I'm the only person she has left in the world."

"It doesn't matter. There are all sorts of rules and procedures, paperwork and all that."

"You just have to pay off the right people. Isn't that how this whole country works?"

"Do you have any money?"

"You know I don't. Peter, is this just another way to humiliate me? Because if it is…"

"Sit down, I haven't finished," and he gently pulled her back onto the seat. "Now, I could lend you the money, or give it to you, whatever, but I can tell you now, on your own you wouldn't get anywhere. They'd rob you blind then laugh in your face. It's not just about money, it's about knowing the right people, having the right connections. It's about being in a position where people who can help you want to help you, either because they think it will be good for them or because they are frightened of what will happen if they don't."

"You are one of those people, Peter, don't you see. You managed to find her, surely you can get her out."

"Part of my family is well connected, it's true, and yes we could almost certainly muster up the money and influence to do what we need. But first I need to ask you something."

"What is that?"

"Do you remember what I said when we first started looking for Angelica about how my help was unconditional? That you didn't have to do anything you didn't want to do in return?"

"Of course."

"Well, it's to do with that. I have a question I want to ask you."

Francesca smiled. "Always asking questions, Peter."

"It is the curse of my life!" His face then set in a serious expression, and he looked directly into her eyes. "Francesca, will you do me the honour of becoming my wife?"

"You want to marry me?"

"Yes, I do, if you will have me."

"I... I... I don't know what to say."

"What about yes?"

"Those other things, those things I told you about, they don't put you off?"

"We never need talk about them again."

"Then I say yes! I am honoured to be your wife." She let him throw his arms around her and hold her before modesty prevailed and compelled her to push him away, albeit kindly. "But what about my job here?"

"Francesca, you have no idea how much your life is about to change. From now on, an amah is something you will have, not something you will be. I promise you, you are never going to have to sleep on a cement floor ever again. I will speak with my mother, you can stay with her until we are married."

"How are we to be married, Peter? You are a Muslim and I was brought up Catholic."

"Does that matter to you?"

"No."

"Me, neither. I don't mind, I am happy to convert. If I can have you, I am willing to take Jesus Christ as part of the deal. Two for the price of one!"

"You had better not let the priest hear you talking like that."

"A mortal sin, eh?"

"I can't remember whether it is a mortal sin or a cardinal sin. But he will tell you all you need to know about that."

"A lot of hocus pocus mumbo jumbo. Don't worry, I will nod and shake my head in all the right places."

"They get very upset if they think you are mocking them."

"I'm not mocking them. I am sure they are good people, just as we are good people too."

"What will your family think?"

"They are Muslims, but they are not especially religious. They won't give us any trouble over it. There are plenty of influential people in this country who have converted to Christianity. Uncle Benny will see it as a way of connecting with them. So long as we attend the right church, he will be happy."

"Why does everything always come back to him?"

"It's just the way things work round here. But even that is changing. He is not the man he used to be. Rollo's death has diminished him greatly. When I went round to offer my condolences, I was shocked at how vulnerable and small he seemed."

"We think we are one thing, then life shows us how little we know about anything."

"I know I love you, Francesca."

"And I think I know I love you, Peter."

"You just think you know?"

"After all I have seen, it is the best I can do."

"Well, that's good enough for me," he said, gently stroking her hand. "Are you ready to tell the rest of the world?"

"Soon," she said. "But first I would like to keep it to ourselves for a while. Perhaps you can get me a ring, then we will announce it properly. It doesn't have to be anything fancy, Peter, just something I can look at and feel to remember your promise by."

"We shall go to the jewellers today. And let's have no more of this talk about nothing fancy. You shall have the finest diamond I can find. After all you have been through, you deserve nothing less."

"And Angelica?" How hard she tried not to make it sound like a condition of her acceptance.

"We will get her back. I will make sure of it, if it's the last thing I do."

25

O nce again, Ron found himself standing at the threshold of the Cole residence; once again Barbara came to the door to greet him herself.

"Is Amanda at home?"

"She's in her room," Barbara replied.

"How has she been?"

"She's taken it hard," Barbara continued. "She's hardly left her room, she cries for hours on end, she's hardly eaten a morsel since it happened. I'm frightened she'll waste away if she carries on like this."

"I met him a couple of times," Ron said, coming into the air conditioned hall and closing the door behind him. "He seemed like a nice enough kind of guy."

"He was too old for her," Barbara said adamantly. "He'd done too much, seen too much. She's not yet eighteen, she needs to experiment with someone more her own age."

"Guy was in 'Nam, wasn't he?"

"Yes."

"Well, it's all academic now."

"Trouble is, she's not going to look at anyone else. In dying he's become some kind of martyred saint in her eyes.

Downright inconsiderate of him, if you ask me. Selfish too. Why couldn't he have just let her get bored of his seedy bachelor ways? She'd have come to her senses soon enough."

"Do you think she would be willing to speak to me?"

"It's certainly worth a try. Dennis, why don't you go and fetch her?"

"It might be better if it was just the two of us," Ron suggested.

"Of course," said Barbara in such a way to let Ron hear the reluctance in her voice.

Dennis shuffled back into the hallway towards his daughter's room. Even if she agreed to come out, he wasn't at all convinced of the wisdom of inveighing this minister's help. They were a tight family unit, the four of them; Amanda's grief wasn't anyone else's business. Thank goodness that dreadful Melanie had gone back to England. A stiff afternoon loomed ahead; if he wasn't careful, the tiresome man would have them all kneeling on the carpet inviting Jesus into their lives.

He tapped on the door, leant down and placed his head next to the handle. "Amanda?"

"Amanda?" he repeated after a moment's pause. "It's me, Daddy."

"What do you want?" Her voice sounded muffled, and he could tell she had been crying again.

"May I come in?"

The lock clicked from the inside and the door cracked to reveal her tear-stained face. Gently, he pushed it open and placed his arm around her shoulders.

"There's someone who's come to see you."

"I don't want to see anyone."

"He might be able to help you."

"Who is he?"

"Ron Milliner, he's the missionary who's been working out in the jungle."

"He's here?"

"Yes. Your mother asked him to come by."

She sniffed, daubing her eyes with a handkerchief. "He came all the way from the jungle to see me?"

"Not exactly, he was in town on business."

"I don't need any help from anyone. Tell him I don't want to see him."

"Amanda, darling, you can't carry on like this forever."

"Why not?"

"Because life goes on. Look, I'm not going to try and force you to see this chap if you don't want to, but one day you're going to have to face the fact that you're going to have to get by without Eddie. I know that sounds cruel, but it's the truth."

"Your life goes on. Mine's over."

"Nonsense."

"It isn't nonsense. Please, Daddy, just leave me alone, will you?" Gently but firmly she pushed him back out of the room and made to close the door.

Dennis placed his foot in the gap just before she managed to shut it. "Promise me one thing, will you? Then I will leave you alone."

"What's that?"

"If you need to talk, you'll come to me."

"I promise, Daddy."

"I understand more than you may think."

"I know you do."

"Don't forget that. Please."

"I won't. Goodbye, Daddy, and thank you."

"Any time, my darling. Any time." He stepped back and the door clicked shut, leaving him to wonder about the chasm that had opened up between them, and whether he would ever be able to penetrate the depths of its void. He was so wrapped up in his thoughts he barely noticed Francesca slip past carrying a pile of freshly ironed clothes. Arriving at Amanda's room, she held the garments into her chest with one hand and tapped softly on the door with the other.

"Is that you again, Daddy?" came the muffled reply.

"No, it's me, Francesca. I have some shirts for you."

The door opened to reveal Amanda's puffy, tear stained face.

"I am sorry, Miss Amanda, I can come back another time."

"No, no, it's fine, come in," replied Amanda, stepping aside to let Francesca through.

Francesca crossed the room to the closet while Amanda shut the door behind her.

"Forgive me, I'm not being rude, Francesca, I just don't feel like speaking to anyone today."

"I understand. I was very sorry to hear about your friend Eddie."

"Thank you." Flopping down on her bed, she looked up at Francesca, who placed the shirts neatly on the shelves then turned to face her. There was an awkward silence, as if neither woman knew who should speak next, or what they should say. Eventually Amanda broke the silence.

"Just so long as you don't tell me I'll get over it."

"I would never say that to you, even if I thought it were true."

"Do you?"

"How could I know?"

"May I ask you something, Francesca?"

"Of course, Miss Amanda?"

"Just call me Amanda. A while ago you said you had no family, that you had left them behind in Timor. What happened to them?"

Francesca took a deep breath and sat down on the bed beside Amanda. "Yes, I did have a family. I had a wonderful family, we were very happy together. Until the Indonesian soldiers came one night and attacked our house."

"They killed them?"

Francesca nodded, unable to help noticing how her revelation had shocked, if only momentarily, Amanda out of her grief.

"My mother, my father, my older brother Antonio, my little brother Marco. The only ones they did not kill were me and my baby sister, Angelica."

"What happened to her?"

"They took her away. Peter and I are trying to get her back. We think we have found her, but it is not easy. So I understand what it is to lose somebody close, Amanda, which is why I would never say to you you will get over it. Maybe you will learn to be happy again, maybe you will not. I cannot tell."

"Oh, my God, Francesca," cried Amanda, "I had no idea." She sat up and placed her arm around her. "How did you manage to carry on?"

"It was only Angelica who gave me the strength. I told myself if I stayed alive maybe I could find her, but if I died then she too would be all alone in the world. And that I could bear even less than the thought of carrying on."

"You have such dignity, Francesca, such poise, such grace in your sorrow. You make me feel ashamed of myself."

"I don't want to do that, Amanda. It is not a competition to see who can suffer the most and stay standing up. You have always been kind to me, you are a good person. I am very sorry for your loss, I don't compare it to my own and say to myself, "She does not know what it is to lose everything". Our life was simple, we did not have much, not like people do here, but we were happy. My father worked in the radio station, my brothers they liked playing football, and they worried there weren't going to be any jobs for them when they grew up, but our house was full of love, and there was often laughter. I, too, do not know if I will ever know that again."

"I hope you do, Francesca. Just as I hope you manage to get your baby sister back. If anyone deserves it, it's you."

"Thank you, Amanda. Now we now know where she is, we just have to persuade them to hand her over."

"If there's anything I can do to help, anything at all, you will tell me? Promise me that."

"I will do that. And again, I thank you."

"It's me who should be thanking you."

"You don't need to thank anyone."

"My mother says you might be leaving us."

"That is true. Peter has asked me to be his wife and I have said yes. When we are married, I will go and live with him."

"I am going to miss you, but I wish you well. Will you still be my friend once you are no longer working for us?"

"Of course."

"May I give you a hug, Francesca?"

Francesca shifted her weight around the bed and placed her arms around the English girl's shoulders, pulling her head into her own chest. As Amanda spread a damp patch across her sarong with her tears, Francesca became conscious of a new stillness welling up from within, and with it a sense that whilst she might never again know the happiness she had lost, somehow she might learn to be at peace with the sadness that had overwhelmed her life.

It was a disheartened Ron who shuffled back from the Cole's residence to his guest apartment, where the company car was waiting to take him down to Base Camp for the helicopter ride back to the fresh clearing near his camp. He glanced at his watch. If he was lucky, they would be there by five, which would allow him to reach the mission station before darkness. Otherwise it would be another night in Bandakan, surrounded by debauched flight crews and off-duty riggers for company. Maybe he'd win a soul for Christ; more likely he'd sit alone at a table in the Base Camp bar with his Bible like some modern day leper, the God-botherer they were all terrified of being cornered by, until he couldn't take it any more and retired to his portakabin. It was disappointing, and hurtful if he was honest about it, to be rebuffed by the Cole girl, but these setbacks had to be weighed against the successes he'd achieved in Katapulu over the past few months. From those tentative beginnings word of the station had spread throughout the kampongs and people were now coming in from miles around. Back home they were delighted with his achievements, and there was even talk of sending a young missionary couple over to assist him.

It was God's will, not his, he reminded himself as he tapped on the door of the helicopter operations room. He waited a moment, then opened the heavy metal door to see Mick sitting at his desk talking on the phone.

Ron signalled his apologies and made to back away, but Mick indicated for him to stay where he was. One minute, he mouthed.

"No problem, Benny, I'll sort it out," he continued into the receiver. "Yeah, there's a bunk here he can crash out in tonight… Don't worry, I'll tell him… Bye."

Mick turned to face Ron. "Sorry about that, Reverend."

"No, I'm sorry for interrupting you."

"You weren't interrupting, in fact your arrival was very timely."

"Why is that?"

"I'm afraid we can't fly you up to Katapulu."

"I appreciate it's getting a little late. That's okay, I can stay here overnight."

Mick shifted uncomfortably in his chair. "You're welcome to find a billet here overnight, but we can't take you in the morning either. Or any other morning, for that matter."

"What?"

"I'm sorry, Ron, orders from above. That was Benny on the phone just now. He doesn't think it's a good idea for you to go back there."

"Why?" Ron struggled to keep the fear out of his voice.

"He didn't say. But he did expressly pass on orders forbidding me from letting any of our pilots fly you up there in company aircraft. Apparently it came right from the top. There's nothing I can do, mate, if I put you in one of our choppers I'm out of a job."

"Where is Benny?" Ron demanded.

"Jakarta. He won't be back until next week. But there's no point in arguing with him, he's just the messenger boy. The decision was made elsewhere."

"I have to go back there. It's my mission, it's where my work is, it's where my people are, it's where my life is!"

Mick shrugged his shoulders. "Well, I can't stop you from doing that. But you heard what he said."

"Is there something you're not telling me?"

"All I'm doing is passing on what I've been told," replied Mick, but Ron could tell from the way his gaze flinched Mick was lying. He fought to keep the panic at bay, to remain calm, to think clearly.

"If I can't use one of your helicopters, how can I get there?"

"You could catch a bus to Samarinda; once you're there I'm sure you'd find someone who would drive you past Gunpura until the road runs out. After that, you're on your own. But, as Benny said, I wouldn't advise it."

"You are hiding something from me."

Mick stood up and shut the door, then turned to face the missionary. "Look, I've been forbidden from providing you with any Constar resources beyond putting you up here for the night, but I also know I can't stop you reaching Katapulu if you're hell bent on getting there. You'll find a way – people like you always do. But you're not going to like what you find if you go."

"What's happened?"

"You didn't hear this from me, Ron, and I only know because a couple of our boys were flying upcountry and heard it on the airwaves. Yesterday, an entire battalion of the Indonesian army dropped in on Katapulu, then fanned out on a search and destroy mission, looking for suspected communists."

"Did they find any?"

"I haven't a clue, mate, but I do hear it wasn't pretty."

"I've got to get up there."

"I understand, but at least give the army time to pull out. Otherwise you could just end up making a bad situation worse. You really don't want to mess with these guys, especially if you don't have a big US company like Constar looking after you."

Defeated, Ron slumped back in his chair and tried to digest this disastrous turn of events. He asked himself how much of it was his fault. How much had he actually told Carl? Looking back, it was so obvious how he had been used. How could he have been so blind, caught up in his egotistical desire to inflate his importance through his geo-political insights and to furnish his mission with modern medicines? In the end, he'd been nothing but a tin-pot empire builder, a harbinger of catastrophe for these innocent people who'd never asked him to be amongst them in the first place.

Three days later Ron sat down on a charred tree stump, surrounded by the ruins of his erstwhile mission station. Like the
rest of the village, the huts had been burnt to the ground, those
villagers who had survived dispersed into the jungle until it was
safe to return. Joseph had been amongst their number, and he
had been patiently waiting for him at the end of the twelve mile
footslog he'd undertaken when the dirt road petered out into a
trail. Grimly, Joseph had filled him in on the details, including
the statistics. A hundred and seventy-four people massacred,
including fifty-three women and twelve children under the age
of fourteen. And that wasn't to mention the women who were
raped by the soldiers as they went through the kampongs, or the
men hauled away for questioning. They hadn't touched Hallie,
who wandered aimlessly around the remains of the camp in a
daze. A couple of soldiers had made for her, but an officer had
quickly pulled them back, mindful of possible consequences.
The last thing any commanders on the ground wanted was an
international incident. According to Joseph, they had commandeered the station as their HQ, ordering the mission staff
to remain within the main hut while they fanned out into the
jungle, shooting anything that moved. When they were done
they ordered Joseph and the three other terrified workers outside, before burning that hut too. They then informed Joseph
they had specific orders not to harm the staff, and provided
they continued to cooperate with the army in the interests of
national security, they were free to carry on with their work.

What work? Ron couldn't understand it any more than the
bewildered Joseph. Every morning he had prayed to God to
guide him. How could he have been led to this? What on earth
was he going to tell the good folks in Oklahoma, who had placed
their faith and their prayers in him? Right now, he had no idea.
Humbled, lost in this new wilderness of his good intentions, he
shook his head and began to weep.

26

A year on, Benny Surikano sat at a table on the club balcony, a half-eaten steak sandwich in front of him. As usual, he'd lost interest in his food after a few bites and shoved the plate to one side, replacing it with one of the Dunhill Internationals he chain-smoked these days. His clothes felt loose around his body; he'd shed forty pounds in the past year without any effort on his part, but not bothered to tailor his wardrobe to his new figure. Likewise, he no longer dyed the grey streaks out of his hair. He knew he had aged a dozen years in as many months, but he simply lacked the will to do anything to reverse the process. People said he was a broken man since he had lost his only son, and people were right. With Rollo gone, Benny was just seeing out his days, like some weary patient flicking through old magazines in the doctor's waiting room, until the time was up for him to go too. Nothing seemed worth the effort any more, by far the hardest part of each day was summoning the strength to rise from his bed in the morning when he came to and realised he was still here. Some days he didn't.

He still had his job, but he performed his duties listlessly, delegating tasks wherever possible and only stepping in when it couldn't be avoided. Peter had taken on most of his responsibilities, and much to Benny's surprise was shaping up well. He had a good intuition for where people were coming from, and now that he'd dropped that ludicrous urge to save the world, his ability to see the other person's point of view meant all parties tended to leave any encounter he chaired feeling they had done well out of it. That lassitude and refusal to try which had so infuriated Benny was gone, banished forever by the Timorese servant girl he had made his wife. It was she who was to be thanked for putting the steel into Peter's spine. Benny retained just enough of his sense of the absurd to appreciate the irony that if anyone could resuscitate the fortunes of this Indonesian dynasty he had struggled so hard to create, it would be her.

From behind the sunglasses that covered his watery eyes he looked over the terrace down to the poolside where she now lay under the shade of an umbrella, not far from that shrivelled up little bitch who'd made such a fool of his precious boy. Well, she'd had her come-uppance for sure, he thought with a sense of satisfaction. If the stories were to be believed she'd already made two attempts to take her life, once with sleeping pills, once with a disposable razor. From what Benny could see, the girl was headed the same way as her mother, only at three times the speed. When she wasn't on the pool deck knocking back vodka martinis, she was in one of the bars, drowning her sorrows and drawing in any loser half-witted enough to listen to her hard luck story in the misplaced belief a gratuitous fuck lay at the end of it. It was the same with all the expats: they thought theirs was the only suffering that counted, whereas most of them hadn't experienced anything that would make the slightest dent on the collective pain register in the country he called his own.

An amah sat in an upright chair at a respectful distance from Francesca minding a bag containing all the necessary accoutrements for two young children on an afternoon out.

Francesca

The little girl, who was just under two, ran around the pool deck in a bright pink swimsuit and a pair of inflatable armbands, joyous in her love of the water. Francesca still held the boy, a little more than eight-weeks-old, carefully shaded from the sun by the umbrella. The more he had come to know Francesca, the greater his sense of shame had grown, for he and his ilk had wrought nothing but catastrophe and death upon her and her kin, while she in turn had regenerated his with her own astonishing life force.

He was spent, and he knew it, his days as a big shot with a pistol and an address book of dangerous friends long behind him. He and his cronies might enjoy a few more years plundering the wealth of the country they had helped build, but it couldn't last forever. The future mocked their base desires, just as it mocked their physical pretensions of invincibility with sagging chests, wheezing lungs and spreading wrinkles. If he could do it again with the knowledge he had now, well, of course he would do it differently. Who but an idiot wouldn't learn from their mistakes, and Benny and his fellow officers had sure made some big ones when they fashioned their notion of a nation out of these thousands of islands wrestled from the hands of the Dutch. Handing over was hard, but just as the Europeans had had to do it when their time was up, so now did he. The future, his country's future, belonged to that little infant lying in his mother's arms, oblivious to everything but Francesca's presence, the sunshine and his own immediate needs for milk, a change and a nap. Benny reached for a fresh cigarette and lit it from the butt of his last one, which he extinguished in the small dollop of ketchup at the edge of his plate. God, he thought, if only the poor mite knew what he was in for, if only he could see the road that lay ahead.

EPILOGUE

Dili, Timor Leste, December 2005

"Madam, this way please."

Amanda stood up and let the receptionist lead her through several corridors which eventually opened out into a large anteroom, where the receptionist showed her to a sofa.

"The Minister will be with you in a minute. Can I get you some refreshment? Tea? Coffee? Juice?"

"Some iced water would be lovely."

"Certainly."

Amanda sat down, glancing around the modern room. Though modestly furnished, it was tended by someone who took considerable pride in it. The walls were freshly painted, and a vase of fresh jasmine stood on the occasional table next to a selection of neatly fanned-out tourist leaflets. Six oil paintings adorned the walls, each one depicting a scene from the quarter century struggle against Mother Indonesia.

The receptionist returned with her water. Amanda thanked her, then stood up and walked across to the window, where she looked out at the immature gardens fronting the brand-new government buildings. She caught her reflection in the glass, and wondered how much she had really changed over the past thirty years. Would she even recognise her? Like any woman approaching fifty, all Amanda saw were unwelcome lines and what used to be there, even though she knew she had aged better than many of her contemporaries. Her hair was cut shorter, and of a darker hue now that it was no longer permanently bleached by the sun and salt water, and she had managed to keep the weight she had put on into single figures, provided you measured in kilos rather than pounds. With some irritation she glanced down at a couple of age spots on her left hand, between her thumb and forefinger. Was it all those years in the harsh sun in the days before anyone worried about skin cancer, or just time itself, not so much the great healer as the great eroder?

Behind her the door clicked open, and she turned to face the receptionist.

"The Minister will see you now, Ms Cole. Please, come this way."

Amanda allowed herself to be shown into the office. Hardly hearing the door close behind her, she smiled as Francesca stood up and walked from behind the huge teak desk to greet her. For a moment they stumbled around the formality of a handshake, before falling into each other's arms in a tight embrace.

To Amanda's eyes, Francesca had retained all the poise and dignity she exuded as a humble amah. However, in place of the fear and the flinch there was now a confidence and a warmth, as she guided them to a pair of occasional chairs. She had hardly aged at all, despite the large photograph proudly displayed on the shelf behind the desk of four handsome grown-up boys. There were a few wrinkles around the eyes, but her hair retained its length and sheen, causing Amanda to wish she had never been so timid about flaunting hers.

"Sit down, sit down, we shall have some tea." Her English was perfect, almost completely devoid of accent. Amanda noticed with some amusement she had assumed the role of mother hen, as she picked up a phone on her desk and issued instructions in Tetum.

"I am so glad you called on me," she said when she finally sat down. "What brings you to Dili?"

"I travel a lot these days," replied Amanda. "It is one of my favourite pastimes. Fortunately, I work for an airline, so I am able to indulge my passion quite cheaply."

"What do you do for them?"

"I look after their international marketing," she said off-handedly. "I've done it for years."

"We could use some international marketing here."

"You seem to be doing pretty well to me."

"It has not been easy, but yes, we do have our accomplishments."

"So, in the end you came back."

"Yes, I came back," Francesca said slowly. "I never thought I would, I swore many times in my life that I would never set foot in Dili again, but here I am." She smiled, and just then there was a soft tap on the door, followed by the receptionist carrying a tea tray and a plate of biscuits. Francesca let her pour the tea, offered Amanda the biscuits which she declined, then waited for the receptionist to shut the door behind them before continuing. "There were too many terrible memories, and we led an enviable life in Bandakan. When Uncle Benny died, he left everything to Peter. It took us nearly two years to untangle the trail of secret offshore bank accounts and businesses he had a stake in. Do you know, he was worth over two million dollars? US dollars, that is, not Singapore or Malay, and there still could be more stashed away somewhere we never unearthed. All I could think of were those motorcycles and TVs and crates of coffee beans looted from my country piled up on board the boat I managed to escape on. Here we were, a young couple just trying to do the right thing in life, sitting on this fortune founded on a thousand thefts and scams."

"Did you keep it?"

"What else could we do with it? We weren't about to hand it over to the Suhartos. No, I decided the best use of it was to provide our children with a first-class education and to spend time with them, hoping they would grow up to be decent human beings who would become part of the solution rather than add to the problem." She pointed to the photograph Amanda had noticed earlier. "I think I didn't do too bad a job. They have all turned out well, I am extremely proud of them."

"And Peter?"

"He lives here with me. He is mostly retired now, but he still takes a few classes at the university. He likes to keep his mind alert. We would both very much like you to come to dinner with us tonight. That is, if you are free."

"I would love that," said Amanda. "Thank you very much."

"We can talk about some of the old times."

Amanda smiled. "It'll be like visiting my parents. They talk about little else."

"They are alive?"

"Oh, yes, they live in Sussex. Not quite in the style they were used to, but well enough none the less."

"Please send them my regards. They treated me well at a time when I had very few friends in the world."

"They'll be tickled pink when they find out you're a government minister. I can't wait to tell them."

"Sometimes I find it hard to believe myself. Quite often, actually. I never meant it to happen. Most of my colleagues spent years in the countryside fighting the Indonesians, and here I was, a wealthy Kalimantan housewife who hadn't set foot in my country since the day after it was invaded. But those of them who know me are aware I suffered every bit as much as them at the hands of the Indonesians."

"Why did you return?"

"I don't know, Amanda, other than I felt I had something to contribute, especially after we finally won our independence in 2002. Maybe it was a way of honouring my family, the family I came from, that is. At first my boys were very much against it, but they've come round to the idea. Angelica understands better, especially now that I have told her everything. I waited until she was seventeen, the same age I was when it happened. I felt it was her right to know, just as it was her right not to know up until that point. I never told you all about it, did I?"

Amanda shook her head. "You told me some things, but not that much. Not that I was in a state to take it in."

"Tonight I will. We will wait until Peter has gone to bed. Then I will tell you everything, and you will finally understand why I will always be so grateful to your family, and why I could never really be with you in your grief."

"Will Angelica be joining us?"

"No, she is living in Sydney. She works for a radio station, just like her father. Of course I'd love her to come back, but she has her own life to live and must make her own choices. Do you have children, Amanda?"

Amanda shook her head. "No, I never did. I was married for a short while back in the mid eighties, but we went our separate ways. After Eddie died, I went wild for a few years, I was all over the place. You probably remember. People kept telling me I'd get over it, I was young, I would recover, sooner or later I would find someone else and settle down. And while I did eventually get over the grief so I could live without feeling as if my insides were being ripped out, I never found anyone like him. He was a soul mate, and although we were only together a very short time it was like we were always meant to be with each other, that our lives up until then had just been about waiting for each other, that we were in fact one. Part of me knew that, despite what everyone was saying, but part of me thought I would find it again. I never did. I guess I was lucky to have it at all, even though I was very young and didn't truly know what I had in my hands. Most people never get to have that."

"When that helicopter went down, it changed everything for both of us forever. Still, no one has a clue why it happened. Eddie never sent a mayday signal, and the investigators never found any reason for it to crash like that. I know it was the beginning of the end for you, but for me it was the beginning of the end of the nightmare."

"Because of Rollo?"

Francesca nodded.

"Why, did he try something on with you? He tried to hit on me, too, you remember."

"No, it was nothing like that. I'll tell you all about it tonight."

"I went to America to visit Eddie's family. I wanted to see the places he'd grown up around, sit in the coffee houses he'd hung out in, talk to people he had known. I found it a very frustrating experience. They were all very kind to me, but it was clear none of them had ever really known him. I was desperate, trying to reach out for any piece of him, any memory I could hold on to, but the truth is it all burnt up back there in the jungle."

"Do you remember that missionary who used to work out there?"

"Yes, I do. The Reverend Ron something or other. He tried to help me, but I wasn't in the mood for a religious transformation. I seem to recall you got to know him quite well. Whatever happened to him?"

"You remember the Indonesian army went through his mission station and destroyed everything, looking for so called communists."

"Yes, I do."

"It turned out Ron had been set up all along. Constar had been asked to help him by the CIA, and in return for all his helicopter rides and medicines and powdered milk, they milked him for information about government resistance in the jungle, which they then passed on to Indonesian intelligence. Apparently they appealed to his sense of patriotism. For a while he was very bitter about it, and he hung around Bandakan ranting and raving about the evils of the government until someone eventually got tired of him and kicked him out of the country. He went back to America and wrote a book about it, called *Humbled at the Foot of the Cross*. Have you ever come across it?"

"Somehow that rings a bell," said Amanda.

"It's sold over ten million copies, and been translated into about thirty different languages. I'm told it's required reading in almost every Protestant seminary in the world. I've got a copy at home, I'll lend it to you. I'd let you have it, but he wrote a rather nice inscription in the front. He married Peter and me, you know."

"Did he really?"

"At first we went to the Catholic church in Bandakan, the one where all Uncle Benny's influential Christian friends worshipped, but we didn't get on very well with the priest. Peter kept on arguing with him and making sarcastic remarks – he was a pompous little ass – and finally he refused to continue Peter's instruction. So we turned to Ron. We still get a Christmas card from him each year, he's eighty-three now, but incredibly fit and alert. I guess that's California for you."

"Timor-Leste seems to have kept you looking young."

Francesca blushed. "Why, thank you. Though, it's not the place that does it, Amanda, it's what lies in your heart. So many people in this country have suffered so much, but we have to move through that if we are going to have any hope of creating a better future. Otherwise we will just recreate more of the same. Peter helped me learn that. I had to forgive the Indonesians for what they did, not for their sake but for mine. It was the hardest thing I've ever had to do, but it was the only way I could find any peace or freedom." Francesca looked up at a small brass clock on the wall, then turned to Amanda. "Do you have time for a little walk?"

"Sure."

"I am meant to be seeing someone at twelve, but my secretary can rearrange it. I'd like to take you for a little stroll, down by the wharf. There's a café run by some people I know where we can have lunch. It looks out onto the harbour."

Amanda stood up and waited while Francesca made a couple of notes on her desk jotter and rang through to her secretary. She watched her close down her laptop and reach under her desk for her handbag.

"Oh, my God," Amanda laughed, "it's that Hermès bag I gave you! You've still got it!"

"I've had to send it away to be repaired three times, but I'll never let go of it. Peter keeps buying me new ones, he's says it's unseemly for a member of the Government to go around with a thirty-year-old handbag, but I don't care. I love it. It reminds me of who I am. It was the first really nice thing anyone gave me. I remember you telling me I could sell it if I didn't want it, and what a kind gesture that was. When I went back to my quarters, I sneaked a look at the price tag, and I was shocked that anyone could have that much money to spend on something they didn't even bother to use."

"I don't know why I never used it," Amanda said. "It was a very nice bag, I remember buying it. I guess it was just waiting for you. It's okay," she laughed, "I'm not going to ask for it back!"

"I'll have you arrested if you so much as try!" Although she was smiling, Amanda noticed the way Francesca instinctively shielded the bag with her forearm.

"Come on, it's time you showed me this capital of yours. I want the full guided tour."

"I don't know about that, but I can show you where it all began." She took Amanda's arm in hers, and led her out of the office, through the anteroom and into the corridor. Behind them the receptionist stared, somewhat perplexed, as the Minister escorted this western tourist out of the building, the pair of them looking for all the world like two giggling teenagers cutting school for an afternoon jaunt in the sun.

AUTHOR'S NOTE

Whilst this is a work of fiction, the story is grounded in a specific time and place, and based around real events. The characters, however, are all fictitious and bear no relation to any individual, living or dead. Neither is Constar intended to be representative of any real life company.

Sadly, the Indonesian invasion of East Timor was all too real, especially for the Timorese people caught in the middle, including the two hundred thousand or so men, women and children (almost a third of the population) who lost their lives during a quarter of a century of conflict. The prologue in which President Suharto discusses the impending invasion with President Ford and Secretary of State Henry Kissinger is also grounded in fact. The setting has been dramatised; however the words spoken by those individuals, if not their thoughts, are drawn from recently declassified documents in the President Ford Library.

I would like to thank all those who have helped me during the research of this novel. In particular, I am grateful to have been able to draw upon Amnesty International's archives on East Timor during the Indonesian occupation. I would like to acknowledge James Dunn's book, *Timor: A People Betrayed*, upon which I drew heavily for background information on East Timor. I can think of no better place to start for anyone wishing to learn more about this particular episode in history. Meanwhile, Roland Challis' *Shadow of a Revolution* provided invaluable material on Indonesia's post-colonial political evolution. I am indebted to Jim Bradin for sharing his own memories as a US Army pilot during the Vietnam War, and for introducing me to a group of veteran pilots from the Army Aviation Heritage Foundation near Atlanta, Georgia. These men generously shared their experiences and insights flying Bell Hueys during that conflict and provided me with a huge amount of technical detail. Any errors are, of course, my own.

Finally I would like to thank Svetlana Pironko, whose patience and perseverance has guided me through numerous drafts and edits. Her encouragement is matched by a razor sharp mind, and it's a rare inconsistency or grammatical error that makes it past her red pencil. I can think of no one with a greater talent for telling a writer what he doesn't necessarily want, but needs, to hear.

ABOUT THE AUTHOR

Donald Finnaeus Mayo was born in London and grew up in Australia and South East Asia, the backdrop for *Francesca*. He was educated in England, where he graduated in Politics and Culture. He has worked variously as a radio journalist for the BBC, a business writer for major corporations, and as a photographer. He currently lives in Hampshire with his wife and three children. You can find out more about the background and history behind *Francesca*, as well as forthcoming titles at *http://donaldfinnaeusmayo.com* and *www.betimesbooks.com*

www.ingramcontent.com/pod-product-compliance
Lightning Source LLC
Chambersburg PA
CBHW030548260626
47157CB00006B/2231